"I *am* a beast. Don't ever forget that."

Mariah sniffed haughtily. "I'm not afraid of you."

Robert's eyes gleamed wolfishly. "You should be."

His mouth captured hers, so quickly, so unexpectedly that she didn't even have time to gasp before his lips molded against hers, stealing her breath away and stunning her senseless. For a long while, she could do nothing in her surprise but stand there while he kissed her. Oh Lord, Carlisle was *kissing* her!

Worse, she was letting him.

And oh, what a kiss... The strength of his mouth on hers contrasted with the softness of his warm lips as they caressed and nibbled against hers, almost coaxing at her to give over to him, yet mercilessly relentless in his pursuit to make her senses flee. And damn him, the devil was succeeding...

HOW I MARRIED A MARQUESS

"Extremely entertaining...I enjoyed this well-written tale."
—RomRevToday.com

ALONG CAME A ROGUE

"Harrington creates fast-paced, lively romances with unconventional characters and plot. For her second novel, she adds heated sensuality and a gothic twist. There is little doubt that she is fast becoming a fan favorite."

—*RT Book Reviews*

"In this thoroughly entertaining story, seduction and adventure take center stage. Nathaniel is far more honorable than he will admit, and Emily far braver than she ever imagined. Together, they form a formidable pair that readers are certain to love."

—*BookPage*

"Harrington has created a richly woven novel, complete with romance, a touch of mystery, and wounded, believable characters."

—*Publishers Weekly*

"A fast-paced, high-action thrill ride punctuated by hot and sexy games."
—FreshFiction.com

DUKES ARE FOREVER

"A touching and tempestuous romance, with all the ingredients Regency fans adore."
—Gaelen Foley, *New York Times* bestselling author

ALSO BY ANNA HARRINGTON

AS THE
DEVIL DARES

ANNA
HARRINGTON

FOREVER

NEW YORK BOSTON

Copyright © 2018 by Anna Harrington
Excerpt from *If the Duke Demands* © 2017 by Anna Harrington
Cover design by Elizabeth Turner
Cover illustration by Chris Cocozza
Title hand lettering by Jen Mussari
Cover copyright © 2018 by Hachette Book Group, Inc.

Forever
Hachette Book Group
1290 Avenue of the Americas, New York, NY 10104
forever-romance.com
twitter.com/foreverromance

First Edition: March 2018

Forever is an imprint of Grand Central Publishing. The Forever name and logo are trademarks of Hachette Book Group, Inc.

The publisher is not responsible for websites (or their content) that are not owned by the publisher.

The Hachette Speakers Bureau provides a wide range of authors for speaking events. To find out more, go to www.hachettespeakersbureau.com or call (866) 376-6591.

ISBN: 978-1-4555-9729-1 (mass market), 978-1-4555-9731-4 (ebook)

Printed in the United States of America

OPM

10 9 8 7 6 5 4 3 2 1

Dedicated to
Sarah Younger,
for urging me to write about the Carlisles

And to my father,
who never once threatened
to send me away to school or to a convent
(although perhaps he wishes he had)

Special thanks to
Michele Bidelspach, Jordan Rubinstein,
and Angelina Krahn
for all your help
in writing and releasing this book

CHAPTER ONE

A Very Wintry Afternoon in London
January 1823

"I suppose you prefer White's," Henry Winslow drawled.

Robert Carlisle's gaze drifted from the smoke curling from the tip of his cigar to the man sitting in the leather chair across from him in the smoking room at Brooks's. Before them, a crackling fire warmed away the chill of the winter afternoon outside the large windows, whose gray sky once more threatened to snow.

"I prefer here, with the real leaders of England," Robert corrected casually. "Businessmen and merchants, traders, importers—the men who make England run."

"Hear! Hear!" Winslow lifted his glass and gasped softly as he took a swallow.

Robert popped the cigar between his teeth before Winslow could see his self-satisfied smile. In truth, he preferred Boodle's, where the gambling required more skill, the stakes were higher, and the women allowed in through the rear entrance were more interesting. But he would gladly flatter the man's choice of club because he needed Henry Winslow.

Rather, he needed Winslow Shipping and Trade.

He eased back in the chair and kicked his Hessians onto the fireplace fender, for all appearances the model of a confident businessman when he was actually anxious as hell. He'd been waiting two years for this. Two years of taking calculated risks to build his wealth and connections, purchasing unproven shares of ships from India and the Far East just so he would have a presence among the men who drove the auctions, buying and selling warehouses full of goods so he could make a name for himself among the traders... all of it coming to this moment. To prospects with the largest merchant company in the British Empire.

He'd be damned if he let it slip away.

He drawled as nonchalantly as possible, "I've heard that you're expanding your shipping routes."

"Ha!" Winslow flicked his ash onto the floor. "Where did you hear that?"

"I have good contacts." The best, in fact. Winslow knew that, too, or he wouldn't have invited him here in the first place. "I've also heard that you're looking for a partner to help you do it."

"I am." Winslow's eyes gleamed, appreciating Robert's bluntness. "I'm looking for new blood to energize my company. Someone with the drive and ambition to make a name for himself." He pushed himself from his chair and stepped forward to the fire, to take the liberty of grasping the brass poker and stirring up the flames. "I have an extraordinary company, and I need extraordinary men to run it."

Robert smiled tightly. *Extraordinary*, all right.

Henry Winslow might have been an arrogant braggart, but as England's most successful businessman, he had every right to be. The sole proprietor of Winslow Shipping and

Trade, he was one of the few import merchants who had managed to emerge from the wars wealthier than before. All due to determination, a willingness to risk capital, and good old-fashioned luck. A titan of fortune and power, Winslow had never taken on a partner before, but Robert had thoroughly studied the company and knew that he would be the perfect man for it.

And that this partnership would be the answer to his prayers.

"I'm offering a limited share, you understand." Winslow puffed out his chest, a gesture more propriety than proud. "A small stake. Perhaps seven percent."

Robert's eyes narrowed. Much smaller than he'd hoped. But it would do. For now. "You've never taken a partner before. Why now?"

Winslow stared into the fire. "Changes need to be made. A man who doesn't recognize when it's time to adjust his ways might as well retire." He jabbed the poker at the logs, sending up a shower of sparks. "But the timing of it— *daughters*." He heaved a hard breath and shook his head. "How does a businessman ensure a legacy for his family when all he has are daughters?"

Robert didn't answer. His own father hadn't worried about such things. Instead, Richard Carlisle had concerned himself with character, hard work, and devotion to his family, and he never considered his daughter to be any less worthy than his sons. They were all his children, all equally able to earn his pride.

And Robert was determined to do exactly that. He *would* become the kind of man his father could take pride in raising, and he would let nothing stop him.

"Perhaps one of them will marry a gentleman you can

bring into your business." For his own selfish sake, Robert prayed that both Winslow daughters were toothless, bald spinsters well into their third decade and beyond the possibility of marrying ambitious upstarts who might snag this opportunity away from him.

"Not into my business. Not sons-in-law," Winslow grumbled as he replaced the poker, then slapped his hands together to remove the soot from his fingers. "You don't know my daughters, do you, Carlisle?"

Robert shook his head. His usual female companionship fell more toward experienced widows than spinster daughters of trade merchants.

"Their reputations precede them, I'm afraid." Winslow folded his hands behind his back and stared grimly down into the flames, his round belly jutting out. "Their mother died when they were young, only ten and eight. I suppose I should have found them a stepmother who could have raised them into proper young ladies, as my late wife wanted. But the business needed my attention, and there was barely enough time to find an appropriate governess, let alone a wife." He paused, then admitted, "And in truth, a part of me didn't want to. It would have felt as if I were attempting to replace my dear Beatrice."

Robert understood that. It was why his own mother would never remarry.

"But now, when I look at my daughters..." Winslow blew out a long-suffering sigh. "I regret that decision."

"Are they both out for the season?" Robert asked curiously. Polite conversation was expected. It was also essential that he get to know Winslow better so no surprises would arise later.

"Yes." The single word was spoken with grim chagrin.

"But it's their seventh and fifth seasons, and I'm afraid it might be too late."

Robert blinked, stunned. Fifth and *seventh*? Good Lord. He'd never heard of young ladies taking that many seasons to find a husband. Especially heiresses. Even if the two possessed second heads, he couldn't fathom why fortune hunters weren't pounding down the man's door to get to them.

"Didn't both of your brothers wed last year?" Winslow inquired, knowing as well as every man in Mayfair that the Carlisle brothers had been picked off one by one. Robert was the last one standing from a threesome that had once been considered the bane of marriage-minded mamas everywhere.

"They did." *And may God rest their bachelor souls.*

Oh, they both seemed happy enough. Sebastian, especially, appeared more relaxed than he'd been in years, which was all due to his wife, Miranda. The perfect duchess she certainly wasn't, although she'd proven completely perfect for Sebastian by being nothing he wanted in a wife yet everything he needed in a woman. His brother had gone happily over to the ranks of the enemy, doting on her like a smitten pup. The attention he heaped on her was now made all the worse by her being with child.

His younger brother, Quinton, was little better. His wife, Annabelle, had him up to his neck in tenant leases, farm improvements, livestock, and crops, yet Quinn had never been more focused on his future and was happy to be shackled to a woman who was more than his match in wits and charm.

"Are you planning to follow suit?" Winslow accepted a fresh drink from the attendant.

Popping the cigar between his teeth, Robert firmly shook his head. "No reason to rush into captivity."

His mother, however, had other ideas. Elizabeth Carlisle was beside herself with joy over having three of her four children happily married, two grandchildren already here and one more on the way—which meant she was determined to bring the same wedded bliss to Robert. Even if it killed him.

He dearly loved his mother. But while he would do anything to make her happy, he drew the line at proposing. Just as he would never enter into a bad business deal, he had no plans to enter into marriage. Especially since he'd come to believe that matrimony was simply another business arrangement, negotiated and bound by contract. Yet one a man could never escape when it went bad.

"Didn't you court General Morgan's daughter last season?" Winslow asked. Apparently, Robert wasn't the only one who had done his research for this meeting.

"Yes," he admitted, a touch ruefully. "But we mutually agreed to break off."

And better for both that they did. Diana had gone on to be courted by the Duke of Wembley's youngest son, and Robert had come to realize that he'd rather remain a bachelor. Their courtship had ended without rancor, the two remaining good acquaintances. A situation much to his relief, as he didn't fancy having to face her brother Garrett over pistols at dawn.

"Be assured that marriage is not in my future and that I will give my full attention to the company." Robert exchanged his empty glass for the full one held out by the attendant and explained, "After all, I had the great fortune to be born a second son."

Winslow guffawed so loudly that he drew an irritated glance from Lord Daubney, who sat in the corner reading the *Times*.

"A second son with a happily married older brother—

very happily married, you understand," he clarified. That innuendo brought another laugh from Winslow. "I am a man in no danger of becoming an heir, so a man in no danger of needing a wife."

But he *was* a man in desperate need of a partnership. And with this company, in particular. Winslow Shipping's interests reached around the globe, with successful ventures in India, the Far East, and the Americas. Already the largest sole proprietorship in the empire, the company was poised to grow exponentially over the coming decades. Gaining a partnership with Winslow would be like finding the Golden Fleece. The best opportunity with the best business.

And the very best way to prove to his father's memory that he was worthy of the Carlisle name. Anything less would be failure.

Which was one reason why he'd not disclosed his plans for the partnership with his family. They were already uneasy about his choice of making business his life's path, rather than the usual posts available to second sons. But he couldn't stomach the law or medicine, and he lacked the discipline necessary for the military and the moral fortitude for the church, with no desire to either end men's lives or save their souls.

Of course, the other reason he hadn't told them was that they still blamed him for Richard Carlisle's death. He knew they did. Because he still blamed himself.

Pushing down the sickening guilt at the thought of that terrible night two years ago, he leaned forward, keen to nail down terms. "So you're considering—"

A clatter went up outside. Angry shouts and jeers joined the loud rattle of running hooves approaching wildly down the cobblestone street.

"What on earth?" Winslow frowned and stepped toward the tall window.

Robert shoved himself out of his chair to join him, tossing the butt of his cigar into the fire. Lord Daubney dropped his newspaper as he finally gave up all hope of reading it and hurried over, joining the group of men gathered at the window, to stare down at the spectacle below.

Daubney uttered in disbelief, "A phaeton—driven by a woman?"

"On St James's Street!" The club manager was appalled.

"That's no woman," another gentleman clarified with a disapproving shake of his head. "That's the Hellion."

Robert watched as the rig raced by. Oh, that was definitely the Hellion.

He'd never spoken to the woman, nor ever laid eyes on her before, knowing her only from idle gossip. But it *had* to be her. No lady would have dared such a thing except her, the notorious woman who delighted in outraging the staid old guard of the *ton*. And judging from the sight of her, she'd proven to be just as beautiful and brazen as the gossips claimed. Had she been at a ball, the dark beauty would have had gentlemen fighting among themselves like dogs to gain the favor of her attentions. But here, on the street that housed London's most exclusive gentlemen's clubs and where a respectable woman would never have dared to venture a slippered foot without a male companion, they openly jeered at her.

Robert couldn't help but smile in admiration, despite knowing firsthand the kind of rumors such an outrageous act might rain down upon her.

"And that is why my daughter is in her seventh season," Winslow muttered beneath his breath as the rest of the men returned to their seats, the excitement over.

"Pardon?"

"That, Carlisle," he explained, his back straightening under the weight of humiliation as he turned away from the window, "is my daughter Mariah."

"The *Hellion*?" Robert exclaimed before he could stop himself, flabbergasted. His mind ran wild searching for the woman's name. Then it hit him—Mariah Winslow.

Winslow Shipping and Trade.

Christ.

Winslow's mouth pressed tight, seemingly offended less by the epithet that the gossips had branded on her and more by his daughter herself. "And beside her sat her sister, Evelyn, who is just as determined to mire herself in scandal."

That certainly explained all those seasons without proposals, and judging by this latest antic, none would be forthcoming this year, either. If the Carlisle brothers were the scourge of Mayfair, these two were its female equivalent. Two young ladies who somehow managed to thumb their noses at the quality yet creatively skirt ruining their reputations completely.

"I promised their mother on her deathbed that I would make proper ladies of them, but I've failed," Winslow lamented with a deep frown. "Especially with Mariah. She has no interest in society events or housekeeping, in fashions or flowers...in none of the things that other young ladies enjoy." He waved a dismissive hand. "Instead, she'd rather be working at the shipping offices, spending her time at the wharves with longshoremen and sailors, or wasting her allowance on urchins."

Robert sympathized with the man, but he couldn't help a touch of admiration for his daughters. They certainly weren't part of the boring misses following the suffocating rules of the marriage market like lambs being led to slaughter. They should consider themselves lucky to have escaped the chains of domesticity that society shackled onto its young ladies, who were expected to do nothing more in life than host parties, birth heirs, and retire quietly into the countryside with their embroidery and watercolors.

"What Mariah needs is a husband to settle her into proper womanhood," Winslow muttered, rubbing at the knot of tension at his nape. "But I've no female relatives in society to give her introductions, so no chance of gaining appropriate suitors for her."

Robert raised his glass to his lips and murmured dryly, "That's a shame." It was hard to commiserate with the man when his daughters had practically glowed with freedom as they'd raced past.

Winslow faced Robert, his gaze hard. "But *you* do."

He choked on his cognac. "*What?*"

"I need a partner with connections in the *ton* and the audacity to use them," he said frankly, laying all his cards on the table. "Call on your relatives to guide Mariah through this season, and I'll guarantee you a partnership. A twenty percent stake is yours if an offer is made from a respectable gentleman by the last day of Parliament."

Robert gaped at him. The man was mad.

And utterly serious.

"A partnership," Robert sputtered, echoing his words to make certain he understood him, "in exchange for marrying off your daughter?"

Winslow nodded curtly, frustration evident in every inch of him.

Robert stared at him, incredulous. The offer was preposterous. A test to prove his abilities wasn't out of line, but *this*? Good Lord.

"There seems to be a mistake," he drawled, forcing a half grin and doing his damnedest to keep his own aggravation from showing. Even now, with the partnership flung down onto the table for him to simply pick up, he felt the opportunity slipping through his fingers. "You've confused me with a matchmaking mama."

Winslow shook his head. "Mariah's behavior has to stop, for her own good, and I am at my wit's end. Finding her a husband is the best way to save her from herself." He pinned Robert beneath a hard gaze. "And you're the man to do it."

Not at all the way he wanted to prove himself. Yet he was tempted. So *very* tempted. Especially when Winslow put it like that.

Mariah Winslow certainly wouldn't find a good husband on her own, and he'd be doing only what other men had done for their female relatives for centuries—ensure a good marriage. And yes, to save her from herself. If she kept on as she was doing, remaining unmarried would be the least of her worries, because her antics would turn her into a social pariah. He'd seen women's lives destroyed over far less scandalous things. It would be a damned shame if that happened to the Hellion.

A much-needed marriage for her, a partnership for him...He'd be a fool to let his conscience interfere. Yet uncertainty gnawed at his gut that this might be a step too far in pursuing his goals.

"Seven months to secure a suitable match doesn't strike me as unreasonable for a man of your connections," Winslow challenged, misreading his hesitation. "*If* you truly possess them as you claim."

His eyes narrowed. "Be assured that I do."

"Then come by the house tomorrow at eleven, and you'll have the chance to prove it."

Oh, he could certainly meet this challenge. Easily. After all, Winslow's daughter might be the Hellion, but she was also a shipping heiress with the beauty of an Incomparable. And he had his mother to help him, a dowager duchess longing for something more interesting to do this season than attend the same boring events. A few balls and teas, some new gowns, and even Mariah Winslow would be offered for by March. April at the latest. The partnership would be his, and he would finally prove himself worthy of the Carlisle name.

"Agreed," Robert said. "I won't let you down."

Winslow dubiously arched a brow, even as the two men shook hands.

But Robert was confident, both in himself and in his mother's matchmaking abilities. After all, if Sebastian and Quinton could be sent packing into matrimonial bliss within three months of each other, how hard could it be to marry off the Hellion by season's end?

Chapter Two

 ⁓   ⁓

$\mathscr{M}$ariah Winslow pressed her ear against the study door, but she could hear nothing of the conversation her father was having with her sister. Or rather, the scolding he was undoubtedly unleashing upon poor Evelyn. With a sigh, she sank onto the chair in the hall to wait her turn.

Another morning, another chastisement from Papa...as predictable as the tide on the Thames. Lately, it seemed as if they spent every morning this way, with Papa demanding that she and Evelyn act like proper young ladies and them promising to behave, while wholly unrepentant for their societal sins.

This time, however, she feared that she and Evie might have gone too far.

Certainly, racing Hugh Whitby's phaeton down St James's Street seemed like a good idea at the time. Something daring and bold, Evie had assured her, that would get their hearts pumping and destroy the boredom of a winter's afternoon. *Something to make us feel alive*, Evie had pleaded. Mariah dearly loved her sister and found it difficult to deny Evie anything. Not when she knew how much their mother's death still affected her, even fifteen years later. And certainly not with that adventurous spirit of hers that was simply contagious. So how could she have refused? After all, if she hadn't joined in, God only knew the trouble her younger sister might have gotten into on her own. So she'd conceded, and they'd launched into the madcap adventure that had proven to be as exhilarating as Evie predicted.

Yet Mariah would also never forgive herself if Evelyn were ever seriously punished by Papa for doing something in which Mariah had taken part.

Pressing the edge of propriety was one thing, but if the two of them ever went too far, there could be dire consequences. Evie might be sent away, most likely back to Miss Pettigrew's School for the Education and Refinement of Young Ladies, which seemed populated more by scandalous daughters whose families wanted them exiled all the way to Cornwall than by young ladies seeking refinement. How would Mariah bear to remain here in London without her sister, especially when Papa barely spent any time with her lately, except to chastise her for her unladylike behavior?

It hadn't always been like that. There was a time when Mariah had been his constant shadow, following after him on the wharves and spending more time at the shipping offices than at home. But then he'd sent her away to school, and when she returned, everything had changed. While she still longed to be at his side, Papa was equally determined that she would lead the life of a fine lady. And reputable ladies didn't work in business.

Which was why Mariah didn't care a fig about becoming a lady. What she wanted—what she'd *always* wanted—was a true partnership in Winslow Shipping. And she was deter-mined to have just that.

The study door opened, and Evelyn slipped into the hall-way, looking as unrepentant as ever.

Mariah darted to her feet. "Is he terribly angry?"

"I should begin packing my things for Miss Pettigrew's," Evie answered matter-of-factly, repeating Papa's words.

A knowing smile tugged at Mariah's lips. "So the usual threat, then?"

With a frown of distraction, Evie nodded. Then she cap-tured Mariah's hands in both of hers, with worry darkening her face. "I'm so sorry, Mariah! He blames you."

Of course he did. But he wasn't completely wrong. As the older sister, wasn't it her responsibility to keep Evie from harm?

Evie's bottom lip quivered with guilt. "He's talking about punishing you this time. *Seriously* punishing you."

"It's all right." She squeezed Evie's hands reassuringly. "What can he do to me? I'm too old to be tossed over his knee and spanked."

Most likely, he would forbid her to spend any time during the next fortnight at the Gatewell School in St Katharine's, where she donated the better share of her time and allowance to keeping the doors open, instructors in the classrooms, and food in the children's hungry bellies. Oh, how she loved St Katharine's! It was the same parish where her mother had been born and raised. The same narrow, winding streets where Mariah had often walked hand in hand with her as a little girl. Now, every time Mariah walked through those streets, she felt connected to her mother. Mama was so dis-tant now that Mariah could no longer remember what she'd looked like, knowing her beautiful features only from the portrait in Papa's study. But in St Katharine's, she could remember her mother as clearly as if she still walked beside her.

She wouldn't like being kept away from the school, certainly, but it would be a fitting punishment, both for her and for Whitby, who assisted her at the school and would miss having her help. After all, he was complicit for letting them borrow his phaeton in the first place.

"Mariah," her father called out, "I will see you now."

"Good luck!" Evie placed a kiss to her cheek, then hurried away to her room as she did after every one of these morning talks with their father. Ostensibly to pack for Cornwall, only to be reprieved by dinnertime when Papa always changed his mind.

Drawing in a deep breath, Mariah walked into the study and stopped in front of her father's large desk. She contritely folded her hands in front of her and awaited the ritual tongue-lashing.

"This time, my dear, you have gone too far."

She resisted the urge to roll her eyes.

He wouldn't be scolding her like this if she were a man. No, he'd have been crowing with pride that his son possessed the skills to match any of the best drivers among the gentry. On the other hand, if he'd treated her with the same respect and pride that he would have treated a son, she would have been too busy with the business to look for ways to disrupt a dull afternoon in the first place.

She swallowed down the bitter taste of frustration. At twenty-five, she should have already been a partner in the company, fulfilling the dream she'd wanted since she was a little girl. To have a serious role in running the family business. To participate in the merchant trade that was such a large part of her father's world and that still connected her to her late mother. Instead, he saw her as nothing more than a young miss to be dressed up in furs and silks like a doll, who should be content wasting away her days at silly teas and boring balls.

But Mariah wasn't like that. Had never been. One good look should have told him that.

These days, however, Papa never truly *saw* her at all. Unless she was standing in front of him, being scolded. Like now. But instead of gaining his attention, he saw her behavior as simply another act of rebellion.

He shook his head. "A phaeton on St James's Street."

"I drove that team well," she countered. "You cannot deny that."

"Yes, you drove well." For a moment, she thought she saw a flicker of pride in his eyes. "But you are not a driver at the Ealing Races. You are a young lady from a respectable family—"

Her chest fell. No, not a flicker of pride after all.

"—one who scandalously flaunted herself by racing down St James's Street—"

"I did not *flaunt* myself," she corrected firmly but quietly. Heavens! He made her sound like an actress strutting the boards at Covent Garden.

"—risking both her neck and her sister's, in addition to ruining their reputations."

"Our reputations are not ruined." *That* was one thing about which she was always careful. No matter how bold her antics, she always danced the fine line that separated acts for idle rumors from acts of ruination. Oh, she'd let the fops and hens of the so-called quality gossip about her behind her back all they wanted to, as if she didn't know that they already did just that. As if she didn't know that they'd nick-named her the Hellion. She couldn't care less what those busybodies thought of her.

But ruining her reputation meant possibly ruining the business's reputation, and she would *never* do anything to harm Winslow Shipping. She loved the company as much as her father did, and what she desired more than anything was to work side by side with him in growing the business for the next generation of Winslows who would continue the com-pany that her grandfather had started. She held no delusions about running the business herself. As a woman, she'd never be able to do that. But it was certainly within her reach to be a partner, one who oversaw day-to-day responsibilities. And then it would truly be a family business in every way.

If Papa would ever let her.

"If you keep behaving like some wild creature without any understanding of her position," Papa continued, exasper-ation heavy in his voice, "how do you ever expect to find a respectable husband?"

She bit back the urge to answer that she hoped to find a *dis*respectable husband, knowing a comment like that would certainly get her sent back to Miss Pettigrew's, right beside Evie.

"How do you expect to receive any invitations for this upcoming season if you behave like this?" he demanded in a tone clearly implying that he did not want an answer. "A lady of quality would never invite someone who cannot con-trol herself to her soiree."

Oh, the devil take society invitations! The very *last* place Mariah wanted to be was at some stuffy, boring ball. If so-ciety cut her completely, what would she care...or notice? After all, it wasn't as if the quality was flooding the front foyer with calling cards and invitations in the first place. Not when they regarded the Winslows as nothing but upstart cits infringing on their hallowed aristocratic ranks. While they couldn't ignore the importance of the company or her family's wealth, they could certainly ignore *her*. And did.

Yet this was the part of Papa's speech that Mariah knew by heart, the same one it seemed lately he'd delivered at least once per sennight and more frequently as the new season approached. Another season in which he hoped she would finally venture into the uncharted waters of society and make her mark, ideally snatching up a fine husband in the process. Mariah couldn't have cared less. But this division between them seemed to be growing wider as the season drew nearer.

This hadn't been an issue before she was sent to Miss Pettigrew's, where she'd received a fine education...*if* all she wanted to know was how to host dinner parties, paint watercolors, and play the pianoforte. So she'd taken it upon herself to carve out a real education through tutors secretly paid to ignore whatever frivolous lesson had been planned that day and teach her useful skills instead. The result was an education that more than prepared her for success in business. And a decided lack of talent at the pianoforte.

But Papa refused to entertain the idea of her working with him. All he wanted to know was how she planned to spend her season, when she would marry and give him grandchildren. Every time she arrived at the office to surprise him, to throw herself into work and show him how capable she was, he promptly told her that the docks were no place for a lady and sent her home.

So last fall, she'd set out to prove to her father that she was far more than just some mindless miss. To finally gain his attention as something other than someone to be molded into a perfect society lady. To show him how important the business was to her.

And so far...

"Mariah, you are embarrassing yourself and this family."

It wasn't going well. At this rate, he might never offer her the partnership she dreamt of.

Yet he hadn't offered one to anyone outside the family, either. She took hope in that. Because perhaps that meant he understood that the best person to guide Winslow Shipping and Trade was a Winslow. To Mariah, the company was so much more than a business. It was her heart and soul, and one of the few connections she had left to that happy time before her mother's death. Surely, Papa was coming around to realizing that.

If not... well, then she'd simply wear him down until he surrendered. Siege warfare worked with medieval castles, after all. And she couldn't imagine a more medieval relic than Henry Winslow.

"So I have decided to make some changes."

Mariah's gaze snapped to his. *That* was different.

Usually this was the part of the speech where he threatened to revoke her allowance, to force her to remain room-ridden for the next fortnight, to send her to a convent even though they were devoutly Church of England—

But this time, there were no empty threats. This time, he stared at her across his desk with the same glint in his eyes that shined whenever he faced down business adversaries.

"I've been listening to you during the past few months," he told her, "to your concerns about how the company needs new blood. How we need a new generation to keep us moving into the future."

"You have?" Hope fluttered low in her belly. She could scarcely believe it!

"And I've decided that you are right. Changes need to be made, ones which will benefit the company while also staying true to what your mother wanted." He started for the door. "Come with me."

He stalked from the room in long strides. She fell into step beside him, yet she felt as if she were flying! Her feet barely touched the Persian rug beneath her in her joy to finally—*finally!*—have this opportunity.

"I have so many wonderful ideas we can discuss," she rushed out, barely able to keep her breath beneath the overwhelming excitement pulsing through her. The same breathless joy as racing the phaeton—oh no, so much better!

"Of course." He dismissed her comment with a wave of his hand as they ascended the marble stairs. "First, however, there is a business associate I want you to meet."

"Oh?" She puzzled as she followed him down the hall to the drawing room. "Who?"

But heavens, she didn't care! At that moment, she didn't want to meet anyone. Not when her chest was bursting with happiness. Instead, she wanted to skip and dance all the way to the company's offices on Wapping High Street and—

Papa smiled proudly. "The man I've selected to be my partner."

Mariah froze as the world plunged away beneath her. A partner? It couldn't be. It simply *couldn't* be true! A *partner* . . .

But not her.

Stunned numb with disbelief, she was helpless to do anything more than stand in the doorway and watch her father stride across the room to greet the man waiting there.

Her vision blurred with frustrated tears, and she forced herself to breathe as the waking nightmare crashed over her, as the numbness slowly gave way to piercing desolation. And grief. The same terrible grief that had overwhelmed her when her mother died.

"Carlisle." Her father enthusiastically shook the man's hand, oblivious to the wretchedness he'd just unwittingly unleashed upon his daughter. "Glad to have you here."

"My pleasure." The man smiled as he released her father's hand, stepping his legs apart and placing his fisted hand at the small of his back in a stance that was one of pure masculine command and ease. As if he had every right to be there, invading her life and stealing away her father's attentions.

Papa gestured for her to approach. "Let me introduce you to my daughter."

But Mariah held her ground near the doorway, for once less from obstinacy and more because she didn't have the strength to come forward without collapsing to the floor in sobs. Instead, she pressed her fist against her chest and willed herself to keep breathing.

"My eldest daughter, Mariah." Her father frowned when she didn't come sweeping across the room to greet their guest as any proper lady of the house would have. To graciously welcome this man into her home. And into a position with the company that should have been hers.

She simply couldn't do it. *Never* that.

Blinking back her tears, she lifted her chin and silently stared at the stranger in cool disdain, even as her heart shattered like ice. She had too much pride to reveal how much this meeting devastated her. She *was* a Winslow, after all. Even if Papa had forgotten what that meant.

"Mariah, this is Lord Robert Carlisle." Her father slapped him on the shoulder. "The man who wants to partner with me to conquer the world's shipping routes!"

A bitter taste formed in her mouth. *Partner.* On what merits? As her eyes raked over him, she saw nothing to believe that this man was any more qualified than she was. Moreover, *she* was a Winslow, entitled by blood and history to take her rightful place at her father's side. While this man was nothing but an opportunistic interloper.

Certainly, he was dressed well, sporting a dark blue cashmere jacket over a blue-and-cream-checkered satin waistcoat, a simply tied cream-colored cravat, and black trousers. The whole effect was one of careful consideration, she was sure, in an attempt to look as if he cared little for appearances while taking great pains to do so. She would have labeled him a dandy if not for the slight scuff to his boots, which showed that he'd actually ridden a horse to the house instead of being brought by carriage. Not a dandy, then, but certainly a Corinthian. One of those physically attractive and stylish young bucks over whom the old hens of the *ton* practically swooned whenever they flashed a charming smile.

If there was one thing she'd come to know since she'd returned to London, however, it was that dandies, Corinthians, and bucks possessed very little intelligence among the lot of them. Certainly not the kind of business acumen that Winslow Shipping needed to flourish. Or the dedication that only a family member possessed.

"Miss Winslow." Carlisle crossed the room to her and bowed graciously. "A pleasure to meet you."

A pleasure. That was a lie if ever she'd heard one. She bobbed a stiff, shallow curtsy. Then purposefully ignored his courtesy title. "*Mr.* Carlisle."

His eyes gleamed with amusement at that, as if he knew what dark thoughts about him lurked inside her.

"A businessman, are you?" she drawled coolly, affecting that same tone that Miss Pettigrew had used at school to keep the girls in line.

"I've dabbled."

"In shipping?" she pressed. Did the man even understand how the day-to-day operations of merchant trade worked? By the looks of him, she doubted he'd ever spent a single day laboring at the quayside or in warehouses. But *she* had, in those few precious weeks after she'd returned from school, before her father decided that a shipping company was no place for a lady.

He modestly shrugged. "A bit."

"Forgive me for doubting your *bit* of competence." His eyes flared, and this time it wasn't with amusement. "But it seems to me that of all the people my father could have chosen—"

"Mariah, give the man peace," Papa ordered, a faint warning underlying his voice. And an even larger warning in the look he shot her. He turned to Carlisle and explained, "Mariah's always been as protective as a bulldog of the company."

Carlisle smiled at her, a charming grin she was certain he used to make his way through the world. And into women's beds. Well, well—a Corinthian *and* a rake. In Winslow Shipping and Trade. Had Papa lost his mind?

"Quite all right," Carlisle asserted, but his eyes never strayed from Mariah. As if he realized that she considered him an adversary. "No offense taken."

"Good," Papa assured him, with an affectionate but frustrated smile at Mariah, "since you're here precisely because of my daughter."

Mariah gaped at that. How on earth could *this* be her fault? "I don't understand."

"Do you think I haven't been listening to you?" He crossed to the tantalus in the corner of the room and removed a bottle of bourbon, then gestured toward Carlisle with it. "Been talking my ear off lately about what the business needs, how to leverage assets, where to create new trade routes…" He poured two glasses and handed one to Carlisle, keeping the other for himself. "That I should take on a partner."

Not allowing humiliation to color her cheeks, Mariah folded her hands in front of her skirts and said quietly, "I meant me."

That drew Carlisle's attention. His gaze snapped to her, narrowing hard for a beat.

So did her father's. For a fleeting moment, she thought she saw longing to do as she asked darken his face, followed by a flash of guilt.

But then it was gone, and he was shaking his head. "A shipping company is not the place for a lady."

"But it *is* the place for a Winslow," she pressed quietly. "A family business should be run by family."

"And a daughter's duty to her family is to be a proper lady." Papa was beginning to lose his patience. "Not a businessman."

"The two do not have to be mutually exclusive," she argued calmly, even as desperation knotted in her belly. She would *not* give up without a fight. "Family should run the company, not outsiders. It was what Grandfather wanted."

"And I promised to raise you into a proper lady," Papa countered. "It was what *your mother* wanted."

His words sliced through her like a knife, cutting down to her heart, and she flinched, unable to answer.

She turned her head away as the tears became dangerously close to falling and blinked furiously. She would *never* let Papa see this weakness in her.

"And that is exactly what I intend to do," Papa promised. "What is best for you *and* for the company. Which is why I chose Carlisle." Hiding his chagrin over the argument they'd just waged in front of the man, her father forced a smile and tapped his glass against Carlisle's. The clink echoed through the silent room and teeth-jarringly rattled all the way down Mariah's spine. "He's the best man to do both. If he can prove himself."

If. Hope sparked inside her. Then the partnership wasn't final? "How?"

"By helping me with a new real estate venture I'm undertaking," her father answered. He leveled his gaze on her, the intensity of it clearly stating that he would brook no argument. "And by giving you a proper season."

She gasped at the unexpectedness—and sheer *absurdity*—of that. "Pardon?"

"My mother is the Dowager Duchess of Trent," Carlisle offered helpfully. "Your father thought you'd appreciate having her support this season."

"Dowager duchess," she repeated, not knowing how her numb lips were able to form the words. Her blood turned to ice, chilling her where she stood.

So Lord Robert Carlisle was the son of a duke. Her father's choice of him for a partner now made sense. Horrible, horrifying sense.

"Mother enjoys helping young ladies with their seasons," Carlisle continued with a smile, unaware that she'd figured out why *him*. "Once I heard that you had no female relatives who could provide introductions, I was certain she'd be willing to assist you."

"I understand." And she did. Perfectly. "How clever of you, Papa," she said quietly, her eyes stinging with fresh tears. What mattered how deep—or shallow—Carlisle's business mind if his connections stretched all the way into the Lords? And to a duke, no less. Her father was doing what was best for the family business, all right. By bringing in the family of a peer.

"Two birds, one stone." Her father gave her a satisfied look, as if he'd arrived at the answers to the world's worst problems. All encapsulated right there in the dashing, golden form of Robert Carlisle. Her father lifted his glass to toast his solution. "Winslow Shipping gets young blood in a much-needed partner, and you get a proper London season at last."

But she didn't want a season. She wanted a role within the company, the chance to work side by side with her father. While this—this *interloper* came waltzing in with his sapphire-blue eyes and his duke of a brother to snatch her dream away.

"To what end?" she asked quietly, too angry and frustrated to think clearly.

Her father blinked, as if the answer were obvious. "Marriage, of course."

The world tilted beneath her, her breath dying in her throat. She reached for the back of a nearby chair to keep from losing her balance and falling to the floor.

"You cannot be serious," she whispered, unable in her surprise to find her voice.

"Very serious." His face turned grim. "Your latest antics

proved that I have not raised you properly, but I will no longer fail you as a father."

She stared at him, stunned. Was that truly what he thought—that he'd *failed* her, when all she'd wanted was to capture his attention?

"No," she whispered, her heart aching with pained misunderstanding, "you *haven't* failed. That wasn't at all what—"

"And I will *not* fail your mother," he added firmly. "She wanted her daughters to be the fine ladies that she could never be as the daughter of a sea captain. And that is exactly what I plan on giving her. Proper ladies with respectable husbands."

"But *I* don't want that," she protested softly, her voice barely louder than a breath. Oh heavens, how much it hurt to defy her mother's wishes! But Mama would also want her to be happy, and nothing in the world would bring her more happiness than being at her father's side.

"Carlisle will make that happen, both for you and your mother," he continued, although Mariah couldn't tell if he'd not heard her or if he'd heard and chosen to ignore her. "Arrangements have been made. It's done now."

"Papa, I will not participate in this," she announced calmly, forcing her voice to remain steady even as her insides roiled with fury and betrayal. And more anguish than she wanted to acknowledge at openly defying him, when all she'd ever wanted was to make him proud of her.

"You do not have a choice."

The sickening realization sank through her that this was the serious punishment Evie had warned her about. Her own special banishment, right into the hell of society.

"You will involve yourself fully in the season—

introductions, balls, breakfasts, soirees... *all* of it—whatever Carlisle and the duchess decide is best for you." His gaze never wavered from hers. "Or I'll cut off your allowance."

The air rushed from her lungs. Her *allowance*, and with it, all the help she provided to the Gatewell School and the children of St Katharine's, children in need just like her mother had been. If Mariah lost the school, dear God, she'd lose her mother all over again!

"You wouldn't," she whispered. Her hands clenched into helpless fists. The same powerless frustration swept over her that she remembered from when she'd been sent away to school, away from Evie and Papa and everything she loved.

Her father said nothing but turned away and tossed back the rest of the bourbon with a gasping swallow. It was impossible to say if the flicker in his eyes came from guilt or resolve.

Mariah stared at him, her chest burning so fiercely that each beat of her heart shattered through her like a hammer against glass. Oh, she'd certainly gotten his attention this time, but the result wasn't at all what she'd hoped. Instead of allowing her to work at his side, he'd turned the distance between them into a chasm.

And right in front of a stranger, no less. At least Carlisle had the decency to say nothing, staring down into his bourbon rather than watching them. Or gloating that he'd won.

A soft scratch sounded at the door. "Excuse me, sir."

Bentley, the butler who had run the household for her family as long as Mariah could remember, stepped into the room.

"What is it?" Papa seemed grateful for the interruption.

"There's a caller at the door, sir." Bentley glanced warily between all three of them, clearly sensing the tension that hung over the room as thick as London fog. "Mr. Ledford from the shipping office."

"I'm afraid I have to see to this." Papa set down his glass and gestured at the two of them. "I'll be gone only a moment. You two need to discuss the upcoming season anyway. Why not get started immediately?"

As her father strode from the room, Mariah narrowed her eyes on Carlisle, turning all of her anger and frustration onto him. Then she smiled slowly, calculatingly…

Why not, indeed?

CHAPTER THREE

$\sim$ $\sim$

$\mathcal{R}$obert gazed at Mariah Winslow over the rim of his glass as he took another swallow of bourbon. He certainly needed a drink after witnessing that familial battle of wills.

He'd anticipated that the Hellion wouldn't be happy to be harnessed by society's rules, but he certainly hadn't expected *this*. Or that she actually thought Winslow would consider her for the partnership. It might have been a family business, but family usually meant sons and sons-in-law. There were few examples of daughters being allowed into businesses as anything more than figureheads, and even then only with small companies. And none that brought them into contact with sailors and longshoremen.

In Winslow's boots, he most likely would have done the same. Yet he understood her frustration.

He slowly lowered the glass. "So you want to be a partner in your father's company." There was no point in dancing around the subject, not when it hung in the air as palpable as the snow falling beyond the bay windows.

"I do." She folded her hands behind her back, although less likely from demureness and more to keep herself from scratching his eyes out. "And you think you're going to be able to marry me off?"

"I do." With the help of his mother, his sister, fate, a prevailing trade wind, and nonstop prayers to God. "I'll certainly give it my best shot."

Her lips curled in amusement, and a low warning prickled at the backs of his knees. "And I as well." Her green eyes gazed at him innocently enough, but something told him that they'd just agreed to two completely different outcomes. She tilted her head thoughtfully. "Lord Robert Carlisle...how do I know that name?"

"My father was the late Duke of Trent." He fought back a grimace. He disliked acknowledging his connection to the title, preferring to be known for his own accomplishments.

"That's not it." Her catlike eyes swept over him, blatantly sizing him up. Like an opponent before a fight.

"My mother is active in society events. Perhaps you two met at a soiree."

"Oh, I'm quite certain *that's* not it. You see, I don't have time for frivolities." Her smile never moved, yet it seemed to harden. Which was a damnable shame, because she had a very sensuous mouth. The kind a man could enjoy kissing for hours. "I'm too busy following the trade business to bother waltzing at balls."

"Of course," he murmured, certain she didn't spend much time at society events. He'd have remembered meeting her...a dark rose among the pastel daisies of the unmarried ladies. And she certainly had thorns. "My brothers, then."

"Pardon?" She blinked, surprised by that sudden turn of conversation.

"The Carlisle brothers," he explained, a touch ruefully. "We made quite a reputation for ourselves in our younger days. That must be where you've heard of me."

"Perhaps." She gave a dismissive sniff. "But I definitely know it wasn't in praise for being a good businessman."

Thorns, indeed. But she'd have to try a lot harder than that tiny prick to wound him. "Your father thinks my business acumen enough to benefit the company."

"Papa thinks he can use you to gain influence in Parliament," she corrected quietly but bluntly.

He finished off the rest of his bourbon, hiding the sting to his pride. "I know."

Surprise flickered in her eyes. Clearly, she'd thought him either too naïve or too daft to have figured out the real reason why he, of all men, was important to Winslow. But he'd known from the beginning.

He crossed the room to the tantalus and refilled his glass. "My brother Sebastian, the current Duke of Trent, sits on several important committees in Parliament, including the committee which governs trade and tariffs. So does the Duke of Chatham, the father of my brother-in-law, the Marquess of Chesney, who will someday take over for him in Parliament." He reached for a second crystal tumbler and splashed in two fingers' worth of bourbon. "And my family maintains a strong friendship with the Duke of Strathmore, although the duke's interests lean more toward the military than commerce, but one never knows when privately held ships might be called into commission or when merchants might need to supply army provisions."

Even though he'd never deign to exploit the connections he'd so glibly listed, he took pleasure in inverting her opinion of him as someone who didn't realize his own worth.

He'd certainly considered the power of all his connections many times while he'd been researching Winslow Shipping.

He continued, "My cousin, Ross Carlisle, Earl of Spalding, is currently a high-level diplomat within the Court of St James's, and my brother Quinton is well on his way to someday being elected an MP from Cumbria, if the villagers don't decide to tar and feather him first." He carried both drinks back to her. "All in all, I'd say those connections are worth a twenty percent stake." He held out the second glass toward her, his eyes not leaving hers. "Don't you agree?"

A burst of satisfaction spun through him at the flash of annoyance in her eyes. If the minx wanted a bare-knuckle fight, he'd give her one that would make Gentleman Jackson take note. This partnership was his best hope to put his father's ghost to rest and repent for his sins, and no one would stand in his way. *No one.* Certainly not some green-eyed harridan, no matter how curvaceous her lithe body or how tempting those berry-red lips, which on any other woman would have appeared too full but on her were succulently ripe.

Her gaze darted suspiciously to the bourbon. "Did you poison it?"

"And ruin fine Kentucky bourbon?" He quirked a brow as if offended. "Do you take me for a heathen?"

A faint smile tugged at her lips, the first genuinely amused expression he'd seen from her since she walked into the room. And it was surprisingly nice.

But it faded quickly, and she coolly accepted the glass. "At least you appreciate good liquor," she grudgingly muttered, then took a sip. "Most Englishmen consider bourbon beneath them, preferring to spend twice as much for cognac that's half as good."

He raised his glass toward her in a casual toast. "I am not one of those men."

Her eyes gleamed at that, as if she might find respect for him after all. "My father deals in the finest bourbons. It's one of the perks of trading with the Americans. That, and we also get the best coffees and cocoas."

"And cigars," he added knowingly. "Winslow Shipping traded more than six thousand pounds in American cigars last year."

"Impressive." The tip of her tongue darted out to innocently lick away a drop of bourbon still clinging to her upper lip, but he felt that small lick burn through him like liquid fire. *Sweet Lucifer.*

If he couldn't find her a husband by August, it would only be because the devil himself wanted to keep her for his own wanton pleasures.

"I've studied your father's company, Miss Winslow, and I know what goods he specializes in, which countries his ships sail to, which merchants he buys from at all ports of call, just as I know the best buyers in England where he can sell those goods for the most profit and how to leverage that profit once we have it. I assure you, he's found a good partner in me."

"But you're not a Winslow." She eyed him over the rim of her glass as she held it thoughtfully to her lips. "Tell me, Lord Robert—"

"Just Robert," he corrected. He hated that appellation, preferring to make his own mark away from the shadow of the title. "Or Carlisle, if you prefer. There's no room for courtesies in business." *Or in war.* And he had the sinking feeling he'd just stumbled unwittingly into the fray.

"Carlisle," she repeated distastefully, nearly making him laugh with how evident her dislike of him was. Not that it

mattered what she thought of him. Certainly, an amiable relationship would make the season easier for both of them,
but he'd walk through the flames of hell to prove himself if
he had to. "Do you take the same position as my father? That
business is the realm of men and that ladies should do nothing more taxing than watercolors?"

"I don't believe that's what your father thinks," he murmured, remembering Winslow's words about fulfilling his
late wife's wishes to turn their daughters into ladies. And
sympathizing immensely with the man's frustrations, now
that he'd met his daughter.

"Do you?" she pressed.

He couldn't help a twitch of his lips at her doggedness.
"One doesn't hold that view among the Carlisle women and
live a long life."

The quick narrowing of her eyes told him she wasn't satisfied with his answer. "Do *you* believe that?"

He took a slow step toward her, inexplicably drawn to
the fight in her. Like a moth to a flame, he was unable to
stop himself, even though he knew the fire would most
likely burn. "I believe, Miss Winslow," he clarified quietly
but firmly, wanting no mistake between them on this point,
"that ladies are capable of holding their own against gentlemen in nearly every endeavor—"

"*Nearly* every?" she echoed.

Good Lord. Was the Hellion a reformer, too? The more
he learned about her, the more he realized exactly how mon-
umental the task was that Winslow had given him to find her
a husband.

"Nearly every," he repeated, thinking of all the antics he
and his brothers had committed during their reign of terror.
Some of those were certainly not fit for ladies. Or most men.

"Including business. I've no doubt that you would make a fine partner."

That surprised her, based on the flicker in her green eyes. "Well, then you concede—"

"But I would be a better one."

With that, he stunned her, and long enough that he was able to take another step to close the distance between them, remove the glass from her hand, and set it aside before she decided to fling its contents at him. Which would be a true waste of fine bourbon.

"I have no intention of surrendering this opportunity," he told her frankly. Directness seemed to garner more of her respect than subtlety, so he'd gladly oblige. And found it surprisingly refreshing to be able to be so blunt with a woman. "Not even to you."

Neither of them moved in the silence that followed that declaration, both unwilling to back down.

As they faced each other, he noted that they were almost evenly matched for height. She barely had to tilt her head back to look up at him, her lips very nearly level with his...those same lips that even now twisted tightly together in an aggravated grimace. What would it taste like, that sensuous mouth of hers that reminded him of a ripe cherry, all dark red and juicy? Inexplicably tart and sweet at the same time? Or would it have the bite of a poison apple?

"Then you're going to have a difficult task ahead of you, I'm afraid," she whispered, and God help him, he leaned in to catch each word.

"Not so difficult," he countered, his deep voice far huskier than he'd intended. But the hellcat had him saying all kinds of things he didn't intend, including, "You're beautiful."

Her lips parted in surprise. He nearly chuckled as he stared at her. For once, he'd left her speechless.

Risking a slap, yet unable to stop himself, he reached to touch one of the ebony tendrils framing the side of her face and rubbed the lock between his thumb and forefinger. His gut tightened at the smooth feel of it. Like black silk. Which immediately made him wonder if her bare skin would feel just as silky beneath his hands.

Her breath hitched, and her wide eyes dropped to his mouth, lingering there on his lips.

Did the minx want him to kiss her? Those lips, that hair…How many men had succumbed to her spell and done just that? And how many hadn't survived?

"Intelligent and sharp," he murmured.

She stood perfectly still beneath his touch, except for a nervous swallow that undulated softly in her throat and had him wanting to place his lips right there against her neck to feel it. And against the pulse he could see racing in the hollow at her collarbone even now. Was it arousal that had her senses alert, her pulse racing? Or fury?

Shamelessly, he didn't care which. Even now she had him longing to take far more intimate touches than the mere stroking of her hair that he was so brazenly stealing.

"And an heiress," he murmured. "What man could resist?"

She blinked, breaking the spell. "An heiress?" she repeated, her breathless voice evidence that she'd been affected by his caress. "Is that what you think?"

"Of course." What would she do if he dared to trace his thumb over her bottom lip? Would this hellcat sigh with pleasure or sink her teeth into his flesh in attack?

"But didn't Papa tell you?" A throaty laugh of surprise fell from her. "I have no dowry."

Clenching his jaw as the lilting sound of her laugh twisted into his gut like a knife, he dropped his hand away. No dowry, with *her* reputation—*Christ*. He'd been bitten, all right.

She clucked her tongue disapprovingly. "First rule of business: never commit to an agreement until you know all the terms." A victorious gleam lit her eyes. "*All* the terms."

Ignoring her baiting, he fought to keep the incredulity from his face. "You don't have a dowry?"

"Not one ha'penny." With the smile of the cat that ate the canary, she turned away from him, snatching up her glass of bourbon as she went. "Neither of us Winslow daughters do. Oh, Papa is wealthy enough to negotiate a fine marriage settlement, but he doesn't believe in them." She paused in front of the fireplace. "Marital bribery, in his opinion." Bracing her arm against the mantel, she gestured with the glass and puffed out her chest in an impression of Henry Winslow. "'If a man wants my money, let him come to work for me to get it!'"

A rather good impression, he admitted grudgingly, as the harsh realization of what he was truly up against spiraled through him.

"'If he wants my daughter, then money shouldn't matter.'" She raised the glass in a toast as she belted out in a deep voice that sounded eerily like her father's, "'And if he wants both my money *and* my daughter, then he is a greedy bastard who deserves neither!'"

With a flourish of the glass in the air, she finished the impression by tossing back the remaining bourbon in a single swallow. And *that* was as equally impressive as the impersonation.

Applauding her performance with a slow clapping of his

hands, he walked toward her. "Very nicely played." He bit back his opinion that she had better odds of becoming a successful actress than she did of gaining the partnership, wanting to escape the afternoon unslapped. "But the man you marry will still become part of Winslow Shipping. His share of the company serves as your dowry."

"No." Her eyes grew serious, all traces of her previous teasing vanishing. "My father will never bring a son-in-law into the business. You see, my grandfather did with the man my aunt married, giving him both her dowry and a large part of the company, only to watch him change into a drunkard and a gambler. He turned my aunt against her family, then ruined the marriage and nearly destroyed the company before they were able to force him out. Until the day she died, my aunt never again spoke to my father." She shook her head sadly, as if grieving for all that her family had lost. "Papa might eventually relent and bestow a dowry, but believe me when I tell you that he will *never* relent on that."

The hole around him grew deeper, and the sensation gripped him that the partnership was once more slipping through his fingers. "Then your husband will wait until your father dies to get his due." He was grasping at straws now. *Anything* to keep hold of this opportunity. "You'll still be an heiress, dowry or not."

"Unlikely. Knowing Papa, he's probably left the company to some distant relative none of us knows just to keep Winslow Shipping out of the hands of fortune hunters."

Which was exactly something Henry Winslow would do. The same things that drew Robert's interest in partnering with him—his success, his shrewdness, his belief that a man needed to prove his worth—now cut like a double-edged sword.

"Doesn't it bother you that he's made it so difficult for you to secure a husband?" he bit out, wanting commiseration in his mounting frustration.

"Actually, in that," she replied with full sincerity, "I agree with him. It would be terrible to wonder which my husband wanted more, my money or me. This way, I'll know he wants me." She gave a soft sigh, as if she'd often pondered exactly that. "So you see, it isn't going to be as easy to marry me off as you think. You'll have to find suitors who want to court me because they actually *like* me, and, well..." She shrugged as if it were the most obvious thing in the world. "I'll make it difficult for anyone to like me."

"Oh, I'm certain of that," he muttered.

She laughed with a genuine amusement that fell through him like a warm summer breeze.

Frustration blistered inside him. If the damned woman wanted to, she could easily find a man willing to take her for her beauty and mind. Dowry be damned. Her wit alone could keep a man happily challenged for years.

Yet he also knew the slim odds of finding a love match for a woman hanging on to the fringe of society by her fingertips.

"Don't you want a husband?" he pressed. "A family and home of your own?"

"I'd rather have Winslow Shipping." Her voice emerged so intensely that it quavered. "The company *is* my family, as much a part of me as any child could ever be." She took a deep breath, and he knew she was genuinely trying to make him understand. "I have wanted to help my father run the business since I was a little girl, since the first time I visited the wharves. I was mesmerized by all those ships, by the sailors and porters as they worked. Papa showed me everything, pointing out all the small details and explaining how trade worked. It was magical, and I have never forgotten it."

Coming from anyone else, he would have called her speech poetic and naïve. But from her, the words landed with quiet authority and heartfelt dedication. She was no simpering debutante bedazzled by the sights of the season; she was a woman in full, one who knew exactly what she wanted. He should have felt the cut of that hard edge to her, yet she fascinated him even more because of it.

"I won't let you take my place at my father's side," she said, as calmly as if stating a fact about the weather. *Rain falls down, winters are cold…I won't let you win.* "The best partner for Winslow Shipping is a Winslow. Always has been, always will be."

At that declaration, he reached past her shoulder to set his glass on the mantel and leaned in close, bringing his face level with hers. Close enough that he could see flecks of gold in her emerald eyes and smell the exotic scent of orange and cinnamon lingering on her skin. He touched her hair again, and this time as he pulled away he let his knuckles caress across her cheek, even as he carefully kept his fingers out of biting range.

"You don't have a choice," he reminded her. A faint blush pinked her cheeks, and he couldn't help but faintly smile at her reaction. That she should react so strongly to such a little touch…*Remarkable.* "Unless you want to be cut off, you have to do as required of you this season."

Her bottom lip jutted up defiantly. "Papa will see sense and relent. He always does."

His gaze fixed on her mouth. If she wasn't careful, a man might just feel compelled to wipe that disobedient smirk off her lips with his. And enjoy it immensely. "Not this time. He's expecting you to fully participate in the season and make a valiant attempt at finding a husband. If you refuse to cooperate, you'll lose."

"Then so will you," she countered, her soft breath spicy-sweet as it fanned his lips and vibrated an electric tingle through him. "Because you won't succeed at your test, and you won't get the partnership."

Unable to resist any longer, and thoroughly willing to risk a bite, he brushed his thumb over her bottom lip.

She gasped, her lips parting in surprise. Yet she didn't step away.

Emboldened by her defiance, and enchanted by the fire inside her, he slowly traced his fingertip around her mouth, drawing the outline of her full lips. When she trembled, the electric tingle inside him turned into a yearning ache. *Never* had he wanted to kiss a woman more than he did at that moment.

"I'm willing to take that chance," he drawled in a low voice, then quirked a brow in challenge. "Are you?"

As if considering her options and finding no escape from her father's plans for her, she stared at him silently, her eyes shining with unshed tears of frustration. She whispered, each word a warm breath against his fingers, "I will *never* surrender."

Admiration for her perseverance flared inside him, and he murmured, "I would be disappointed if you did."

He dropped his hand to his side and stepped back. Oh, certainly to keep from touching her again, although this time more than likely to throttle her. Then he turned on his heel and walked away.

"I might have to participate in this fiasco of a season," she called after him as he headed toward the door, "but I certainly don't have to make it easy on you."

"From you, Miss Winslow," he replied with a heavy sigh, acknowledging her tenacity if not the aggravation she sparked inside him, "I would expect nothing less."

With that declaration of war, he politely inclined his head and stepped from the room.

*   *   *

Still muttering to herself as she'd done during the entire hour-long carriage ride from Mayfair to St Katharine's, Mariah hurried up the front steps of the massive stone house that served as the Gatewell School for Orphans of the Sea, cursing Robert Carlisle, his connections in Parliament, and every one of his ancestors whose procreation culminated in *him*. A man so infuriating that she could barely see straight by the time he'd so arrogantly sauntered from the drawing room.

The audacity of that man! To come sweeping into her life to take the company away from her. To turn her father against her. To force a season upon her, with the end goal of marrying her off...oh, the mortification of it! And to dare to touch her the way he did—

Well, perhaps *that* wasn't so awful. Except that behind the caresses stood the devil himself, gleefully ready to take her soul.

She swiped at her eyes as she hurried through the maze of rooms that comprised both school and safe haven to children whose fathers had died at sea or working on the wharves. The solidity of this old house with its sagging roof and cracked walls had always brought her comfort. So had the knowledge that she was helping children just like her mother, who had lost her own father to the sea. Every time

Mariah entered this building, she felt Mama smile, as if she were watching over her from heaven.

But today, even the school couldn't bring her peace.

Doing her best to force from her mind the image of Carlisle's infuriating grin, she ran down the back stairs and into the kitchen in search of Mrs. Smith, the woman who served as both housekeeper and cook for the school. On the tip of her tongue she held an angry rant about Carlisle so venomous that she was certain it would peel the whitewash from the walls once she unleashed it.

But she halted in the middle of the doorway. Inside the kitchen, Mrs. Smith pulled a fresh sheet of biscuits from the oven, and Hugh Whitby sat perched on a stool at the table, relating some juicy bit of gossip while rolling out little balls of dough.

At the sight of her two dearest friends, an anguished sob tore from her.

Mrs. Smith looked up and dropped the sheet onto the table with a clatter. "Mariah!" Concern instantly gripped her. "My dear, whatever is the—"

But Whitby had already sprung to his feet and hurried to her, to slip an arm around her shoulders and gently help her sit on one of the chairs. By then, she was sobbing uncontrollably. All the anger and betrayal from that morning's introduction to that horrible man came surging out of her in an unbridled wave of wretchedness.

"Mariah?" Whitby's face paled at her tears, making his sky-blue eyes and shock of ginger hair stand out even more than usual as he knelt in front of her and fished a handkerchief from his waistcoat pocket. "What's happened?"

Blowing her nose on the handkerchief, she poured out a

description of that morning's events, carefully leaving out the part when that rake had touched her.

When she finished her story, her shoulders were straighter, and her chest was lighter. She felt better, as she always did after unburdening herself to her friends. Yet she wasn't naïve enough to dismiss so easily the oncoming storm set to rush over her during the months to come.

"*Robert* Carlisle?" Whitby repeated incredulously, moving back to his stool as Mrs. Smith set a cup of tea on the table in front of her.

She sniffed. "You know him?"

"My brothers knew him at Eton. They told all kinds of stories about the Carlisles and how they were always being reprimanded by the prefect." He grinned, a goofy smile that was all big teeth and dimples and somehow just as gangly as the rest of him. "Don't know how they never got expelled."

Her fingers tightened around the handkerchief. *This* was the man her father wanted to run Winslow Shipping?

"Of course, I don't believe all those stories." Whitby shook his head as he logically deduced, "I mean, how could a cow fit inside a carriage?"

Her tear-blurred eyes widened.

"And as for those Chinese acrobats, why, I don't think there are that many in all of England. Certainly not enough to fill an entire vicarage!"

Mariah's heart lurched.

"Now, Mr. Whitby," Mrs. Smith scolded lightly, setting a plate of warm biscuits on the table, "Mariah doesn't want to hear stories like that."

Certainly not!

"She wants to hear about the man's character," the housekeeper explained, "and be assured of his good intentions."

"*Robert Carlisle?*" Whitby blurted out. "I'm not certain he has any—"

"Whitby!" Mariah pleaded. He was a dear friend, but if he didn't stop talking, she might very well have to shove a biscuit into his mouth to silence him. She groaned and hung her head in her hands. "What am I going to do?"

"There, there now." Mrs. Smith put her arm around her shoulders and gave her a squeeze. "'Twill work out all right in the end. You'll see."

Mariah shook her head and reached for the cup of tea, to hold it between her trembling hands and take comfort in its warmth. "How can it? I'm being compelled into a season against my will at the hands of a horrible man." One who apparently forced innocent cows into carriages and hordes of acrobats onto parish vicars. God only knew what that portended for *her*. "I'm caught. Either way I lose the partnership."

Whitby's face softened sympathetically. He knew how much that dream meant to her of being the next generation of Winslows to guide the business into the future, to have once more that feeling of closeness with her father that she'd experienced so long ago. But she also suspected, despite Whitby's ever-present optimism, that he'd never truly expected it to come true.

"You don't have to go through with this, Mariah," he told her.

"If I don't, I lose my allowance," she reminded him quietly. "And if I lose my allowance..." She waved her hand at the old house around them. "Then Gatewell loses, too. And we cannot afford to lose a single farthing."

"I'll ask my father to—"

"No." She affectionately squeezed his hand. "Your father

has already been extremely generous." The baron owned the building and let the school use it for free as long as they kept up the property. Without Whitby's father, the school would have to relocate. But without her allowance, it would have to close completely. "This is my problem, and I'll find a solution."

Whitby's boyish face turned uncharacteristically solemn as he popped one of the biscuits into his mouth and chewed thoughtfully, his mind racing to solve her problem. That was what she loved most about Whitby. He was loyal beyond measure.

Mrs. Smith sat in the chair across the table from Whitby and reached for the bowl of dough, keeping her flour-whitened hands busy rolling out balls. And *that* was what Mariah loved most about Mrs. Smith—her unfailing belief that tea and biscuits could solve any dilemma. "You know, it might not be as bad as you think."

"Because it might be even worse?" she sighed out miserably.

Mrs. Smith's lips twisted into an expression of motherly disapproval. "You've never had a real season."

"I've had six," Mariah reminded her with chagrin.

"No, my dear." She placed a ball on the sheet and pushed the bowl toward Whitby to once more get his help, although Mariah suspected it was done more to keep him from eating up all the biscuits that were already cooling. "You've never had a proper season. Not the kind you deserve."

She countered defensively, "My seasons were just fine."

"You had no invitations, no gowns, absolutely no suitors—"

"Thank you," Mariah grumbled sardonically.

"And you deserve to have it all. To be Cinderella in the fairy tale." Mrs. Smith gave a dreamy sigh. "Now you have the opportunity for a proper introduction, and under the guidance of a duchess, no less! A chance to meet all the most eligible gentlemen, attend all the best events, perhaps waltz with a duke—"

Mariah laughed at that.

"And what's so amusing? A duke should consider himself lucky to dance with a beautiful lady like you." When Mariah rolled her eyes, Mrs. Smith gently kicked Whitby under the table. "Tell her, Mr. Whitby, how beautiful she is."

"What?" Whitby glanced up and blinked, startled from his own thoughts.

"Don't you think that Mariah's beautiful?" Mrs. Smith prompted.

He glanced at Mariah and blinked again. "Oh yeah, sure." Then he reached for another biscuit.

Mariah smiled. Whitby, always true to form.

She took the biscuit from his fingers just as he was about to pop it into his mouth and broke it in two, then handed him half. He grinned at her and gobbled it down, while she nibbled slowly at her own half.

"And what's the worst that can happen, truly?" Mrs. Smith placed the last ball on the sheet, then pressed a spoon gently down on each to flatten them. "At the very worst, you have a boring time. And at best..." She shrugged and pushed herself away from the table to carry the baking sheet to the oven. "You might find a husband."

Mariah choked.

"Not if you don't want to, of course, but one whom you love," Mrs. Smith corrected quickly as Whitby slapped Mariah on the back as she coughed. "No one can force you into marriage against your will, not even your father."

True. Although it certainly felt like it.

"But to meet a man whom you might actually *want* to marry...," Mrs. Smith pondered gently, refilling her teacup. "Wouldn't that be wonderful?"

Whitby grinned. "Mariah get married? Now *that's* a society event I'd pay to attend!"

Scowling, Mariah threw her biscuit at him. He caught it and popped it into his mouth.

Mrs. Smith sighed heavily. "Stranger things have been known to happen." She fetched a baked sheet of biscuits from the oven and spooned each one carefully onto the rack, smacking Whitby's fingers when he reached for one. "Besides, this might work to your advantage."

"How so?" She couldn't imagine any scenario in which being paraded about for men to gawk at, like some creature from the Tower Menagerie, could possibly be an advantage.

"It might prove to your father that you're willing to do as he asks instead of rebelling, which might be exactly what he wants in a business partner."

"I wasn't *rebelling*," she muttered and risked a smack of the spoon by reaching for a warm biscuit herself. "But even Cinderella rebelled, first against her wicked stepmother and then by pretending to be something she wasn't." She shook the biscuit at Mrs. Smith to make her point. "Do you really think the prince would have danced with her if he'd known she was only a scullery maid? Then, afterward, when she pretended to be a dutiful stepdaughter again only to hide—"

She stopped suddenly, her eyes darting between her two friends as a wonderful idea popped into her head. A wonderfully, deliciously *devilish* idea!

"Oh, that's it," she practically purred, resting the biscuit thoughtfully against her lips. "That's what I'll do..."

"Pardon?" Mrs. Smith's mouth drew down warily.

Mariah sent her a sly smile. "I'm going to do *exactly* as you suggested."

Her frown deepened with suspicion. "How so?"

Pretending to be a dutiful daughter. Of course, she'd have to walk a very fine line. On the surface, she'd make it look as if she were going along with Papa's plans, participating in the season and doing whatever Carlisle and his mother asked of her, so that Papa couldn't find fault. But underneath, she'd do everything she could to throw enough rocks under Carlisle's wheels to prevent him from finding any suitors for her. When August arrived without a single marriage offer, he would be denied the partnership, and she would be happily *un*married, her allowance still firmly in place. And she'd have a brand-new opportunity to convince her father that she should be allowed to help run the company.

Oh, it was simply perfect!

With a happy laugh, she announced, "I am going to be just like Cinderella!"

Except that when her fairy godmother waved her magic wand, it wouldn't be a princess she turned into but her father's business partner. And when the clock struck midnight, she'd make certain it was Carlisle who turned into a pumpkin.

"Whitby," she pleaded, excitement bubbling in her voice, "tell me everything you know about the Carlisles."

"Everything?" He blinked, surprised that for once someone was actually asking to hear his stories.

She smiled and handed over her last biscuit. "*Everything.*"

CHAPTER FOUR

~~~ ~~~

*R*obert!" Elizabeth Carlisle, Duchess of Trent, smiled broadly as she swept into the drawing room at Park Place the following afternoon, as bright as the winter sunlight slanting through the tall windows. "Good to see that you haven't burned down the house." She stopped in the center of the room and pointedly arched a brow as she clarified, "That was not meant as a challenge."

"None taken." Robert strode forward to greet her, then grinned as he added, just to tease her, "Not until May Day at least."

She narrowed her eyes. "*Absolutely* no donkey races. The rear garden still has hoofprints all over it from last year, and I fear the chestnut tree is never going to recover."

Yet she placed an affectionate kiss on his cheek.

That was what he loved best about his mother. Beneath her regal façade lurked the most loving, most forgiving woman he'd ever known. And certainly the most distrustful of her sons, although admittedly they'd given her plenty of cause over the years. Like last season. He had a rather fuzzy but pleasant memory of the revelries that had terrorized the neighbors last May after Sebastian left London in pursuit of Miranda. All in all an amazing fortnight, although in retrospect perhaps renting an elephant hadn't been such a brilliant idea. Thank God his mother hadn't found out about *that*.

But he couldn't bring himself to regret it, because last summer had proven to be the final bachelor season he and Quinton would ever share. Even then it was far tamer than what they'd done before Father died, because Robert had learned well his lesson on the dangers of excess.

His mother glanced around the room. "Where is this young lady of yours?"

"She isn't *my* anything," he corrected.

He wanted Mariah's season to go well enough to secure a marriage offer from some unsuspecting clodpole who had no idea what he was getting himself into. He had no thoughts of her beyond that.

Folding his arms across his chest, he sat lazily on the arm of the settee. "She's due to arrive at any minute. You'll like her." Dear God, he hoped she did! If his mother didn't agree to help, the season—and the partnership—was as good as dead.

She eyed him suspiciously as she sank gracefully onto the settee. "What trouble have you gotten yourself into this time?"

"None," he assured her. Which was the truth. He hadn't gotten himself into trouble; he was correcting past wrongs.

She accepted the cup of tea he poured for her from the tray and dubiously asked, "So I'm to believe you've suddenly taken a selfless interest in debutantes?"

His lips twisted. Annoyingly, his mother knew him too

well. "I said I wasn't in trouble. I never said I had no personal interest."

"Oh?" Her brow lifted curiously.

A curiosity he knew he had to firmly quash. "*Not* in Miss Winslow. Not like that."

A fortnight ago, he would have said he found Mariah interesting. Tall, ebony-haired...intriguing. Perhaps enough to call on her. But now he knew better. The Hellion was a hellcat in disguise. After their previous encounter, he was certain that if he removed his shirt, he'd have the claw marks to prove it.

"Her father is Henry Winslow," he explained, pinning today's introduction over tea to nothing more than business. "Of Winslow Shipping and Trade." He paused, then added unassumingly, "He's offered me a partnership."

His mother's face shined. "That's wonderful news, Robert! Your father would be so proud of you."

He averted his eyes. He wasn't at all certain of that himself. Especially after the last conversation they'd shared, when Father led him stumbling out of the gambling hell where he'd racked up three days' worth of debt, reeking of cheap whiskey and even cheaper prostitutes. Mother hadn't been there, hadn't seen the look of frustration on Father's face, hadn't heard his words...*I am disappointed in you.*

But Robert had worked hard to pay off every penny of that debt, and now he was working even harder to secure his place as one of England's top businessmen. He wouldn't stop pushing himself until he was certain Father would be proud of the man he'd become. Without hesitation.

Which was why it had to be *this* partnership with *this* company. Only the best would do. Because then there could be no debating the measure of his success.

With a loving smile, Elizabeth Carlisle placed her hand over his. "He would have been so pleased to see the man you've become."

"He will be," he resolved, affectionately squeezing her hand. "So will you."

"I already am, darling." But her assurance didn't ease the guilt sitting on his chest like a lead ball. Certainly not when concern for him darkened her brow.

Dear God, how he regretted hurting her! Oh, she'd never openly blamed him for Father's death, had repeatedly insisted to him in the dark days that followed that it was an accident. That no one was to blame. But he knew better. If not for him, Father wouldn't have been out at midnight, wouldn't have been in the street when the pistol was fired, wouldn't have been thrown from his horse...would still be alive.

This partnership with Winslow could never make up for the damage he'd done that night, the grief and pain he'd caused—nothing could bring his father back or heal his mother's heart. But he could prove to his family that he'd become the kind of man of whom Richard Carlisle would *never* be ashamed again.

Mother frowned, puzzled, and slowly withdrew her hand. "But what does a business venture have to do with a season for Mr. Winslow's daughter?"

Everything. Instead he answered, "I'm attempting to do a good deed."

Not a lie. Mariah had never had a proper society introduction nor the opportunity to meet prospective suitors, and didn't all ladies deserve a fairy-tale season, complete with gowns, dancing, and courtship? Of course, a triumphant season for Mariah also meant a solid future for him. If he had his way, by August they would both be happy—she'd have a husband whom she adored, and he'd be at Winslow's side.

When her frown deepened, he reminded her, "You've always said that those of us whom life has blessed are obliged to help the less fortunate."

"I *meant* orphans and war widows, not daughters of shipping magnates." Her lips twisted into a grimace. "But I suppose I should be grateful that you were listening at all."

He grinned.

"So. What do I need to know about her?"

"Her name is Mariah."

"Mariah Winslow..." Her brow scrunched as she tried to place the name. "Why does that sound so familiar?"

His grin faded, all amusement vanishing. "The Hellion."

"Oh dear." Her eyes widened.

He nodded. "Which is why I need your help."

"I see," she murmured gravely. "But surely her mother or an aunt can give her a season."

"Her mother passed away when she was ten, and she has no aunts or cousins among the *ton*. She's been out for six seasons, but never with proper introductions or presentations." He shook his head. "I'm not certain she's ever been to a ball, actually."

Her face softened, with sympathy shining in her cornflower-blue eyes. "We have quite a challenge ahead of us, then."

He dragged in a deep breath and tried to ignore the dread squeezing at his chest. "Worse."

"Worse?" Her brows shot up. "How can it be *worse*?"

"She has no dowry," he admitted grimly.

She blinked, incredulous. "None at all?"

"Not one ha'penny," he repeated Mariah's words. "And

whomever she marries will not be let into the company. Her father thinks sons-in-law and business shouldn't mix." Her face paled, and he nodded, wordlessly confirming her unspoken concerns. "So you can see why your help is so vital. She needs a true season this year, complete with balls, gowns, introductions...everything."

She *did* deserve a real season. He certainly held little sympathy for the hellcat, but growing up without a mother couldn't have been easy. Or having Henry Winslow for a father.

"If anyone can give her a proper season, it's you." He emphasized, "And it's essential that she attract suitors."

"Oh? Why is that?"

He paused as he hunted for a way to phrase his answer that wouldn't sound as if he were a marriage broker. Not at all. He truly wanted her to be happy. But her future happiness now coincided with his.

"She's twenty-five." He shrugged, as if that explained everything.

Mother nodded gravely, understanding perfectly. By twenty-five, most unmarried ladies were placed on the shelf, relegated to the invisible ranks of spinsters and companions for the rest of their lives. This season would most likely be Mariah's last chance to find a husband. "What else do we know about her?"

He smiled with a masochistic bent, remembering how much he'd enjoyed their sparring. "She's quite witty." When she wasn't making him want to throttle her.

"Well, that's something at least." Although his mother didn't seemed pleased about it. "In moderation."

That surprised him. "I thought you admired intelligent women."

"*I* do." She gave a long-suffering sigh. "Most gentlemen, however, do *not*."

"True," he agreed ruefully.

Yet the sheep of Mayfair weren't the most intelligent creatures themselves, certainly not if they wanted to spend their time with dumb women.

But with Mariah, a man could appreciate the quickness of her mind. After all, he'd certainly enjoyed their war of words. Every question was an offensive salvo, every answer a returning volley of fire... When was the last time a woman had challenged him so brazenly and had him liking it?

"No," he countered, "let her be as witty as she wants." And damn those men who weren't manly enough to rise to the challenge.

"What else?"

Intelligent, independent to a fault, with the tongue of a she-devil and no sense of restraint, no care for society's rules... With a frown, he admitted to what had been foremost in his mind since he met her, "She's beautiful."

A knowing smile tugged at his mother's lips. "I see."

"No, you don't," he corrected firmly, wanting no misunderstanding. From the look Mother gave him, he wasn't certain if she believed he had no personal interest in Mariah, but *he* was certain. "So give her the season of a lifetime," he encouraged as he lifted a strawberry tartlet from the tray. "Gowns, slippers, all the ribbons her heart desires, all the invitations she can manage—"

"But leave you completely out of it?" she interjected dryly.

He grinned and popped the tiny tart into his mouth.

A soft knock sounded at the door.

"Your Grace." The butler nodded politely to the duchess, then to Robert. "Sir. Miss Winslow has arrived."

And so it begins.

Robert rose to his feet. "Show her in, Saunders."

The man nodded and disappeared back into the hallway. A few moments later, he reappeared to formally announce, "Miss Mariah Winslow."

She swept into the room with the intensity of a summer storm. For a moment, Robert was taken aback and could only stare. *Good Lord*, she was lovely.

She'd had presence yesterday, but now self-assuredness practically dripped from her. Which was even more surprising given her choice of attire—a pale pink muslin dress with dark pink trim and matching pelisse, kid gloves embroidered with roses, and that ebony hair of hers upswept in a demure chignon. She looked for all the world like any young miss out for her season in pastels and ribbons, all primped and innocently perfect, with no trace of the true minx she was showing through the carefully constructed façade.

"Lord Robert." She kept her gaze lowered as she dropped into a curtsy. "How lovely to see you again. Thank you ever so much for the invitation to tea."

He paused. She was being...*nice*. His eyes narrowed. What game was she playing? "Thank you for accepting." Then he smiled as he came forward to formally greet her. After all, she wasn't the only one who could play at manners. "A more welcome visitor to Park Place we've never had."

Her lips twisted at the private meaning behind his comment. "Surely you have more visitors than that!"

"None like you, I assure you," he returned the volley, noting the gleam in her eyes that they'd fallen so easily back into yesterday's sparring. And liking it. Only the Hellion could make him look forward to battle. One he planned on decisively winning.

From the look in her eyes, however, so did she.

But he was also aware of his mother's puzzled frown as she watched them curiously. Not wanting to explain their war to the duchess, he took her arm and led her across the room. "Mother, may I introduce you to Miss Mariah Winslow? Miss Winslow, my mother, Elizabeth Carlisle, Duchess of Trent."

"Your Grace." As Mariah dropped into a low curtsy, genuine nervousness danced across her face. That the Hellion would be nervous about meeting anyone... *Interesting.*

"Miss Winslow." His mother smiled and reached to squeeze both of Mariah's hands. "Welcome to Park Place."

"Thank you." Her nervous smile turned into a full-out beaming beneath his mother's warm welcome. "I'm quite beside myself to be here."

Oh, Robert was certain of *that*. But how much of that glow on her face was nothing but pretense?

If his mother noted anything peculiar in Mariah's remark, though, she didn't comment. But then, she wouldn't. His mother exuded a sense of natural elegance that most women could only envy, yet one that Mariah seemed to match grace for grace.

"Sit here by me." His mother gestured to the settee. "Tea?"

Mariah sank gracefully onto the cushions while Robert collapsed into the chair opposite them. "Yes, thank you."

His mother smiled and poured cups, handing one to Robert and a second to Mariah. "So, Miss Winslow—"

"Mariah, please," she interjected. "I would be honored if Your Grace would use my Christian name."

Robert choked on his tea. And on her flattery.

But his mother didn't seem to notice. Instead, her smile

brightened. "It is indeed a pleasure to have you here at Park Place, Mariah."

"Thank you, ma'am."

Robert studied her closely. The smile she gave the duchess seemed wholly genuine. And lovely. What would it feel like to have her guilelessness aimed at him for once, instead of her rancor?

Mariah offered politely, "Your house is beautiful. I'd heard stories about how grand it is, but they certainly didn't do it justice." She trailed her gaze admiringly around the room. "I'm so fortunate to be here this afternoon."

Robert fixed his gaze on her, wariness nipping at his heels. "Why is that?"

She smiled patronizingly at him. As if he were a bedlamite. "Because Her Grace has so graciously offered to help with my season."

"It's my pleasure, my dear," Mother assured her and gained Mariah's grateful smile.

Robert tightened his jaw. How could she do it, be so sincere and polite to his mother yet remain ready to sink her claws into him the moment his guard slipped? She was more cunning than he'd given her credit for.

"When Robert asked me if I would help with your season, I wanted to have this opportunity for us to meet, to see if we would be a good fit to take on society together." His mother rested her hand on Mariah's arm and softly assured her with sympathetic understanding, "I would never attempt to take the place that your mother should have had, but perhaps we can work to give you the kind of season she would have wanted for you."

Mariah's lips parted slightly as she stared at the duchess, absorbing the offer she'd just made, and the glistening of emotion in her eyes struck him with unexpected force. She'd truly been affected by his mother's kindness.

Perhaps beneath her thorns, the Hellion possessed a real heart after all.

"Thank you, Your Grace," Mariah whispered, so softly that Robert barely heard her. "I think Mama would have liked that, very much."

His mother's eyes softened on Mariah. "I understand that you've had quite a difficult time with your seasons in the past."

Mariah nodded, turning her face away. Despite the torment she'd unleashed upon him, his chest tightened in quick sympathy for her. "As I'm sure Your Grace knows, it can be hard to make a proper introduction without the right connections." She looked down at her tea as she admitted to his mother, "And perhaps my sister, Evelyn, and I have behaved a bit...well..."

"Scandalously?" he prompted, wanting an end to that behavior before the season started. They had enough of an uphill battle before them already. He didn't need any more phaeton races to tarnish her introduction.

"*Impetuously*," she corrected, shooting him a peeved glance. "But we've never really had proper guidance in the niceties of society. We're a shipping merchant's daughters." She gave a faint, rueful smile. "The Winslow women have always been more concerned with docks than drawing rooms."

"Until now," he added, subtly reminding her of her father's ultimatum. "When you're embarking on a new life as a respectable lady."

At that, she stiffened, her shoulders and spine going ramrod straight. But she didn't deign to look at him as she explained to the duchess, "I'm afraid that Papa's never known what to do with us. We were sent away to school, to Miss Pettigrew's in Cornwall. When I came back, I was ready for my debut, but I had no female relatives to help me. As you know, a season can be overwhelming, and I felt lost in the middle of all of it."

"Oh, you poor dear!" His mother's face fell as she reached to squeeze Mariah's elbow.

Robert narrowed his eyes over the rim of his teacup. How much of her confessions were genuine, and how much nothing more than an attempt to wrap his mother around her finger? He didn't trust one pink-ribbon-clad inch of her.

"But that's all in the past now," his mother murmured, sympathetically patting the back of Mariah's hand. "You must look forward to a brand-new season."

"That's why I'm so grateful to *you*, Your Grace." The prick of that cut to him was carefully mitigated by an appreciative smile for his mother.

Robert's mouth twisted as he watched her. She might have genuinely appreciated his mother's kindness, yet clearly, she still viewed him as the enemy. And he suspected that the performance of a proper debutante that she was putting on this afternoon was purely for his punishment. He might as well be wearing a target on his back.

But she was mistaken if she thought she could declare hunting season on him.

"You see, this is my . . ." Mariah lowered her voice. "My *seventh* season."

"Seventh time's the charm," Robert muttered behind the rim of his teacup.

"Oh, I certainly hope so!" she exclaimed with a deep, heartfelt sigh.

He bared his teeth in a crocodile smile and mumbled, "*I* certainly hope so."

Her shoulders stiffened. She'd heard him all right, even though she didn't spare him a glance.

"Well, we will do the best we can." His mother offered her the plate of cucumber sandwiches. "And how exactly do you know my son, Mariah?"

Blinking, she swung her gaze to him, as if surprised to find him there. "You mean Lord Robert?"

He smiled patronizingly. He *was* the only man in the room, after all.

She delicately selected a tiny sandwich and placed it on the edge of her saucer. "He's a business acquaintance of some sort of my father's, aren't you, Lord Robert?"

"Yes." His lips tightened in irritation, both at her and at her repeated use of his courtesy title. "Of some sort."

He couldn't contradict her, nor could he reveal the truth. He needed the duchess to take her on for the season, and any hint of a squabble between them would have Mother refusing immediately in his defense.

Rather, he *hoped* that she'd defend him. From the way she kept smiling so warmly at Mariah, he wasn't certain.

"My apologies." She gave a shrug of her slender shoulders, the innocent gesture made even more unassuming by the bows of pink ribbons adorning her puffy sleeve caps. "My father has so many hangers-on of all kinds these days that I simply cannot keep them all straight!"

He smiled smugly. "Then you'll be happy to know that there will be considerably fewer hangers-on"—setting his tea aside, he leaned confidently back in the chair and quirked a brow to emphasize his words—"once your father confirms my partnership."

"A partnership?" she repeated in a pleased drawl, one that curled dread through him and announced that the minx had figured out that he wanted to keep Winslow's challenge to him secret from his mother. "Are you certain?"

"Yes," he answered, annoyed that she dared to question it.

"Truly?"

"Verily."

"Impossible!"

"Highly probable."

"I don't believe it."

"You should."

His mother silently followed the back-and-forth volleys as if she were watching a tennis match.

"Well, goodness." Mariah blinked. "I thought you were to be a *clerk*!"

Clenching his jaw in anger, Robert leaned forward, a cutting reply on his tongue—

"Have a tart, dear." His mother shoved the plate beneath his nose.

He snapped back his head, nearly inhaling a strawberry. "What the—"

"Oh yes, Lord Robert." Mariah smiled ingenuously at him. "I've heard how much you enjoy tarts."

"Take *several*, dear." His mother shoved the plate at him again until he had no choice but to accept the entire thing in his hands. Which meant he couldn't lunge across the tea table and throttle the minx.

"A partnership," Mariah prattled on. "Well, that's quite something, I daresay. Papa's never offered a partnership before. My! You must be truly special." She tilted her head, deviously feigning naïve curiosity as she skillfully plunged the dagger into his belly—"And what is it, *exactly*, that you've agreed to do for my father to secure it?"

Damn her. He couldn't answer. If Mother learned the truth, she might very well refuse to be a part of this fiasco. And without the duchess, he didn't stand a chance of winning.

The infuriating woman knew it, too.

So he forced an unconcerned shrug. "Oh, the usual...to take care of problems that have grown far too troublesome for their own good."

That barb certainly hit home, and her eyes darkened angrily.

The duchess blinked, completely lost in their private conversation and unable to find any clues to read the subtext.

With a smile that didn't bother to hide his pleasure at one-upping Mariah, Robert returned the plate of tarts to the tray and leaned confidently back in his chair. "I was thrilled when he asked me to help with your season. A husband would do you wonders, Miss Winslow."

"And you, a wife," Mariah purred with a calculating smile, turning the conversation back on him.

"Most certainly," his mother agreed, and far too quickly for Robert's comfort. "I've been saying so myself since last winter that—"

"Plenty of time later to marry me off, Mother," he interjected gently with as much pretense of helpfulness as he could muster in order to change the subject away from him and back to Mariah. "Today is all about Miss Winslow and making a match for *her.*"

"Indeed." She turned her attention to Mariah with a happy smile, then reached for the pot to refill Mariah's cup, not noticing the glare the hellcat shot him. His lips twitched with amusement.

"So, my dear," his mother asked, "what skills do you possess?"

"Let's see..." She added a dollop of honey to her cup and watched the tea thoughtfully as she stirred it. "I speak Spanish and French fluently and have completed advanced studies in mathematics and bookkeeping, along with law, politics, philosophy, the natural sciences..."

With each skill she reported, his mother's face paled a shade lighter with distress. But Robert found the list intriguing and hid his admiration for her by raising his cup to his lips—

"And a smattering of knowledge of naval warfare."

At *that* he nearly spilled his tea.

His eyes darted between the two women. His mother's face had turned completely white at that bit of information, but as far as he could discern, Mariah had told the truth.

"Oh dear," his mother whispered, as if Mariah had just admitted to stealing the crown jewels.

She blinked, confused. "You did say *skills*, ma'am."

"I meant those belonging to young ladies in pursuit of suitable husbands." She clarified in a hushed tone, as if Robert shouldn't overhear, "You know...watercolors, sketching, flower arranging..."

"I'm afraid not," she answered a bit ruefully.

"Not even the pianoforte?"

Mariah's cheeks pinked with honest embarrassment. "I am not musical."

"But you attended Miss Pettigrew's, and all the young ladies from there are quite proficient musicians." His mother stated that as if it were a universal truth.

"Not one note," Mariah admitted with a grimace.

His mother was aghast. "Surely, you attended lessons."

"W-Well, I—I...that is..." Mariah's eyes widened

with the look of a caught doe. "Every time I had a scheduled lesson, the pianoforte would unexpectedly...break."

Mariah guiltily averted her eyes. Robert struggled to fight back a grin as he imagined a young Mariah gleefully breaking keys and stopping up hammers at every opportunity.

"Break?" His mother puzzled, "How on earth does a pianoforte *break*?"

"With much perseverance," Mariah answered gravely.

Robert laughed.

For one fleeting moment, their gazes met, and for once not with animosity. Her eyes twinkled knowingly, and her berry-red lips began to curl into the start of a smile for him, as if they were co-conspirators in some kind of innocuous prank rather than fierce adversaries. The momentary connection pulsed a pleasant heat low inside him.

But then her teacup was at her mouth, and whatever shared amusement he'd seen vanished like the morning fog.

His mother ignored him, having long ago learned not to encourage her sons' improper behavior by acknowledging it. "You do dance, though, do you not?"

"Oh yes!" Mariah smiled, and a genuine warmth radiated from her as her face lit up. Grudgingly, Robert had to acknowledge that she could be quite beautiful. When she wasn't being infuriating. "I enjoy dancing very much."

The duchess breathed a loud sigh of relief. "Thank goodness for that! Then we'll start making plans right away for your debut ball."

Mariah paled. "My debut ball?"

"Of course. Every young lady should be presented at a ball."

She shifted uncomfortably. "But I've been out for six seasons already, Your Grace."

"As far as I'm concerned, those seasons never happened." She patted Mariah's hand. "And I see no reason why we shouldn't start preparations right away. I'm certain Madame Bernaise can fit you in tomorrow for a consultation. She's the best mantua-maker in England."

"I'm sorry, but I already have a commitment for tomorrow." Mariah hesitated, then ventured carefully, as if she wasn't certain yet how much she could trust his mother, "You see, I'm a patroness for the Gatewell School for Orphans of the Sea. I'd planned to work at the school, and I'm afraid it's going to take all day."

"You're a patroness for a school for orphans?" His mother seemed as surprised by that bit of news as Robert.

His suspicious gaze raked over Mariah, but he found nothing in her that indicated she was lying. And she'd damned well better not be. Not when it came to orphans. Not with his family.

Mariah nodded. Encouraged by his mother's interest, she explained, "We provide practical education for children who have lost their fathers in the shipping industry. It isn't a very large school, but we do all we can." She bit her lip uncertainly. Then, as if deciding she could trust his mother with this private part of her life, she offered, "Of course, if you'd ever like to visit the school, I'd be honored to give you a tour."

"I would like that." Mother smiled affectionately, her eyes glistening. "Very much."

If there were any doubts that the duchess might give up on Mariah and pull out of the season, they all vanished. As far as Robert could tell, Mariah wasn't even aware of her coup as she returned his mother's smile, a faint bewilderment furrowing her brow.

"Perhaps, Your Grace, we could visit your dressmaker the following day instead?" Mariah offered.

"Of course." She gave Mariah's hand an affectionate squeeze. "And please, call me Elizabeth. I insist."

A grand coup, indeed.

Mariah set her cup aside as his mother busily described her plans for the ball and how she counted on involving the Countess of St James and his sister, Josephine, in the festivities. Robert was unable to decipher the expression on Mariah's face, whether she was happy about her season or furious that she was being force-marched into it. Either one made no difference to him. But his mother was a miracle worker, and he had no doubt that Mariah would be enjoying herself thoroughly by February and engaged by April.

Without pausing in her long list of preparations, his mother slowly rose to her feet and gently led Mariah to hers. Which forced Robert to his. Yet it also meant that tea was over and that the aggravating minx was leaving. *Good.* After today, he hoped never to have to deal directly with her again.

"Thank you so much for a wonderful afternoon, Your Grace—I mean, Elizabeth." Mariah smiled warmly at the duchess. Then she turned to him and coldly bobbed a half-hearted attempt at a disdainful curtsy as she muttered, "Lord Robert."

His lips tightened. Only Mariah Winslow could turn his name into an accusation. "Miss Winslow." He inclined his head. "Good day." *And good riddance.*

She turned to leave, assuring his mother that she could see herself out.

But just as she reached the doorway, she stopped. Then she turned slowly to look back. Not at him or his mother, but to let her gaze drift curiously around the room. The grand space was garishly decorated in a riot of gold gilding, with naked cherubs frolicking across the painted ceiling, and he didn't blame her for being a bit stunned by it.

"Hmm." She tilted her head and mumbled contemplatively, "I'm beginning to think that all those stories I've heard about Park Place must be apocryphal."

"Oh?" his mother asked, perplexed. "Why is that?"

With a smile aimed directly at Robert and the intent to cause as much trouble for him as possible, she announced, "I simply don't think it's possible that an elephant could have fit into the gardens!"

Then she slipped out the door.

His mother slid her imperious gaze sideways at him. "Robert Spenser Carlisle, *what* does she mean?"

His patience snapped. Biting back a curse, he charged after her.

* * *

Laughing to herself, Mariah bounced down the hallway toward the front door. Oh, the look on Carlisle's face— *priceless*. Whitby was right, she could hardly believe it. An elephant! She would have admired Carlisle for his audacity if she didn't dislike him so—

A strong hand closed over her elbow and propelled her into a side room before she could protest. The door slammed shut with a bang.

Robert Carlisle stepped her back against the wall and pressed his hands against the paneling at her shoulders, trapping her with his broad body. Raw anger pulsated from him.

As she stared at him, her heart lodged in her throat even as it lurched into a furious tattoo.

"Quite the little show you put on back there," he drawled, his deep voice even more terrifying for all of its control.

"You're the one who declared war, Carlisle," she countered, the fight rising in her. She refused to be cowed. Certainly not by him! "I'm merely playing by your rules of—"

He placed a fingertip to her lips. She fell silent, more from the furious flicker in his eyes than the resistance of his finger. "Our *war*," he said, surprisingly icily given the hot anger that radiated from him, "does not involve my mother. Understand?"

She glared at him through eyes narrowed to slits, but nodded. When he pulled his finger away, she resisted the urge to bite it.

"I would *never* dream of upsetting your mother." How dare he suggest such a thing! Indignantly, she threw back, "I like the duchess. She's a lovely woman with a caring heart."

Which was the truth. Mariah had expected a pinch-faced, boring matron as pompous as her son and was prepared to hate the woman on sight. Instead, she found herself liking Elizabeth Carlisle a great deal. Everything Whitby had told her about the woman—her elegance, her graciousness, her generosity—had proven true.

So had the arrogance and wicked reputation of her son, who stood far too close for comfort. Close enough that she could smell the faint bergamot scent of his shaving soap still clinging to his skin.

"And that bit about the orphans?" His jaw tightened. "How were you trying to manipulate my mother with that?"

"I wasn't. I *am* a patroness of the Gatewell School." Something pricked shamefully inside her that he'd think her so evil as to use orphans to her advantage. His low opinion of her bothered her more than she wanted to acknowledge.

"And that parting shot about the elephant?" he pressed.

She flashed him a saccharine smile and purred, "Pure spite."

He leaned toward her to bring his flashing eyes level with hers. His mouth was so close that the warmth of his breath tickled against her lips. "Did it ever occur to you, Mariah, that I'm on your side?"

Ha! Did he truly think her so simple as to believe that? She arched a brow. "By driving a wedge between me and my father?"

"You don't need me for that." A dark light glinted knowingly in his eyes. "You've done a fine job of turning your father against you yourself."

Beast! Anger spun through her, and she drew her hands into fists. "I don't need *you* for any—"

"You need my help more than you realize."

His *help*? She was certain that the kind of help he'd offer would only cause problems. She scoffed. "What could you possibly do for me?"

His gaze dropped to her shoulder, where his fingers plucked at the bow decorating her capped sleeve. He drawled in a husky voice, "Save you from yourself."

"I'm not in need of a savior." She swatted his hand away with a warning scowl. "Nor do I seek absolution from society or the blessings of its good graces."

"Good." Condescending amusement sounded in his voice. "Because you're never going to get any."

That was painfully blunt. So much so that her lips parted as she stared at him, astonished by his brutal honesty.

He took advantage of her momentary shock to reach up again to her shoulder. "Not with your family's wealth." He teased the satin ribbon around his fingers, then trailed his hand over to the neckline of her bodice. "And certainly not with your beauty."

She swallowed, hard, not knowing what to say to that. Or to the heat of his fingertips as they traced over the lace edging of her bodice and seared the skin near her collarbone. Her traitorous heart pounded so furiously that he could most likely feel it, and she prayed he recognized it for what it was—anger. Nothing else. Certainly *not* attraction to this damnable devil.

His sapphire blue eyes followed the tracing of his fingertip back and forth over her neckline. She cursed herself for not wearing an old-fashioned fichu. Next time, she'd come properly prepared for battle, with a spencer buttoned up to her chin and a sword hidden in her skirts.

"Society's watching every move you make," he cautioned, "all those gossips, just waiting to pounce. You're only one misstep away from crossing a line from which you'll never be able to step back."

Despite the harshness of that warning, his deep voice came smooth and soft. Like a velvet cape wrapping itself warmly around her. She trembled. *Heavens.* If this much masculinity radiated from him when he was attempting to persuade her into behaving decorously, what must he be like when he'd set his mind on seduction?

"All it would take is a new rumor or two." His fingers stroked lightly up her neckline to her shoulder, and a faint ache tightened low in her belly. "About you gambling alone in some seedy hell in Covent Garden or getting foxed in a private box at Vauxhall—after all, everyone knows how you raced that phaeton down St James's Street. It wouldn't take much for those bitter old hens and jealous misses to have everyone believing you'd done something even worse."

His forefinger slipped teasingly beneath the sleeve cap of her dress to caress bare skin. She inhaled sharply, both at the silken slide of his fingertip and at his brazen audacity.

His eyes flickered darkly, which only grew the hot blush at her cheeks. "Or something even more sordid." His fingertip trailed down over her bare arm as he murmured, "Something wanton."

"They wouldn't dare," she whispered. Her breath now came in harsh little pants. Every inch of her throbbed with a mix of frustration and anger. And something else just as intense, just as aching...something triggered by his nearness that set her trembling.

"I've seen them ruin ladies for offenses far more slight than what they'll believe you're attempting to do to them this season," he warned, "as an upstart cit invading their ranks, with the audacity to think she can steal away one of their gentlemen." He leaned in farther until the heat of his breath shivered across her lips. "Those women will shred you, and the men will ruin your reputation without taking a single touch." His gaze fell to her mouth, the heat of his stare burning her lips. "Although I'm certain the alternative might be damnably fun with a hellcat like you, *if* a man could survive your claws."

Her breath hitched with a jerking gasp. That was no mere innuendo, but pure masculine assertion. One that coiled through her, stirring up an inexplicable feminine longing inside her.

"But you won't let that happen," she countered in a voice far huskier than she intended, "or your own prospects will be ruined. After all, if you can't even protect me from—what was it again? Gambling, drinking, or—" She jutted up her chin, too much of a lady to repeat his words. "Something *intimate*...How would you ever be able to convince my father that you're capable of protecting all of Winslow Shipping?"

"Don't worry, I'll do exactly that," he promised. "And you'll do what my mother asks of you this season and convey yourself as a proper lady, or losing your allowance will be the least of the punishments from your father." In that moment's pause, something haunted and remorseful flickered deep in the sapphire depths of his eyes. Something so pained that her breath caught with surprise. "Because you'll also lose all his pride in you, and he'll be disappointed to have you as a daughter."

Her heart stuttered at the way he said that and at the darkness she glimpsed inside him.

But whatever fleeting sympathy she felt for him wasn't enough to tamp down her own rising anger. Or the sharp wariness that squeezed her heart at the possibility that this arrogant interloper might be right.

"I'll do whatever *your mother* asks of me," she promised. And with that, laid down a clear line of demarcation between what he wanted from her and what she planned on giving. They'd declared war, and battle lines had to be drawn. "After all, it isn't her fault that her son is such a beast."

"That's right." Shifting closer to her, so close that she could feel the heat of him along her front, he took her chin and lifted her face toward him. "I *am* a beast." His thumb strummed over her bottom lip and made her tremble. "Don't ever forget that."

She forced a laugh, suddenly and inexplicably nervous. Instead of the haughty insult she'd intended, it emerged as a throaty rasp. "I'm not afraid of you."

His eyes gleamed wolfishly and fixed on her lips, staring

at her hungrily as if he wanted to devour her. He drawled huskily, "You should be."

Then he lowered his head and captured her mouth beneath his.

The kiss came so unexpectedly that she didn't have time to gasp before he stole her breath away and stunned her senseless. For a long while, she could do nothing in her surprise but stand there and absorb the strange and delicious feel of his mouth on hers.

Then all her senses flooded back with the force of a tidal wave. Pushing her hands against his chest, she tried to shove him away, but the man was a mountain, solid and immovable. He didn't budge as he continued to feast on her lips, kissing her more thoroughly than she'd ever experienced in her life.

And oh, what a kiss! The strength of his mouth contrasted with the softness of his warm lips as they caressed and nibbled against hers, almost cajoling her to give over to him, yet mercilessly relentless in his pursuit to make her senses flee yet again. And drat him, he was succeeding. His nearness intoxicated her until she stopped pushing and instead snaked her arms around his neck to hold him close. He smelled delicious, a masculine mix of leather, soap, and tobacco that made her head spin, and on his lips she tasted the sweet yet earthy flavors of honey and tea. A slow heat seeped into her from the tips of her fingers and toes, until it met in the middle and turned into a throbbing ache.

She shuddered with mortification. She couldn't possibly find his embrace stirring. Not him of all men! Surely she wasn't aching from his kisses, didn't find his nearness intoxicating— A low sound came from the back of her throat in response, half a moan of desire and half a groan of shame.

Then he slowly pulled away. The loss of his heat stunned her, and she was barely able to stifle a whimper of protest on her lips. She stared up at him, wide-eyed and blinking with utter bewilderment.

But at least he had the decency to look just as astonished. If only for a fleeting beat before he collected himself and banished the shocked expression from his face beneath a confident smile.

"Let that be a warning to you," he said in a hoarse whisper, "about exactly what kind of beast I am."

Her heart stuttered, a jarring beat that jolted painfully through her. Was that all this was—an object lesson to make her behave? Her bafflement turned instantly to the anger of a pricked pride and her thoughts to retaliation. If he thought she could be managed so easily with only heated kisses and charming smiles, then he certainly had another think coming!

Fighting down her rising blush, she forced a blank expression onto her face and asked with false naïveté, "Let *what* be a warning?" When his jaw clenched, she let fly her arrow—"You mean that little kiss?"

Ignoring the way his eyes narrowed on her, she laughed lightly with forced embarrassment for him. When what she really felt was an inexplicable yet hungry desire to have his mouth on hers again. But her pride was too wounded to admit it.

"I'm so sorry! I didn't realize…Perhaps," she offered with feigned helpfulness, "you should try that again, and this time, I promise, I'll pretend to be contrite. So go on." She closed her eyes and puckered her lips in flagrant exaggeration. "Go on, then—kiss me."

When he didn't move, just as she knew he wouldn't, she

cracked open one eye to peer at him. Oh, the fury on his face! Exactly what he deserved.

"Well, then." She stepped sideways to free herself from the barricade of his body. "I believe we're done here." Perhaps next time he'd think twice before—

He grabbed her shoulders and pressed her back against the wall, his mouth seizing hers.

No, she realized as she melted bonelessly against him, he was not the kind of man to think twice before claiming what he wanted. And what he seemed to want—she trembled— was *her*.

She once more slipped her arms around his neck, once more leaned up to eagerly meet the delicious onslaught of his mouth against hers. He was a scoundrel, a cad, a rake, but his kisses—oh, sweet heavens, his *kisses*! They left her breathless and weak, her mind spinning with a swirling rush of emotions and sensations, until all she knew was the persistent warmth of his lips enjoying hers and the electric tingle that sparked from every place their bodies touched.

But this time, he was different. Instead of the raw anger and frustration that had driven him to demand that first embrace from her, this one was softer. As if he were attempting to persuade rather than conquer. To entreat her to melt beneath his embrace. And, God help her, that was exactly what she was doing. She went limp in his arms even as she yearned for more.

When the tip of his tongue traced along the seam of her lips and coaxed her to open, he gave her exactly what she wanted—*more*. More heat as his tongue invaded her mouth to claim the entire kiss. More aching in her loins as he explored every dark recess of her mouth and made her shiver when he swept his tongue across her inner lip. And even more dizziness and weak knees, until she melted against the wall behind her and didn't fight him at all as his hand slipped behind her nape and his strong fingers kneaded seductively at the base of her skull.

Her last thread of resistance snapped at that surprisingly erotic caress, which joined rhythmically with the slow but steady thrust of his tongue between her lips and the increasing throbbing between her legs. His mouth slid away from hers, and a soft whimper of loss fell from her parted lips.

"Mariah." He smiled against her cheek.

A stab of defeat pierced her. So Carlisle thought he'd won, did he? Well, she'd prove to him that it would take more than that to convince her to surrender.

This time when he stepped back, Mariah advanced.

She wrapped her arms around his shoulders and delved her fingertips through the golden curls at his nape, then pressed her body so tightly against his front that she felt his heart slamming furiously against her chest. When she brushed her hips against his, a low groan tore from the back of his throat. Emboldened, she brazenly kissed him, and in that moment's hesitation, when he was too stunned to move, she slipped her tongue between his lips the way he'd done to her.

That was enough to snap him out of his reverie.

He grabbed her shoulders and set her away, demanding in a raspy voice, "What the hell do you think you're doing?"

Despite the racing of her heart and the need to gulp back the air he'd stolen, she forced a shrug of her shoulders. As if it were the most obvious thing in the world. "Kissing you."

Then she pressed against him again, her lips managing to barely make contact with his before he set her away. An angry scowl hardened his face.

"Don't you want me to?" she prompted as innocently as possible.

Something dark and heated flickered in his eyes, and thinking it was anger, she thrilled at finally gaining the upper hand. Hiding her own shaking and quaking brought on by the heat of his embrace, she leaned toward him as far as his restraining hands would allow.

She purred huskily, "Surely the notorious Robert Carlisle knows what to do with a woman who wants to kiss him."

Despite gritting his teeth, his gaze fell longingly to her mouth, and for a moment, she thought he might just kiss her senseless again. And if he did, she wasn't certain that she could withstand it this time without falling completely apart in his arms.

"Don't tease me, Mariah," he warned in a murmur. "You're playing with fire."

"Am I?" Pretending that he hadn't affected her, even as that tingling heat still throbbed achingly between her thighs, she sadly shook her head. "Well, I certainly hope the other gentlemen I'll meet this season are better at kissing than you." She slipped away from him before he could reach for her again. Or she for him. "Or I'll be too bored to consider marrying any of them."

He stared at her coolly as he wiped his mouth with the back of his hand. "You *will* be married by season's end, I promise you."

This time when he took her arm, instead of angling her against him to embrace her, he pulled her toward the door. He flung it open and led her into the hall so quickly that she struggled to keep up with his determined strides.

Robert snatched her bonnet and cloak from the waiting butler, who wisely averted his eyes, then slung the cloak around her shoulders and unchivalrously slapped her bonnet on her head. Then he pulled her toward the front door again. Anger radiated from him as he led her across the small portico and down to the carriage waiting in the street.

Ignoring the tiger, he placed her inside the carriage himself. But when she yanked her arm away, it wasn't relief she felt but an inexplicable sense of loss. For one maddening moment, she wanted to blurt out an apology, to beg him to crawl inside the compartment with her and keep kissing her just as he'd done before, all the way home to her doorstep.

But the devil inside her couldn't help one last parting jab, and she sniffed with mock disappointment, "If I'm going to be forced to give my first waltz to such a boorish man, I certainly hope you're far better at dancing."

He rose up onto the step and leaned into the compartment, bringing himself close to her in the small space. "Don't you worry, minx," he assured her in a husky voice that twined down her spine. "When it comes to having a woman in my arms, I do *everything* well."

Her breath strangled in her throat. Leaving her to gape at him in stunned mortification at her own heated reaction to the beastliness in him, he closed the door, then ordered the coachman to drive off.

The carriage rolled forward, and she slumped against the squabs. A curse left her lips at him, followed immediately by several more at herself.

They'd fought their second battle, yet for the life of her she couldn't have said which of them had emerged the victor.

CHAPTER FIVE

One Cold Day Later

*H*enry Winslow poured two glasses of bourbon. "The first thing you need to learn about Winslow Shipping, Carlisle," he instructed, "is that we always make room for good Kentucky bourbon in our ships returning from the United States." He looked up at Robert, a teasing gleam in his eyes. "Even if we have to tow it behind in a dinghy!"

Robert laughed and accepted the second glass.

Around them, the shipping offices on Wapping High Street were quiet and empty, which made for the perfect time for Winslow to meet with him. For once, all the employees were out for the afternoon, including John Ledford, the man who managed the day-to-day office operations. And who didn't seem at all happy to have Robert joining the company.

Not that Robert was much bothered by it. Ledford would accept him once he proved his worth. The same way that Mariah would once she gave up her fight against her father and realized that his partnership was in the company's best interests.

"The king wants new docks close to the Tower," Winslow explained, jumping straight into the reason for this meeting. "With the current Parliament, whatever King George wants, he gets. And *I* want to make certain that Winslow Shipping benefits."

Robert had heard the rumors himself about the king's desire to expand the Thames waterfront, but he'd chalked it up to nothing more than royal egotism. If new docks were built at all, they'd have to be much farther downstream toward Millwall. "There's no room for more docks at the Tower."

"There is at St Katharine's," Winslow countered in a knowing drawl.

Robert narrowed his eyes. New docks at St Katharine's? *Impossible.* The London embankment was already filled to capacity with wharves and quays so busy that ships often had to wait at anchor mid-river for days before they could unload. Including the stretch fronting St Katharine's.

Robert shook his head. "The only way that more docks can be made in London is if God himself moves the river, to carve out miles of new embankment where it doesn't exist."

Winslow paused, the glass of bourbon raised halfway to his lips. A slow, devious smile spread across his face as he pinned Robert knowingly over the rim, then finished taking his sip.

"Good God," he murmured as the full realization of what Winslow was insinuating washed through him, sending up a tingle of excitement in its wake. New docks...*in the city*. God didn't make enough river for that, but King George could, by digging out a basin just inland along the riverside that would create miles of new riverbank. And miles of new riverbank meant miles of new quayside and warehouses—and tremendous new profits for Winslow Shipping. *If* they were bold enough to seize the opportunity.

"It's the real estate buy of the century," Winslow assured him, putting voice to the thoughts swirling through Robert's head. He strode behind his desk and sank down into the large leather chair, smiling like the cat who got into the cream. "When Lord Whitby complained to me over dinner about how the king wanted Parliament to raise money so he could build new docks near the Tower, I knew exactly what King George was planning. Just as I know that they'll be built at St Katharine's."

Robert leaned forward. Calculations and scenarios were already running through his mind on the best way to leverage the company's assets to free up enough capital for the kind of venture Winslow was proposing. A commitment of hundreds of thousands of pounds—

A *loss* of hundreds of thousands of pounds if they weren't careful.

He knew how fickle King George could be, how royal projects were often abandoned or changed halfway through, until they resembled nothing of the original concept. "New basins can be built anywhere," he cautioned.

"Have to be built at St Katharine's," Winslow assured him, slumping down in his chair and resting his glass on his round belly. "Only the northern bank can support that kind of construction, and they can't be built any closer in due to the tides and the bridge. Anything further downstream is too far away from the City and too close to Greenwich. The king will also have to reimburse landholders for the properties he puts underwater, so for his purse, what better place to build than a slum?"

And *that*, Robert realized, was how Henry Winslow had taken his father's small shipping interest and grown it into the largest sole proprietorship in the empire. By recognizing that something as inconsequential as Baron Whitby's complaint could be turned into an opportunity for tremendous profit.

If Robert had any doubts that working with Winslow wasn't the best for him—an opportunity that could *never* be matched with any other company—this meeting erased them all. And only increased his determination to secure that partnership.

"So you plan to buy up as many properties in St Katharine's as you can for pennies on the pound," Robert drawled with admiration. *Like scattered pearls on the ground…* "Then sell them to the crown for profit when the docks go in."

"I plan for *you* to buy up as many properties for *us* as you can, while also identifying those at the edges that will make for good warehouses," Winslow corrected with an eager glint in his eyes. "After all, we'll need somewhere to store the goods we'll unload from that fleet of new ships we'll be able to buy." Then he pulled a sheet of paper from his desk drawer and handed it to Robert. "And make us a fortune in the process."

Hiding the simmering excitement that pulsed through him, he glanced at the paper. A list of street names where Winslow assumed the basins would be built. A long list.

"I want you to track down the owners of every property on those streets and find out how much it would take to convince them to sell," Winslow ordered.

He frowned, feeling his excitement wane sharply. "Parliament has to approve the docks first." Judging from the length of the list, it encompassed the entire area of St Katharine's. He tossed it onto the desk. "They'll never agree to destroy an area this large."

Winslow gave a curt nod. "Which is why you must convince them."

His heart stuttered. In that pain-filled beat, all the connections between his partnership and the properties in St Katharine's instantly crystallized, and a bitter taste rose in his mouth. He felt like a fool for thinking Winslow appreciated his business acumen. "Is that the only reason you offered that partnership to me, my influence with Parliament?"

"Not at all." Winslow straightened in his chair, his no-nonsense gaze fixing on Robert across the desk. "You possess a sharp business mind and the zeal to work hard. You'll be an asset to me long after those docks are built. But you also know how business works, Carlisle. To be successful, a man has to use every tool at his disposal. Including his connections."

"Including applying pressure to my friends and family until they support the new docks, you mean," he drawled, carefully keeping the distaste from his expression.

Winslow leaned back in his chair with a dismissive wave of his hand. "It happens all the time. Canal bills, import tariffs, taxes…it's how politics works. Ask your brother. I'm certain Trent witnesses it every day." He shook his head. "The current London docks and wharves cannot handle the amount of ships which need to use them, and new docks *will* be built. It's as simple as that. If we don't benefit, someone else will. Why not let the profits be ours?"

Robert felt as if the devil himself were tempting him to make a deal for his soul. A tantalizing deal he very much wanted to accept. "We'll destroy the borough and chase thousands of poor from their homes."

"We'll bring new jobs with good wages. The sailors, longshoremen, and their families will have better lives than they have now."

Something else pricked at his conscience... "Isn't the Gatewell School located in St Katharine's?"

Winslow's eyes flickered, and for a heartbeat, Robert thought he saw remorse on the man's face. "It is. But running a charity school isn't what a proper young lady like Mariah should be doing in the first place." He rubbed his temples with his thumb and forefinger, as if working down a headache. But then, Robert conceded, hadn't Mariah given him his own headache since the moment he met her? "Neither is running a shipping company."

Robert swirled the bourbon in his glass and ventured diplomatically, "Your daughter seems to think differently."

"A thought that I should have discouraged years ago." Winslow blew out a long-suffering sigh. "When she was a little girl, I used to bring her to work with me." A touch of pride filled his voice. "I loved taking her down to the wharves, to let her watch the workers and ships coming and going. Her face would light up whenever she saw all the strange, new things being unloaded. Once we even saw a camel." He chuckled at the memory. "I'll never forget the way she stared at it. Not frightened at all—oh no, not Mariah. *She* wanted to ride it like a pony!"

Robert smiled, easily imagining her as a little girl who wanted to do just that.

"My wife cautioned me about letting Mariah get too attached to the company. But she was only a child then, and I enjoyed having her at my side. At the time I thought, what harm could it do, to let her see that side of life? To let her experience the world as much as she could?" His voice quieted as his face grew dark. "But then her mother died, and everything changed."

Winslow fell silent as he tossed back the rest of his bourbon in a gasping swallow. Then he pushed himself out of his chair to refill his glass.

"Mariah followed me everywhere after that—around the house, to the offices, down to the quays. I think she was terrified that if she let me out of her sight that she'd lose me as well, so I let her. But by the time she turned thirteen, I knew I'd made a mistake. She was more comfortable with sailors than she was with society ladies, more interested in learning about shipping routes and auction houses than about running a household."

Robert resisted the urge to state that she still was.

"I'd promised Beatrice on her deathbed that I'd raise our two girls into fine ladies who would be welcomed into any drawing room in England. And I had failed." He returned to his chair but paused to glance out the window at the few snowflakes that were making a half-hearted attempt to fall. "So I stopped bringing her to the offices, forbade her to visit the quayside and warehouses...but it was Mariah." He grimaced with exasperation. "So of course she defied me and came anyway."

"Of course," Robert mumbled against the rim of his glass as he took a sip to hide his smile. Her determination was one of the things Robert liked best about her. When she wasn't using it against him, that is.

"I had no choice but to send her away to school, hoping Miss Pettigrew could make a lady of her. I'd hoped that years away with other young ladies from England's finest families would turn her attentions to becoming a proper miss, with prospects for a good marriage. That she'd forget this nonsense about her running the company."

Well, that certainly didn't happen. As far as Robert could tell, her desire to do just that was as strong as ever.

"But when she returned, she was determined to have a real hand in running the company rather than simply offering advice whenever we'd discuss business over dinner." He gave another bewildered shake of his head, and Robert sympathized with the man. "Her sister, Evelyn, has always been a handful, too, and I worry about her just as much. But Mariah—always so willful! Determined to let nothing stop her from getting what she wants."

Robert shrugged a shoulder. "She is her father's daughter."

Winslow laughed. "If she is, then she'll eventually listen to reason. She'll understand that fine ladies do not run shipping companies, nor do they spend their days with urchins." He arched a brow. "Oh, she'll be angry at first. But in time she'll come to realize the benefit of those new docks to the company, especially when she sees how much money she'll have to donate. She'll be able to support dozens of charities then, if she wishes. Besides," he said, his lips curling into a pleased smile, "no gentleman wants a wife who spends her days among street urchins. Closing down that school will only make it that much easier for you to find her a husband."

And with that, to earn the partnership.

The words hung in the air as plainly as if Winslow had spoken them aloud, the implication clear. For all that he was eager to bring Robert into the fold, the position was still tentative. Still wholly dependent upon a marriage offer for Mariah.

"The duchess has agreed to sponsor her," Robert reported, erasing any doubts regarding the outcome of the season. "And I'll get started right away on the properties." And with that, erasing any doubts that he deserved to be Winslow's partner.

"Good."

"But understand that any influence I exert on my friends and family in Parliament will be completely aboveboard." He wouldn't compromise on that. Doing so would completely negate any strides he'd made toward proving himself worthy of his father's pride.

"We'll keep it between the two of us, then, until it becomes necessary to involve others." Winslow stared down into his bourbon, watching as he swirled it in his glass. "Mariah also doesn't need to know about the school. Not yet. For now, let her think the project is only about purchasing a few warehouses and stores."

"Understood." Not a difficult condition to agree to, given that the entire project was still nothing but rumor and speculation, with the possibility of disintegrating long before any of it came to fruition. No need to unduly upset her before they had to. If at all.

Winslow set down his glass and rose from his chair, ending their meeting as he lifted his overcoat and hat from the coat stand. "I'm going home. Ledford will be back at sundown to lock up."

Robert followed him into the outer office. Through the wide window, he saw the snow coming down at a faster pace, but not enough to stick to the bricks and stones of London.

"Offering you the partnership was the best move I've made in a long time," Winslow admitted as he signaled to his driver through the window that he was ready to leave. He opened the door, then paused to glance back at Robert. "Do not disappoint me."

Robert froze as a flash of emotion jarred through him. Disappoint... *The hell he would.* His days of disappointing anyone were long over.

When Winslow's carriage pulled away, he closed the outer door and crossed to the shelves covering the end wall, where the company's maps and charts were kept. He quickly found what he sought—a detailed map of the Tower hamlets. Then he grabbed up the list of streets and sat down to work in the small side room where he'd set up his own office. Not that he needed to work here. The study at Park Place would have done just as well. But he wanted to establish himself here so that there would be no mistaking his intent to play a hands-on role in the company.

He made his way down the list, marking off each street on the map with a pencil. But his thoughts kept straying... to the school, to Mariah, to the thousands of families who would be displaced by the new docks, to Mariah... *always* to Mariah.

After an hour of being unable to concentrate, Robert shoved himself away from the desk and stood, to rub at his nape and pace the frustratingly short length of the room. He couldn't force her out of his head. He hadn't had a moment's peace since she sauntered in for tea yesterday afternoon, draped in pastels and ribbons as if she were nothing more than an ordinary debutante. But nothing about her was ordinary. He'd known better than to let her get beneath his skin, but every taunting remark she made, every flutter of those long lashes and curl of her berry-ripe lips stirred the irritation inside him.

He grimaced at the memory of kissing her. Apparently, she'd stirred something else as well.

It was madness to go running after her like that, to ravish her mouth until she melted against him and had him wanting to ravish her body just as thoroughly. But she possessed a fire inside her that drew him unlike any other woman. A confidence that radiated from her. A fierce resolve to fight for what she wanted. The woman was pure determination and challenge. And when she'd practically thrown herself into his arms, then dared him to kiss her—good God.

He raked shaking fingers through his hair. She'd left him furious and pacing all the rest of yesterday, with a frustration that even a night at Boodle's couldn't ease. When he'd finally gone home and crawled into bed, the damnable woman had the audacity to come to him in his dreams, giving him that same breathtaking kiss. And more.

Good God, indeed.

A clatter rose from the street. He glanced up. And froze. *Speak of the devil . . .*

He had a clear view of Mariah through the window as she perched high on a phaeton stopped in the street. A tall, lanky gentleman beside her gave orders to the groom, who ran forward to hold the team. Then he took her hand to help her gracefully to the ground.

Robert's eyes narrowed. Who was this fop? A suitor of some sort. And a serious one judging from the familiar way the man rested his hand against the small of her back as he leaned down and said something that made her laugh.

Who was he? And why hadn't she told him about this man before?

The door opened, and Mariah glided inside, her soft laughter surrounding her like a cloud. She released the dandy's arm and tugged off her gloves, then unfastened the gold clip of her rabbit-fur-edged cape to slip it off. All the while she wore a beaming smile that lit her face, her cheeks pinked from the winter air.

"Papa?" she called out, sticking her head into her father's office.

Robert sauntered forward to lean his shoulder against the doorway. "You just missed him," he called out to her, casually crossing his arms.

She whirled around. Her smile vanished. "You," she whispered, too surprised to find her voice.

"Me." He grinned and glanced past her at the lanky fop in the tall beaver hat. A poor fashion choice that made him appear even taller and ganglier than he actually was.

Then the man smiled and awkwardly glanced from one to the other, sensing the tension between them. "Mariah?" he asked quietly.

With a hard sigh, she grudgingly introduced them. "Whitby, Lord Robert Carlisle. Carlisle"—heavens, how the woman could make his name sound like an insult!—"this is Hugh Whitby, Baron Whitby's son."

"Robert Carlisle!" Whitby exclaimed. "So good to see you again."

They'd met before? Robert raked his gaze over the man. How could he have forgotten this dandy?

"I attended last summer's spread at Park Place with my brothers." Whitby grinned, wide and beaming, so much so that the apples in his cheeks reddened. "Deuces, Carlisle! You certainly know how to throw a party."

So *that* was how the little minx knew about the elephant. She had an informant. "Good to see you, too, Whitby." His eyes drifted to Mariah. She looked fresh and beautiful, with snowflakes melting delicately on her lashes, and surprisingly soft with her velvet cape and rabbit fur muff and hat. "And you, Miss Winslow."

"I stopped by to speak with my father," she said defensively. "And to my surprise found you." Her brow quirked. "And *why* are you here, exactly, Carlisle?"

He hesitated, uncertain how much to share. But she was certain to find out soon that he was already working with her father, if not the exact nature of the work. "I'm researching a project for the company."

She froze. Only for a beat, but in that unguarded moment he saw hurt flash in her eyes, before she said quietly, "I see."

Oddly enough, he felt no satisfaction at gaining the upper hand over her. After all, he was only here, too, because of his own father.

"And what kind of project is it?" she asked. He had to give her credit for keeping the anger from her voice.

"Real estate," he answered simply, reluctant to offer more.

"Of course. Warehouses and stores." Her green eyes shined with understanding. "Papa and I have been discussing that for the past two years. But it was only speculative."

"It still is," he admitted, reminding himself of how very far the docks were from actually being built. "But I'm investigating possibilities."

"I see," she repeated tightly.

Oh, there was jealousy in her, although the minx would never admit it. But could he use that to forge a bit of peace between them? He'd promised Winslow to keep the project's end goals secret, but there was no reason to hide its beginnings. Certainly not when the minx might be able to provide helpful insight.

He offered casually, "Perhaps you'd like to look at it and give me your opinion?"

That stunned her into silence, her lips parting delicately as she stared at him.

He stepped back to invite her into his office. Casting a yearning glance into the room, she hesitated. He could practically see her thoughts whirling as she tried to decide if she could trust him.

But the temptation proved too great. She turned to Whitby and rested her hand affectionately on his arm. "Do you mind waiting? I'll only be a moment."

"Of course not." Whitby shrugged, as if used to her whims. Apparently, the milksop was well trained.

Tilting up her chin haughtily, as if to remind him that he was an intruder in her family's offices, she swept past him into the inner room.

Which immediately felt a hundred times smaller with the two of them inside it. He was instantly aware of every inch of her, from the ebony tendrils framing her oval face all the way down to the half boots poking out from beneath the hem of her cream-colored driving coat, whose form-fitting silhouette molded to her figure like a glove and left no doubt of the full curves beneath.

She removed her gloves, then laid them with the muff and hat on the corner of the desk to free her hands as she reached for the papers he'd been working on. Pages with scrawled notes to himself of what he knew about the hamlet, its most important buildings, ways to scout out the properties in the upcoming days...Her catlike green eyes scanned over his notes.

He came up beside her and pretended to read over her shoulder, careful to remain far enough away to keep a respectable distance, yet close enough to catch the spicy-sweet scent of oranges and cinnamon that lingered around her.

"Did you truly spend the day at the school," he began in a voice low enough to keep Whitby from overhearing, "or is that the story you tell when you want to spend the day driving with Prince George out there?"

Her eyes narrowed icily. "I spent the entire day working on the school's accounts. Since breakfast, in fact." She returned her attention to the papers as she shuffled through them. "*Whitby*," she emphasized, "was visiting the school and was gracious enough to drive me home in his phaeton."

"The same phaeton you used to race down St James's Street," he murmured, reaching over her shoulder to draw her attention to the set of first-guess figures he'd calculated at the bottom of one of the pages.

"He let Evie and me borrow it." She smiled affectionately. "Whitby is quite generous."

His chest tightened inexplicably at the offhanded comment, one that implied an intimacy of thought between the pair, if not of body. And it bothered him. Immensely.

"So generous, in fact, that he encouraged me to speak with Papa about the possibility of him buying unwanted goods from the warehouses to donate to the school."

Of course he did. The dandy certainly knew how to curry her affections. "Is he courting you?"

Surprise flashed over her face at that blunt question. "Whitby?" Then a soft laugh fell from her lips. "He's a dear friend who helps me at the school. That's all. Sorry to disappoint you, Carlisle, but you don't get to marry me off as quickly as that."

His lips twisted at the fight in her. He was very much

beginning to appreciate her fire. "You won't be able to discuss the warehouse stores this afternoon, I'm afraid. Your father already left for home."

"And while the cat's away...," she taunted, then reached to dip the quill in the inkwell and correct his last sum. Although, he noted with amusement, she didn't fix his figures so much as trace over them. "The rat takes over the world."

"Not the world," he corrected in a low murmur, sliding his hand down her arm to take away the quill before she could make more notations. Or stab him with it. "Just the largest shipping company in England."

She yanked her hand away, her cheeks reddening as she fumed. "Why you *arrogant*—"

"Apologies," he interjected quickly, stopping her before she got completely wound up and brought Prince George running to her rescue. As if this lioness needed a cub like him to defend her. "I meant no offense." Well, hardly none. "Let's declare the shipping offices neutral ground, shall we?" When she didn't immediately agree, he added, "After all, we need at least one place where we're not at each other's throats."

She grudgingly conceded, "I suppose... but I'll still quarrel with you everywhere else."

"Oh, I have no doubt of that." Yet the possibility of future sparring sent a thrill of anticipation coursing through him.

A faint smile played at her lips. "Truce, then?"

"Truce," he agreed.

With an uncertain glance at him, as if she didn't quite trust him even that far, she gestured at the papers. "Quite a project. It will test your skills, I'm sure."

Letting that bit of baiting slide by unchallenged, he set his notes aside and revealed the map he'd begun to mark up. Always easier to draw flies with honey instead of vinegar. Or in this case, a bee who possessed a sharp sting. "Which is why I could use your help." He rolled up his shirtsleeves, having removed his jacket hours ago. There was no need for formality in a shipping office, and Mariah wouldn't expect him to put it back on. "He's tasked me with finding landowners and preparing estimates of purchase prices."

She nodded as her eyes moved over the map. A happy smile tugged at her lips, like a proud mother. "The company must be on the verge of expanding."

You have no idea. Guilt pricked at him that he couldn't share Winslow's plans with her. But it was one thing to tell her that he'd embarked on a scouting mission of the area, quite another to reveal the true motivations. Later. Winslow would divulge everything to her later, when the project and its profits were assured. And judging from the way she smiled at the possibility of expansion, her heart would lie exactly where Winslow said it would. With the company.

"Your father is targeting St Katharine's," he told her. "I know that you're familiar with the area and thought you might be able to provide insight."

"I do know this neighborhood," she confirmed, with a pleased smile. She tapped her finger against the map. "There's the hospital and church, the brewery, the school," she murmured, her eyes shining. "My mother was born and raised here, you know."

"I didn't know," he said quietly, his stare transfixed on her delicate profile. Fate must be laughing at him to make his rival so alluring.

She nodded. "Her father was a ship's captain who sailed for my grandfather. That's how she and Papa met. Mama said it was love at first sight, although Papa was twenty at the time and she only thirteen. But five years later, they were married, right there in St Katharine's by the Tower."

He watched the emotions flit across her face, struck by each captivating one. She'd shared practically nothing about herself with him until today, as if unwilling to reveal a soft underbelly to her enemy. But now, her openness surprised the devil out of him. Because it was a whole new side to the Hellion that he never would have suspected.

"The company's important to you because of your parents," he murmured thoughtfully.

She drew her finger lovingly over the familiar streets on the map. "Yes, it is. And so is the school."

"More important than Winslow Shipping?" he asked casually, but he held his breath, waiting for her answer.

A smile teased at her lips. "That's like asking a mother to choose between her children."

He supposed it was. But the answer was important. Watching her closely, he asked as hypothetically as possible, "What would you do if you had to relocate the school?"

She paused her finger on the map and looked up at him quizzically. "Why would I have to do that?"

He shrugged, to hide both the importance of his question and the niggling prick of remorse in his gut over keeping the truth from her. "Because London is changing, and St Katharine's can't remain as it is forever."

"There's a medieval church next door to the school." She gave him a knowing smile, one that warmed through him but did little to quell his guilt. "Nothing changes quickly in St Katharine's."

He smiled faintly in response. Perhaps she was right. It might be years before the docks were built. By then, she'd most likely be married and have children of her own, and she'd be thrilled to know the company was thriving and profiting, securing the future for her own sons and daughters.

He was worrying over a future flood when it hadn't yet begun to rain.

He leaned back against the desk, facing her as she studied the map. Her pretty little brow creased intriguingly, and he had a glimpse of what she must have been like as a pupil, poring over her books.

"Is it really true," he wondered softly, "all that knowledge you told my mother you possess?"

"Yes," she replied, her concentration not straying from the map.

"*Fluency* in Spanish and French?"

"The wars were ending, and I knew my father would want to recapture lost trade with France and perhaps expand further into the Americas."

Amused admiration sparked inside him. Only Mariah would become fluent in two languages in order to increase trade opportunities. "And the rest?"

"Bookkeeping because one should never completely trust accountants, law and politics because of contracts and negotiations, philosophy and the natural sciences in order to study human nature and the world..." She sent him a chagrined glance. "Although I must admit that my knowledge of naval warfare comes secondhand from eavesdropping on sailors."

"Of course," he muttered, struggling to keep from smiling.

She folded her arms across her chest and cocked her head suspiciously. A lock of ebony hair had loosened from its pin and dangled against the side of her neck, and he itched to touch it, even knowing the slap that might very well result.

"Why do I think you're not really interested in learning about my school days, Carlisle?"

"But I am." *Know thy enemy.* And at that moment, he wanted to know everything about her.

"Then you should know that everything I have ever studied was to make myself more valuable to this company," she declared with a quiet intensity, her eyes flashing with fire and determination. "I have dreamt of working beside my father since I was a little girl. It's all I've ever wanted, and I won't surrender that dream."

Then they were in trouble. Because no matter how much he was coming to understand now why the company meant so much to her, Robert had no intention of surrendering it himself.

"It must have been difficult for you," he said sympathetically, keeping the conversation focused on her instead of putting them at odds again. Because when she wasn't fighting him, she was quite enjoyable. "Losing your mother at such a tender age."

Grief flashed across her face, but it was gone in an instant, leaving only a lingering sadness behind. She shrugged a shoulder and looked away. "I suppose it's difficult to lose one's parent no matter how old you are."

His chest tightened, and he admitted quietly, "It is."

"Mama was a wonderful woman," she continued, reaching for her muff to keep her fingers busy by pulling idly at the fur. "I cannot imagine how different my life might have been had she not caught that fever—" Her voice broke, and she froze, her fingers stilling. Then she drew a deep breath and divulged softly, "It was harder for Evelyn. She was younger, and at first, she couldn't understand what happened, why Mama had gone away."

Her eyes glistened with unshed tears, and Robert's heart went out to her. He'd witnessed firsthand the grief that his own sister had suffered upon his father's death. He would have done anything to bring her solace, just as he was certain Mariah would have done for Evelyn. In that, at least, they agreed.

"I'm worried about her," she confessed in a whisper. "She seems so . . . *lost* these days." She looked up at him hopefully, a thought striking her. "Would your mother mind if Evie benefits from my season, too? The distraction might do her good. Perhaps she could come to the soirees and events that I'm forced to attend."

Forced to attend. He fought back a smile at her defiance. Even in the midst of concern over her sister, she'd bared her claws.

"*Two* young ladies to fuss over?" he teased. "My mother would adore it."

"Good. Evie needs guidance, and—"

She turned toward him, stopping in mid-sentence with a soft hitch of her breath at finding him so close. Her green eyes dropped to stare at his mouth, and she swallowed hard, as if remembering the taste of him and longing to experience it again. God certainly knew he wanted to.

"You were saying?" he prompted when she continued to stare at him, as if trying to fathom him and yesterday's embrace.

Then her gaze darted over his shoulder toward the outer office, checking up on the dandy out there. And gauging the privacy between them in here.

"Tell me, Carlisle . . . why do you want this partnership so much?" she whispered, her gaze intense. "Why would it matter to someone like you?"

"Someone like me?" A touch of pique sparked inside him.

"The brother of a duke, wealthy, educated, refined—when he wants to be," she added quickly in afterthought, which drew a crooked grin of amusement from him, despite himself. "Why would you want to work with a shipping company?"

"Why not?" he evaded with a small shrug. The last thing he would do was share his need to prove himself. They were beginning to trust each other, albeit tentatively, but he would never share that.

Her eyes narrowed. She was too sharp to fall for prevarication. She opened her mouth to press—

"Mariah?" Whitby stuck his ginger-haired head into the inner office. "Are you going to be much longer? We really should get on to Mayfair."

"Just one moment," she called out over Robert's shoulder, her gaze never leaving his.

"All right," Whitby acquiesced, and Robert nearly rolled his eyes at the man's lack of spine. What could she possibly see in that milksop? "But I'm to meet up with my brothers at Boodle's soon."

Ignoring Whitby, she whispered low enough that he could barely hear, "This partnership can't possibly mean that much to you."

"More than you know," he answered in the same intense voice, his gaze once more drawn to her sensuous mouth. Just a small lowering of his head, and his lips would be on hers, tasting again that spicy-sweetness he'd begun to crave—

"Mariah?" Whitby called out again, and Robert gritted his teeth. Forget siege warfare. Apparently Whitby's weapon of choice was hounding one to death.

"You should go," he urged her quietly, then pushed himself away from the desk, ending their conversation before she could trap him into other topics he had no intention of discussing. "Whitby!" he called out with far more jocularity than he felt. "Nice to see you again."

"And you, Carlisle." A toothy grin blossomed on his ruddy face. "Say, we should meet up at Boodle's sometime—"

"Have a safe drive to Mayfair," he interrupted, unable to imagine a worse outing than a night spent prowling the clubs with Mariah's dandy in tow. "Miss Winslow." He bowed his head and ignored the irritation that once more flitted across her face as he murmured, "I'd stay away from the phaeton's ribbons, if I were you."

With a soft *humph*, she flipped up her cape hood and flounced from the room. "We're not through with this discussion," she warned as she pulled on her kid gloves.

Oh yes, they were. Yet he tossed out an olive branch. "I'd appreciate any further insight you could give about St Katharine's."

She paused as she reached for the door and shot him a look of annoyance over her shoulder as he stood in the middle of the office, his feet wide and one hand closed in a fist against the small of his back.

But she'd better get used to seeing him here. Because he'd determined to make this business his life's work, and no one was going to stop him. Not even a hellcat with emerald eyes and ebony hair, a mouth that would have tempted a saint, and an attitude as hot to match. Not even the vulnerable woman beneath, of whom he'd had a fleeting but striking glimpse.

"Don't get too comfortable here, Carlisle," she warned

as Whitby rushed to escort her out. "The season is far from over."

The door closed behind her.

Robert blew out a harsh breath and a soft curse.

Through the office's front window he watched Whitby help her onto the seat, then settle in beside her. As the groom scurried to the rear, the dandy leaned over to say something in her ear that earned him a laugh and a bright smile. And her hand resting far too familiarly on his arm. Robert felt that touch from twenty feet away, its heat pouring through him as palpably as if she'd reached for him instead of that fop at her side.

His eyes narrowed as they drove away. What did a woman like Mariah see in a pup like Whitby? For the life of him, he couldn't imagine.

But he sure as hell understood what Whitby saw in her. The magnetic attraction she stirred in men was undeniable. He knew firsthand how she challenged them with her cleverness, always keeping them on their toes and leaving them wanting more. How much she made them long to lay her down, peel away the layers, have her panting—

Christ. Mariah was the last woman he should be thinking about as . . . well, a *woman*.

He'd been too long without the physical pleasures of a woman, that was all. Because of the long hours he'd spent managing his business ventures, he'd not been with a woman since he returned from Quinton's wedding in Cumbria nearly four months ago. That was all that was the matter with him. Nothing else.

Because the alternative—that he truly desired the Hellion—was simply unthinkable.

*   *   *

The next afternoon, Mariah stood in front of a full-length mirror in the private salon of Madame Bernaise, wearing only her stockings, stays, and shift. Around her, a small army of French assistants scurried to take her measurements, present bolts of the finest satins and muslins for approval, and make certain that the tea never cooled.

Sitting on the settee and calmly sipping her tea, Elizabeth Carlisle seemed right at home amid the flurry of activity. She had a list of all the dresses and accessories Mariah would need for the start of her season, in specific colors and fabrics, right down to the ribbons on her slippers. She gave orders to the assistants as firmly and without compromise as Madame Bernaise herself.

Madame, meanwhile, draped fabric after fabric over Mariah's shoulders so that Elizabeth could see how each one complemented her complexion. Those deemed acceptable were whisked away by the assistants though a rear door, where seamstresses immediately set to work to fashion gowns from them. Those that were rejected were sent away by Madame with a dismissive wave of her hand, never to be seen again.

"I have the perfect material for her ball gown!" Madame raved. She snapped her fingers and spoke in street French to one of the shopgirls, threatening that she would have the chit's hide if she didn't fetch the bolt of copper satin.

Mariah bit back the smile at her lips. Madame didn't know she could understand every word. When the assistant complained that she had no idea which fabric Madame meant, Madame called her a worthless cow whom she should have left behind in Marseilles.

"I shall fetch it myself," Madame declared to the duchess, as if the material were too special to trust to an assistant. Then she swept through the room with the imperial air of a woman who had dressed the finest ladies at the French court, rather than the displaced seamstress she was who had been lucky to flee from France with her life.

Elizabeth set down her teacup and stood. Smiling warmly as she approached Mariah, she reached for a length of cream-colored lace, decorated intricately with tiny pearls and silk ribbons.

"Are you having a good time?" she asked as she draped the lace over Mariah's shoulders, possessing an eye for fashion and quality that rivaled Madame's.

She beamed. "I am."

Truly, she was. Her past fittings had been rushed affairs filled with pinpricks and admonishments from the dressmaker that she was too tall to be fashionable, her hair too dark to complement any of the fabrics on hand, her tastes too simplistic. Today, though, there was none of that, and Mariah suspected that if she told Madame that she wanted to attend her debut ball wearing a burlap bag, the Frenchwoman would have fallen over herself in her hurry to recommend a matching wrap of flour sack.

But most of her enjoyment was due to Elizabeth. She loved her role as duchess, and her eyes sparkled whenever she mentioned the season's upcoming events. She also dearly loved her family, glowing with pride whenever she spoke of them. The same proud way she now looked at Mariah. Amid the flurry of preparing for her season, Elizabeth made her feel special, beautiful, and oddly excited about it, the way her mother surely would have if she'd lived.

A knot of emotion tightened in her throat. Did the

Carlisles realize how lucky they were to have her for their mother?

Elizabeth smiled. "Good. That's what a season is for, after all. To enjoy oneself."

As the duchess wrapped the end of the material over her hair like a wedding veil, Mariah mumbled pointedly, "Not to marry me off, then?"

Realizing with a jolt what she'd done with the lace, Elizabeth quickly lowered it away with a chagrined grimace. "Well, yes, I suppose that, too." Then she paused, her brow creasing as she looked closely at Mariah. "Robert said you wanted suitors, but you've never shared those same sentiments. You *do* want to marry, do you not?"

Mariah uncomfortably averted her eyes. "I suppose." Only a small dissembling, although she still couldn't bring herself to look at Elizabeth as she said it. Because she *did* want a husband, family, and home of her own. "But only to the right man."

One who didn't mind sharing her with a shipping company.

Elizabeth nodded, as if that were obvious. "Of course, dear."

"No, I meant…" Her cheeks pinked as she admitted, "I want a love match." The words came hesitantly. Evelyn had been her only confidante in matters of the heart until this season, when she'd begun to confide in Elizabeth, and she dared not tell Evie a breath of how she truly felt about marriage. Oh, she'd never hear the end of it from her overly romantic sister! "Is it silly to wish for that?"

"Not at all." Elizabeth gave her a melancholy smile, yet one full of affection. "My marriage was a love match."

Mariah took hope in that. Her own parents had married for love, but with Mama dying so young and Papa working such long hours, she could barely remember seeing them to-gether. She'd been too young to ask her mother about such things. But Elizabeth instinctively understood her need to learn about marriage and love, and Mariah treasured this moment of shared female intimacy more than she could ex-press. "The duke loved you?"

"Deeply, but he wasn't a duke when we married. Richard wasn't even a baron yet." Her eyes softened as they took on a faraway look. "He was an officer in the army, and I was so proud to have him for my husband. Then they sent him to war, and he returned a hero." She smiled. "King George made him a baron. We already had Sebastian by then. Robert arrived the following spring, Quinton the year after that. A few years later we adopted Josephine."

Adopted? No wonder Robert had behaved so peculiarly about the orphans she helped at the school. Mariah's blos-soming love for the duchess grew even stronger at discover-ing this.

"We were so very happy." Despite her smile, her voice trembled with grief. "Richard's been gone over two years, and I miss him more with each day that passes."

"I'm sorry," Mariah whispered, tears for the duchess stinging in her eyes. She knew how grief lessened but never vanished. For all their fighting, that was one thing that she and Carlisle had in common.

Elizabeth's face melted at the tears she could so easily glimpse in Mariah's eyes. With motherly affection, she lov-ingly brushed a stray lock away from her cheek. "I agreed to help with your season because I knew how difficult it would be…for me, not having Richard at my side, and for you, not having your mother to share this special time." She smiled then, with such love and affection that Mariah lost her breath. "But, Mariah, I'm also enjoying simply spending time with you." Her eyes glistened. "Very much."

"Me, too," she whispered, unable to find her voice.

In only a few days, Elizabeth Carlisle had found her way into Mariah's heart. She finally had someone she could talk with about dresses and dances, flowers and fashion, love and grief . . . all those things mothers and daughters were supposed to share. She might never like Robert Carlisle, but because of him, she'd met his mother. For that, she would always be grateful to him.

An assistant brought over a dress for inspection, one Madame had already made for another client. Emerald-green silk with cream lace, a tight-fitted bodice, an old-fashioned waist . . . The entirety created a shimmering gown that reminded Mariah of something from a book of fairy tales.

Standing behind her so she could look over Mariah's shoulder at her reflection, Elizabeth held the dress in front of her.

Mariah caught her breath at the sight. *That* was definitely not burlap and flour sack.

Elizabeth's eyes sparkled with pleased amusement at her reaction. "So you like it?"

Oh, she absolutely adored it! It was the most beautiful dress she'd ever seen, and selfish longing to wear it ached in her chest. Yet she gave a wistful shake of her head. "I don't need any more dresses."

"Of course you don't *need* it." The duchess's lips curled into a conspiratorial smile. "But wouldn't it be wonderful to have anyway?"

Mariah stared at her reflection in the mirror and bit her lip. Such a beautiful dress, and so tempting . . . but she should say no. She already had enough dresses and accessories ordered to give Papa a fit of apoplexy when he saw the tallies.

Yet it was such a lovely dress, the color perfectly matching her eyes. And Elizabeth wanted so badly for her to have it...

"All right," she acquiesced with a sigh.

"Good. Because we could all use some pleasant distractions this season, even in the form of a gown." Elizabeth smiled at her as she fussed happily with the dress. "And I think that this season will be a good distraction for Robert, as well."

Her mouth fell open. *Carlisle?* Well, the duchess was completely wrong about that! His interest in her season was purely mercenary. "What could *he* possibly need to be distracted from?"

"Oh, lots of things." Elizabeth's attention strayed to the drape of the dress, her gaze moving away from Mariah's. She busied herself with adjusting the bodice, but Mariah could see a troubled concern cloud the duchess's face. "His father's death, for one."

A stab of shame pierced her. She should have thought of that immediately. She'd lost her mother fifteen years ago, yet she still carried grief inside her and feared she always would. Of course Robert still mourned his father. The fact that he had been twenty-five instead of ten wouldn't have lessened his loss.

"Richard's death devastated all of us," Elizabeth explained. Avoiding Mariah's gaze, she picked up a velvet wrap from a nearby chair and placed it over her shoulders. "It was an accident. There was absolutely nothing that could have been done, but—" She choked off, then inhaled a deep breath before continuing, and the glimpse of pain Mariah saw in her at that moment ached into her own chest. "Robert blamed himself."

Mariah's gaze snapped to the duchess's reflection in the mirror. Good God, to blame himself for that...For the first time, she felt a prick of empathy for him, and she understood completely why his mother believed he needed to be distracted.

"He seldom speaks of it," Elizabeth continued, "yet it changed him. He's not the same man he was before. For the longest time, I was so very worried about him." Finally, she raised her eyes to meet Mariah's, and hope sparkled in their cornflower-blue depths. "But this year, he's finally setting a path for himself."

"Oh?" Dread at what the duchess meant panged dully inside her. Because Mariah knew full well that Robert's path drove right through her own.

Elizabeth smiled at their reflection, oblivious to the way that the hope for her son underpinning her expression sliced into Mariah's heart. "This business venture with your father could prove to be the purpose he's been searching for."

Robert wanted purpose, and she understood that. But at what cost to her own dream?

Fresh frustration swelled inside her. *Why* did he have to pick Winslow Shipping? He could find another partnership in no time at all, while she...Well, it was the family business or nothing. She only wished Robert would realize that and gracefully concede.

Elizabeth smoothed down the skirt to check its fall around Mariah's legs. "Then there was Diana Morgan, of course."

"Of course," she mumbled. Who on earth was Diana Morgan?

"You might know her. I believe she's your sister's age.

Blond, very attractive..." She played with the drape of the gown. "A lovely girl."

"No, I'm afraid I don't." What the deuces did a very attractive blonde have to do with Robert?

"He courted her last season." Elizabeth frowned as her attention fell to the skirt. "Do you like the hem? The pattern is awfully busy. We could ask Madame for a plain one, if you'd rather."

"It's fine." She didn't care a fig about the hem. What was this about Carlisle having courted someone? "And Miss Morgan?"

"We all thought he'd offer for her."

A marriage offer from Robert Carlisle? Her chest squeezed, surely in sympathy for the poor girl. Without thinking, she blurted out, "I'm glad she escaped."

With a gasp, she realized what she'd said. Her hand flew over her mouth in mortification. Heavens, how could she have been so thoughtless? To insult him like that in front of his mother, in such a cruel slap to her kindness—

"Me, too," Elizabeth agreed, lowering her voice conspiratorially.

Mariah gaped at her. Instead of being angry, Elizabeth looked...relieved. "*Pardon?*"

"I agree with you completely, my dear. Miss Morgan isn't at all the sort of woman Robert needs in a wife."

Her mind reeled as she tried to follow this strange turn of conversation. And with his mother, no less. "Lovely, attractive...?"

"Unsuspecting," Elizabeth confirmed somberly.

She choked on her surprise. Perhaps Carlisle hadn't pulled the wool over his mother's eyes quite as thoroughly as he'd thought.

"Robert doesn't need a wife who agrees with him. What he needs is one who won't hesitate to keep him in line, who knows her own mind and isn't afraid to speak it. I'm hoping that this season he finds just that woman." She paused, her gaze flicking to Mariah's in the mirror. "Did you know that he was quite a handful as a child?" A faint smile played at her lips, as if she were amused by his behavior but afraid a full smile would condone it. "Always stirring up trouble of one kind or another, but never getting caught."

That sounded exactly like him. Mariah couldn't help the urge to hear more and cajoled, "Tell me?"

Elizabeth hesitated, as if uncertain whether she should give up secrets on her children. Then she lowered her voice and launched into a story about how his tutor had once fallen asleep after stealing a sticky bun from the kitchen, only to wake with his fingers glued to two rulers. "Which were also smeared with icing," she finished, "so of course poor Mr. Fitzwater couldn't blame Robert."

Mariah laughed. It sounded exactly like something she would have done herself at Miss Pettigrew's.

"And then, there was that incident with the piglets…"

By the time Madame returned, Elizabeth had shared over a half dozen stories about Robert and the tricks he'd played, both as a boy at home and later as a student at Eton and Oxford. Mariah was beginning to see him in a whole new light. One in which he wasn't the selfish blackguard she so very much wanted him to be.

Of course, that didn't mean that she would call an end to their war. If he continued to believe he had a claim to the company, then she had a right to fight back. And she certainly wouldn't let him unsettle her again with any of those sinful kisses that left her weak-kneed and aching.

Madame held up the copper-colored satin and draped it across her shoulders. Her black hair shined exotically next to its shimmer, and her green eyes glowed.

"Ah, *mademoiselle*," she purred ingratiatingly. "*Très belle, non?*"

"It's lovely," Elizabeth agreed, her eyes shining with approval. "Make her a ball gown in that, please, with all the accessories. Whatever you think she needs for her introduction."

Madame smiled. "Of course."

Elizabeth gestured toward the green-and-cream-silk dress that Mariah held in her hands. "That one, too, and the wrap. And make that one first, will you?" She nodded at Mariah as Madame hurried off to add the latest two outfits to their growing list. "This dress will be perfect for your first soiree." Then the happy shine in her eyes turned to something even deeper, something Mariah couldn't quite identify . . . "All the gentlemen will be flocking to your side after a glimpse of you in it."

Mariah stared at her reflection and inhaled a trembling breath. It wasn't the flocks of men who worried her. It was *one* man who bothered her to distraction, and it wasn't the good kind of diversion that Elizabeth wanted for her season, either.

Because Robert Carlisle was certainly proving to be a distraction all right—of the worst kind.

CHAPTER SIX

❧ ⁓ ⁓

One Week Later

*R*obert's jaw tightened as he stared at Mariah. Thanks to that little hellcat, the evening was quickly becoming a disaster.

His gaze never strayed from her as she stood on the far side of Lady Gantry's music room, not even when he secured a glass of Madeira from a passing footman. If he looked away, God only knew what she'd do. Especially tonight, surrounded by gentlemen eager to curry her favor.

Sheep. The lot of them. And not one had any idea of the she-wolf in green silk she really was.

"Don't you agree, Robert?"

He was startled back to attention by his sister, Josephine, his gaze darting down to her at his side. "Pardon?"

She sighed at having to repeat herself, and not for the first time during their brief conversation. "The soprano Lady Gantry hired this evening sings beautifully, don't you think?"

"Yes, fine voice," he agreed distractedly.

His gaze returned to Mariah just in time to see her smile at a man whom Robert knew to be a fortune hunter with a trail of debts from here to Yorkshire. A man whose suit her father would never accept. And she knew it, too. Which was probably why she was chatting with him.

The entire time Robert had been watching her, she'd never looked his way. But of course she wouldn't dare. She was purposefully ignoring him, just as she'd done all evening, except for that moment immediately after they arrived when the footmen brought around trays of champagne. She'd certainly paid attention to him then, all right, as she'd spilled her flute down his arm.

The damned minx actually had the gall to look apologetic, although he knew from the gleam in her eyes that she wasn't at all repentant. Most likely, she'd been waiting for the first opportunity to douse his sleeve so she could send him away and escape. But he didn't trust her enough to leave and simply shrugged away the spill as inconsequential, even though he could still feel the cold champagne against his forearm.

Leave it to Mariah to have him reeking like a St Giles gin palace. He would have admired her audacity if he didn't want to throttle her for it.

Josie continued, "The way she sang the Queen of the Night aria was simply breathtaking."

Robert muttered his agreement, only half listening. One would have thought Mariah was the queen of the night herself from the way she drew attention. From the moment they arrived, she'd garnered the interest of nearly every gentleman in the room and hadn't lost it since. They'd all wanted introductions to her before the musicale began, and during the intermission, several of the more eager dandies had embarrassed themselves by stealing chairs from one another in order to gain a closer seat.

And speaking of dandies... *Whitby*.

He'd arrived outfitted in a purple and orange waistcoat and jacket so garish that Robert wondered if Whitby's valet was going blind. But he seemed to be having a grand time, chatting to everyone in the room and never straying far from Mariah's side. Anyone who saw the two of them together, so mismatched, would never presume anything more between them than friendship. And yet—

Josie touched his arm.

He glanced down at her. "Pardon?"

"Don Juan," she said pointedly, once more repeating herself.

"Who?" He jerked his attention back to Mariah. Which one of those sheep had overstepped now?

"Goose!" She laughed at him, a knowing sound that reminded him of all the torment they'd inflicted on each other as children. "*Don Giovanni*, the opera!"

His shoulders slumped with chagrin, and he shook his head. "I'm sorry, Josie," he apologized sincerely. "I'm distracted tonight."

"Well," she conceded grudgingly with understanding, "you do have your hands full with Miss Winslow."

"More than you realize," he muttered.

"Hmm." The sound was a low disagreement, but one tempered by an amused curl of her lips. "Poor Signorina Pergoli." She raised the flute to her mouth as she murmured, low enough that only Robert could hear, "For once, she isn't the only prima donna in the room. Miss Winslow is forcing her to compete for attention, and I don't believe she knows what to do about it."

No, except to send scathing glances in Mariah's direction.

"Mama seems to like her, though," she commented, nodding toward their mother.

"Yes, she does." *Thank God.*

That was one thing that was going well so far this season, that Mariah and his mother had already developed an affection for each other. And tonight, the duchess appeared blissfully happy with the whole situation. Even now, as she chatted with Lady Sydney Reed and the Duchess of Strathmore, she seemed pleased as punch. He'd nearly spit out his wine earlier when she'd leaned over to whisper to him between music sets, *Doesn't Mariah look beautiful?*

And damnation, she did, too.

Madame Bernaise had outdone herself with a drape that perfectly highlighted the fullness of Mariah's bosom beneath the gown's tight bodice, before falling straight to the floor in yards of green silk that only accentuated how tall and graceful she was. A shade of dark green that drew attention to her catlike eyes and ebony hair. A green that any other young miss wouldn't have had the presence to carry off but that Mariah wore like her birthright.

Beautiful?

No. Simply enthralling.

But if she wanted to avoid marriage, she'd have been better off in worsted wool, because all she'd done by wearing that dress tonight was make herself even more alluring. None of the sheep here tonight would do. Yet talk would spread about her, and she'd soon have every curious gentleman in London calling on her, to see for himself the woman who was on her way to becoming that season's Incomparable. Exactly as he wanted.

So why did that aggravate the hell out of him?

"And do *you* like her?" Josie asked.

Robert sputtered at his sister's question. "*Pardon?*"

"You've been staring at her all night," she commented with a knowing glint in her eyes.

Good Lord. When it came to marrying him off, Josie was nearly as bad as Mother.

"Because I don't trust her enough to look away," he answered grimly, wanting no mistake on this point. He was *not* captivated by Mariah Winslow. "A gentleman stares at a woman because she's beautiful," he admitted with a small lift of his glass to her, earning himself a sardonic *humph*. Then he narrowed his aggravated gaze on Mariah. "A man stares at the Hellion—"

"Because he cannot help himself?" The teasing gleam in her eyes drew a scowl from him. And *that* caused her to laugh at him. Again.

He said nothing and raised the wine to his lips. There was no good reply to that.

She sobered quickly as her gaze drifted around the room. "I'm afraid your attention might be misplaced this evening."

He frowned. "What do you mean?"

She gestured her champagne flute toward the corner of the room. "That's her sister, isn't it?"

His gaze followed where she'd indicated. That was Evelyn Winslow, all right. He'd been too concerned tonight with watching Mariah to worry about the other Winslow daughter, who now stood chatting with Burton Williams, Viscount Houghton's youngest son. Not a wise choice for her, considering the man's reputation and Sebastian's inexplicable hatred of him.

He grimaced. Mariah was his primary concern, but if anything happened to Evelyn tonight, Henry Winslow would blame him. "Josie, do me a favor? Make certain Evelyn Winslow stays out of trouble tonight."

"Of course."

He kissed her cheek. "Thank you," he murmured gratefully, putting out one fire only to turn his attention back to Mariah.

And finding a bonfire.

Whitby was at her side with a fresh glass of champagne for her and whispering something in her ear that made her cheeks flush nearly as red as her lips.

Enough.

Tossing back the last of his wine, he set his glass aside and started toward her.

* * *

"Why, Mr. Lawton, you must be especially lucky to have purchased such a fine hunter." Mariah's compliment fell over the man as nothing but empty flattery, yet he didn't seem to notice. "And from Jackson Shaw, no less!"

"Not luck, Miss Winslow." Lawton bragged, "I'm a skilled purveyor of horseflesh." He smiled broadly with arrogant pride. "I know how to find my way around bow hocks and cow hocks."

"Yes," she mumbled stoically, yet was unable to keep the wry tone from her voice, "I'm certain you do."

Her cheeks were on the verge of breaking from the unceasing smile she'd worn on her face all evening. And now, so was her patience.

Oh, she'd had a simply marvelous time earlier, listening to the Italian opera singer perform. She was so grateful to Elizabeth for allowing her and Evie to accompany the duchess to Lady Gantry's annual musicale tonight, and when the woman sang, her voice was so beautiful that it nearly brought Mariah to tears.

But now, she was surrounded by nearly a dozen young men, all finely educated at Oxford and Cambridge, whose conversation sparked not one bit of interest from her. All they wanted to talk about was who belonged to which clubs, who raced the fastest carriages, who owned the best hunting packs—as if the ability to simply *buy* things proved anyone's merit. Of course, she hadn't expected profound debate on opera or philosophy, yet not one of them thought to bring up topics that really mattered, such as charity work, politics, the plight of the poor, or the changes to England during the past few tumultuous years. Which left her wondering...did they think she was too dimwitted to carry off those kinds of topics, or were they?

In fact, all the polite conversations she'd been forced into this evening had bored her stiff, when what she really wanted was to dive into the kinds of verbal sparring that she always fell into with Carlisle. *That* type of conversation she thoroughly enjoyed, and she didn't let herself ponder what it meant that it was that aggravating devil, of all the gentlemen here tonight, who was the only one capable of holding her interest. It pained her to admit it, but in comparison, the gentlemen around her simply couldn't keep up with Carlisle's skill for debate, and none of them possessed the sharp wit that he wielded in spades, matching her own, barb for barb.

Robert Carlisle. The man was a menace. Yet she had to give him credit for his mind.

And for his control. After all, he'd barely flinched when she'd inaugurated the start of her season by spilling her champagne on him.

"Do you ride, Miss Winslow?" one of the sons of the Duke of Heatherton asked.

"Not at all, I'm afraid," she answered, taking another sip of champagne. Drink might be the only thing that saved her sanity this evening. God help her—she had the rest of a very long season ahead of her of equally superficial, painfully polite conversations that characterized society events. At this rate, she wouldn't have to worry about avoiding marriage proposals. She was certain to be dead of boredom by March. "I've never liked horses."

He puffed out his chest like a strutting peacock. "Only because you've never been riding with me."

And never will. She smiled politely, then took another sip of champagne.

"A turn about the room, Miss Winslow?" From behind her, the deep voice twined down her spine and hummed through her blood. She didn't have to look to know—

"Carlisle," she whispered.

Finally the evening had taken a turn toward the interesting.

She casually glanced over her shoulder at him, as if he were simply another one of the men flocking around her tonight, when in reality his appearance at her side sent her pulse spiking. "I'm terribly sorry, but Lord Gregory was in the middle of a story about horses." She turned her attention back to the dandy and smiled at him to continue. After all, if Carlisle was set on subjecting her to such dull conversations this season, then he could suffer right along with her. "Lord Gregory, you were saying?"

"I'd asked if you—"

"A turn about the room." His hand clasped her elbow from behind. "Please."

"Come now, Carlisle," Lawton interjected good-naturedly,

but with a prick of annoyance in his voice. "You've already had Miss Winslow to yourself enough this season. The rest of us would like more time in her delightful company."

She glanced over her shoulder just in time to see a dark look flash across Carlisle's face.

Her heart skipped. Oh, that was not a happy mood! *Good.* The blasted devil deserved every prick he received for parading her through society like this.

He ignored the men around her and fixed her beneath his gaze. "Now."

The anger seething behind the single word sent an ice-cold warning slithering through her, and she knew not to press her luck by refusing. She might be willing to cast caution to the winds, but she was no fool.

"Of course, Lord Robert." She placed her hand on his arm, ignoring his narrowed eyes as she pretended that nothing was wrong. "I'd be honored to take a turn with you." With an apologetic smile for the group, she slowly dropped into a curtsy. "Gentlemen, if you'll excuse me."

Carlisle nodded coldly to the others and led her away, ostensibly for a slow stroll around the room. He steered her toward the open French doors that let in the cool night air and eased the stifling heat of the crush of bodies and lamps blazing throughout the room.

When they were just out of earshot of the other guests, she muttered, "So our truce is over, then?" A part of her was sad to see it go. A very *small* part, because the rest of her burned to give him the thrashing he deserved.

He slid a sideways glance at her. "Oh, I think that truce ended the moment you decided to serve me champagne, don't you?"

A pang of remorse pinged inside her, but she'd never

acknowledge it in front of him. "Come now, Carlisle. Surely, you've had women spill drinks on you before."

His jaw tightened as he drawled sarcastically, "Never with such targeted aim."

"Thank you." She beamed brightly, as if he'd truly meant that as a compliment. To her delight, that only irritated him more.

Unfortunately, he wasn't going to let that barb pass unanswered and smiled coldly. "Quite a dress you're wearing."

"Why, this old thing?" she asked with mock innocence.

"Yes, that old thing," he drawled. Then, with all the conservative pomposity of an octogenarian, he added, "Which belongs on a French courtesan."

She sighed in aggravation, although she couldn't help the thrill that sped through her that he'd noticed how she looked tonight. That he thought she was attractive enough in this dress to cause a stir, even though there was nothing improper at all about it. His mother would never have allowed her to wear it if there were.

No. What upset him about the dress was that *she* was in it. She could have donned a nun's habit, and he would have found fault.

Deciding the aggravating scoundrel deserved to be irritated even more, she trailed her hand over her neckline and asked with false artlessness, "Whatever do you mean?"

"You know damned well," he ground out. "Any man who gets close enough to you has a view all the way down to your navel."

She stifled a victorious laugh at raising his hackles and tossed out recklessly, "If that's only as far as he can see, then he isn't standing close enough."

His eyes flared at her bold innuendo. Then he murmured, "Oh, I'm standing pretty close."

He took the invitation she'd so thoughtlessly delivered and lowered his gaze to her breasts.

A shivering heat prickled beneath her skin, and her nipples puckered against the bodice. Something tightened low in her belly, something hot and intense. And it stunned the breath from her.

So did the compelling urge to whisper, "So how's the view?"

His eyes snapped up to hers, and she saw a desire in their sapphire depths so raw that she gasped.

Impossible. Carlisle couldn't desire her. Would *never*—

Yet the way he stared at her triggered a dull throbbing inside her, when the other gentlemen tonight had barely raised enough interest from her to garner a second glance. But then, Carlisle wasn't looking at her the same way the other men did.

No, behind his gaze simmered a ravenous hunger that was simply predacious. As if he wanted to drape her across the dining table and feast on her.

For one breathless heartbeat, she wanted to let him do just that. Something dark and wild inside her wanted to lay herself bare to this man who titillated her so wickedly and continuously kept her dancing on the razor's edge.

Then his hand tightened on her arm to lead her on, and the moment vanished.

As she fell into step beside him as they continued their turn about the room, she stole a surreptitious glance at him. He kept his gaze straight ahead, an inscrutable expression on his handsome face.

Where was the amiable man he seemed to be with everyone but her? When Carlisle wasn't being a beast, he could be quite charming. She'd seen it herself tonight when he'd talked with his mother, in the way he'd laughed so easily with his sister and charmingly chatted with the opera singer. And heaven knew Mariah had experienced his passion herself and knew all too well the appealing charms of that side of his character.

No, it was *this* side of him that aggravated her to no end. The cold, arrogant man who brought out her ire. His mother was certain that he needed to be distracted this season, and perhaps he did. Perhaps he was still suffering from the loss of his father and feeling adrift, needing purpose.

But why did his lack of purpose have to result in suffering for her?

"Be assured that there is only one man's attention I'm interested in gaining," she declared. "Tonight and any other."

His face hardened with a strange expression she couldn't place, and he ground out through a clenched jaw, "Who?"

Was that jealousy she saw in him? No, certainly she was mistaken. The only emotion Carlisle would feel about such a declaration would be relief.

"*My father*," she emphasized, "and doing so by behaving exactly as your mother has asked of me."

When they reached the French doors, he released her and stepped away. Far enough to quell any gossip that might arise about them by stopping to speak privately, yet close enough that she could still smell the masculine scent of him swirling around her like fog on the cool night air that seeped in from the garden.

Then the blasted devil had the audacity to lean his hip casually against the doorway, in a pose so wickedly rakish that her belly clenched.

"Whatever game you're playing at," he warned in a low voice, "you won't win."

"But I will," she countered, her own voice just as soft. "It's going perfectly, in fact."

"For me." He shrugged, which only drew her attention to the fine cut of his cashmere jacket across his broad shoulders. "By the end of the week, gentlemen will be calling on you in droves."

Although something peculiar in the tone of his voice told her that he wasn't at all happy about that. Was Carlisle regretting his decision to find her a husband?

She shook her head. "And fleeing just as quickly when they learn that I have no dowry and that Papa will never allow a son-in-law into the company." If she had her way, enough of tonight's gentlemen would call on her in the days to come to spread that bit of news throughout the *ton*. By the end of the fortnight, not one gentleman would be daft enough to pursue her, and August would arrive without a single suitor in sight. *Perfect.*

"You underestimate your worth," he assured her, his gaze traveling deliberately over her. His blue eyes shined like the devil's own in the flickering light of the chandeliers.

Her pulse jumped in foolish response. "You're mistaken," she answered as icily as she could manage, although her words infuriatingly came out sounding more like a purr than a setdown. "No gentleman will want me when he discovers that I'll enter marriage as penniless as a beggar."

"A woman who looks the way you do, with a sharp mind that's a constant challenge..." His deep voice swirled through her and raised goose bumps across her skin. "You're an unpredictable beauty who keeps a man on his toes," he murmured, his dark gaze dropping to her mouth. "They'll certainly want you."

As he stared at her, a wolfish gleam lit his eyes. Oh, how she remembered that look! She'd seen it before... when he'd pushed her against the wall and plundered her mouth, as if to devour her one breath-stealing kiss at a time.

"Wanting and having are two very different things," she reminded him, unable to keep the trembling from her voice. She'd learned that lesson the hard way when her father refused to let her work with him. But now, with every moment she spent in Carlisle's presence, she was beginning to realize so much more about the difference. "What do *you* want from me, Carlisle?"

He froze. Only a heartbeat, not long enough that anyone else would have noticed—but Mariah did. Just as she noticed the heated look that darkened his face. One that made her tremble.

"I want you to realize that your father and I have only the best intentions for you," he answered, yet she had the distinct impression that he'd wanted to say something very different but censored himself. "That fighting against us will come to no good."

"I will not give up." She wouldn't—*couldn't*—surrender her dream.

"You should," he countered firmly, pushing himself away from the doorframe and once more taking her arm to walk on. But she refused to go.

Despite the low warning licking at the backs of her knees that she was poking a stick at a tiger, she was spurred on by her anger. Both at him and at herself for being drawn so inexplicably to such a coldhearted devil, to the tingles of his casual touches and the heat of his not-so-casual kisses.

"What truly frustrates you, Carlisle?" She slowly moved her arm away from him. But because he didn't drop his hand away, he caressed all the way down her forearm and sparked the unsettling sensation of his fingers continuing to caress her long after she'd shifted away. "That I'm doing exactly what any young lady should do to find a husband?" Her voice lowered to a breathless whisper. "Or the knowledge that it ultimately won't work?"

Anger instantly lit his eyes with a gleam so intense that they glowed like brimstone. "Do not play games with me, Mariah," he warned, his voice more frightening for all its cold control.

"Then call off this foolish season." She smiled as if they were discussing nothing more innocuous than the weather.

"You know I won't do that," he bit out.

She countered acerbically, "And you know you won't win."

Then she sauntered away, not caring that she'd given him a public cut right there in Baron Gantry's music room. The beast deserved far more than that!

As she walked away, Mariah felt the heat of his furious gaze on her. She'd successfully revealed to him tonight what kind of opponent he had in her. One who would never admit defeat.

Robert Carlisle might have declared war, but victory would be hers.

CHAPTER SEVEN

Four Aggravating Days Later

*P*lease, Uncle Robert?" Clara looked up at him beseechingly through nine-year-old eyes, but the tug at his heart
told him that she'd already mastered the womanly skill of
wrapping men around her finger. When she finally became
old enough to debut, the gentlemen of the *ton* wouldn't
stand a chance of resisting her. "Daisy's all alone and
frightened."

As if on cue, the kitten gave a heartrending cry from the
chestnut tree in the far corner of the garden, where it had
gotten itself stuck by not having enough sense to use its
claws to climb down. Clara tugged at his jacket sleeve to
convince him to help.

"Sweeting, she's a cat," he tried to explain logically. "If
she can climb up, she'll eventually climb back down."

Clara let out a soft sob. "Please, Uncle Robert!"

His shoulders sagged. Apparently, logic didn't work on
nine-year-old girls.

"Yes," a soft voice called out with amusement, and he

glanced down the garden path to see Mariah strolling toward them. She reached Clara and knelt down to pull the girl into her arms to comfort her. "Please, Uncle Robert."

He clenched his jaw. Leave it to the Hellion to sneak away from the tea his sister, Josephine, was hosting in the drawing room at Audley House and make a beeline to him to cause trouble. He'd come out into the garden to enjoy the air—and to escape the women, most of whom seemed to think he needed to meet one of their unmarried female relations—only to be assailed by two of their kind.

"I was just explaining to Clara that the kitten will come down when it's ready," he said, pointing to the small puff of white fur clinging to one of the high boughs.

His niece gave a hiccupping sob and wrapped her arms around Mariah's neck, turning away from him to focus all her charms on her new ally. "Daisy's just a baby, and she's frightened," Clara choked out softly, in that I-am-a-helpless-female-who-needs-a-hero voice she'd practiced to perfection on all three of her uncles since Josie and Chesney adopted her shortly after they married. All golden curls and big blue eyes, she'd learned quickly how to manipulate the three men to get whatever she wanted.

Then her mouth hardened in cold accusation. "But Uncle Robert wants to leave her up there!"

He blinked. Apparently, he and his brothers had created a monster.

"It's a *cat*," he reminded them with exasperation. "They climb trees. It's what they do."

Mariah narrowed her eyes on him in disapproval. Apparently, logic didn't work on twenty-five-year-old hellions, either.

She tucked one of Clara's curls behind her ear. "Well,

it seems that Daisy's gotten herself into quite the predicament."

"Yes." Clara sighed, the long-suffering sound of a mother whose child often misbehaved.

"Have you tried calling to her?"

She nodded.

"What about tempting her with a treat?"

Another nod, this time accompanied by a finger pointing at a saucer of cream on the grass beneath the tree.

"I see." Mariah commented gravely, "She must be *very* stuck, then."

He heaved out a breath of aggravation. "Oh, for Lucif—"

"Uncle Robert," Mariah interrupted sharply, shooting him a warning look at the curse he was about to unthinkingly spit out in front of his young niece. Then she smiled, one that curled forebodingly down his spine. "It seems the only way to save Daisy is for you to climb up after her."

Aware that his niece was listening, he forced a smile and said as sweetly as possible, "You really expect me to climb a tree to rescue a cat?"

"Saving a damsel in distress seems a perfectly heroic thing for a dashing gentleman to do," she pointed out ingenuously.

Clara nodded her agreement with a loud sniff.

His smile tightened. "It's a cat. With claws. Twenty feet in the air."

Mariah's mouth rounded into an exaggerated O of shock. "So you're just going to leave the poor thing stranded up there?"

He saw a gleam of amusement dance in her eyes. The damnable woman was enjoying this! He bit back his growing irritation and ground out, "It will come down when it's ready."

"When anything might happen by and hurt it?" Her smile faltered with an expression of inflated dread. "Including a pack of wild wolves?"

"Wild *wolves*?" He spit out in half anger, half surprise. "For God's sake, we're in a walled garden in the middle of Mayfair!"

But the worried look Clara gave him nearly broke his heart.

Good Lord. It was bad enough when just one of the pair beset him. Together they were deadly.

"Fine." He rolled his eyes. "I'll climb up after it."

Mariah gave a deep sigh. "My hero."

The glare he shot her was murderous. But the minx only stifled a laugh.

"Thank you, Uncle Robert!" Clara threw her arms around his legs to hug him.

His shoulders sagged. Hadn't he been defeated from the beginning? "When I fall and break my leg, imp," he teased grimly, giving a tug to one of her curls, "you'll be the one bringing me breakfast in bed for the next six months."

She giggled and placed her hand over her lips in a gesture of pure flirtatious femininity as she retreated back to Mariah. He felt a pang of sympathy for her father when in ten years the gentlemen would be flocking to his door to court her. But knowing Chesney's former reputation as a rake, Robert suspected the universe had a grand sense of humor and was simply getting even.

Mariah smiled victoriously at him as she hugged Clara.

He grimaced. Perhaps not so grand, after all.

"You two stay back," he ordered as he shrugged off his jacket and tossed it over the stone bench at the side of the path. "I don't want you to get hurt."

"Oh no," Mariah affirmed with an exaggerated shake of her head. "We certainly wouldn't want *anyone* to get hurt."

Gritting his teeth, he ignored her baiting and rolled up his shirtsleeves to his elbows. "Just stay back, all right?"

Both females nodded gravely, although one was on the verge of bursting into laughter at his expense. *Damned minx.*

He walked up to the tree and jumped to catch the lowest of the branches, then pulled himself up onto the bough. In a matter of seconds, he was in the midst of the tree and making his way carefully up toward the ball of white fur, which now meowed such plaintive cries that he would have sworn that wolves truly were stalking it. Far below on the path, Mariah held Clara wrapped securely in her arms to keep the girl from attempting to climb up after him. Both sets of female eyes followed him closely.

Slowly and carefully, encumbered by the smooth soles of his boots, which were not made for climbing trees, he made his way up to the top boughs where the kitten clung from its claws on the side of the trunk. Its tail lay curled between its legs, its eyes wide with fear.

"There now, you little fur ball," he cooed softly to the kitten as he reached his hand toward it. "It's all right. I've got you."

The cat let out one more cry for help as he caught it by the scruff of its neck and lifted it from the tree. But when he pulled it against him to free his hand and lower himself out of the tree, the terrified kitten let out a teeth-jarring howl and sank all eighteen claws deep into his forearm.

He bit out a curse, but the kitten clung on, undeterred, leaving him no choice but to climb down with the little beastie firmly attached to his flesh.

When he reached the lowest rung of branches, the cat

retracted its claws and leapt onto the bough, then quickly shimmied down the tree. It ran straight to Clara and jumped into her arms, purring so loudly that Robert could hear it as he dropped to the ground.

"Oh, thank you, Uncle Robert!" Clara gushed as the kitten rubbed itself beneath her chin, the long tail flicking against the girl's cheek. She cradled it against her chest as if it were a baby.

"Oh yes," Mariah seconded as he approached, with blood beginning to dot the scratches on his forearm and streaks of dirt marring his white shirt. She plucked a leaf from his hair. "Thank you, Uncle Robert."

Before he could give her the tongue-lashing she deserved, Clara hugged him in gratitude, the kitten still held tightly in her little arms. Then she skipped off happily toward the house.

When she reached the edge of the terrace, she put the kitten down and hurried on inside. It raced up the nearest tree, where it stopped halfway to the top and, once again stuck, began to cry out for help.

Robert slid a narrowed gaze at Mariah as she pressed her hand against her mouth to keep from laughing.

"Glad I could offer you amusement," he grumbled as he reached to snatch up his discarded jacket.

"Sometimes, Carlisle," she admitted with a sigh, "you simply make it too easy."

Muttering a string of curses beneath his breath, he began to unroll his sleeves.

"Wait!" She placed her hand on his arm to stop him. "You'll get blood all over your shirt. Let's get you into the house and cleaned up."

He lifted a dubious brow. "Concerned about me?"

She sniffed and released his arm, as if insulted at the idea. "Concerned about your poor valet, who has to wash out all that blood."

"Of course." But he didn't believe her. For all that the Hellion was prickly as a cactus around him, there was also a softer side to her. One that had her genuinely comforting Clara only a few moments ago, showing affection to his mother, and worrying about her sister. He only wished she'd show that softer side more often, especially to him, and when she did that it didn't involve blood.

"This way." She started toward the house. "There's bound to be salve in the kitchen."

He followed her into the house, noting that she carefully skirted the drawing room and the three dozen society matrons packed inside.

"Shouldn't you be in with the ladies"—he jerked his head in the general direction of the soiree—"rather than haunting the garden?"

"I suppose." She carefully kept her voice low. "But there's only so much talk about muslin that a woman can tolerate before she goes mad."

He smiled at that, despite himself. Her wit was one of the things he liked best about her.

"And why were *you* in the garden?" she pressed. "The ladies were all asking where my handsome escort had gone."

There was poison somewhere in that, he was certain, but he knew not to antagonize. Instead, he drawled, "There's only so much talk about muslin a man can tolerate before he goes mad."

When she opened her mouth to give that the retort it deserved, he took her arm. "In here."

He pulled her out of the hall and through a double doorway.

She stopped in surprise to gaze at the room. "The library?"

In answer, he tugged at one of the books. With a soft click, a hidden door opened and the false façade of the bookcase gave way to reveal a shelf filled with crystal tumblers and bottles of all kinds. He grinned. "Where Chesney keeps his best liquor."

She swept her gaze around the room. "It's amazing," she whispered, a touch of awe in her voice. "I don't think I've seen a private library in London to match it."

"My family believes in the value of books." He liberated one of the bottles and a crystal tumbler from the stash and set them on the nearby reading table. "They also believe in the value of good drink." When her eyes met his as a smile of amusement tugged at her ripe lips, her glance warmed through him. Spurred on by that moment's quiet connection, he revealed a private part of himself by admitting, "I'm hoping to have a grand library myself someday."

"I believe you will," she murmured, turning her attention back to the room around her.

She slowly circled the room, taking in the floor-to-ceiling mahogany shelves, the dark walnut paneling and wine-colored drapes, the Turkish rug... She stopped in front of the marble fireplace and looked up at the painting hanging over it.

His gaze followed hers—

His father's portrait. His heart skipped with a pained ache. *Good God.* For the first time, he'd walked into this room and forgotten that portrait was here, and he wasn't prepared for the rush of guilt that swept over him because of it. Or the grief.

"Richard Carlisle, Duke of Trent, Baron Althorpe," he offered in explanation, hoping his voice sounded normal. Then added quietly, "My father."

She threw him a surprised glance over her shoulder before returning her attention to the painting. "It's a lovely portrait."

A copy of the one his father sat for when he was granted the dukedom, the painting had been commissioned by Josephine when he died. She'd wanted it simply because she wanted a portrait of her father in her home to remember him by, never suspecting how the sight of it cut raw slices into Robert's heart. Nor would he ever tell her. Richard Carlisle had been the man who saved her from the hell of the orphanage, loving and raising her as one of his own, while Robert was the man who took all that away.

"Your father was a very handsome man," she commented softly.

He forced a grin as he splashed the whiskey into his glass, not feeling at all jocular. "People say I resemble him."

She sniffed and turned away from the portrait. "I don't see it."

His lips twisted at that. Mariah, true to form.

"Sit down so I can clean you up," she ordered gently, gesturing at two leather chairs pulled up to the reading table. When he hesitated, she heaved out an exasperated breath. "Oh, don't worry! You're safe with me." As he began to sit, she added, "After all, I haven't murdered anyone in a library all week."

He froze for a heartbeat, then pinned her with a look as he finished lowering himself into the chair. "Just the garden, then?"

Her eyes danced mischievously as she took the chair next to his. "Death by kitten."

Damnable woman. When he clenched his jaw and began to rise from his chair, she placed a hand on his shoulder to stop him and softened her gaze as she looked up at him. Faint remorse shone in her eyes for teasing him.

He let out a patient breath and settled into the chair.

"Show me your arm," she ordered gently.

He stretched his forearm across the reading table toward her, then raised the glass and gratefully took a long swallow. Both to ease the pain of the scratches on his arm and the hollow ache in his heart.

"You did get quite a wounding, didn't you?" She pulled a handkerchief from the pocket of her pelisse and gently dabbed at his arm to clean off the droplets of blood clinging to the jagged scratches. "Who knew a tiny kitten could be so lethal to such a big, strong man?"

Enough. With an aggravated sigh, he began to rise from the chair.

"Carlisle." She brushed her hand down his forearm before he could pull away completely, a soft caress that tickled up his arm and made his breath hitch. Her hand slid into his, palm to palm, and he felt her pulse beating gently against his own where their wrists touched. She gave an apologetic squeeze to his fingers, one that sped through him with a heated electricity that tingled at the backs of his knees.

He slowly eased back down.

She once more rested his arm across the table between them, but this time, she kept her left hand holding his, their fingers entwined, even as she continued to dab gently at the scratches farther up his forearm. Only to keep him still. Certainly not out of any thoughts of affection.

"The duchess speaks of your father quite often," she said quietly, her voice growing serious as she let the teasing fall away. She didn't look at him, her eyes focused on his arm, but he suspected that she was keenly aware of the reaction that talk of his father drew from him. There was little that sharp mind of hers missed.

"They were very much in love." He watched her face as she focused her attention on his arm. He had to admit that she was quite beautiful... when she wasn't set on torturing him. "His death was hard on her."

"And on you," she commented, not raising her gaze from the scratches.

He tensed, dread freezing his blood. How much did she know? Surely, his mother hadn't shared the details of his father's death with her. "On *all* of us," he corrected, deflecting attention from himself.

When she lifted her gaze to meet his, a faint plea to share more revealed itself in her eyes. But that sure as hell wasn't going to happen. The *very* last thing he wanted to discuss with her was his feelings about his father's death.

"Your mother said it was an accident," she told him quietly.

"Yes." A damned lie. His father's death wasn't an accident.

Her green eyes stared at him for several long moments, as if she knew he had just lied to her. But instead of challenging him, she gave a faint nod of understanding and lowered her gaze back to his arm.

"When my mother died," she shared softly, "her death was also unexpected."

With her head bowed so he couldn't see the expression on her face, she slowly pulled her hands away from him. Suddenly, the inexplicable urge gripped him to grab her hands and hold on tight, so that she couldn't take the comfort of her touch away. But it vanished a heartbeat later and left him feeling like a fool.

Christ! To take comfort in this hellcat—what on earth was wrong with him?

Completely unaware of the turmoil her nearness stirred inside him, she reached for the bottle of whiskey. "She'd taken Evie and me to the park just that morning, in fact. It was a dreary day, cold and damp, but we didn't want to stay inside and hounded her until she relented." She fell silent as she placed the handkerchief over the end of the bottle and turned it upside down to wet the cloth. When she continued, her voice was much softer. "That afternoon she said she was tired and went upstairs to rest. She never got out of bed again."

His chest tightened in grief for her. He'd lost his father, but for a little girl to lose her mother . . . "I'm so sorry."

Her only acknowledgment of his sympathy was a tight nod. "The doctors said it was a fever, that there was nothing anyone could do." She didn't raise her eyes, sitting perfectly still as she whispered, "By dawn, she was gone."

Her shoulders shook as she inhaled a deep breath to collect herself. Then, without meeting his gaze, she returned to her task and dabbed the whiskey-soaked linen against the scratches.

He sucked in a mouthful of air through clenched teeth at the bite of the liquor. Knowing the Hellion, he would have said she was torturing him on purpose, except for the grief that hung heavy on her brow. Not even Mariah could fake that.

"You must have been inconsolable," he commented gently, remembering the cries of grief from his mother and Josie when his father died. Hearing them had made him feel like a piece of glass, shattered from the inside out.

"I was, because I blamed myself," she whispered. "If I hadn't insisted that she take us to the park, she would have still been alive."

"You don't know that," he reassured her quietly. "Fevers come from all places."

She nodded slowly. "And in time I came to accept that."

She paused, mid-dab, her eyes not lifting from his arm. In that moment's hesitation, he had the feeling that she wanted to say something that she wasn't certain he wanted to hear.

Instead, she commented, "It's been even worse for Evelyn. She was only eight and couldn't really comprehend what death meant, except that Mama fell asleep and never woke up. For weeks afterward, she was terrified of going to sleep. After all these years, she still has trouble sleeping, and even now, she'll sometimes stay in my room with me, especially when she has nightmares."

The sting of the whiskey weakened as she continued to gently cleanse the scratches, but his sympathy for the Winslow sisters grew. Especially for Mariah, knowing how close she was to Evelyn, how much it must upset her not to be able to help her sister more.

"That's why I spend so much time at the school, I suppose," she reflected softly. "I want to help others through their grief, to let them know they're not alone."

Not alone. But she was wrong. In the end, everyone grieved alone. Even surrounded by a crowd of friends and family. He'd certainly learned that lesson well.

"I wish Evie could take solace in the school the way I do. But seeing the children reminds her too much of Mama, and she can't bear it." She paused and stilled the handkerchief against his skin. "I wonder…does the duchess ever experience that side of grief? When she looks at her sons, she must see your father in you and miss him terribly."

"I'm certain of it," he murmured. Mother often commented on how much her sons reminded her of their father.

Especially him. She always said that with pride, not realizing how that simple comment shredded his insides. Because he'd proven himself to be nothing like the good and respectable man Richard Carlisle had been.

She set the handkerchief aside. "What was he like?"

His gut tightened as he hesitated to answer. The last person he wanted to talk with about his father was Mariah Winslow. Yet she knew the pain of losing a parent, and he ached with the harsh guilt that he kept bottled inside him. Finally, he offered succinctly, "He was a hero."

"Oh?" She looked up at him, her eyes bright.

The sight of her unshed tears for him and his family made his own eyes sting, and he had to look away. "In the first war with the Americans. He fought at Saratoga and gave an order that ended up saving the lives of nearly every man in his regiment." A melancholy smile tugged at his lips. "He'd been just a young officer then, but when the war ended, King George rewarded him with a barony."

"That's how your family ended up at Chestnut Hill." Her fingertip traced delicately over the scratches now, ostensibly checking to make certain that she'd tended to each one, yet completely unaware of how much those soothing caresses gave him the strength to share so much about his father with her. How much they inexplicably consoled him.

"Where my father earned a reputation for being a good landowner," he added.

Goose bumps sprang up in the wake of her fingers, but if she noticed his reaction to so slight a caress, she didn't comment. "And a wonderful husband and father, I understand."

"The very best," he murmured. Could she feel his racing pulse beneath her fingertips as they grazed his wrist? It was mystifying, that this same woman who infuriated the daylights out of him also left him aching beneath her touch.

"How did he die?"

He froze. His body flashed numb at her unexpected question. Not that... *Dear God, not that.* He would tell her anything else she wanted to know about his father, but *never* that.

But her whisper came so softly, so innocently that he couldn't bear not to answer her. She'd opened her own grieving heart to him, and she deserved better than any kind of dodging or dissembling.

He slowly pulled his arm away from her. "He was mounting his horse when someone fired off a pistol," he said quietly. The truth—although Robert had no intention of telling her that the reason he had been mounting his horse was because Father had ridden out to find him at a gambling hell where he'd wasted away three days in drink, cards, and whores. "The horse startled. He lost his balance and fell." He took a gasping swallow of the whiskey. "He hit his head."

She asked softly, "Were you there when it happened?"

"Yes." He'd been standing only a few feet away, but he might as well have been on the moon for all the difference it made.

She gently squeezed his fingers. "I'm sorry, Robert," she whispered. "It must have been so terrible for you."

He tossed back the rest of the whiskey. *Terrible?* No. It had been pure hell.

They sat there silently for several long moments. There was nothing to say, but he took an odd comfort in their shared silence. Could it be possible that Mariah Winslow, of all people, might be the only one able to empathize with the grief and guilt he still carried inside him and always would?

The one who understood the need he felt to prove himself to his father's memory? After all, she struggled herself to prove her worth to her own father.

No. He'd trusted her as far as he dared. Sharing any more with her would only make him more vulnerable to wounding when she next decided to bare her claws.

He rolled down his sleeves, then stood and pulled on his jacket. He tugged at his cuffs to bring them into proper place, until there were no visible signs that he'd climbed a tree to appease a nine-year-old. And an ebony-haired minx.

"So what next, then, Carlisle?" As if she sensed the change in him and realized as he did that the tender moment between them had ended, Mariah reached for the bottle to refill his glass. "Where do we go from here?"

He forced a grin at her. "I stay right here in hiding from those women for the rest of the afternoon."

But the sobriety of her expression didn't change at his teasing, and she gravely shook her head. "That's not what I meant."

"I know," he answered quietly, his grin fading. There were some topics he had no intention of raising this afternoon with her, and settling the terms of surrender on the season and the partnership was one of them. She might have raised the topic of his father in order to share their grief, but that conversation only reminded him of how much he owed to his father's memory. And how very far he still was from reaching it. He repeated, brooking no argument, "I stay right here in hiding, and you return to your tea." He snatched the glass out of her hand as she raised it to her lips. "*Without* the scent of whiskey on your breath, or my mother will never forgive me."

"Ah!" Her eyes sparkled, and his heart thumped hard

against his ribs. He much preferred that unrepentant gleam of mischief in her eyes to grief. "Then you've not had tea with Lady Agnes Sinclair."

He shook his head. "Those stories that she puts whiskey in her tea are apocryphal."

"They're true, actually," his brother-in-law, Thomas Matteson, Marquess of Chesney, corrected as he sauntered into his library. "The woman once put so much whiskey into the tea that she nearly drank two of us under the table." He fetched himself a glass from the shelf and filled it from their bottle. When they both looked at him disbelievingly, he added, "Why do you think Josie always seats herself next to the woman?"

With a soft laugh, Mariah rose and dropped into a belated curtsy.

Chesney waved off the formality. "Don't mind me. I'm only here to rescue Robert from the ladies." Then he pinned him with a no-nonsense look. "And you'll return the favor at Lady Grenadine's dinner party next week."

"Of course." The dinner party...just one of the many events during the next fortnight to which his mother had insisted Robert escort Mariah. Apparently, his mother hadn't understood when he said he wanted to be left completely out of her season.

A smile pulled at her red lips as Mariah glanced between the two men. "Do the ladies know how much scheming you gentlemen employ to avoid them?"

"Self-preservation, Miss Winslow," Chesney replied with exaggerated profundity. "If we didn't, the males of our species would die out, and then where would England be?"

Another laugh fell from her lips, and this time, Chesney's eyes lit up as if he found her absolutely charming.

Robert supposed she was, despite the untamed hellcat that lurked within.

"Papa!" Clara ran into the library.

"Walk inside the house," Chesney ordered patiently.

She slowed to a walk, yet her feet still somehow managed to propel her across the room as fast as one of Jackson Shaw's racehorses. "Papa, it's Daisy," she choked out. She beseechingly wrapped her arms around Chesney's legs, with a trembling bottom lip and large eyes round with worry. "She's climbed up a tree again and gotten stuck. You have to get her down!"

"That cat will find its own way down in an hour or so. It always does," he answered firmly.

Robert slid a sideways glance at Mariah, who wisely kept staring straight ahead, and mumbled, "Always, huh?"

Chesney placed a loving kiss on his daughter's forehead. "Now stop worrying about that cat and go find Nanny. Tell her I said you could have an extra sweet roll this afternoon."

Clara beamed, then turned to run from the library without a worry in the world.

"Walk."

She walked slowly until she reached the hallway where, thinking that she couldn't be seen, she launched into a bouncing, high-stepping skip as she hurried away.

Robert rolled his eyes. Women would be the death of him yet.

"Robert, join me upstairs in my study. The women won't come looking for us for at least another hour." Chesney nodded his head politely at Mariah. "Miss Winslow, it was a pleasure to see you again."

"And you, my lord."

Chesney took both his glass and the bottle, then headed

toward the door. Clara burst into happy song from some-where down the hallway, and he paused to shake his head with fatherly pride.

He glanced back at Robert and Mariah. "Clara worries about that cat, but it's been stuck in a tree every day for the past fortnight, yet it always manages to get itself down." He grinned as he stepped from the room. "I'd have to be a nod-cock to climb up after it!"

Robert pinned a narrowed glare on Mariah, her lips twitching with suppressed laughter.

"You will pay for that," he warned.

"Undoubtedly." She nodded with mock gravity, her bottom lip trembling as she forced out, "Uncle Robert."

Damned minx.

"I do hope your arm isn't too painful," she offered, an apologetic tone lacing her voice. "If I had known..."

He lifted a brow. "You still would have sent me up that tree?"

"Oh, most certainly," she heaved out in a sigh, as if she simply couldn't have helped herself.

"Mariah—"

She touched his bicep, silencing him. The teasing glint in her eyes dulled into quiet sincerity, and she admitted quietly, "But I *am* glad that you shared your memories of your father with me."

The genuineness behind that comment surprised the hell out of him. So did the demure way she folded her hands in front of her as she dropped her gaze to the rug.

"And thank you for listening in kind about my mother," she added. "I find that it helps sometimes to talk about her."

"I suppose it does." Although he hadn't yet gotten to that point himself. Oh, sharing with her how wonderful Richard

Carlisle's life had been was far easier than he'd suspected, but he wasn't prepared yet to reveal the truth about his death. If he ever could.

"I can't do that with Evie or Papa, you see, because they have their own pain over losing her. I assume it's the same for you, with your family."

"Certainly." Except that he'd never tried to talk about his father with them. And *never* planned to.

She gave a slow nod, turning her head slightly toward him but not yet raising her gaze to look fully at him. "We might never be anything more than adversaries," she confided softly, "but you can trust me with this." Then she lifted her gaze, and the compassion for him on her face struck him like a blow. "If you ever need to talk about your father and what—"

"I don't," he interrupted, the force of his reply silencing her.

A tense stillness settled over the library, broken only by the muted ticking of the mantel clock that pulsed on like a relentless heartbeat. She wordlessly held his gaze, clearly not believing him.

But instead of challenging him, she whispered gently, "All right." She let her hand fall slowly away from his arm and retreated toward the door. "Then I'll go and leave you men to your kittens."

He rolled his eyes and drawled with a grimace, "Thank you."

She paused in the doorway to look back at him. "Chesney isn't completely right, you know," she said, almost as an afterthought, "about leaving a cat to climb down on its own. Oh, usually they get down just fine." A knowing but melancholy smile pulled faintly at the corners of her mouth. They both knew she wasn't speaking of cats. "But sometimes they need help."

With a lingering glance at him, as if she still hoped he would stop her from leaving and share everything about that night, she disappeared into the hallway. Moments later, he heard her voice rising sweetly as she joined Clara in song.

With a fierce curse, he tossed back the glass of whiskey in a harsh, gasping swallow.

Damn that woman, with her prodding and pressing! She didn't understand the first thing about what he'd gone through, how it ate at him even now. How he'd never be able to purge from his mind the sight of his father falling from his horse, striking his head, then lying so still as a puddle of blood seeped onto the cobblestones beneath him. How every time one of his family mentioned Richard Carlisle it felt as if that night had happened all over again.

He didn't need her platitudes and that nonsense about unburdening himself by sharing his grief—for Christ's sake! *She* didn't kill her mother, and *he* wasn't some helpless cat stuck up a tree.

Robert had killed him as surely as if he'd pulled the trigger himself. And he was in hell.

CHAPTER EIGHT

~~~~~~

One Very Long Week Later

$\mathcal{R}$obert sank heavily into the leather chair in front of the fire at White's. He heaved out a sigh as he let his head fall back, but the knotted frustration inside him didn't ease away.

The past three days spent escorting the ladies across London had been excruciating. He'd managed to sneak away this afternoon only by claiming that he had an important appointment at the club, then sending a message to his cousin Ross to meet him here so that he wouldn't technically be lying to his mother.

As if having to escort Mariah to his sister's tea hadn't been bad enough, the week had only grown worse from there. Daily afternoon drives with her through the park in the barouche. Breakfast with Lady Sydney Reed. Dinner with the Duke and Duchess of Chatham and thirty of their closest acquaintances. A morning call on Lady Elizabeth Mullins and her aunt, Lady Agnes Sinclair, where Robert learned firsthand that the stories about her whiskey-drenched tea were indeed true. Lunch with Mrs. Peterson and her niece

Iphigenia Dunwoody, a very near-sighted, very nice—and oddly colorless—girl, for whom Mrs. Peterson clearly had designs on him, much to his terror and to Mariah's delight.

Today, though, had been the last straw.

An entire morning spent shopping on Bond Street. *Good Lord.* If he had to see one more display of shoes and parasols, he would go mad. He couldn't even sneak away for ten minutes' peace into the bookseller's to study *Peveril of the Peak*, the new novel by Walter Scott, without his mother sending the footman to fetch him back to the milliner's so he could give his opinion on several bonnets the two women couldn't decide between on their own, only for them to reject outright every choice he made.

That was when he sent the message to Ross and dared to make his escape. And he hadn't looked back.

"Cognac," he called out to the attendant.

"Good God, you look awful." Ross Carlisle, Earl of Spalding, sank into the chair opposite him. "Bring the whole bottle," he ordered the attendant, with an amused gleam in his eyes at his cousin's expense. "This could turn into a wake."

"Very funny," Robert muttered.

Kicking his long legs out in front of him, Ross sent him a slow grin.

"Mock me all you want, but I needed you to save my life." He shot Ross a pointed look. "And you still owed me for saving yours that day in York."

"You mean from the Scot?" His sandy-colored brow jutted into the air, his blue eyes sparkling. Although the Spalding side of the family had darker features than the Trent side, they all possessed the same blue eyes. And the same penchant for stirring up trouble. "I would have been just fine on my own."

"He was coming after you with a claymore—"

"That had last been used at Culloden," Ross interjected.

"That was still sharp enough to chop through your door—"

"That he could barely lift to swing—"

"Enough to have you backed against the wall and sending up a prayer."

Ross grinned. That same charming smile that had broken a string of hearts across the continent, including those of two princesses, if rumors could be believed. "Perhaps I shouldn't have made that comment about kilts and sheep."

Robert drawled wryly, "Perhaps you shouldn't have bedded the man's wife."

His cousin gave a long and happy sigh at the memory. There was as little guilt on his face today as there had been that night in York. "I did a fine job of talking him out of killing me, you have to admit."

"And a career diplomat was born," Robert concluded ironically, taking his glass of brandy from the attendant.

"Scots with claymores, Americans with rifles, French with cannons..." Ross shrugged, accepting the bottle and setting it on the table beside his chair. "In the end, it's all the same."

Robert arched a dubious brow. "Angry non-English husbands who want to kill you?"

"Exactly," Ross answered, deadpan.

But Robert knew the truth. For all that Ross had earned a rakish reputation that followed him into life as a diplomat, he was dedicated to England. Always had been, since the day he left university and took an officer's commission in the army. Neither did he let inheriting the title keep him from continuing his work for his country, because he now served under the British ambassador to France. Even now, he was in London only for a short stay before heading back to Paris.

Robert shook his head and grumbled, "At least you've only got wars and armies to worry about."

"And your foes are worse?" Ross hid a knowing grin behind the rim of his glass as he took a sip.

"Yes." Robert closed his eyes against the headache pounding at the back of his skull. "The petticoat set." He groaned with a pained shake of his head. When had his perfectly normal life spiraled out of control? "Good Lord, you have no idea the hell of it."

And it *was* hell, but not just the socializing and shopping. There were also the implications behind it. He was forced to escort Mariah about the city to introduce her to all their family's friends in order to spread the news that she was out for the season and thus also accepting suitors. Every marriage-minded mama they came across eyed her up and down…those with sons to decide if her family's fortune might just be worth overlooking her reputation, and those with daughters to snub her once they saw for themselves how engaging she was. How attractive in her yellow muslin day dress and blue satin dinner gown. How light her laughter and bright her smile.

How truly enjoyable her company.

That grated Robert most of all, because when she wanted, the woman could be downright enchanting.

"Well," Ross muttered with deadpan sarcasm, "I've heard that Wellington once considered sending misses and their mamas into battle, but the carnage from parasols alone would have been unfathomable." The clink of glass and soft splash of liquid signaled a refilling of their drinks. "Not even the French deserved that."

"Thank you," he drawled, cracking open one eye to glare half-heartedly at his cousin.

With a grin at Robert's expense, Ross pushed himself to his feet and crossed to the ivory inlaid cabinet in the corner to help himself to two of the cigars stored within. "And does your current state have anything to do with this petticoat of yours whom you've been—"

"She isn't *my* anything." He tossed back the brandy in a gasping swallow.

"So this petticoat who *isn't* yours but whom you've been escorting around London as if she were," Ross corrected, then chuckled with amusement at the glower he elicited from Robert. "Is she the reason you're halfway to the bottom of a bottle of cognac in the middle of the afternoon and lying to your mother about appointments at the club?"

Hell no. He'd never let a woman affect him before in his life, and he certainly wasn't going to start now with Mariah.

But when Ross put it like that...*Damnation.*

He admitted with a grumble, "It's complicated."

"The best women always are." Ross cut off the tips of the two cheroots and handed one to Robert as he returned to his chair. "And what do you plan to do with her?"

Leaning forward to light his cigar, he blinked, taken aback by that. "*I* don't plan to do anything." *Except make her some other man's problem.*

Ross slid him a disbelieving glance. "And what does she plan to do with you?"

"A slow and torturous death," he muttered, then popped the cigar between his teeth. At this rate, certainly, one of them would kill the other by June.

With a quiet laugh, Ross lit his cigar on the lamp, then

kicked his boots onto the fireplace fender, settling in for the afternoon.

"Her father offered me a partnership with his company," Robert admitted, omitting several details he preferred not to share. Not even with his cousin. Lately, the challenge Winslow had given him had begun to feel more like a deal with the devil than a chance to prove himself. "That's why I've been escorting her this season. He hopes she'll find a husband and settle down. There's nothing more to it than that."

Ross said nothing, but the expression on his face told Robert that he didn't believe him.

"Lord Robert?" The club's manager strode into the room, carrying a small, paper-and-string-wrapped package. "This arrived for you, sir."

"Thank you." Puzzled, he accepted it. He pulled loose the string, and the paper fell away. *Peveril of the Peak.* The Walter Scott novel he'd been perusing at the bookseller.

"A book?" Ross sat up curiously at that. The gentlemen at White's were notorious for committing infamous firsts. The first man to ride a horse backward to Richmond, the first to wear trousers to dinner, the first to bet on a race of raindrops sliding down a window...but a book delivered to the club? Certainly this was the first time *that* had ever happened. "Who would send that to you here?"

"No idea," he mumbled and removed a note card that had been stuck between the pages.

*In your desperation to flee from us women
and our shopping, you forgot this. Consider
it the start of your grand library.*

—M. W.

"Mariah," he murmured, stunned that she would have thought of this.

Ross asked with surprise, "The Hellion's sending you gifts?"

"It's not a gift." He tossed it onto the table with a grimace. "It's a portent."

With a knowing shake of his head, Ross pointed at the book with his cigar. "That doesn't seem the action of a woman set on your slow and torturous death."

No, it certainly didn't. Which only made him even more suspicious.

If they weren't at odds, he might have taken the gift as nothing more than a kindness. Just as he would have genuinely found her likeable. But in his fight with Mariah, there truly was no judging a book by its cover.

"This season is going to end badly for you," Ross assured him, flicking ash from the end of his cigar. "And I don't mean your business interests." His eyes softened on Robert in that same contemplative diplomatic expression he used at court when he wanted to sway opinions on whatever new political stance King George wanted to take. "Either you're going to be blamed by her father when she finishes her last season as a spinster and lose the partnership, or she accepts a marriage offer and you lose her."

"Don't be daft. I don't want her for myself." He glared at his cousin for even suggesting such a thing. "She's a hell-cat."

Ross smiled slyly, studying the glowing tip of his cigar. "And what's wrong with a woman with spirit?"

For a moment, his mind blanked, and he couldn't find an answer.

What *was* wrong with Mariah, except that she would do

anything to work at her father's side? That ebony hair and creamy pale skin, those berry-red lips that tasted as spicy-sweet as they looked... and to his great surprise, a brilliant mind. She wasn't some simpering young miss; she was a confident woman, one who donated her time and most of her allowance to helping children. For heaven's sake, she knew naval battle strategy. And wasn't afraid to use it.

She was pure challenge, every breathtaking inch of her.

If she had been any other woman except for Henry Winslow's daughter, he would have pursued her. Without hesitation.

But she wasn't any other woman. Mariah was the only obstacle preventing him from proving that he deserved the Carlisle name. And *no one*, not even an intelligent, intriguing, and achingly beautiful woman, would stop him from doing exactly that.

"Everything," he muttered as he shoved himself out of the chair and walked away.

Ross called out after him, "Aren't you bothered that she's refused her invitation to St James's ball?"

He halted in mid-step and craned around to gape at his cousin. "*What* did you say?"

"She declined Olivia Sinclair's invitation," Ross explained as Robert slowly stalked back to him.

"Impossible." Because he divided his time between Parliament and court, Ross often heard news before the rest of Mayfair. But this time, he'd gotten it wrong. *Completely* wrong. "That ball's to be her formal introduction. Mother personally arranged it with Lady St James."

"And yet, Miss Winslow refused," Ross insisted as he rolled the cigar between his fingers. "St James was grumbling about it yesterday in the Lords. Seems the countess was beside herself wondering what the proper protocol is for a seventh-season debutante who refuses her own introduction, while St James didn't know whether to take it as an insult or a disaster averted." With a shake of his head, he lifted his glass in a toast. "Foreign armies and women, Robert. Best to avoid engaging with either of them."

Without a word, his teeth clenched so hard that the muscles in his neck jumped, Robert spun on his heel and stormed from the club.

This time, the little minx had finally gone too far.

* * *

An hour later, Robert charged up the main stairs at the Gatewell School, taking them three at a time. The housekeeper who'd answered the door said he could find Mariah on the second floor in the schoolroom. And God help her when he did.

How dare she attempt to ruin her introduction like this—refusing an invitation to her own debut ball! And what did she hope to gain by it? To destroy both of them? Because that was *exactly* what would happen if word of this got back to her father. Winslow would blame her for purposefully sabotaging her season, then blame him for failing to keep her in line.

He halted in the doorway and stared into the room. What had once been the nursery of the rambling house had been transformed into a schoolroom, filled with little desks that were now all pushed to the edges of the room and the teacher's desk sitting before a large blackboard. Sets of rough-hewn shelves lined the walls, filled to bursting with books and stacks of slates. There was even a globe in the corner.

And in the middle of the floor, on her hands and knees, was Mariah.

She scrubbed vigorously at the floorboards with a large brush, spreading the soapy water around herself in a widening puddle. Dressed in an old blouse and soiled apron, with her skirt tied up to keep it out of her way, she looked like a scullery maid, right down to the streak of dirt across her left cheek and a mobcap perched on her head to keep her ebony hair contained. As she moved slowly forward, inch by hard-labored inch, she hummed softly to herself, and her bare legs peeked out from beneath the hitched-up skirt. With the disheveled way she looked, all sweaty and soapy and bare beneath the skirt, from her toes all the way up to where her legs disappeared beneath the hem just above the knees... *Sweet Lucifer.*

Only the Hellion could look more erotic dressed like a scullery maid than in a ball gown. Like a sailor lured by a Greek siren into dangerous waters, he had the sinking feeling in his knotting gut that she was drawing him toward his own destruction. Because he wanted nothing more than to join her right there in the middle of the floor, wrap those bare legs around his waist, peel away that wet blouse—

She lifted her eyes and froze at the sight of him. For a moment, as if reading his heated thoughts, she returned his stare with an unguarded expression of longing... only for it to vanish with a frown.

She sat back on her heels. "Shouldn't you be off somewhere reading your book?"

"And miss this show?" He gestured at the floor and her smack in the middle of it. "Not for the world."

"So glad I can provide entertainment for you." She

dropped the brush into the bucket of water. "Good to know I have a future at Vauxhall."

His lips twisted. He would have enjoyed her dry wit, if she didn't infuriate him so much. And if she wasn't so alluring, even sitting in a puddle of dirty water. "I was thinking Covent Garden."

"Wise choice. The crowds will be so much larger there." Her eyes gleamed devilishly. "All kinds of people lining up to witness something never before seen in England."

Over his dead body. *No one* would ever see her looking like this. He forced a tight smile and ground out, "And what's that?"

Her brow rose. "A society lady doing work." She reached back into the bucket and fished out the brush. "Must be quite unsettling for your gentleman's sensibilities."

It wasn't his sensibilities that were unsettled. "You don't know the women in my family very well if you think that."

She gave a faint *humph* and began to work the brush against the floor again, harder than before. Most likely imagining his face there beneath the grinding bristles. "Why are you here, Carlisle?"

"To save you from yourself."

She stopped in mid-stroke. With both arms extended in front of her and her round bottom lifted beguilingly into the air behind her, she eyed him with distrust. "Like a damsel in distress? I don't believe I need to be saved."

Then she set about scrubbing the floor again as if he wasn't there, once more humming the same lilting song she'd been half singing when he'd interrupted her.

Damn her for being so challenging! And double damn himself for letting her prick at him.

"Miss Winslow," he began, chewing each word out through clenched teeth, "if you think—"

"Oh, Good Lord!" In frustration, she slapped down the brush and sat back to glare at him, this time so fiercely that she folded her arms across her chest and blocked his view of that tantalizingly wet blouse. "I very much appreciated the fact that you spent the morning on Bond Street, escorting the duchess and me." She sniffed haughtily, as if it pained her to admit it. "In fact, at certain times, being in your company was surprisingly enjoyable."

Well. That was the most backhanded compliment he'd ever gotten, but at least it was a compliment. Which was far more than he'd expected from her. His lips curled into a half grin. "Only certain times, eh?"

She ignored that and arched a brow. "Which is why I gave you that book. You were quite gracious." She grudgingly made a half-hearted attempt at a shrug. "I *thought* you might like it. And now, here you are." She dismissingly waved a hand at him. "Disrupting my afternoon *and* my work, to tell me how unladylike it was of me to send it to you."

"Actually, I like the book," he admitted. It was a nice gesture. And a wholly surprising one.

She blinked, bewildered. "You do?" Another blink, and her shoulders eased down from their defensive posture. "Then why are you here?"

He stalked slowly toward her, stopping his boots at the edge of the puddle. "Olivia Sinclair."

"Olivi— *Oh.*" Her anger-flushed cheeks blanched pale as understanding dawned on her. Then, in a frantic attempt to ward off the argument that was coming, she grabbed for the brush and began to scrub at the floor again. "I'm glad you liked the book. I had to send the tiger to buy—"

"Olivia Sinclair," he repeated, this time louder and more slowly. "Countess of St James."

She scrubbed furiously, refusing to look up as she mumbled, "I've never met her."

"And you never will if you refuse the invitation to her ball." He frowned down at her. "The same ball which is also your introduction."

She stopped, freezing in place like a startled doe, but he knew her sharp mind was whirling at a million miles a minute to find a way out of this latest mess she'd placed herself into.

Then, drawing a deep breath, she sat back on her heels and folded her hands contritely in her lap. "Now, Robert, please understand—"

"Your own introduction," he bit out, not allowing himself to be distracted by her use of his given name. Or her captivating mix of innocence and wickedness as she gazed up at him through lowered lashes. "Are you trying to end your season before it's even begun?"

He squatted down onto the balls of his feet and brought his eyes level with hers. The angry glare she must have seen on his face kept her silent. For once. *Wise woman.* He was through playing games.

"Lord and Lady St James have been kind enough to allow the use of their ball to introduce you. So you will accept the invitation," he ordered, his voice far more controlled than he felt. But then, he was rarely in control of himself around her. "And you will send a note to the countess apologizing for the confusion and any distress you have caused."

Defiance flared in her eyes. "No, I won't."

Damnable woman. Challenging and obstinate at every turn. "And my mother?" he pressed, playing his trump card.

"Should she be gossiped about because you refuse to attend?"

Guilt flitted across her face, and he felt a small surge of satisfaction. But when she bit her bottom lip and drew his attention to her ripe mouth, he felt something else pulse through him, this time tingling down to the tip of his cock and leaving him achingly *un*satisfied.

"You are going to that ball," he warned, his blood beginning to heat from the irritation she stirred inside him, and from the way her wet clothes clung to her, "even if I have to toss you over my shoulder and carry you inside the ballroom myself."

Her chin raised stubbornly. "I'd like to see you try!"

He growled out through bared teeth, "Mariah, if you don't—"

"Miss!" A child's high-pitched yell cut through their argument, followed by the sound of footsteps pounding up the stairs. A wailing cry echoed through the rooms. "*MMMMIIIISSSS!*"

A little girl raced into the room and sped right past Robert without a glance as she launched herself at Mariah, who caught the child in her arms. She pulled the girl close as violent sobs poured from the skinny creature with mussed blond braids, who couldn't have been more than four or five. The girl's left arm wrapped tightly around Mariah's neck while her right arm gripped a headless doll.

Mariah cooed soothingly and pulled the girl onto her lap. She cradled her in her arms, rocking her softly until the worst of the wailing ceased and the cries gentled into strangled sobs.

Her eyes lifted to meet Robert's, and she held his gaze for a moment over the little girl's head. Her concern for the child and her wariness that he was witnessing the incident were both unmistakable.

"What is it, Polly?" She carefully unwrapped the little girl's arm from its death grip around her neck and set her away just far enough to look down into her tear-streaked face. With a worried frown, she smoothed the girl's hair away from her forehead. "What's happened?"

"It's—it's Lu-Lucy," Polly choked out between hiccupping sobs. Her nose glowed red. "The boys took her, and they—they—" She thrust the headless doll at Mariah, as if that said it all. So did the angry "Boys!" that she bit out.

Then Polly glared over her shoulder at Robert, as if he embodied all the most horrible aspects of his sex. The ferocity of her look set him rocking back onto his heels.

"Not all boys are bad," Mariah assured her, the fleeting glance she spared him inscrutable. "What did they do?"

"They hurt her!" Polly thrust the doll at her again. "See?"

Robert's chest panged at the girl's grief over her doll. The boys hadn't hurt the pathetic little collection of stuffed rags in a dirty blue dress—they'd decapitated it.

"Where?" Mariah asked, her brow furrowing.

Where? Good Lord, it was obvious. But he had to give her credit for her composure in front of the child, the way she lovingly brushed her fingertips over the girl's hair and calmly soothed away her tears. It was a caring, maternal side to her. And it stunned him to see it.

"Right here." Polly lifted the mangled doll and pointed to a spot on its arm. "See?"

"Oh dear," Mariah said with deep concern, taking the piece of stuffed rags gently into her hands. "She's cut her arm."

Her arm? The doll was missing its *head*, for heaven's

sake! But Mariah seemed as nonplussed about the decapitation as the girl.

"They *hurt* her," Polly whispered, so intensely that Robert feared she might start wailing again.

"I'm certain they didn't mean to," Mariah assured her gently.

And Robert was certain the boys had intended much worse. He remembered every doll of Josie's that he and his brothers had shaved bald, dragged from ropes behind their ponies, strapped to an archery target to take turns shooting arrows at it...They'd even blown one up with gunpowder. *Boys*, indeed.

"Will she get better?" Polly wiped the back of her dirty hand across her eyes.

"She needs surgery, but I'm certain she'll be fine," Mariah told her softly, kindness lacing her voice. "Go down to the kitchen and show Mrs. Smith. Tell her that I said it was okay if you have a biscuit while you wait for her to stitch up Lucy's arm, all right?"

The girl nodded with a loud sniff. Mariah hugged her once more, then placed a kiss on her forehead and set the girl on her feet. With a parting glower at Robert, Polly ran from the room with her doll clasped tightly to her chest.

Mariah kept her gaze on the doorway long after the little girl disappeared as a quiet stillness fell over them. "Go on," she urged softly, not looking at him. "Say it."

"That doll's missing its head," he returned in the same solemn voice.

She sighed heavily. "I know." Her slender shoulders deflated. "Polly's father died when the *Mary Grace* went down last year. That doll was the last present her father gave her. It's falling apart and lost its head last month, but she refuses to part with it, no matter that I've promised her a new doll to replace it."

Robert understood that. Even now he carried with him the pocket watch his father had given him when he was graduated from Oxford. The same pocket watch that hadn't worked in years.

"You can say the other, too." Her gaze found him then, and wariness flickered in her green depths as if she expected him to attack. "That I'm wasting my time and money on this school. That I'm a fool to think that I can make any difference. That one little girl means nothing when so many are on the streets."

Beneath her defensiveness, he glimpsed vulnerability, and it took his breath away. No one in the *ton* would have ever suspected that this softer side existed to the Hellion. *He* certainly hadn't, and it surprised the hell out of him. So did the gnawing realization that he liked it.

He reached out and covered her hand with his. "I would never say that."

She looked down at their hands, as if surprised at the tender gesture, but didn't pull hers away. Then she stunned him by slowly bringing her other hand to cover his. The sudden connection that blossomed between them was undeniable.

"Why not?" she challenged softly, watching as she trailed a fingertip over the back of his hand. "My father would. In fact, he's said so several times." She gave a defeated glance at the dirty puddle around her. "Perhaps he's right."

"He's not," he assured her quietly, giving a small squeeze to her fingers as he thought of his sister and the orphans she'd helped in their village. One kind soul could change the path of every life it touched.

She slowly pulled her hands away, and immediately, he

missed the warmth of her understanding touch. "Better not let Papa hear you disagreeing with him, Carlisle," she warned, but with more teasing than reprimand. "You'll lose your partnership." She paused a beat for effect. "On second thought…"

He ignored that barb, not wanting to engage in battle, not when they were finally beginning to understand each other.

But something about her teasing bothered him. "Is that why you care so much about this place?" Had he completely misunderstood the complicated relationship she had with Henry Winslow? "Because it irritates your father?"

"No." A conspiratorial smile played at her lips. "That's just a delightful bonus."

He grinned. *There* was the minx he knew, in the mischievous gleam of her eyes and the impish twist to her lips. His gut tightened to see such stubborn resolve matched with feminine vulnerability. The combination was bewitching.

"My mother grew up two streets from here." She turned her face away to avoid his gaze, but not quickly enough to prevent him from seeing the glistening in her eyes. He recognized that grief. It was the same that he carried for his father. "It sounds foolish, I suppose, but after she died, whenever I missed her so terribly that I thought I might die myself, I would come here to St Katharine's and feel close to her again."

"Not foolish at all," he murmured. After all, hadn't he done the same thing, by living at Park Place, by working at the same desk where his father had?

When she glanced at him, a shared understanding softened her features, and he once again felt that inexplicable connection between them. Once again saw the vulnerability in her that she tried so hard to hide from the world.

"When I returned from Miss Pettigrew's, I wanted to help the families of St Katharine's," she explained. "I finally had the financial means and plenty of time on my hands, so we decided to open the Gatewell School."

"We?" he asked gently.

"Hugh Whitby and me."

So that's how the dandy had first worked his way into her heart. Yet even knowing his charitable bent, it was deuced hard to like him. Or acknowledge the flash of jealousy toward the man.

"Baron Whitby lets us stay here rent-free in return for keeping up the building, so the children help with the maintenance. They learn carpentry and masonry, housekeeping skills, how to raise vegetables and herbs in the garden..."

As he watched her speak about the school, admiration for her began to warm inside him. She certainly wasn't some idle society daughter whose only forays into charity were hosting teas and ladies' circles. No, Mariah preferred to *work*. That was one of the most unconventional aspects to her. One Robert found himself liking a great deal.

She shrugged her slender shoulders. "Whenever we can, we turn the work into a lesson."

"That's an unusual education." And ingenious.

"It fits our mission. Primarily, we run a vocational school. We teach work skills, as well as a foundational education in the basic subjects." She looked down at her hands. "We also provide an afternoon tea, which for some of the children might be the only meal they have all day, and we offer a safe haven during the day while their mothers work."

Judging from the chagrined expression that flitted over her face and the way she refused to meet his gaze, the school also provided a place for the children when their mothers couldn't find honest work and had to sell their bodies to survive.

"As soon as they're old enough, we find them positions... the girls as maids or shopgirls, the boys as porters or apprentices. We've placed five children this winter alone." Pride flashed across her face at that, but then vanished just as quickly beneath a tired sigh. "We can only help a few, but I'd like to think that the work we do here is important."

"It is," he murmured.

Slowly, she raised her gaze to meet his.

For a heartbeat, the vulnerability in her emerald depths rose unrestrained to the surface, and he saw her as more than the adversary set on ruining the future he wanted for himself, as more than the daughter desperately fighting for her father's approval. What he saw was a kind and capable woman with dreams of her own, one who gave her heart and soul to the people she loved... A beautiful rose in the middle of a puddle of dirty water.

And he'd never met a more enthralling woman in his life.

She shook her head. "You don't have to pretend to like the school. I know what you really think of me."

No, he was certain she didn't. Because at that moment, he was no longer certain himself. Not of her, not of Henry Winslow... not of his task to find her a husband. And certainly not of Winslow's plan to benefit from the destruction of St Katharine's. Her father was so confident that she'd accept relocating the school, so certain she'd put the company first. But as Robert stared at her now, a jumble of doubts twisted inside him.

Had he and her father misread her? Was longing to work at her father's side a great deal more than wanting to prove a point, and far more important than simply rebelling when Winslow tried to turn her away?

"I like you, Mariah," he answered, finally acknowledging the truth. Ignoring the puddle and what it would do to his breeches, he lowered himself to the floor until he was sitting close, hip to hip at her side, facing her. Close enough that he could see her swallow nervously as he placed his hand onto the floor on the other side of her, surrounding her on three sides with his body. "God help me, but I do."

Her eyes widened, but for once, she didn't attack. Or pull away. A small thrill of victory sped through him. Emboldened, he leaned closer.

His mouth lingered near enough to hers that he felt each of her warm breaths tease across his lips, and he sensed the moment when her breathing turned into shallow pants. The delicate sensation was maddening. So was the way she gazed at his mouth, as if half-afraid he would kiss her again. And half-afraid that he wouldn't.

"Doesn't it bother you at all, then," she challenged softly, "that you want to marry me off for your own gain?"

"It isn't like that." She damned well knew it, too. But he couldn't quash the flash of anger at that quiet accusation. Most likely because he'd wondered himself if that was exactly what he'd been doing since Henry Winslow challenged him with that task. He'd only been able to justify it by clinging to what he knew to be true—"Your father would never force you to wed a man you didn't want to marry."

"No." Her voice emerged as little more than a whisper filled with hopeless exasperation. "Only take my allowance away and close the school."

She unflinchingly held his gaze, as if daring him to deny

it. But he couldn't. If she ever decided to openly defy her father and refuse to participate another day this season, Henry Winslow might do just that. And it would have absolutely nothing to do with him or the partnership.

"I'm not your enemy, Mariah. I'm trying to help you." He softened his tone, knowing that fighting against her only made her dig in deeper. "Tell me the truth now. Why did you refuse Olivia Sinclair's invitation?"

Uncertainty darkened her face as she hesitated, then admitted softly, "Evelyn."

He blinked. What did her sister have to do with this?

"Lady St James didn't invite Evie," she explained, pride and indignation lacing her voice. "If my sister isn't good enough to attend her ball, then neither am I."

He studied her face. That's what this was about—a snub to Evelyn? The realization struck him of just how fiercely loyal she was to her sister, the same loyalty he and his brothers shared, and understanding settled over him. Her connections to her family were proving to be deeper than anyone gave her credit for. Including her own family.

Yet her younger sister's reputation was as tarnished as her own, if rumors could be believed, since Evelyn was equally as adventurous and daring as her sister. He couldn't blame the Sinclairs if they didn't want either Winslow daughter at their ball. But knowing how gracious the countess was, he was certain she'd simply forgotten about Evelyn.

"It was an oversight," he assured her. "Nothing more."

A sniff declared that she didn't believe him.

"Mother will secure an invitation for her. I'll make certain of it." He reached up to tuck a stray curl of black silk beneath the edge of her cap. Her siren song was irresistible, even all dirty and wet. "All right?"

She gave a curt nod, as if doing what he wanted cost her greatly. "Then I'll send a note to Lady St James."

He smiled faintly with relief. "Thank you."

"But only because I don't want to harm the duchess," she clarified. Then, because the war between them mandated it—"I couldn't care less what you want."

Of course not. His mouth twisted with chagrin. "From you, Mariah, I would expect no less."

Her red lips tugged upward in the start of a smile. No doubt the minx took his comment as a compliment. Perhaps it was. Although he was loath to admit it, he'd become fond of her stubbornness. And the challenge she presented because of it. No other woman had kept him on his toes the way she did.

Then she playfully swatted at his shoulder, as if signaling that this tender moment of understanding had ended and that they could resume the fighting they'd grown accustomed to.

But he didn't move away. Nor did he want to when he saw her flash of realization that the rapport between them had just irreversibly changed. An undeniable electricity tingled between them. And instead of pushing him away, her hands trailed slowly down to his lapels.

"It's nice when we don't fight," he murmured. Unable to keep from touching her again, he rubbed his thumb over the dirt smear on her cheek. "If we keep this up, things between us might even become halfway pleasant."

"Optimist," she muttered dryly. Then she glanced down at him, all the way to where he sat next to her in the puddle. "Looks like I've dragged you down with me and made you all dirty."

His thumb continued to brush over her cheek, long after the mark was gone, caressing slowly over her smooth, warm skin, then back along her jaw and down her slender neck. She was a wonder, that she could be such a claws-bared hell-cat one moment yet so soft and vulnerable the next. And he liked this soft side of her. Very much.

He murmured, "Perhaps I like being dirty."

She caught her breath, and her fingers tightened on his lapels.

He hadn't meant his reply as an innuendo, but when he saw the pretty flush to her cheeks, he was glad he'd said it. And even more so when her gaze darted to his mouth and her lips parted delicately in invitation.

His heart thumped with yearning. She wanted him to kiss her... and who was he to deny a woman what she desired?

Slipping his hand behind her nape to gently tug her to him, he lowered his head and brought his mouth to hers.

As he kissed her, he wanted to savor the moment, make it as tender and special as the hidden side of her that she'd just shared. But the spicy heat of her lips ached through him, and he couldn't stop himself from ravenously devouring her kiss, his hands cupping her face to hold her mouth still beneath his. Reckless from the frustration and arousal in which she'd kept him from the moment they met, he only half cared as his lips molded against hers that another child might come running into the room and see them. He wanted this—he wanted *her*—too desperately to be cautious.

When her lips softened beneath his with a whimpering sigh, he stopped caring completely.

He smiled against her mouth and teased, "Boys?" Then he licked the tip of his tongue across the seam of her lips, daring her to open so he could taste the sweetness hidden inside.

"Boys," she purred, the single word an aching declaration

of how delicious she found boys to be. As if she found him the most delicious boy of all. She slipped her hand behind his neck and parted her lips eagerly beneath his.

He groaned and plunged inside, taking decadent sweeps across her smooth inner lip and entangling his tongue with hers. She was so unbelievably spicy on the surface, so undeniably sweet beneath. The combination was simply addictive.

Breathless, he tore his mouth away from hers to nip at her throat as he tugged her fully onto his lap. His hands swept up the sides of her body, to explore all of her.

"Not all boys are bad," he reminded her, daring to brush against the side swells of her breasts. "Some of us can be nice." When she arched herself closer, inviting more than a glancing caress, desire flared through him, and he gladly obliged by capturing her breasts fully in his hands. "*Very* nice."

"You're...not nice," she forced out between pants as he massaged her fullness in his palms. She clutched at the lapels of his jacket with one hand to keep him close while the other combed through the hair at his nape, silently encouraging him. "You're wicked."

"Very much so." To prove it, he cupped her buttocks, then squeezed. A throaty gasp tore from her, the breathlessly erotic sound spiraling through him. "But I think you like being wicked, too."

She stiffened, and he worried she might deny it, that she would order him to stop touching her. Instead her gaze locked heatedly on his lips, and she admitted, "Perhaps a little. With you."

He groaned and seized her mouth for another blistering kiss. He was drowning in the inexplicable wonder of her, swimming in her taste and touch, and lost in that heady combination of spicy-sweetness that had come to represent everything about her. That arousing incongruity of a kind and caring heart lurking beneath a prickly façade. More than anything, he wanted to delve beneath her surface and reveal the true Mariah, to peel back the layers until he found the pure woman beneath.

But for now, he'd settle for peeling back that wet blouse and shamelessly taking whatever small glimpse of her she'd allow.

He unfastened the top three buttons of her blouse and tugged it down past the swells of her breasts, then scooped his fingers inside her stays. Her right breast sprang free yet remained hidden beneath her chemise. Frustrated at being unable to bare her to him without stripping her to her waist, he pulled the chemise taut across her breast until the dusky-rose outline of her nipple strained against the thin cotton.

So unbelievably lovely...He traced his fingertip around the dark pink circle and delighted when she shivered. He watched as her nipple pebbled beneath his fingertip, and an ache twisted through his gut, tightening all the way to the tip of his cock like a coiling spring.

"A touch of wickedness in a woman is what a man likes best," he murmured, lowering his head until his breath fanned over her breast. "And I like you wicked, Mariah. Very." He placed a light kiss on her pointed nipple and smiled at the way it quivered. "Very." He nipped at her through the chemise and drew a surprised gasp from her. "Much."

Then his hot mouth closed over her and sucked boldly, at last taking the forbidden taste of her that he craved.

With a soft moan, she shuddered and arched herself

against him. Her fingers twined in his hair and tugged his head down to bring his mouth tighter against her in a silent plea for pleasure. He groaned at her eager reaction and took her breast deep into his mouth, blissfully yielding to her desires.

He had no right to have his mouth on her like this, but she'd tempted him too devilishly for too long. Now that he'd captured her, he wouldn't miss this chance to revel in the taste of her as she gave herself over so willingly to the nips of his teeth against her soft flesh, to each lick of his tongue and suck of his lips until the cotton surrounding her nipple was thoroughly soaked. And transparent enough to reveal her dark nipple completely to his greedy eyes as he drank in the sight of her.

"Is that how you think of me?" She shuddered in a gasping shiver when he blew a stream of cool air across the wet fabric and the hot nipple beneath. "As wicked?"

He stroked his hands down her body, and each caress had her writhing on his lap. *Sweet Lucifer.* She was so wonderfully responsive, positively bewitching... "You're a genuine she-devil," he admitted honestly. *This* she-devil certainly took a pleasing shape, and if she kept wiggling her bottom against him, she'd learn what shapes an aroused man could take, as well. "A seductress who leaves men panting in her wake."

"I don't...do that," she protested, her own shallow breaths undercutting the primness of her answer.

She tore her mouth away to catch her breath, but that only gave him access to her slender throat. When he tongued her racing pulse, growing conceitedly proud to know that he made it pound so furiously, a soft moan rose from her and fell achingly through him. God help him, he wanted to lick her *everywhere*, just to hear in her mewlings the pleasure he brought her.

"Oh yes, you do," he assured her as she pressed herself tighter against his chest, so tight he was afraid she might be able to feel the way she made his heart pound for her. "You have men making fools of themselves over you everywhere you go."

He'd seen the effect she had on men, how she left them all lathered and bothered with nothing more than a smile. The same effect she had on *him*. But he was helpless to resist, craving her more than any other woman in his life, and he couldn't stop kissing her. Like chocolate spiced with pepper, each forbidden taste filled him with a burning sweetness that left him greedy for more.

"The thoughts you put into their heads," he rasped hoarsely as he placed a trail of kisses between her breasts. "The way you make them itch to touch you, how they long to be alone with you—you drive them mad trying to get to you."

The dandies who had ogled her on Bond Street, the old men who had leered at her at all the soirees they'd attended, even the damnable footmen who had tried to catch a glimpse down her dress when they leaned over to serve her dinner...they all wanted her, but none stood a chance. A woman like her would chew them up and spit them out as if they were nothing at all.

"I thought that was what you wanted," she said huskily, then bit her bottom lip to fight back a throaty gasp of pleasure when he returned to worshipping at her breast.

"Hell no," he growled against her fullness at the thought of one of those fop dandies kissing her like this.

"But wasn't that your diabolical plan?" she taunted, her

voice thick with arousal but light with something else...Happiness? Enjoyment? Whatever it was, he liked it. And longed to hear more of it. "Marry me off to the first gentleman who offers?"

"That is *not* my plan." He once more seized her mouth in a fierce kiss. One set on silencing her teasing. And on purging away the flash of guilt that he'd once considered doing exactly that.

But not now. Marry her off to one of those self-proclaimed Corinthians who saw her as nothing more than an object to possess? Or chain her to some milk-and-honey dandy like Whitby who would never provide her with the challenge and purpose she craved? *Never.* Those men cared nothing for the loving woman he now knew lurked within. She deserved better, she deserved—

"Someone like you, then?"

He jerked back from her, his hand stilling where it had drifted beneath her skirt to her thigh. His eyes narrowed as he searched her face and tried to slow the furious beating of his startled heart. Where on earth had *that* question come from?

With a soft laugh at the stunned expression on his face, she placed a kiss to the tip of his nose. "A rakehell and scapegrace?"

But the knot in his belly only tightened, instead of easing with the relief he should have felt to realize that she was merely bamming him. Not allowing himself to think about what that meant, he nuzzled his face into her hair so she couldn't see how much her innocent question had unsettled him. "*Not* someone like me," he corrected ruefully. "My job is to keep men like me away from you."

"No." Sadness touched her voice. Immediately he

missed the lightness and delight he'd heard there only moments before. "Your job is to marry me off, no matter who offers."

Never. He'd never ask her to marry a man she didn't love. But based on the interest she garnered wherever she went, that wouldn't be a problem. "By the end of the ball, you'll have your pick of the best gentlemen in England. You'll meet someone you want to marry, who will spend the rest of his life making you happy."

But knowing Mariah would be happy didn't ease the leaden thud of this heart when he thought about her being in the arms of one of those men.

He cupped her face in his hands and danced his lips across her cheeks and mouth, to kiss away the unhappiness on her face and bring back the wonderful passion he'd tasted in her just moments ago. "Already, fine gentlemen are flocking around you," he murmured, as much to convince himself as her of the inevitability of her season. "Begging for time alone with you, falling all over themselves for the favor of one of your smiles."

He flicked the tip of his tongue against the corner of her mouth and drank up the sweetness there, fighting back a groan at how delicious she was. At how much desire he felt growing inside her. So much that she trembled with it.

"You set them on fire, Mariah," he whispered.

"And you?" She licked her lips—a purely nervous motion, yet the erotic sight of it ripped straight through him. "Do I set you on fire, too, Robert?"

God, yes. A bonfire raged inside him. He'd thought she was trouble when she'd been nothing more than a hellcat. Now that he'd glimpsed this other side of her, one that was loving and vulnerable, happy and relaxed, she was down-right dangerous.

But he'd be damned if he'd admit it. "Playing with fire gets a man burned," he dodged, lowering his head to nibble at her throat.

She stiffened in his arms. "Oh?"

"And I have no intention of getting burned."

But he had every intention of feeling the heat. His hand stroked boldly over her leg, and he desperately wished her skirts weren't between them. At the very least that she'd thought to hitch them higher to make it easier for him to explore beneath—

A rush of cold water splashed over his head.

"What the *hell*?" Robert scrambled to his feet as the dirty mop water ran down his body and puddled around his boots on the floor.

Wiping the water off his face, his clothes drenched, he glared down at Mariah as she held the empty bucket in her hands.

"Then it's a good thing I also know how to put fires out!" she snapped, then tossed the bucket aside and straightened her stays and blouse with shaking fingers. Instead of the triumphant gleam he expected to see on her flushed face, what he saw was anger and...*hurt*?

His mind reeled. She'd doused him with the bucket, for heaven's sake! And *she* had the nerve to feel hurt?

Confusion mixed with sharp rejection. He clenched his teeth. "For God's sake, why did you—"

The shouts and clatter of children split the stillness of the upper floors as a dozen students raced up the stairs. Their feet pounded like a herd of cattle as they stormed into the classroom and scrambled to find their desks and chairs for the last lesson of the day, somehow not noticing that Mariah was sitting in the middle of the floor and that he resembled a drowned rat.

She jutted a brow into the air, as if daring him to come after her now that she was surrounded by a pack of pixie-size guard dogs.

Knowing he was beaten—for now—and not having the slightest clue what he'd done wrong, he sucked in a deep, steadying breath. Then he shook his arms to fling away as much dirty water as he could.

"Don't worry, Mariah. I won't marry you off to the first man who offers," he promised as he sauntered toward the door, as casually as a man could with dirty water squishing between his toes. "But definitely the second."

CHAPTER NINE

$\mathcal{D}$usk was falling by the time Mariah arrived home. She smiled weakly at the butler as he opened the door for her. She was cold and wet, covered with dirt, and thoroughly exhausted. At that moment, nothing in the world sounded better than sinking into a hot bath, then falling into bed.

"Shall I send Alice to your room, miss?" Bentley asked, taking her coat and hat.

"Please." She smiled gratefully, then hesitated before asking, "Is my family home?"

"Miss Evelyn is upstairs, and Mr. Winslow is in his study."

Her chest fell. She'd been hoping to have the house to herself so she could wallow in her misery in peace. And try to sort through the confusion that had gripped her since the moment Robert Carlisle walked into her life.

"Thank you. Tell Alice I'll be up in a moment, and take this down to Cook, will you?" She held up the cloth-covered basket she'd carried in from the carriage. "Mrs. Smith sent a pie for Papa." She lowered her voice with a conspiratorial smile. "And I put in a second pie for you and the servants, too."

"You're a kind one, miss." He gave her an affectionate wink as he accepted the basket, then he snapped back into his role as a dignified butler and bowed his head formally. He retreated toward the rear stairs.

With a long sigh, she moved slowly down the hall toward Papa's study. Soon, the footmen would light the lamp in the foyer and the sconces along the hallways, but for now, the house was still dark and quiet, and she was glad for it. A headache had threatened to engulf her since the moment she said her good-byes at Gatewell.

No. The headache had arrived well before that, since the moment Robert Carlisle destroyed a perfectly wonderful moment by calling her the kind of woman on whom a man could get burned.

"I'm not a flatiron, for heaven's sake," she muttered, letting her anger push down any lingering hurt at the accusation. Because it *had* hurt. A great deal. And just when she was beginning to think that she could trust him, that he might finally understand her.

Apparently, he didn't understand her at all.

The study door stood open, and Mariah stopped to lean against the doorframe and gaze in at her father.

Whenever she imagined Papa in his study, she pictured him like this, sitting right there behind his large desk, busy at work. A Chippendale piece made of mahogany with black leather inlay across the top, complete with carved lion's paws for feet, the desk was Papa's most treasured belonging next to his wedding ring and the place where he felt most at home in the world. How many hours had she played on the rug in front of the fire while he pored over the company's books at that desk? How many plans and hopes for the future had he shared with her during those quiet afternoons? Her love for the company had come as naturally as loving her father, which wasn't surprising because the two were inseparable. During all the years spent shadowing her father, even before Mama passed away, she'd loved simply being in the same room with him, dreaming of ships and faraway places.

Her chest squeezed. When had their relationship gone so wrong? When had Papa stopped being the man she admired and become an adversary?

Her shoulders sagged. She was so very tired of fighting him, of struggling to earn his attention. It hadn't always been that way. When she was a child, she was his joy, and he would take her with him wherever he went, whether for a stroll through the park or to meet with his captains and warehouse managers. Until she turned thirteen, when he sent her away to Miss Pettigrew's. When she returned, nothing was the same. She was a grown woman, and Papa couldn't fathom why she wanted to spend time at the offices or wharves when she could have been out shopping or attending parties. Just as she simply couldn't fathom any other life for herself but working at his side.

Perhaps Robert was right. Perhaps it was time she stopped trying to bring back those old days.

But how did one give up a dream held for so very long and survive?

As if sensing her presence, her father glanced up from the papers he was reading and smiled at her. "So you're home," he announced.

"And you're working," she commented in a gentle chastisement. "As always."

"Because there is always work to be done," he answered with a tired but happy sigh, his smile growing.

Her heart panged and reminded her that they weren't always at each other's throats, that they often shared quiet moments like this. Unfortunately, those moments seemed preciously few these days and never managed to last long.

She shook her head. "Then don't let me interrupt. I just wanted to let you know that I'd returned."

"Nonsense." He set the papers down and leaned back in his chair. "Seeing my daughter is never an interruption."

At that, she disbelievingly arched a brow, yet she pushed away from the doorframe and came forward into the room.

"Well, a very welcome interruption at any rate," he conceded as he rose from the desk and crossed to the liquor cabinet. "You were at Gatewell?"

"Yes. And thank you for sending the bags of flour and the sugar."

He paused in the middle of pouring bourbon into two crystal tumblers and threw her a pointed glance. "And?"

A knowing smile spread across her face. "And Mrs. Smith sent along a quince pie to you in gratitude."

"Ah!" he replied happily, holding out the second glass to her. "Mrs. Smith has a kind soul."

She accepted the drink with a twitch of her lips. "And knows exactly how to target the soft spot in yours."

He laughed, a warm and carefree sound that reminded her of the man he was before her mother's death, when he laughed more and worried less. "Never underestimate the value of finding a man's soft spot, my dear." He tapped his glass against hers, more to emphasize his point than to toast. "It makes for more favorable business deals and a much happier marriage."

She gave a small laugh and took a sip of the golden liquid, savoring its sweet warmth, then gestured toward the desk. "How's business?"

"The usual. Too many goods coming in, too few going out." He slumped down heavily in his chair, leaning back and folding his hands across his stomach, with his glass perched on his waistcoat buttons. "The bane of a trader's life."

"Will we be able to purchase a new ship this spring?" Her question was disguised as casual interest, but she was checking up on the company as she always did whenever she had a chance. She couldn't help herself. She loved Winslow Shipping and always would. Despite the torture he was putting her through this season, she still loved her father, too. Every misguided bit of him.

He glanced down at the stack of papers and grimaced. "Not this spring, I'm afraid. I need to free up monies for another project I'm considering."

Curiosity pricked at her. "Would that be the real estate project in St Katharine's?"

He glanced up, frowning. "What do you know about that?"

"Not much." She shrugged her shoulders and took another sip of bourbon. "Carlisle said you had him investigating properties, and he asked if I had any insights I might be able to share."

He studied her closely. "Did you?"

"Nothing that was helpful, I'm afraid." She sent him a rueful smile. "I'd be better at stocking stores than buying them."

"You would be wonderful at it."

Despite the affection in his voice, the compliment landed hollowly. Because he was still unwilling to let her attempt it—or any company project, for that matter. She swallowed down her bitterness with a sip of bourbon and asked, "So we're expanding our warehouse holdings, then?"

"Just exploring possibilities. Ones that might prove extremely lucrative for the company."

"That's wonderful." And it was. She only wished that she could play a larger role in it.

"As your grandfather always said," he reminded her, "what's good for Winslow Shipping—"

"Is good for the Winslows," they finished together, then shared a nostalgic smile. Mariah was certain that the look of love in her eyes shined just as brightly as the one in Papa's.

"I've not settled on anything yet." He leaned forward in his chair, set down his glass, and reached for the papers to pick up where he'd left off. "But when I do, I'll be certain to tell you."

She knew he would. Keeping her informed about the company was the one area in which he always considered Mariah's concerns. "How *are* the warehouse stores?"

"Favorable. We'll start moving out the coffee next week and taking in cotton from Alexandria and silk from China. We have a buyer in Boston for the lot of it."

"Good," she said, pleased to hear it. The merchandise had always been her favorite part of the business, all those exotic goods from far-flung corners of the globe. Every ship was a treasure trove. At the thought of how many thousands of miles those goods had traveled, she murmured, "Chinese silks to Boston . . . amazing."

"I'll hold back one of the bolts for you, if you'd like."

"If it's no trouble." Mariah planned to give it to Elizabeth Carlisle as a token of appreciation for all the duchess had done for her. She'd come to like the woman a great deal. Her son, on the other hand...well, she was certain she would like him, too, if he ever stopped infuriating the daylights out of her.

"And Robert Carlisle?" she asked, unable to resist. "You gave him that project, so you must think he's showing promise." It stung to say that, when Papa had never given her an opportunity to demonstrate her own worth.

He grunted affirmatively. "He is."

Her shoulders sagged. *Of course.* Robert was capable and hardworking, with solid connections and a sharp mind that would help the company thrive. She couldn't begrudge him this chance to prove himself. She just didn't want him to keep her from being able to do the same.

She held her breath. "So you think he's doing well enough for a partnership?"

"We'll see," he answered noncommittally.

But her foolish heart didn't leap with hope at that dangled carrot. Instead, she sucked in a deep breath and tried to hold on to the resolve that had been driving her since Papa's mad scheme for her season had been unleashed. "You still think I should find a husband, then?"

"A husband would be good for you." His voice softened. "And what your mother wanted for you, to have your own family and home." Oblivious to the distress his comment spiraled through her, he looked up and met her gaze. Affectionate worry darkened his face. "You *are* enjoying yourself this season, are you not?"

More than she would have thought possible, but that was only due to the duchess. And to a certain extent, she realized grudgingly, to Robert. She *had* enjoyed his company at the soirees and dinners, and even when he'd accompanied them shopping, he'd shown more patience than most men would have. And his kisses...she very much enjoyed those.

"Yes," she answered honestly, "I am."

He nodded curtly, looking back down at the papers, satisfied at her answer. But then a frown creased his brow. "Speaking of potential husbands...Burton Williams came to the house this afternoon to call on Evelyn."

"Oh?" Unease pricked at the backs of her knees. Evie had spent quite a bit of time with Williams recently, talking alone with him at all the events they'd attended. While Mariah couldn't say exactly what it was about him that she distrusted, she didn't like that he was now calling on her sister. Evie certainly deserved suitors, but Mariah would have preferred someone else.

"I think he plans to ask my permission to court her."

Her chest tightened with worry. "And what will you say?"

"Yes, I suppose," he sighed out heavily. "Evelyn likes him. Although to be truthful, I don't really care for the man. There's something about him that doesn't sit right."

"Yes, there is," she confirmed quietly, glad that she and Papa agreed on this. But Evie was intelligent and knew to be cautious, and she wouldn't let Williams take advantage.

At least Mariah hoped not.

"Does he know that he won't be brought into the company if he marries her?" Papa asked. "I won't allow a repeat of what happened with your aunt Charlotte and that man she married."

That man. She smiled to herself. The years were mellowing Papa. His descriptions of her scapegrace uncle used to be much more colorful.

"I don't know." Mariah shook her head, not knowing what—if anything—her sister had told Williams. "But I don't think we need to worry about that." Williams had never struck her as the kind of man who was eager to work on the quaysides. For that matter, to work at all.

Papa answered that with a faint *humph*. Then he asked, "You have plans for the evening?"

"I'm staying in."

"Looking forward to a night in front of the fire with a good book, are you?"

A good book…*Robert*. She bit back a frustrated sigh and swallowed the last of her bourbon, then set the glass down and turned to head upstairs. She was more than ready to put this day—and Carlisle—behind her.

"Be nice to Carlisle," Papa called out in gentle warning.

"I will," she answered. Although, considering what they'd shared that afternoon, she doubted it was possible to be any nicer to him and keep from being ruined.

She stopped in the doorway as a desperate urge rose inside her. One that told her that it was now or never. Turning to face him, she inhaled a deep breath to find the courage to finally put voice to her dearest dreams.

"I've always wanted to work with you, Papa." She looked away when he glanced up at that soft and unexpected declaration, unable to face whatever shock or recrimination she might see in him. Or utter disappointment. "Since I was a little girl, I wanted to be part of Winslow Shipping. A *real* part of it," she rushed out quietly, afraid that if she stopped, the words might never come. After all, how could she continue to press Robert to talk about his father, if she didn't have the courage to talk with hers? "Is there any way—any way at all—" Her voice choked.

With her fingers twisting nervously in her dirty skirt, she forced herself to look up at him. The regret and pain she saw in him nearly undid her.

"Oh, Mariah," he murmured, his shoulders sagging. "I wish things could be different, I truly do." He looked away, but not before she saw the glistening of tears in his eyes. "But shipping is a dangerous world, not at all fit for any woman, let alone the lady you deserve to be. The one your mother wanted you to be." He shook his head. "I was never able to deny your mother anything she wanted. It seems I still can't." Clearing the knot of emotion from his throat, he looked down at his hands as he folded them together over the stack of papers, interlacing his shaking fingers in a failed attempt to hide his emotion from her. "Can you understand?"

With a jerking nod, she blinked back the hot tears of exhaustion and frustration.

Weeks had passed since he'd made his decision that she should marry, and she was no closer to convincing him to relent. But instead of the piercing anguish she'd expected at his new refusal, only a hollow emptiness panged inside her. She shuddered to think that perhaps she was coming to accept the inevitable. That she would never have a real role in the company.

Keeping her back straight, with too much pride to let her shoulders slump even now, she left the study and made her way upstairs to her room. Surprisingly, no sobs came, but she couldn't have said whether she didn't cry because she was still foolishly clinging to her dream or because she'd already given up and so had no more grief left inside her for it.

Not letting herself contemplate which, she sat at her writing desk and reached for a sheet of stationery to write out the apology to Olivia Sinclair that Robert had instructed her to send. She carefully blotted, folded, and sealed it.

Her maid stepped out from the adjoining dressing room, drying her hands on her apron. "Your bath is ready, miss."

"Thank you, Alice." She handed her the note. "Would you ask one of the footmen to take this to St James House? It needs to be delivered this evening."

"Yes, miss." She hurried toward the door. "I'll be right back to help you undress."

"No need. I'll be fine on my own this evening." She didn't want anyone's company tonight, preferring to be alone so she could sort out her thoughts. "Just ask Cook to send up a dinner tray, will you?"

"Yes, miss." Alice bobbed a curtsy, then left.

Mariah rose and went into the dressing room she shared with Evelyn, whose bedroom adjoined it from the other side. These rooms should have been for the gentleman and lady of the house, but Papa had wisely given them up, knowing his two daughters would need them more than he. Of course, he also knew they'd use the dressing room to sneak into each other's bedrooms, talking together and staying up late into the night. Thank goodness he'd had the foresight to realize how much they would need that.

Her bath waited in the large tub that was permanently installed with its special drainage pipes—one of the many advantages of living in a newly built London town house. The servants didn't have to haul down all the water they'd carried up, which resulted in larger, more luxurious baths. She allowed herself this special treat on those days when she knew she'd be working at Gatewell, when Alice had special instructions to have it ready for her at five o'clock. Like today, when her bath awaited all steamy hot and scented with the orange and cinnamon oil one of Papa's captains had given her when he'd brought several bottles of the stuff back from India.

Breathing in the spicy-sweet scent, she smiled to herself. Being the daughter of a shipping merchant held very nice benefits.

She felt better with each layer of wet clothing she peeled away, and when she stepped into the tub and sank into the hot water up to her neck, the warming sensation was exquisite. She hadn't realized exactly how cold and tired she was—how physically exhausted and emotionally drained—until that moment, when she could let all the fatigue and confusion seep out of her.

She closed her eyes…

…and once again saw Robert Carlisle's face.

She groaned with frustration. Even now, finally warm and at home and ready to put this day behind her, the man still invaded her thoughts. Was there no end to the ways he could irritate her?

Or confuse her?

Because he truly confounded her. One moment, she was certain he was Lucifer himself, come to wreak havoc on her life, and the next he was an angel, with a love for his family she'd rarely seen in a gentleman. In one heartbeat he could go from being dashing and charming to spitting fire at her— although, if she were to be honest, *that* she mostly brought on herself. And at one instant he was set on marrying her off to whatever man he could find, but at the next, he was kissing her himself and enjoying it.

At least she hoped he'd enjoyed it. Because she certainly had.

She hated to admit it, even to herself, but when she was with Robert, she felt alluring, intelligent, and so very feminine, even while sitting in a dirty puddle. He made her feel the way no other man ever had, and she liked it. A great deal.

And she would have liked *him* a great deal, too, if he wasn't set on taking her dream away.

Well, *perhaps* he wasn't taking it away. It was impossible to steal something that didn't exist, after all. But he was trampling all over it, for certain.

Yet she was finding it hard to hold even that against him. During the past few weeks, she'd come to know him quite well through the stories Elizabeth shared of him, of a man who was loyal, kind, and generous to his friends and family, despite a reputation that painted him as a scapegrace and rakehell. What she'd seen of him had borne it out, as he seemed charming and gracious to everyone.

Everyone but *her*, that is. To her, he was a six-foot-tall, golden-blond conundrum, aggravated with her at one moment and kissing her passionately the next. Kissing her passionately *especially* when he was aggravated with her.

And this afternoon at Gatewell, for one mad moment they hadn't been enemies, and the connection between them was breathtakingly tender. So much so that she was ready to acknowledge that she'd been wrong to torment him...until he ruined it by making that hurtful comment about how she set men on fire.

Worse, that he wouldn't let himself get burned by her.

Oh, how it had hurt! His arrogant self had returned in full force, and spurred on by anger, she'd dumped the mop water over his head.

A twinge of guilt pricked her. *Perhaps* she shouldn't have done that. But blast him! He'd made her so furious. And furious most of all at herself for falling for his charms. Because when she was in his arms, she'd wanted so much more from him than just a few kisses.

Thinking like that was dangerous, but she couldn't help

it. Just thinking about him stirred the same tingling ache between her legs that she suspected he'd wanted to touch when
his hand had slipped beneath her skirt. If she hadn't stopped
him, would he have touched her *there*?

She wickedly let herself contemplate what it would feel
like to have his hand between her thighs, and with her eyes
closed, in the darkness of her mind, she imagined just
that...his hand caressing at the tingling ache until it turned
into a hot throbbing, long fingers teasing wickedly at her
most intimate place. More...his mouth kissing her there,
doing to her there what he'd done with her breasts—

The soft click of the turning door handle shot through her.
Her eyes flew open, and she gasped, as if actually caught doing what she had only imagined.

Thank God that the heat of the bath hid whatever scarlet
blush darkened her face, although it couldn't hide the self-
recrimination. Fantasizing about Robert Carlisle like that—
had she gone *mad*?

"There you are." Evelyn entered with an affectionate
smile. She sank gracefully to the floor beside the tub to talk
to Mariah, just as they'd always done during baths since they
were children. In the past, such uninvited visits were done
more to aggravate whoever was in the tub and couldn't escape, but since they'd returned from Miss Pettigrew's, these
chats had become opportunities for sisterly heart-to-heart
conversations.

Mariah's chest tightened ruefully. As with quiet moments
with Papa, these talks with Evie had also grown fewer and
farther between.

"Bentley said you were home." Evie dipped her fingers
into the water to test the temperature. "How was Gatewell?"

"It was fine," she dismissed.

Evie's lips curled knowingly. "Why don't I believe you?"

For a moment, Mariah considered dissembling, but Evelyn knew her well enough to spot a lie from a mile away. "Robert Carlisle stopped by."

Her sister's eyes shined with a romantic gleam. "To see you?"

"To tell me that there was an oversight," she corrected firmly. The last thing she needed was for Evie to play at matchmaker. "You've been invited to the ball after all."

Evie shrugged a slender shoulder. "I told you that I didn't mind."

"But I did," she said quietly. Then forced a lightness into her voice. "So now you can be the evening's Incomparable, and no one will pay me a second glance. Perfect for both of us."

Her sister sighed dreamily. "Or we could both meet wonderful gentlemen who sweep us off our feet."

"Glass slippers will cut you, Cinderella," Mariah warned wryly.

"Not if we're swept off our feet."

"*Especially* then."

Ignoring that, Evelyn idly swirled her fingers in the water. A dreamy expression lit her face. "And speaking of handsome gentlemen—"

Mariah frowned. "I didn't realize we were."

"Robert Carlisle."

She heaved out a breath and closed her eyes, doing her best to ignore her sister as she sank deeper into the water. Evie was a hopeless romantic, but she'd have to look elsewhere if she wanted to play fairy godmother.

"I don't think he's nearly as unpleasant as you make him

out to be, Mariah." She lowered her voice secretively. "In fact, I think he's quite wonderful."

She cracked open one eye and gazed at Evie suspiciously. "How would you know?"

"I've had several conversations with him and the duchess since the season began, and he was very charming. He seems to know a great deal about shipping and trade—"

If it were possible to roll only one eye, Mariah did so, then closed it again.

"And he's quite captivated by you."

That brought both eyes open wide. "Rubbish," she denied, ignoring the sudden pounding of her foolish heart. "The man cannot stand me."

"Oh, so much more than you think," Evie practically purred, so caught up in the idea of romance that she didn't realize the impossibility of what she was suggesting. Her and Carlisle—*ludicrous*. "He doesn't take his eyes off you whenever you're together."

Ha! "Only because he thinks I'm plotting against him."

A hint of surprise laced her sister's voice. "Are you?"

Of course, but... "That doesn't signify." She frowned, ignoring the stab of hurt to her chest as she acknowledged, "I'm nothing to him but a problem to be dealt with."

"Hmm." Evie rested her cheek on her arm as it stretched across the edge of the tub, and gazed doubtfully at her sister. "Then for your sake, Mariah, I certainly hope the man knows how to deal with you successfully."

Mariah scowled at her. Evelyn could be annoying, especially so when she was right. But Mariah was done talking about Robert Carlisle. "And how do you plan on dealing with Burton Williams?"

Evie's smile glowed with confidence. "Successfully."

Her heart skipped in warning. Apparently, Evelyn was more attached to Williams than she and her father realized. "And what, exactly, are his intentions toward you?"

"Honorable," she answered tersely, miffed that Mariah would insinuate otherwise. Yet when it came to Burton Williams's intentions, Mariah suspected that the man was motivated more by fortune than affection. "And I like him." Dreaminess softened her eyes. "He's so handsome and dashing."

Oh, Mariah was certain of that.

"He's from a good family and has real prospects."

She was far less certain of *that*. "Does he know that he won't be allowed to be part of Winslow Shipping?" When Papa looked at Williams, she was certain he saw her uncle and suspected Williams might cause the same kind of turmoil within the family. So did Mariah.

"He isn't a fortune hunter." With a flash of hurt darkening her eyes, Evie scolded, "You really should get to know him before you dismiss him so out of hand."

Remorse pricked at her. Perhaps she had judged Williams too quickly. "I will," Mariah agreed, although she was a bit alarmed that Evie was already considering the possibility of marrying the man.

"Good." A beaming smile lit her face. "Because I think he likes me, too."

"I'm sure he does," she agreed, and meant every word.

What surprised Mariah wasn't that a man like Burton Williams found Evelyn interesting, but that more men hadn't yet discovered how truly lovely her younger sister was.

Even now, leaning casually against the tub, Evelyn possessed a smoldering allure born of a natural grace and ease of presence that even Miss Pettigrew and all her hours of

deportment lessons hadn't been able to beat out of her. Instead of inheriting their mother's green eyes and raven locks
as Mariah had, Evelyn had received their father's fairer col-
oring, with amber eyes and red-brown hair that could never
decide whether to shine softly like honey in the sunlight or
blaze like copper. And for all of her poor marks at school—
which Mariah suspected resulted from sheer boredom—her
mind was sharp enough to keep any prince on his toes. So
was her love of excitement, sense of adventure, and exuberant desire to fully embrace life. And all of it wrapped inside
the heart of a hopeless romantic.

"Wouldn't it be grand," Evie purred dreamily, "if we both
found husbands this season?"

"Bite your tongue!" Mariah splashed water at her.

She laughed and wisely sat back out of splashing range.
"Give Burton a chance," she urged. "You'll like him, I
promise. He's not at all like the rest of those society
dullards."

Which was exactly what worried her.

Still, Williams epitomized what a young lady of Evelyn's
status should be hoping for in a husband. The younger son
of a peer, who fit well into society and belonged to a respectable family, he should have been able to provide a good
position and comfortable living for her and their children.

And yet..."Be careful with the man, Evie," Mariah
warned gently.

With a smile, she arched a brow. "I'll be careful with Burton as long as you're careful with Robert Carlisle."

"Carlisle needs to be careful with *me*," she muttered.

Evelyn clicked her tongue with mocking sympathy.
"How horrible it must be to have to spend time with the
handsome son of a duke, one who escorts you to balls and

fancy dinners and engages you in serious conversations about trade and politics."

"Sheer torture," she answered with a heavy sigh.

Evelyn paused, her voice softening, "Is he really so bad as all that, Mariah?"

At the serious tone in Evie's voice, she lifted her gaze slowly, and the sardonic insult that had been poised on her tongue at Robert's expense fell away beneath the unconcealed hope and concern for her in Evie's eyes. Her sister might have been a hopeless romantic, determined to find them both a fairy-tale ending, complete with a knight in shining armor, but her love for Mariah was undeniable.

"No," she answered, although it cost her a great deal of pride to say it. "He's actually a very nice man who loves his mother dearly and dotes on his niece and nephew." She remembered Papa's words about him, and it cost her even more to admit, "And he'll bring great benefits to the company."

"Do you like him?" Evie asked.

What Mariah felt for him was far more complicated than simple *like*. She shook her head. "He wants the partnership for himself."

Evelyn smiled softly at that and repeated, "But you do like him, Mariah?"

She hesitated, then answered softly, "I do." And felt like a traitor, both to the company and to herself, for admitting it aloud.

"And he likes you?" More of an assertion than a question, Mariah noticed, just as she noticed the hopeful gleam in her sister's eyes. Evelyn wouldn't be satisfied until she had both of them married off, with a babe on each hip.

"I think so," she whispered, afraid to put voice to it for fear of tempting fate to prove her wrong.

Evie pressed, her voice as low as Mariah's, "What are you going to do about him, then?"

"I don't know," she answered honestly, all her confusion about Robert encapsulated in those three small words. When Evelyn's smile began to broaden, Mariah scowled at her. "But I've had more than enough of Robert Carlisle for one day, and enough of you, so out you go so I can finish bathing in peace. Out, out!" She waved a dripping hand, shooing her sister toward the door. Then she relented, as always. "But ask Cook to send up a second tray, and we'll eat dinner together in front of the fire."

Evie sent her a smile over her shoulder as she shut the door after herself.

With a heavy sigh, Mariah closed her eyes and sank down into the water until only her nose poked through the surface, content to suffer alone in her emotional turmoil.

In the fight with Robert, she'd won their latest skirmish.

So why did she feel as if she were losing the war?

Over the past few weeks, she'd grown battle weary and dreaded the long siege of the season ahead. She'd never realized before how difficult and draining it could be to fight for a dream, or battle her growing feelings for a man. And she *did* have feelings for him, blast him. She hadn't lied to Evie. The more time she spent with him, the harder it became to see him as a heartless devil. And each time she saw him at work in the offices, her conviction that he wasn't good enough for the company fractured a tiny bit more.

She groaned with frustration. What *was* she going to do?

CHAPTER TEN

⌒ ⌒

The Night of Mariah's Ball

The quadrille's ending notes died away, and Mariah curtsied to her partner. She smiled gratefully when he placed her hand on his arm to lead her off the floor.

The ball proved to be a crush and was well on its way to being the event of the season. London society crowded into the ballroom in a sea of dazzling satins and jewels beneath glowing chandeliers, attended by an army of footmen bearing trays of champagne, and entertained by the orchestra playing from the landing above. An entire side room had been dedicated for refreshments, with even more rooms serving tonight as drawing rooms, game rooms, gentlemen's smoking rooms, and ladies' retiring rooms. Three sets of French doors stood open wide to the terrace and the dark garden beyond to let in the cool winter air and tamp down the stifling heat.

It was a grand celebration for her introduction, one she never would have dreamt possible six weeks ago. Or ever thought that she would actually find herself enjoying. But much to her own surprise, she was. Immensely. Even more so because Evie was here to share it with her. Her father had stayed home because he said he wanted her to enjoy the evening without being nervous by having him there. But Mariah knew the truth. Papa had never felt comfortable among the *ton*, and her chest panged with a hollow ache that he was determined to make her into a society lady and part of the people who would never accept him as one of them.

The ball wasn't only for her, of course. Lady St James's annual party was always one of the season's most anticipated events, but the countess's kindness in letting her be a special guest of honor touched Mariah. So did the way that Lord St James stopped the festivities to let Elizabeth give a special announcement to introduce her, then led the room in a toast to her. Oh, the moment had been simply magical! She'd felt like a princess in a fairy tale, and she wasn't willing to let this wonderful night slip by without enjoying it.

Not even Robert Carlisle's uncharacteristic moodiness could upset her tonight.

He'd been brooding since he arrived to collect her and Evelyn for the ball. Mariah thought they'd reached an understanding in their standoff...or at least a lessening of personal resentment, despite the bucket of dirty water. Apparently not, because from the moment he saw her descend the stairs in her ball gown, an odd grumpiness had fallen over him. He'd uttered not a spare word to anyone during the ride to St James House and maintained a pensive silence once they'd arrived, including during the opening dance when, as her escort, he'd been obliged to partner with her. Nothing seemed to please him tonight. He frowned in displeasure whenever anyone commented on how splendid she looked, how she would take society by storm, how she was certain to have dozens of gentlemen calling on her...as if the compliments were somehow *her* fault.

Heavens, would she *never* understand the man?

Elizabeth looped her arm through hers. "Are you having a good time, my dear?"

"A grand time," she answered honestly with a beaming smile. She waved a gloved hand to indicate the room around them. "If I had known balls could be this much fun, I'd have begged to attend one long before now." She placed her hand affectionately over Elizabeth's. "But all of it is only due to you. I cannot tell you how grateful I am."

Elizabeth glowed at the compliment, then slid her a sly glance. "Even if the purpose of the game is marriage?"

"That might be the path of the arrow," Mariah countered with a clever smile of her own, "but we're a long way from striking the target."

With a light laugh, Elizabeth squeezed her arm. "There are more people I'd like you to meet." She led her toward a group of ladies gathered a short distance away.

As they wove through the crush, Mariah made a furtive search but didn't spot Robert anywhere. *Not* that she particularly wanted to see him, especially if he remained so dour. She only wanted a moment in private to thank him for what he'd done for Gatewell, that was all. Since his visit last week, he'd surprised her by sending several shipments of goods for the children, including a barrel of supplies for the schoolroom and a trunk filled with coats and boots of all sizes.

He'd also sent a special gift for Polly—a doll with rosy cheeks and blond curls, wearing a pretty pink dress. But it was the note that made Mariah tear up. A letter explaining that the doll's name was Sarah and describing how Robert had met her just that morning in a lane in Clerkenwell, that she told him how she wanted to go to school to be with other children but was afraid of not having any friends…*Perhaps Lucy could be her friend?* With that introduction, Polly took to the doll immediately, and now everywhere she went she carried the blond Sarah under one arm and the headless Lucy under the other. It was the most thoughtful gift Mariah had ever seen.

Unable to resist, she asked as nonchalantly as possible, "And where is Robert?"

"Most likely in the smoking room, hiding away from marriage-minded mamas and their daughters who are shamelessly on the prowl for husbands."

Mariah sent a suspicious glance at her, knowing how much Elizabeth wanted Robert to settle down with a wife and give her more grandchildren. "Aren't you a marriage-minded mama?"

"Tonight I'm one by proxy for *you*, my dear." Elizabeth gave a motherly squeeze to her arm. "Which isn't the same thing at all."

"I see." She fought back a smile at how the irony of the situation went right over the duchess's head.

No matter. Tonight, she planned to enjoy herself and ignore Robert, while simultaneously watching his every move.

And somehow keep an eye on Evelyn, even in the midst of the crush.

In her pale pink dress, her sister wasn't easy to spot among a sea of pastel-colored misses crowding the room. Which was probably why Evelyn had chosen that specific dress in the first place—so that Mariah would be less able to keep watch over her if she wanted to sneak away with Burton Williams. Because of that, Mariah had tasked Whitby with guarding Evie tonight, to make certain her sister didn't get into trouble at her first ball.

Fortunately, Evie was easier to track than anticipated, because *unfortunately* she never strayed far from Williams. But at least she was heeding Mariah's warning to be careful. She'd danced only one turn with him so far, knowing what it meant if she gave him too many dances, and she'd not attempted to wander off alone with him. Yet.

Turning her attention away from her sister, Mariah smiled graciously as Elizabeth introduced her to a new group of ladies, whose names she would never be able to remember when added to the hundred other people she'd already met tonight. It was always the same...a flash of surprised recognition as they suddenly realized who she was and remembered the reputation she'd garnered for herself, followed immediately by acceptance because the Duchess of Trent was at her side. Mariah suspected that she could have danced through St Paul's in her night rail and all would be excused as long as Elizabeth vouched for her.

As she rose from her curtsy, the crowd parted in front of her. The gap lasted only a heartbeat, but it was long enough for her to glimpse Robert across the room. In his formal attire, he stole her breath away. Snow-white breeches that hugged his muscular thighs beneath a white satin waistcoat and intricately knotted cravat, a dark blue cashmere jacket and sapphire cravat pin that matched the blue of his eyes, rakishly mussed hair that shined golden in the light of the chandeliers and had her longing to run her fingers through it...*Heavens.*

As if feeling her gaze on him, he looked up, meeting her stare across the room. A flash of heated longing fell through her so intensely that she shivered.

"There you are, Mariah! I've been looking for you everywhere."

A hand at her elbow snatched her attention away. When she glanced back, the crowd had pushed in, and Robert had disappeared.

Squashing a surprising pang of loss, she turned and smiled. "Whitby, you know—" She bit off her words as her chest tightened with dread. "You've left your post. What did Evie do?"

"Nothing." He jerked a thumb toward the corner of the room. "She's chatting with the Marchioness of Chesney."

He gave her a silly grin that caused his dimples to deepen and made him appear even more boyish than usual. His clothes didn't help. He wore the same style of evening attire as every other gentleman in the room—although in decidedly brighter colors and a plethora of patterns that made Mariah wonder if his tailor had gone mad—but on Whitby, his clothes made him look as if someone had stretched Beau Brummell on the rack.

"I'm here for our dance." He gave an elaborate bow from the waist, which nearly toppled him over, then held out his hand with decorum. "Miss Winslow, our waltz."

Her heart tugged for him. "I would be honored, Mr. Whitby."

With a beaming smile, he placed her hand on his arm and led her toward the dance floor as the master of ceremonies announced the first waltz. Other couples took their places around them until the floor was as crowded as the rest of the room. But when the music began and the men whirled their partners into their steps, the others wisely made room for an exuberant Whitby as he charged across the floor with her at more than double the tempo of the waltz.

Laughing at his enthusiasm, and wondering if the metronome was broken when he learned to dance, Mariah gave herself over to the sheer fun of the moment and simply tried to keep up. They'd cleared a path down the floor and back when she spied Robert. She craned her neck for a better look just as Whitby twirled her into a circle, just as she caught a glimpse of the beautiful woman in Robert's arms—

With a gasp, Mariah stumbled, and Whitby flayed his arms in an uncoordinated grab to catch her. That brought them both to a sudden halt, which in turn sent several couples who had been bravely attempting to pace them careening in all directions.

Concern tightened Whitby's face. "Are you all right?"

She looked up sheepishly at him. Thank goodness the shock heating her cheeks of seeing Robert dancing with another woman was hidden by the embarrassment of her stumble. "I'm fine. Just tripped over my own feet." She moved back into position. "Shall we?"

He nodded, but a perturbed frown pulled at his brow. Leading her more slowly now, he shot a glance behind her to where she'd been gazing when she stumbled. "You were looking at Carlisle."

"Can you blame me?" Perturbed at being so easily caught gawking after the man, she arched a brow and pretended her attentions were simply part of their war. "A wise admiral always knows where the enemy's fleet is anchored."

He nodded but wisely kept them moving at a slower pace so she wouldn't trip again, which was now at half speed to the orchestra and bottlenecked the couples behind them. She affectionately squeezed his hand. Whitby was a dear friend but an absolute menace on the dance floor.

"Didn't you expect to see him waltzing?" he asked, as persistent as a dog after a bone.

Not at all. But she refused to admit that. "I'm only concerned about his unfortunate partner." She sniffed and gave a haughty toss of her head. "That the poor girl must suffer his boorish attentions."

He hee-hawed a laugh. "You're jealous!"

Horror sank through her. "I most certainly am not!"

"Oh, you *are*." He grinned like the cat who caught the canary. "Mrs. Smith is going to crow when I tell her!"

"I am *not* interested in Carlisle," she hissed out, with a smile still firmly glued in place for anyone who was watching and a small pang of remorse for lying to her best friend. Whitby didn't deserve her dissembling, but neither did she want to discuss Robert Carlisle with him. "That man has made my life a confused mess since the moment he walked into it." And that was most definitely *not* a lie.

"Yes. But you're *still* jealous that he's waltzing with someone else, while you only had the opening quadrille."

Blast him for being right! She *was* jealous. Whitby knew her too well not to notice that it pricked at her. But she would *never* tell him that she'd found herself attracted to Carlisle, enough that she'd let him kiss her so passionately in the schoolroom. Or admit to the hurt he'd inflicted when he'd made that callous comment about how he didn't want to burn himself on her.

That other woman was welcome to him. Mariah certainly did *not* want that intolerable man for herself...but drat it, she didn't want anyone else to have him, either.

"I will admit," she answered, deliberately choosing her words, "that Robert Carlisle is an attractive man, if a lady likes that golden Adonis sort." Which she did. A great deal. "And he does appear to have some fine qualities, if a person is able to overlook that prickly personality of his."

"Prickly?" He glanced curiously in Robert's direction. "That's some neat trick."

She puzzled. "What is?"

"How a man can turn himself into a cactus," he goaded teasingly. "But then, Adonis was the god of plants."

She rolled her eyes with failing patience. "*Not* of plants, Whitby. The god of spring's rebirth."

"So you admit that Carlisle is a god?"

"Robert Carlisle is *not* an Adonis!"

The aggravated words flew out before she could stop them, and in her pique, just loudly enough for all the nearby couples to hear. The women tittered at her embarrassment, while the men smiled smugly to have their jealous opinions of Robert confirmed.

A hot blush heated the back of her neck. For once, Whitby's antics were not amusing. She lowered her voice and glared daggers at him, which only broadened his grin. Drat him.

"Robert Carlisle is attempting to take Winslow Shipping away from me," she reminded him. "And his goal is to marry me off, don't forget."

That vanished his grin. He said somberly. "Not if you don't want to."

"And risk losing my allowance?" The severity of that thought landed hard on her shoulders, which sagged beneath the weight of it. That was still a very real threat. Papa would never force her to marry the first man who came along just to be wed and out of his house. But if a proper gentleman with a solid reputation and financial resources offered for her, then he might very well carry out his threat rather than let her refuse. "What would Gatewell do then? And all the children? Where would they go if they didn't have us to shelter them? What would happen to them?"

When he couldn't answer, she looked away as fresh frustration knotted inside her. Over a month had passed since Papa laid down his ultimatum, and nothing about her situation had changed. Her allowance was still as tenuous as ever, and Whitby certainly wasn't helping with all his taunts about Robert.

"Then marry me instead," he proposed earnestly.

Her chest tightened at the sweetness of his offer. One she would never accept. For all that she didn't want marriage forced upon her, she still held out hope that one day she might find a husband who loved her. Whom she loved in return. And that man was not Hugh Whitby.

With a shake of her head, she answered gently, "You don't love me."

"Not romantically," he admitted, giving her hand a squeeze, "but I do care about you. And I don't want you to be hurt by Carlisle."

Her eyes blurred. He no longer wore that silly grin but looked down at her with complete sincerity...and an expression lying somewhere between dreadful expectation and sheer terror that she might just accept. His offer to marry her only proved what a good man he was. And someday he would make a very wonderful husband. To some other woman.

"Oh, Whitby," she whispered, "I love you."

His face turned white. "You—you do?"

She gave a choking laugh. "As a dear *friend*." She laid her hand against his cheek, then stifled another laugh as relief flooded through him and the ruddy hue returned to his face. "That you would offer marriage to help me means more to me than I can say. But I don't think that's the right solution."

"Are you certain?" Even as he asked, she knew he was sending up a silent prayer that she wouldn't change her mind.

"I can hold my own against Robert Carlisle," she assured him.

The waltz ended. As Mariah stepped back and sank into a low curtsy to match Whitby's overly enthusiastic bow, she glanced across the dance floor... and directly into Robert's eyes as he took his partner's hand to lead her off.

Despite her anger at him, attraction spiraled through her, only to turn to icy jealousy when he leaned down to whisper something into the woman's ear that made her smile.

Hold her own? She bit her lip. If only she could convince herself of that as easily as Whitby.

*   *   *

Three dances later, Robert watched Mariah over the rim of his wineglass as he raised it to his lips. Tonight she looked like a goddess as she glided across the floor, one fully aware of the heated effect she had on every man in the room.

Except for him. He'd gained immunity to her charms the hard way.

She was the shining star of tonight's ball, and everyone wanted to be at her side. A few lucky men had been favored enough to partner with her for a dance. Even now she stepped gracefully through a set with the Duke of Wembley. His Grace was twice her age, but she smiled at him as if he were a young buck, putting him into her thrall. The way she had every man she'd danced with tonight. Just as his mother had hoped. After all, the duchess had been very busy working to ensure that all of Mariah's dances were taken by only the most eligible gentlemen.

And Whitby.

His eyes narrowed on the dandy as he stood beside Evelyn

Winslow in the corner of the ballroom. Mariah had made a complete spectacle of herself with him, whirling around the room so recklessly in his arms, laughing easily and glowing with delight. He was certain everyone in the room had seen the way she'd flirted…every casual touch to Whitby's shoulders as they'd crossed the floor, each laugh and smile she gave him, dancing so close that her skirt brushed his legs with every turn. And the way she'd touched his cheek, staring up at him as if the rest of the world didn't exist—shameless.

So was the way that Whitby and the gentlemen threw their attentions on her. Even now half a dozen men were descending upon her to offer glasses of punch as soon as the dance ended and Wembley escorted her off. The clodpoles hadn't even bothered to get to know her well enough to learn that she preferred champagne.

"Sheep," he muttered as she turned heads when she glided past.

So far, though, he had to admit that Mariah's plan for the season was working—the gentlemen who called on her at home had abandoned all thoughts of courting her the moment they discovered she provided no inroads to the Winslow fortune. But it wouldn't always be that way. There must have been one or two men present tonight who cared nothing about money who were casting their attentions on her. One or two who would be bold enough to call on her. Most likely as soon as tomorrow. And then it would be only a few weeks until the first marriage offers were made.

Exactly what he'd hoped when Henry Winslow challenged him with this task—Mariah wedded, his partnership secured, and indisputable proof held in his hands that he was worthy of being Richard Carlisle's son.

So why was he so damnably annoyed about it?

He watched Mariah as she made her way off the floor with Wembley, then moved away from the crowd to catch a moment's solitude by the open French doors. She wasn't beautiful—tonight she was simply incomparable. And that dress... *God's mercy* that dress.

Elegantly cut from copper satin, the gown draped dramatically from its high waist to the tips of her slippers and shimmered like molten gold. Daringly sleeveless yet with a modest neckline that only hinted at her breasts beneath, the tantalizing contradiction of satin and bare flesh was arresting. But it was the utter lack of embellishment that captured his attention most. The simple beauty of it was breathtaking.

Damnation, *she* was breathtaking in it. And he longed to strip it off her. With his teeth.

But remembering how she'd so furiously poured water over his head for daring to kiss her breast, he feared he'd most likely die in an attempt to undress her.

He was sorely tempted to try anyway. Because even now he could taste the spicy-sweet flavor of her, that exotic mix of cinnamon and oranges that drove him mad. Because even now he craved to unleash that sharp wit of hers and engage in the kind of sparring that sent excitement pulsating through him.

She turned gracefully with a smile as the orchestra played a fanfare, and yearning twisted through him so intensely that it took his breath away.

Sweet Lucifer. Some victories were worth the sacrifice of a man's life.

Tossing back the last of his wine, he placed his empty glass onto the tray of a passing footman, snatched up a flute of champagne, and headed directly toward her.

Her back was to him, her body turned toward the open

French doors so that she could catch some of the cool air and seize a moment's reprieve from the party. She didn't see him approach.

Hooking his arm past her shoulder, Robert silently held the glass in front of her.

Laughter lilted from her like music. "Whitby," she chided playfully as she turned around, "liking French champagne does not make me a traitor—"

When she saw him, her laughter choked. The friendly smile turned into a look of surprise. Then into a scowl of irritation.

"Champagne. Your favorite," he commented, dismissing the men with their punch.

"Yes, it is. Thank you." As she icily took the glass, she asked tightly, "Is this bribery for my continued good behavior this evening?"

He nodded at the flute. "If that's all it takes to keep you in line, Mariah, I'd purchase an entire vineyard."

At his quip, a dark smile of amusement danced at her lips. She murmured dryly, "And here I thought my good behavior justified only a case."

"Or ten," he corrected, unable to keep from returning her smile.

Her eyes swept over him. For once beneath her gaze, he didn't feel as if he were an opponent being sized up before a fight. But anger at him still lingered visibly within her. And still aggravated the hell out of him, that she could keep punishing him for what had been little more than a kiss. An encounter she'd seemed to enjoy, too, until the minx dumped mop water over his head.

"What did you wish to speak to me about?" she asked, ending their banter.

But he enjoyed sparring with her and glimpsing her fire.

One lacking in every other miss in attendance tonight. He couldn't help himself and drawled with amusement, "I hear you think I'm an Adonis."

Her eyes widened in a beat of unguarded embarrassment. Then she effortlessly recovered and coolly took a sip of champagne, with only a faint pinking of her cheeks showing any trace of her self-consciousness. "Once again the gossips have the story completely wrong."

He arched an amused brow. "So you think I'm Venus?"

That sent her into a seething pique. She exhaled a hard breath. "*I* think you're the most arrogant, frustrating man who—"

"You look beautiful tonight," he interrupted.

Her eyes flared. "Ha! You're only saying that because—"

"Because I think you look beautiful," he repeated quietly. He'd never uttered a more honest statement in his life.

She froze, for a moment speechless as she stared at him. Yet she refused to thank him, as if knowing he hadn't meant it as a compliment. And he hadn't. Tonight, her beauty was his curse.

"And so does every man in this room." Every last one she'd been so torturously gracing all evening with her brilliant smiles and lilting laughs, with her elegant dancing and witty conversation—except him. Even now, the openly interested stares of the gentlemen standing nearby proved him right. They wanted her.

And God help him, so did he.

"Be careful, Mariah." He felt a dark urge to warn her about the men circling her tonight, like wolves hunting prey. The same warning that applied to himself, as well. "Gentlemen of the *ton* are used to getting whatever they want simply because of who they are."

She sighed impatiently. "Of course they—"

"And what they want," he murmured, his voice far huskier than he intended in its certainty, "is you."

Her lips parted delicately as she stared at him, as if she couldn't believe his audacity to assert such a thing. But thankfully, she didn't slap him for it. Nor did she did turn away, standing perfectly still except for the increased rhythm of her breathing as it grew shallow and fast, her eyes locked with his.

Then she slowly took a long sip of champagne, doing her best to appear as if his words hadn't flustered her, but she couldn't hide the pinking in her cheeks or the shaking of her hand as she raised the flute to her mouth. When she lowered the drink away, finally having collected herself enough to reply, she assured him, "Then they'll be very disappointed to discover they can't have what they want."

He was certain she'd tried for haughty contempt, but her voice emerged as a throaty purr, one that made her impossibly more alluring despite the flicker of ire in her eyes.

"I don't need any of your warnings, Robert. Tonight, I am behaving exactly as everyone wants me to behave." Her fingers tightened around the stem of her champagne flute. "I'm pleasing your mother by dancing with dukes and engaging in the most boring conversations with matrons about afternoon teas and rose gardens. I'm pleasing my father by encouraging gentlemen to call on me, while simultaneously keeping my sister out of trouble with Burton Williams."

Her words were calm, but she ticked off each point with a frustrated tap of her fingertip against her glass.

"And I'm doing it all with a smile on my face, because until five minutes ago I was also enjoying myself. I'm pleasing everyone tonight." Her brow lifted with that look of practiced disdain that aggravated the daylights out of him. "Except you. But then, nothing short of my eloping to Scotland would please you."

Unwittingly punctuating her words, the orchestra struck up the first notes for the next dance with a loud flourish that sent a ripple of excitement through the room. A waltz.

She turned to walk away, but he took her elbow and stopped her. He felt the tension flash through her like lightning, all of her stiffening with a sharp inhalation. She trembled beneath his hand, and that soft tremor shivered through his fingers, down his arm, and into him, like a ribbon twining heatedly through both of them.

"If you want to please me," he told her quietly as the crowd began to shift and couples moved toward the dance floor, the music swirling around them like a swift current, "then dance with me."

She gaped over her shoulder at him, eyes wide with surprise. "Pardon?"

"Give me the pleasure of your company tonight," he ordered enticingly. He stole a caress down her arm and felt her pulse spike beneath his fingertips at her wrist as he repeated in a low drawl, "Dance with me, Mariah."

She hesitated, with a look of uncertain longing clouding her face. His lips curved into the start of a pleased smile, knowing she was on the verge of capitulating.

But pride got the better of the obstinate hellcat, and she gave a tight shake of her head. "I don't want to dance with you."

He clenched his jaw against the mounting frustration. *Oh no.* The little minx wasn't going to succeed in refusing him so easily. Not tonight. Not when he ached to have her close.

Knowing she couldn't resist a challenge, he lowered his

mouth to her ear and murmured, "What's stopping you, Mariah?" The spicy scent of oranges and cinnamon intoxicated him, pulling straight through him until his gut tightened into a knot of desire. Until it was far more than dancing that he wanted to do with her. "Afraid you might enjoy being in my arms?"

Her eyes flashed with an angry intensity. "Are *you* still afraid of getting burned?" she threw back.

He snapped up straight at her unexpected accusation. "Burned?" he repeated, puzzled. "What do you—"

Christ.

The realization struck him as forcefully as if she'd slapped him. Her words echoed inside him, the same ones he'd used against her at the school when she'd gotten too close. When his attraction for her had gone beyond the merely physical and was becoming so great that he'd desperately needed a reminder of who she was and the threat she posed.

His chest sank with leaden remorse as he watched the hurt dance like green flames in her eyes, the defensive lift of her chin in an attempt to replace the pain with pride. She'd opened her heart to him, sharing with him her love for the children of St Katharine's and her worry about her sister, only for him to callously shatter that tender trust. And the way she'd let him kiss her, trusting him enough to bare herself to his eyes and mouth—

No wonder she'd showered him with cold water. When she'd been at her most vulnerable, he was a thoughtless cad.

"I was wrong to think that and an arse to say it," he admitted with chagrin. Shifting as close as propriety allowed, he felt her soften at his apology. "It's the other men who can't tolerate the heat of you, who aren't up to the challenge. Who aren't man enough to handle a woman like you." He paused, then admitted hoarsely, "You know the effect you have on me. I can't think straight when you're near."

She caught her breath in surprise, but he couldn't deny it. She drove him out of his right mind, until he didn't know what to think or say. For God's sake, he wanted nothing more whenever he was alone with her than to fall into a verbal sparring match, then pull her into his arms and kiss over every inch of her. And to his utter bewilderment, she was the only woman he'd ever met who gave him hope that he, too, could eventually overcome the death of a parent.

Even now he was unable to keep from touching her and dared to caress his hand against the small of her back. "I crave your fire, Mariah."

She swallowed. Sudden nervousness spread over her and mixed with the alluring vulnerability that drew him so strongly. Yet she managed to reply acerbically, "And risk a second dousing?"

"For a taste of you?" he drawled rakishly, his gaze falling longingly to her ripe mouth. "Absolutely."

She inhaled a ragged breath. For one unguarded heartbeat, a look of longing sparked in the green depths of her eyes, and her pulse raced in the hollow at the base of her neck. In that fleeting moment he also saw a flash of the same brashness that had led her to push her behavior to the edge of propriety, the same passion that had made her return the boldness of his kisses—it was a look of pure temptation.

But in a single breath it vanished, and her damnable pride rose once more to the surface.

She slipped her arm away from his hold and handed him her half-empty glass of champagne. The gesture was one of dismissal, but the way that her fingers shook told him that their brief conversation had affected her. "Then you'll be very disappointed to discover that *you* can't have what you want, either."

She turned on her heel and without a backward glance walked through the open French doors and out into the dark night.

His eyes narrowed to slits as he stared after her, long after her slender form had vanished into the shadows of the garden. *Damn her.* For her to think that she could prick at him so freely, that she could make his heart pound and his blood boil with both desire and fury, then simply walk away—

Not this time.

He tossed back the rest of the champagne and stalked after her.

* * *

Mariah ducked beneath an overgrown willow tree in the far corner of the garden, the dark shadows and the tree's thick branches that bent to the ground hiding her from view.

Grateful to be alone, she leaned against the trunk and sucked in a deep breath of air so cold that it tingled in her lungs. Thankfully, the garden was empty, with no one there to witness her confusion and frustration. Only a handful of couples were outside, and they remained on the terrace and close to the house. She thought she'd spied Evie standing among them with Burton Williams, but she couldn't stop to make certain. Not when she'd so desperately needed to flee before she screamed.

Oh, what a rake Robert was! To say those things to her, to gaze at her in that heated way—he made her long for all kinds of things she could never have. Not least of all *him*. Because it would have been so very easy to capitulate to the desire she saw in those blue eyes, to his charm and intelligence, to the love and fierce loyalty he held for his family . . . to the thoughtfulness in sending a doll to a little girl.

She groaned in frustration. Blast him for confusing her so much! And the devil take him for making her want to kiss him, to let him touch her and make her feel special. She wanted to laugh with him and see the way his eyes crinkled when he smiled. And God help her, she wanted to simply spend time in the man's company, doing anything besides arguing.

But while she might have wanted him, he wanted Winslow Shipping. And it was time she accepted, once and for all, that the two would never mix.

"Mariah."

She startled, her racing heart leaping into her throat. Through the black shadows of the winter-barren branches, a shadowy form was silhouetted against the midnight sky, dark yet unmistakable . . .

"Robert," she whispered.

He slipped slowly beneath the branches to join her in the secret bower. The space immediately became much smaller and far more intimate, and her heart began to race for a very different reason.

"You followed me," she accused softly, but even that whisper seemed thunderous in the silent stillness of the wintry garden.

He arched a brow in challenge. "I had no choice. You left."

"I told you." She shivered, more from his nearness than the cold. "I don't want to dance with you."

"Too bad." His blue eyes shined impossibly bright in the darkness as he slowly moved closer, one stalking step at a time. His voice lowered to a deep purr as his gaze raked down the front of her, but she didn't turn away, because a dark and wanton part of her thrilled when he stared at her like that. As if she were a sugary treat he wanted to devour. "Because I very much want to dance with you."

The innuendo shivered through her as he stopped in front of her. She prayed he couldn't see in the shadows the same heated desire on her own face that she heard in his voice.

"You can't charm your way into the partnership." *Or into my heart.* Although she suspected that the frustrating man was already there. When he shifted closer, as if taking her words as a challenge instead of an indictment, she warned breathlessly, "I won't let you."

"I wouldn't dare try." He stood so close now that the heat of his body warmed down her front and made her tremble. "Not with a woman as formidable as you."

With his eyes not leaving hers, he shrugged out of his jacket.

Nervousness spiked inside her. She demanded, "What are you doing?"

"It's cold." He placed the jacket around her shoulders. "And you came outside without your wrap."

The jacket was still warm from his body, and the masculine scent of him clung to it. Both of which made her want to wrap it around herself like a blanket even as she argued weakly, "I don't need your concern."

His mouth twisted into a grin of amused aggravation. "And yet you have it anyway."

Along with another painful reminder of how considerate he was. "Please go away," she whispered, her words lacking all conviction, even to her own ears. "I came out here to be alone."

Instead of leaving, he shifted even closer and drawled huskily, "So now you're alone with me."

Drat him for twisting her words! And for looking so dashing in the shadows, so warm and inviting amid the winter night. She forced herself to say, "I don't want you here."

"I don't believe you." He lowered his head until his mouth was even with hers, and his warm breath tickled against her lips. "You like being alone with me as much as I do." With his eyes locked on hers in the shadows, he dared to brush his thumb over her bottom lip, and she shivered. "What are you afraid of, Mariah?" His voice seeped warmly into her, a tantalizingly masculine sound that left her aching. "That I'll try to kiss you again... or that I won't?"

"That's not it." If it were only kissing that she wanted from him, she'd gladly let him do just that and take pleasure in it, wanting nothing more than what he gave her at this moment. But her attraction to him had gone beyond that. She wanted to share quiet moments with him, morning walks through the park, and evenings together at the theater. She wanted to argue politics with him over breakfast, discover his opinions about art and music, and let him teach her how to ride a horse. God help her, she wanted *all of him*. His mind, his laughter, his affections—

"You'd rather be with Whitby," he bit out, his face hardening at her dissembling. "Is that it?"

She blinked. "Whitby?" she repeated, incredulous. Surely, he didn't mean... "*Hugh* Whitby?"

His eyes fixed on hers in the shadows, his hands slipping beneath the jacket to rest on her hips. "I see how you are with him, how you two laugh and carry on." He gave a small tug and brought her soft body against his. She would have gasped at the contact, except that she was too stunned by his words. "How freely you behave when you're with him."

With *Whitby*? Good Lord, Carlisle was mad! And tantalizingly muscular as he leaned her back against the tree trunk, trapping her between it and his body. The contradiction of his absurd accusation and the heat of his thumbs stroking slow circles over her ribs made her head spin.

"Do you have an understanding with him?" He pressed himself along the length of her, leaving her no choice but to entwine her arms around his neck. When she did, he rewarded her with a slow caress of his hands up her body that left shivers in its wake.

"Whitby is…just a friend," she forced out between increasingly shallow breaths, then gasped as his thumbs stroked the undersides of her breasts.

"I don't believe you," he murmured against her ear, then swirled the tip of his tongue along the outer curl and sent a hot shudder shivering through her. "I saw the way you two danced together."

She would have laughed at the jealousy behind his accusation, if not for the fire flaming in her belly at the way his lips placed sultry kisses along the side of her face.

"We were only dancing." She fought to keep her voice steady. To keep from whimpering with the need to have his mouth possessing hers. "Talking."

"I'm certain of that. He whispered all kinds of scandalous things to you, didn't he?" His words were surely meant as an accusation, yet the jealousy behind them stirred the growing ache inside her and sent her head whirling. That Robert Carlisle was jealous over her—*unbelievable*. "Like how beautiful you look when you dance, how lithe and graceful…"

She bit her lip. If she denied it, he would stop, and the last thing she wanted was for him to stop. Not when his hands were caressing over her in slow, heated strokes. Not when she could close her eyes and fantasize that he wasn't making accusations but murmuring words of seduction.

"How much he wants to kiss you," he whispered as his lips finally found hers. "Like this."

She lost her breath beneath his heated mouth and melted so bonelessly in his arms that she had to tighten her hold around his shoulders to keep from falling away. When his tongue teased her lips apart and slipped inside, she tasted the burning jealousy in his kiss. And she thrilled with it.

Unable to deny herself the pleasures of being in his arms, she twined her fingers in his silky hair and welcomed the deep, steady thrusts of his tongue between her lips. The heady way he kissed her made her feel as light and dizzy as if she were drunk on champagne, the flavor of him on her lips just as sweet.

Then his kiss changed. He cupped the back of her neck to hold her head still as the thrusts turned into exploring little licks that delved into the secret recesses of her mouth, swept over her inner lip, and teased at her tongue until she dared to lick back.

He groaned at her boldness and pressed closer. The rough bark scratched and snagged at the cashmere of his jacket between her shoulder blades. But she simply didn't care. She arched herself against him, reveling in the decadent feel of his hard body against hers, craving more of the delicious ache that coiled inside her—

And moaning with satisfaction when his hands cupped her breasts.

Smiling against her temple at her reaction, he teased her

nipples through the smooth satin with his thumbs until they puckered into hard points. Her flesh warmed beneath the heat of his hands, as if no barrier existed at all between his palms and her bare skin. She dragged in a deep, jerking breath. Thank God that the jacket prevented him from unbuttoning her dress and baring her breasts to kiss them as he did before, or she would have been begging him to do just that. And with that, cross the line they were rapidly approaching when they would have to stop.

As if he realized that, too, he reluctantly released her. Placing one hand on the trunk over her shoulder while the other slid down her side to her waist, he paused only a heartbeat before slipping his hand between their bodies and resting it on her lower belly. Just inches from the throbbing ache between her legs.

She caught her breath. Apparently, the rake inside him didn't understand lines of demarcation at all.

"Did he tell you how alluring he finds you, Mariah?" he murmured hotly against her temple in a throaty rasp. "What an absolute challenge you pose? How great a temptation to his sensibilities?" His mouth slid down to hers, to nibble featherlight kisses against her lips that were even more erotic for all their chasteness, even as his hand brushed slow circles over her abdomen. "Because you are all that, minx. And so much more."

Her heart pounded fiercely. Each slow circle over her belly brought his hand tantalizingly closer to the throbbing ache waiting between her legs for his touch.

She squeezed her eyes shut in a desperate attempt to fight back the longing rising inside her to give over completely to her desires. No matter how much pleasure he gave her, he was still her enemy . . . wasn't he?

"You're wrong," she forced out in a breathless whisper. She was desperate to find port in the storm before the fog of desire could close over her again, before she lost herself completely in his arms. "Whitby didn't say any of those things." Longing to see any kind of reaction in him that she could read to understand what, if anything, he felt for her, she announced, "He proposed."

His hand stilled against her. For a heartbeat neither of them moved.

She held her breath and waited for the jealousy she'd glimpsed in him earlier to rise to the surface, for him to declare that he would never allow her to marry Whitby or any other man—that he wanted her for himself. Winslow Shipping and her father both be damned.

Oh, how wonderful if he would do exactly that! If he would look past her frayed reputation and wild antics, past the hard façade she showed to the world, to see who she truly was beneath. If he could accept her as she was, all uncertain and confused and wanting him in her life the way she'd never wanted any other man…

If he would give up the partnership and choose her.

Instead, he dropped his hand away and shifted back just far enough to stare down into her face. Just far enough that he was no longer touching her, and the sudden absence of his body against hers left her feeling cold and inexplicably alone, even though he stood mere inches away. The small space between them gaped as wide as a chasm.

He asked quietly, "Did you accept?"

Rejection pierced her. The heat he'd flamed inside her only moments before now turned as cold as the wintry night around them. But even as she blinked hard to clear away the sudden stinging in her eyes, she knew she was a fool to hope for any other reaction. Even if a tiger could change its stripes, it would still be a beast.

With her foolish heart breaking, her pride got the best of her. "You'd like that, wouldn't you?" she whispered, knowing her voice would break if she spoke any louder. Thank God for the shadows that hid any traces of anguish visible on her face and how much his indifference pained her. How foolish she'd been to think she might be special to him! "Then you'd get the partnership so easily."

"This isn't about business." He reached up to rub a stray tendril of her hair between his thumb and forefinger. "I want you to be happy with whomever you decide to marry." Although, from the way he said that, he didn't seem pleased at all at the idea. After a pause, he admitted, "I know you, Mariah, and you'd never be happy with a man like Whitby."

She swallowed hard as he trailed his fingers down her throat, as if he couldn't keep himself from touching her. He was far less dangerous when he was only her enemy. "You don't know me."

"So much better than you think." He leaned closer, so close that the warmth of his lips tickled hers. "You need a husband who loves you, who challenges you. One who brings out the passion in you."

Her heart skipped. She very much wanted a husband who would give her all of that. And not just the intimate pleasures he'd so rakishly insinuated, but quieter moments born of laughter and teasing, challenging conversations, support and advice...a shared empathy over losing a parent. And when she thought of children and how caring and kind Robert was with Polly, how much love and devotion he showed to his niece and nephew—

She wanted those things with *him*.

The realization tore through her so unexpectedly that it ripped her breath away.

God help her, she wanted a life with Robert Carlisle, the most impossible man in the world for her. She shook at all that implied, trembling so violently that goose bumps dotted her skin, and in her shock, she could do nothing more than stare at him, wide-eyed and lips parted, and somehow remember to breathe.

All she'd wanted her entire life was to work for Winslow Shipping. Yet somehow during the past few weeks that dream had changed, and now she wanted more than simply a role within the company. She wanted the company *and* Robert, wanted both a home with him and a place at her father's side. Dear heavens, she wanted it all.

Instead of filling her with happiness, that thought made tears sting at her eyes and nose, and her throat tightened with the threat of sobs. She pressed her clenched fist hard against her chest to try to ease the pain. But every breath burned in her lungs, every beat of her heart was excruciating—

Because that life would never be hers. Because Robert didn't want *her*.

He wanted Winslow Shipping.

Misunderstanding her silence as loyalty to Whitby, he demanded quietly, "Does he challenge you intellectually or make you feel safe when you're with him? Does he make you laugh with abandon and smile until your face aches?"

"None of that matters," she lied, blinking rapidly, her voice a hoarse rasp. All this time she'd been fighting against him, when he now stood in front of her as the only man she wanted for her husband. The only man capable of bringing her all the joys and pleasures he'd listed.

"More than you realize." He stepped closer and made her

yearn for what she could never have—his affections. "Do you find yourself wanting to run to him to share something amusing? Is he the man you think of when you're upset and need to be comforted?"

You! I think of you. But if he discovered how she truly felt, she would never live down the humiliation. So she forced out, "Yes!"

"You're lying." Another step closer, this one so close that she could feel the heat of him radiating down her front, and she longed to take a single step forward to place herself into his arms. "I know for certain that he doesn't make you crave his touch." His voice grew husky as he lowered his mouth to her ear, his warm breath tickling over her skin so deliciously that she shivered. "That it's not him you dream of at night making you cry out in passion."

"*None* of that matters." Her hands clenched into fists at her side to keep herself from reaching for him. "Whitby is a kind and generous man. Unlike you," she accused unfairly, yet wanting desperately to make him angry. When they were furious at each other, she didn't long to be in his embrace, didn't crave his mouth and hands on her, didn't yearn to hear words of love fall from his lips. "You think you have a right to possess anything you want."

His eyes flared with a predacious heat that made her shudder "Yes." He closed the distance between them, wrapping his arms around her waist and tugging her hard against him. His head lowered so close to hers that she felt each word caress over her lips when he murmured, "And what I want is you."

His mouth captured hers, hot and hungry, once again making her head spin. He kissed her breath away, and she trembled when his hands reached up to cup her face between his palms to hold her mouth still beneath the intensity of his kiss. With her breasts pressed against the hard planes of his chest, she could feel his heart slamming against his ribs, each beat pulsing into her until she couldn't tell if the pounding heartbeat was hers or his.

She tore her mouth away and panted for breath, desperately needing air to clear away the swirling confusion spinning through her. Her hands grasped his wrists to keep him from reaching for her again, because this time she didn't think she'd have the strength to stop him.

"But you also want the partnership, and you cannot have both," she countered in a whisper filled with pain as the impossible truth sliced brutally into her. "Which do you want more, Robert?" Her voice was little more than a breathless whisper as she laid out the choice for him, the one she feared she would lose—"Winslow Shipping or me?"

He stared down at her, his face unreadable in the shadows.

But that moment's indecision ripped through her soul like a dagger of ice. Shaking her head, with tears blurring her eyes no matter how fiercely she blinked them away, she pushed against him to slip out of his arms—

"Mariah?" A feminine voice broke the silence of the garden. "Where are you?"

She startled with a surprised gasp. Then she moved away from Robert to put several feet between them. But there wasn't room in all of London to hide what they'd been doing if anyone came upon them.

"Robert?" The woman called out. Then faint irritation darkened her voice, "For goodness' sake! *One* of you has to be out here. I've searched everywhere else."

Oh God…*the duchess*. Mortification swept through her so strongly that she thought she might be ill. With all of her shaking, Mariah frantically shed Robert's jacket and shoved it at him. "Go," she urged in a fierce whisper. "Go to her."

He shook his head and reached for her. "Mariah—"

"Just go!" she choked out. "We can't let her find us like this. You'll lose the partnership, and I'll—" *I'll lose everything.* Her cheeks heated with humiliation. And panic. If the duchess stumbled upon them like this, they'd be forced to marry; she'd cost him the partnership, and he'd resent her for it. She couldn't bear that! "Tell her that I'm inside in the retiring room, or off with Evie. Tell her *anything*." She shoved him away. "Please, Robert, go!"

As his mother called out again, this time from much closer, he grudgingly capitulated with a curse. He ducked beneath the branches and paused only a moment to cast her a parting glance.

"This isn't over," he warned, then walked away into the garden, toward the duchess.

Sucking in a ragged breath, Mariah collapsed against the tree trunk and hung her head in her hands. All of her shook as the emotions raged inside her, as humiliation and desire and loss all threatened to overwhelm her.

Not over. Exactly what worried her.

When her breathing had calmed and her heart no longer pounded so hard that each beat sent a jolt of pain echoing through her chest, she drew her spine up straight and moved out from beneath the tree. The shadow-filled garden was once again silent and empty. For a moment, she stared at the house, lit like a glowing beacon in the night.

Then she turned away and slipped into the darkness.

CHAPTER ELEVEN

❧◦~~◦~~◦❧

$\mathcal{A}$n hour later, Robert opened the door of the shipping office and met Mariah's gaze in the dim light from the stove's coals. He'd spent the last hour crossing London in the dark of night—and the last half of it beneath a flurry of falling snow—yet the sight of her instantly warmed away the cold.

"You've found me," she murmured, her voice as soft as the shadows.

"I told you." He stepped inside and closed the door. "I know you better than you think."

When she didn't return from the garden, he'd searched for her, only to find her missing from the ball. He knew she hadn't gone home. That she'd be here instead, seeking comfort in the place she loved most in the world.

Yet he wasn't prepared for the sharp pang in his gut at finding her sitting on the floor like that in front of the small fire, still wearing her ball gown and looking so vulnerable. Or for the intense desire he felt to sweep her into his arms, to give her strength and solace until the wounded fragility in her vanished.

The sensation stunned him. He'd known lots of women, but he'd never wanted to protect or comfort one of them before. That it was Mariah, of all women, surprised the devil out of him. But the minx had him longing to do just that. The desire to keep her safe, to hear her laughter and see the spark of amusement inside her, to share ideas and debates with her—all of that outweighed the far simpler desire to make love to her. He wanted her for the woman she was. *All* of her. Every last aggravating, troublemaking, wickedly daring inch of her.

As he stared at her, he knew the truth. That after tonight, one way or another, there would be no going back.

He leaned against the door, keeping his distance. For now. "Where else would you have gone but here?"

"The school." Her chin lifted slightly in proud defiance, and he smiled at the fight in her, even now.

"Not at midnight," he countered gently. "The children aren't there." She drew her strength from those children. That school was her heart.

But this office...*this* was her soul.

She turned away to stare at the coals glowing in the stove. "You must think me a goose to come here."

"Not at all," he answered softly.

She sent him a disbelieving glance over her shoulder, but for once, she didn't argue. Instead, she drew her knees to her chest and admitted, "I love it here, you know. Papa doesn't understand that. He thinks this place is just an office like any other, but it's not. It's so much more."

He said nothing, afraid to break the fragile trust she was placing in him. But when she reached up to remove the pins from her hair, he nearly groaned.

Tonight had left him aggravated and aching, from the moment he first saw her when he arrived at her house to escort her to the ball. The tension inside him wasn't helped by that heated encounter in the garden, or by having to lie to his mother to explain her disappearance afterward. Somehow he'd managed to convince her that Mariah had taken ill and, not wanting to cut her sister's evening short, had asked him to send her home alone in the carriage, only to then have to think up an excuse for himself to leave, so that he could go after her.

Now she sat there on the floor in front of him, the sight of her knotting the frustration inside him even tighter. How was it possible that she could appear both so inviting yet untouchable? That she could twist his insides and anger him to the point of desire? When he saw her dance with those other men and give them the beautiful smiles she kept from him, *that* had nearly undone him.

No wonder he'd lost his mind in the garden. She simply inverted his world.

"When I was a little girl, whenever something happened to upset me," she shared as she carefully removed her hairpins, "I always came here. This place comforted me. All those familiar scents and sounds, all the possibilities of what the ships carried from around the world. Because they didn't carry only goods." She set the pins aside on the floor. "They carried dreams. And if they could bring such exotic promises from the far corners of the world, then I could believe that anything was possible."

She ran her fingers through her hair, and his gut squeezed. Hard. She had no idea what she did to him, the flames she fanned inside him even now as she shook free her hair until it fell in loose waves down her back.

"I came here when Mama died," she admitted in a whisper. "I ran away from the house and didn't stop running until I reached the office. I stayed here all day and night, refusing to go home. Papa finally had to carry me out to the carriage. But as soon as we arrived home, I came right back."

He smiled faintly, easily imagining her doing just that. Based on how obstinate she could be as an adult, he had no doubt that she was willful as a child. Just another part of the strong, independent woman she'd become.

"This business has been my life," she explained softly. "It's been here as long as I can remember—my first memory, in fact, is of Papa coming home from work with a Chinese marionette." She gave a melancholy smile. "One of the captains had brought it back as a gift for Evie and me. It was the funniest thing, watching Papa sitting there on the nursery floor with us, trying to make it dance by jiggling all those strings." Her smile faded, and her eyes grew intense. "This business is all I've ever known, Robert. I would never do anything to harm it."

"Neither would I," he promised.

"But it's not part of you." She shook her head, closing her eyes. "You don't love it."

"I wouldn't say that," he murmured, trailing his gaze affectionately over her and noticing everything about her... from the graceful curve of her neck to the way she tucked her knees to her chest, from the delicate way she parted her lips to the long lashes lying beneath eyes softly closed in this moment of vulnerability.

She was so much more than only the Hellion, and he was a damned fool for not seeing it sooner. Just like her father, he'd convinced himself that she had no business running the company. That a harridan with a tongue as sharp as a dagger and a personality as prickly as a cactus deserved whatever clodpole of a husband fate thrust upon her.

But that was before he'd discovered what she was truly like. Before he'd come to realize exactly how brilliant she was, how much she cared for the sailors and longshoremen and their families. Before he learned of her work with the school.

Before he'd come to care about her.

Her slender shoulders sagged wearily, and she whispered, "I don't want to fight with you anymore, Robert."

"That's too bad," he said quietly, knowing how the spirit inside Mariah drew him the way no other woman ever had. All the others simply paled in comparison to her fire. "Because I like the fight in you."

She opened her eyes and quirked a disbelieving brow. "You like kissing me when I make you angry."

He nodded, deadpan. "That, too."

She laughed faintly, then tilted her head as she studied him, as if finally seeing him as the man he was instead of as her enemy.

"You chased after me all the way from Mayfair when you could have let me go." She shook her head. "When you *should* have let me go." Her eyes glistened in the light from the coals. "Why?"

His chest clenched hollowly at the sight of her, so vulnerable and delicate, so undeniably alluring, even sitting in the middle of the floor. He remembered the spicy-sweet taste of her on his lips and the softness of her curves pressed against his hard body as much as he remembered the way she'd held and comforted Polly at the school, her concern for her sister, her affection for his mother and niece…He'd never met a more complicated and intriguing woman in his life.

He couldn't hide the husky rasp of his voice as he answered, "Because I couldn't help myself."

From across the room, he felt her catch her breath, so connected was he to this woman and every move she made.

"When we were in the garden," she whispered, her gaze not leaving his, "you said you wanted me."

"Yes," he admitted quietly. There was no point in denying it.

"But you don't."

His brow lifted. "Oh, I think I do."

"No," she argued in whispers. "You want the partnership."

"So do you," he countered quietly. "Why is that wrong?"

Her cheeks darkened self-consciously in the shadows, but she didn't look away. Nor did she deny wanting him, and his heart thumped hopefully at that.

"Because you also want... tonight."

"So do you," he repeated in a low drawl.

She hesitated, and in that moment's pause, she proved him correct, which pleased him far more than he wanted to admit.

"I do want the partnership," he explained quietly, the resolve inside him to possess it as fierce as ever. "I will continue to pursue it no matter what happens between us." His gaze held hers, refusing to let her look away. "But make no mistake, Mariah, about how much I also want you."

Blinking, she asked with utter bewilderment, "*Why?*"

He bit back a tender laugh. Only Mariah would ask that question.

A grin he wasn't able to quash tugged at his lips. "I shouldn't. You're the last woman in the world I should find alluring. Stubborn and challenging, far too intelligent for her own good, a woman who doesn't know her place—"

"Thank you," she drawled dryly with a peeved sniff.

"Yet I find myself drawn to you precisely because you're that challenging and intelligent woman who doesn't know her place." His gaze dropped to her luscious mouth. "And I know you want me as much as I want you."

Her lips parted delicately at his audacity, and she stared at him, for once speechless.

"I'm a rakehell, remember? I know women, and I know you most of all." Sweet Lucifer, she was breathtaking as she stared up at him, stunned into flustered silence. Never...*never* had he seen a more beautiful woman. "I've held you in my arms and felt the way you've craved my kiss. I've felt your pulse race beneath my lips when I kissed your throat and the panting of your breath when you pressed against me. And when I dared to touch you in the garden, I felt how much you wanted me. *That's* why I'm here, Mariah." His gaze swept over her, greedily drinking in the enticing sight of her. She trembled beneath his boldness, and his gut burned at the desire he saw in her. "To finish what we started."

For a moment, neither of them moved. They held each other's gaze across the dimly lit room, and the silence around them was interrupted only by the pounding rush of blood through his ears. Outside, the snow continued to fall and blanket the city, further muting the noise of the night and cocooning them together in the soft shadows cast by the stove's coals.

As he stared at her, his thoughts roiled in a mess of doubts and uncertainties. The affections he held for her went beyond the merely physical—they had become a longing to be with her in every way. He wanted Mariah in his arms, wanted to erase the confusion inside him with her kisses and soft touches. He wanted to take solace in wrapping her body around his and melding together, losing himself in her kindness and comfort.

He prayed to God that she wanted the same.

"Yes," she whispered, the single word of permission tearing through him with the force of a lightning bolt.

He reached for the door and flipped the lock.

* * *

Mariah caught her breath as Robert stalked across the office toward her.

She scrambled to her feet. The tension between them was so strong that she found it impossible to sit still, and nervous excitement swept through her, making her tremble. But she didn't back away, not when he slipped his arms around her waist and pulled her against him. Not when his mouth descended upon hers in a kiss filled with such tenderness and heated promise that she whimpered beneath the intensity of it.

"If you don't want this, say so now, Mariah." He cupped her face against his palm. As his lips nibbled at her ear, his thumb traced over her bottom lip, already hot and moist from his mouth on hers. Each word flamed a primal longing inside her. "Stop me before I lose control completely over you."

"I won't stop you," she breathed, her voice too full of desire and anticipation to speak any louder. "I want tonight... with you."

He scooped her into his arms and carried her up the stairs to a small room at the top of the building, where a simple, narrow bed waited.

With a thin mattress over an old rope-strung frame and

scratchy wool blankets, the bed was used on those nights when her father or Mr. Ledford worked too late into the evening to travel home. But as Robert lowered her onto the bed and followed down over her, kissing her hungrily as she ran her trembling fingers anxiously through the soft hair at his nape, Mariah couldn't imagine a more special place.

"You're shivering," he murmured against her lips as he stroked his hand down her side.

"I'm cold," she dissembled, unwilling to admit how nervous she was. He was a Carlisle, after all. He'd been with more women than she wanted to acknowledge, and if the kisses and touches he'd given her before were any indication, the man was an expert when it came to intimacy. While she— *Good Lord*, how much she shook!

"You won't be cold for long," he teased with an impish grin.

Blushing, she slapped his shoulder. "Robert!"

When he laughed and nuzzled her neck, the teasing was infectious, and she giggled softly. The nervousness eased away until there was only happiness and certainty inside her that this night was good and right, with this man.

He kissed her again, this time flicking his tongue across her lips entreatingly until she parted them with a sigh. His tongue thrust inside in a possessive rhythm that sent her heart racing and her breath panting, and she forgot about the cold and the darkness, knowing only the heat and solidity of his body next to hers.

But even that wasn't enough. She wanted the warmth of his bare skin against hers and longed for more of the aching heat he flamed inside her. She wanted the barrier of her gown and his finery gone from between them, along with all their competition and fighting, until it was only the two of them... man and woman, bared to each other.

She slid off the bed and moved away just far enough to kick off her slippers, then reached behind her back for the tiny buttons—

"Oh no, you don't." He caught her from behind and slipped his arms around her waist. "I get the pleasure of undressing you tonight."

As his rakish words curled through her, anticipation fluttered low in her belly, and she ordered breathlessly, "Then undress me." She thrilled at the control she possessed over him. "And take your pleasure."

He growled in a mix of affection and devilish appreciation, "Minx."

She laughed, delighted at the reckless excitement that pulsed through her. But when he unfastened the first button and placed a hot kiss between her bared shoulder blades, the laughter choked in her throat. Then it turned into a deep sigh when he kissed lower down her spine with each inch of flesh he revealed.

Her bodice fell loose around her shoulders, and he pushed the dress down to puddle on the floor around her feet. She shivered as he knelt behind her and placed a kiss against the small of her back, just below the end of her short stays. She closed her eyes. His mouth on her body... simply heavenly!

His hands slipped beneath her shift to caress her legs—

She jumped with a gasp. "Robert!"

He took her hips in his hands to calm her as he explained in a raspy voice, "Stockings."

That single word was enough to understand why he'd been sliding his hands up her legs, but it didn't ease the nervous fluttering in her belly. "Of course," she whispered breathlessly, not wanting him to think her a complete goose when it came to men.

"I'll leave them on, if you prefer." He placed a tender kiss against the base of her spine, and it twined its way up her back, leaving goose bumps in its wake. "After all, what matters isn't the stockings but the woman inside them."

Her eyes stung at the soft compliment, and she whispered, "Then take them off...if you'd like."

"I'd like it a great deal," he murmured, and his hands once more slid beneath her shift and up her legs.

With a small tug of his fingers, the garter holding the stocking in place slipped free. He traced his fingertips over the lace edge encircling her thigh, then slowly rolled the silk material down her calves, over her feet, and off. One leg, then the other, just as torturously seductive...

When he'd finished, he rose to his full height behind her and stroked his hands up her body and against the side swells of her breasts.

Mariah caught her breath. She barely dared to believe that this was happening. That Robert truly found her desirable. But when he began to pull free the lace of her stays with both hands, each pull coming faster than the one before in his eagerness to have her undressed, his desire filled her with a longing so intense that her eyes blurred with emotion. *This* was what she'd dreamt about, the moment when she could come to him bare and without pretense, as a lover instead of an enemy. And now that it was truly happening, oh, it was simply divine!

She closed her eyes, overwhelmed by nervous anticipation as her stays fell away, leaving her in only her thin shift. Then that, too, was slowly peeled away. The cold air tickled over her bare skin, and excitement pulsed through her as she stood naked in front of him in the shadows of the dark room.

"Dear God, Mariah." He sucked in a ragged breath. "You are so beautiful..."

Stepping forward to bring her into his arms, he captured both breasts against his palms and leaned her back against his chest. The buttons of his waistcoat scraped cold against her spine as he kneaded her fullness, and the wanton sensation sped through her with a yearning ache. She couldn't believe how wonderful the heat of his large hands against her breasts, how tantalizing his fingers teasing at her nipples until they grew hard and aching. Then he pinched them, and a pulse of pleasure-pain shot through her, landing hard between her legs.

"Robert," she whispered, her lips thick with arousal as she arched her back to bring his hands harder against her. There was no shame in so boldly giving herself like this, not to him. No shame in encouraging him to find pleasure in her the way she knew she would find the same in him. Delicious tingles danced through her, and having his hands on her naked body exceeded her wildest fantasies. "I want...I want you to..."

"This?" He slid his hand down her belly and through the triangle of curls, to slip gently into the valley between her thighs.

"Yes," she panted out as his fingers stroked against her, each caress delving deeper into her folds and flaming the throbbing at his fingertips. He touched her confidently, as if he already knew her intimately. Instead of frightening her, that thought completely eased away her nervousness. She closed her eyes as her head rolled back, giving herself over to pure pleasure. "Oh yes...exactly that."

"You are lovely, Mariah," he whispered achingly, his mouth resting at her temple while his hands continued to explore her body and stoke the arousal burning inside her. "So much spirit in you, so much daring, yet still soft and feminine."

Encouraged by his words, she drew a breath to calm the pounding of her heart and shifted her legs farther apart. Her pulse spiked when he groaned softly at her boldness, and a shivering thrill raced through her. His tender caresses intensified against her, harder and deeper, until one finger slipped inside.

She gasped, all of her tensing. It was a sensation unlike any she'd ever experienced, making her feel inexplicably vulnerable and emboldened at the same time. Both wanton and wanted. But when he began to stroke inside her, she melted with a soft sigh and shivered as a delicious warmth spread through her, all the way out to the tips of her fingers and toes.

"So many nights I fantasized about being with you," he murmured as he tenderly kissed the side of her face. "Holding you in my arms, making you happy."

"So did I," she admitted, her eyes stinging at his words. He *was* making her so very happy tonight...although she'd certainly never imagined it feeling as good as this. Each swirling plunge and retreat of his finger came as a tender caress that left her tingling with pleasure and yearning for more, for something she couldn't name but felt approaching with the intensity of an oncoming storm.

"Did you fantasize about me kissing you, too?" His lips nibbled at her earlobe and elicited a tremble from her. "Kissing every inch of you?"

She knew what he meant, and a blush heated her cheeks

and all the way down to her breasts. "Yes," she whispered, "that, too."

Turning her in his arms, he kissed her hungrily as he stepped her backward to the bed. This time when he lowered her to the mattress, he left hot, open-mouthed kisses down her front. He suckled at her breasts until she moaned and her back arched off the bed in sweet torture. Then he continued downward over her belly, lower and lower...

She held her breath as his mouth found the aching place between her thighs, only to exhale with a soft shudder when he placed a tender kiss there. But when he continued to kiss her intimately, she squeezed her eyes closed and bit back a moan. Never...oh, *never* had she imagined being with a man could be both so heavenly yet so wicked at the same time! But only because of Robert. He made her feel beautiful and desired, the way no man ever had before. And as she knew in her heart, the way no other man ever would again.

With alternating kisses and licks, he flamed the fire inside her until all of her shook with an increasing need that begged to be released. She pulsed electric, every nerve ending in her body tingling. The world receded until all she knew was the exquisite feel of his mouth against her, the softness of his hair as she reached down to run her fingers through it, the solidity of his hands stroking her inner thighs and holding her open to his ravishing lips.

When he closed his mouth over the little nub buried within her folds and sucked, her hips bucked off the bed.

"Robert!" she cried out, her fingernails digging into his shoulders.

"Relax, Mariah," he cajoled, each word a hot tickle that pulled tighter the knot in her lower belly. "Let yourself go and enjoy it."

Heavens, if she enjoyed it any more, she'd jump right out of her skin! But she couldn't fight back the flames licking at her toes as he continued to kiss between her thighs. Or the overwhelming urge to wiggle her hips against his mouth.

An appreciative groan escaped him. "It's all your fault, you know," he whispered against her.

"How…is this…my fault?" she panted out between gasping breaths.

"Because you're so delicious that you make me want to devour you."

The brazen audacity of his words poured liquid flames through her, and when he sucked at her again, a shuddering wave of pleasure crashed over her. Her breath came in large gasps as her thighs quivered against his shoulders. She felt as if she were levitating weightlessly off the bed, with only her hands clenching the blanket beneath her to keep her from floating away to heaven.

When the exquisite release waned, she lay still on the mattress. Her eyelids were too heavy to lift as she drank in the residual waves of pleasure lapping softly through her.

Then her desire-fogged mind registered that he had slipped away from her. "Robert?" she whispered anxiously, afraid that he'd changed his mind. That he didn't want her after all.

"I'm right here," he assured her. "I'm not leaving you tonight."

When he returned a few moments later, his clothes were gone, and his naked body was warm and hard and so very large as he slid up the length of hers. Everywhere their bodies touched, heat prickled her skin, and a new, even more intense ache sprang up inside her.

"You are beautiful, Mariah," he murmured.

She opened her eyes. His blue gaze was haunting in the darkness as he stared down at her. The enemy she'd known was completely gone now, and in his place was this wonderful man who was making tonight perfect for her.

He kissed her, with more tenderness and desire than she ever imagined possible. No more animosity between them, no more clothes, no more words...only bare body to bare body, both exposed and vulnerable. Certain that this night with him was good and right, more certain than she'd ever been of anything in her life, she wrapped her arms around him and welcomed him into the cradle of her thighs.

He reached between them to gently caress her as he shifted his body over hers. Her already sensitized flesh ached from even this light touch, yet she yearned for more. She knew how men and women took their pleasure in each other, and if having his mouth on her had been that exquisite, then his body inside hers would surely be bliss.

His hand slipped away from her. Instantly bereft, she let a whimper of protest rise to her lips—

Then a hardness nestled down against her sex, and she tensed as he lowered his hips and slipped inside her warmth, inch by slow inch. She held her breath at the unfamiliar sensation of being filled and stretched as her body expanded around his.

She squirmed beneath him. Not uncomfortable exactly, but neither was it the same wonderful pleasure he'd given her with his hand and mouth. She blinked back the hot tears of disappointment threatening at her lashes, not wanting him to see how upset she was.

Holding himself over her on his forearms, he lifted his hips to retreat, then lowered himself again, this time sinking deeper and causing her to spread her legs wider around his hips to be more comfortable. All of him shook, and the way his body clenched so stiffly over hers only added to her discomfort. She bit back the urge to tell him to relax, just as he'd done to her.

A low groan escaped him. "Sweet Jesus... you're so hot and tight."

"I'm sorry," she choked out, no longer able to hold back tears that he should find her so disappointing.

Despite his grim smile, he gave a tense laugh and placed a quick kiss to her lips to reassure her. "That's a good thing, minx."

She didn't believe him. "Is it?"

"A *very* good thing." He squeezed his eyes shut and repeated the slow retreat and plunge. This time he slid deeper, her body forced to stretch even wider to accommodate him.

She wiggled her hips beneath him to ease the pressure—

"Mariah," he rasped out. Then he lost his fight for restraint and shoved his hips forward, plunging inside her to the hilt.

The thin barrier inside her tore, and she gasped at the sharp pinch. He froze, as if her pain had pierced into him. When she was finally able to catch her breath again and the pounding heartbeat in her ears subsided with the pain, she heard him whispering over and over how special she was, how beautiful...

This time, her tears had nothing to do with disappointment.

Slowly, he stroked his hips again in the same rising and falling motion as before, but now there was none of the uncomfortable pressure, none of that feeling of being stretched to the breaking point. Now, there was only smooth, strong glides of his body inside hers. Oh, how wonderful it was!

His manhood filled her completely, and each caressing plunge and retreat created a tingling friction inside her that was so much better than what he'd done to her before. That had been wonderful, but this—this was heavenly!

"Robert." His name emerged as single word of satisfaction and encouragement.

She locked her ankles against the small of his back and arched herself off the mattress to meet each downward stroke of his hips, each one coming faster and deeper than the one before. She clung to him, reveling in the hardness of his muscular body, in the familiar scent of him that filled up her senses, and in the weight of his body pressing deliciously down onto her. Never, *never* had she imagined being with a man would be so freeing, somehow both tender and primal at the same time.

The gentleness between them grew into something more fervent, something she couldn't name but that swelled inside her until she wanted to burst from the intensity of it.

"So good," he murmured into her hair. "So unbelievably good...only with you, Mariah."

A tear of joy rolled down her cheek. She buried her face against his shoulder as a rush of happiness swept through her, and her heart sang.

Then his rhythm changed. Now with every deep thrust, he ground his pelvis against her to rub at that aching nub where he'd so wickedly sucked before. Each thrust sent a tingle of heat shooting through her, like a spark struck from a flint. She tensed in his arms, her body bearing down shamelessly around him—

Wildfire flashed through her, and she cried out as she broke.

All her muscles clenched and released in a pulsating

wave that crashed over her and filled up her soul. She could do nothing more than cling to him, helpless and breathless, as spots flashed before her eyes. All of her shook in a delicious contradiction of mindless satiation and soaring joy.

He thrust hard inside her now, driving toward his own release. Once, twice—he strained against her on the final plunge, holding himself deep, and his thighs and buttocks clenched as a low growl tore from him. She felt his essence spilling inside her, filling her as deliciously as if he'd poured his soul into her. Then he collapsed on top of her, panting hard to catch his breath as their heartbeats pounded into each other.

Sliding her arms up to encircle his neck, she wanted to keep him close in her embrace for as long as possible. She had no idea what would happen between them when dawn came. But tonight he belonged to her, and she refused to let him go a moment sooner than she had to.

Tonight, for the first time in her life, she'd dared to imagine a different future for herself than the one she'd always wanted. A future not running Winslow Shipping but one with Robert, one in which they laughed together during the day and shared their passions at night.

Her heart ached, overwhelmed both by the joy he'd just given her and by the uncertainty of tomorrow. Because somehow, amid all the arguments and fighting, during all the dinners and balls and teas, she'd fallen in love with Robert Carlisle.

CHAPTER TWELVE

Robert nuzzled Mariah's hair as she lay nestled against him and tightened his arms around her. Making love to her had been nothing short of breathtaking, but holding her like this afterward, when he'd never before wanted to remain with a woman after the act itself was over...

Heaven.

But what came next? Everything had irrevocably changed between them. Oh, they would still fight, he had no doubt about that. But now he hoped they could turn that anger into passion, because while he had no idea what would happen between them going forward, he knew he couldn't give her up.

Give her up? Hell, he couldn't bring himself to leave the bed! Even now he preferred to shiver in the cold darkness rather than part from her to start a fire. And that troubled him, because if he felt this strongly connected to her, what did she feel toward him?

A true gentleman would marry her for taking her

innocence. March straight to her father, offer for her hand, then get a special license and wed her as soon as possible, especially since he'd not taken precautions. But he couldn't offer without looking like an opportunistic fortune hunter in Winslow's eyes. And *that* bothered him more than he wanted to admit. So did the knowledge that in doing so he would most likely lose both Mariah and the partnership.

She stirred and wiggled toward the edge of the bed.

"Don't go." He pulled her back into his arms, but his heart pounded with worry that he was already losing her. "I want you right here with me."

She rolled onto her back and stared up at him, a moment's hesitation on her beautiful face.

He held his breath, waiting for her to speak. To say *anything*. She'd been silent since the moment she'd cried out in pleasure, and he wasn't used to such silence from the women he bedded. Or from Mariah.

What was going through her mind? She'd been an innocent, not some jaded society lady looking to ease an evening's boredom. Despite his reputation as a rake, he'd never taken a woman's innocence before, and he didn't know what to expect from her now. Tears, anger...regret?

When she smiled and reached to brush a lock of hair away from his forehead, the worry in his chest eased away. "But it's cold," she explained. "Which is all your fault."

He grinned. Typical Mariah, to blame him for the winter. "How is that my fault?"

"You had me undressed and in bed before I could light a fire."

He grinned and nuzzled her bare shoulder. "You lit a bonfire, minx."

"Robert!" A hot blush of embarrassment colored her

cheeks. Then she giggled and smiled happily against his mouth when he kissed her.

"I'll light a fire, then, shall I?" he offered.

She stared up at him through lowered lashes in a look of wanton innocence that stole his breath away. "Please do."

With a playful growl at her innuendo, he kissed her again, hot and open-mouthed, plundering her lips until she moaned.

Then he slid off her and out from beneath the scratchy blanket. He reached for the tinderbox on the shelf over the little stove in the corner. In a few minutes, he had a fire going, small but enough to keep her warm.

"Robert?"

"Hmm?" He jabbed the poker into the stove at the coals.

She sat up, clutching the wool blanket to her breasts to cover herself. A pang of regret stabbed him that she'd lost her innocence in that poor excuse for a bed, with wool and straw scratching at her soft skin, when she should have had satin, velvet, and down. Yet she would have looked like a goddess even wrapped in burlap.

"You courted Diana Morgan last season," she said quietly. A strange quality filled her voice that he couldn't quite place. "Did you and she ever spend time together…like this?"

Understanding fell through him, and he realized that what he'd heard in her was insecurity, something he'd not witnessed in her before. It had never occurred to him until right then that the Hellion might have been just as jealous of Diana as he was of Whitby.

"Nothing happened between us," he assured her gently. He set down the poker and admitted with a heavy sigh, "In fact, I never should have courted her at all." He shook his head. Looking back now, he realized just how wrong he'd been. "I thought I needed to put a stop to all the wildness of my younger days and settle down. Diana seemed a good way to do that, but I was wrong. Thank God we both realized it in time."

"Stop your wildness?" She dubiously arched a brow. "Didn't you rent an elephant for a party last May?"

He grinned and flipped closed the stove door. "I was easing into it."

When he stood and turned around to rejoin her in bed, she gasped. Her eyes flared wide with surprise, and her red lips pulled into a round O.

He stopped. And frowned. What on earth...?

Then her gaze slowly sank down his front, and the realization hit him that she was seeing him clearly for the first time. *All* of him. From her surprised reaction, she was taking her first-ever glimpses of a naked man. And if she kept staring at him like that, with her gaze fixed on his cock and her curiosity filling him with immense pleasure, she'd also have her first glimpse of a fully aroused naked man.

When she nervously licked her lips, he groaned and lost the battle to stay flaccid beneath her gaze. He stalked toward her, then crawled onto the mattress and up the length of her on hands and knees, until she lay completely on her back beneath him. Her hands still clutched the blanket shyly to her chest.

But she persisted with their conversation, as if it were perfectly normal to have a naked man poised over her on all fours. "But Diana is so lovely and you—"

He silenced her with a kiss. "I came to realize that Diana isn't the type of woman I want in a wife," he concluded with finality. The last thing he wanted to think about tonight was a past courtship, not when he had Mariah naked in bed and the rest of the night ahead of them. He hooked a finger beneath the edge of the blanket and tugged it down until he'd exposed a single full breast.

She closed her eyes, and her breath came ragged as he circled his fingertip around her dusky nipple. It drew up taut. Like magic.

She arched her back and panted out, "Then what…do you want…in a wife?"

He grinned. "I want—"

You.

He froze, stunned at the slip he'd almost made.

Good God, where had *that* come from? True, if she were anyone other than Winslow's daughter, he would offer marriage to her without hesitation. Because he wanted to protect her reputation and his honor. Because she challenged him intellectually while also stirring his passions. Because he'd come to care about her, more than any other woman.

But to *want* her for a wife implied a lasting devotion he couldn't yet bring himself to acknowledge. No matter his growing affections for her.

"An Italian opera singer," he replied instead, forcing a teasing tone as he placed a kiss to her breast.

She slapped lightly at his shoulder. "Be serious."

"I am." He tongued her nipple and drew a shiver from her that made his heart skip. "I've never been more serious about anything in my life."

"An Italian opera singer?" she challenged and ran her fingers appreciatively through his hair as he took her nipple fully into his mouth and suckled at her.

"Nothing puts more fire into a man's blood than hearing all those high notes fall from a woman's lips." As he laved her left nipple, his other hand moved up to caress her right one. His thumb strummed across the taut bud as he teased, "You can't expect to ask a man to give that up for something as inconsequential as marriage."

"Of course not," she agreed with mock solemnity. "That would be like asking the tide not to rise or the sun not to set."

He grinned against her breast. "An act of futility?"

"An act against nature." When he shifted to worship the other breast, she sighed and wrapped her arms around his neck to keep him close, then whispered sincerely, "I wouldn't change a single thing about you."

Stunned by that, he stilled as the simple compliment warmed his insides. Perhaps she held an affection for him after all. And at that, his heart skipped for an altogether new reason.

He buried his face in her shoulder. He felt satiated and relaxed. No. So much more than that—he felt happier than he'd been in a very long time. The fact that Mariah, of all women, was responsible for it made his head spin.

She drew a deep breath, then admitted softly, "I think Diana was in love with you."

At the somber tone of her voice, he raised his head and gazed down at her. Then frowned. Because it wasn't insecure jealousy that he saw in her now, but something else...something warm and affectionate that made him tremble. "What makes you so certain?"

She stared into his eyes, so intensely that she stole his breath away. "Because I—" She cut herself off. Whatever she was about to say was lost as she amended with a smile, "Because I've heard all your mother's stories about you and—"

He kissed her to silence her, then lingered with his mouth against hers, drinking in the spicy-sweetness of her kiss until he went light-headed with arousal. "Please don't mention my mother when you're naked with me."

She laughed, then wiggled wantonly and elicited a groan from him. "You expect this to happen again, then?"

He grinned down at her. "Sweet Lucifer, I hope so."

She inhaled sharply as he tenderly traced his fingertips across her nipples, then closed her eyes and whispered, "So we've become lovers, then."

"We have." He lowered his head to dance kisses across her bared breasts, unable to get enough of her. Lovers…*his* lover. A satisfying sense of masculine possession flamed inside him.

"Good," she whispered, and he thrilled at that single word, reveling in her uninhibited boldness with him.

This was what attracted him to her, that the same beautiful woman who could be so prickly and distant held within her a fierce passion waiting to be unlocked and a vulnerable heart that she'd now placed into his care. So many facets to her that every moment brought a new discovery about the woman beneath.

"But I won't…surrender," she panted out, her voice full of resolve even as she arched herself against him. "No matter what…happens between us…"

"No matter what?" Devilishly, he slipped his hand between her legs. "Even this?" He stroked his thumb across the little nub buried at the top of her folds, and her hips bucked.

She tightened her arms around his shoulders and buried her face against his neck. "Even that," she forced out. Then she inhaled sharply and shivered. "Oh, Robert, do that again!"

Biting his cheek to keep from laughing, he did as she bade. This time, a whimper of need fell from her lips.

"You're not my enemy, Mariah," he murmured against her temple as he slowly withdrew his hand. Making love to her again was so very tempting. But it was too soon, and she would be too sore. The last thing he wanted to do was hurt her, in any way. "You mean so much more to me than that."

She pulled back just far enough to look up at him, and her eyes searched his face, as if she couldn't quite believe him. "Do I?"

"A great deal," he assured her, tenderly brushing an ebony curl from her cheek.

Yet her face fell as she whispered, "But you don't trust me."

"I do," he insisted, having given her no reason to doubt him in that.

But she slowly shook her head, and sadness darkened her face as she whispered, "Not about your father. You still haven't told me everything about the day he died." She hesitated. "Or why your mother thinks you blame yourself."

He froze, his hand stilling against her cheek. The soft accusation in her words cut into him like shards of glass, and he hesitated, needing a moment to steady himself before explaining, "I don't want to burden you when you won't understand."

Her eyes softened as they searched his face, her fingers combing tenderly through the hair at his temple. "Are you so very hard to understand, Robert?"

His chest squeezed painfully, not to hold in the anguish he'd suffered for the past two years but with a desperate desire to share it. Perhaps she *would* understand the horror of that day and the weight of the blame he carried. After all, she knew the frustration of trying to please a father, just as he did, and she knew the loss of a parent.

"Richard Carlisle," he offered cautiously, carefully

testing the new trust forming between them, "was a good man and a kind husband, a concerned father..." He sucked in a deep breath. "And I disappointed him."

She rested her palm sympathetically against his cheek. "You didn't disappoint him."

"A great deal." He shook his head in self-recrimination. "I was always the one who caused the most trouble, thought up the pranks, planned all the games and wagers. Quinton would agree with whatever wild scheme I'd concocted, and Sebastian would go along to keep us from harming ourselves too badly. But I was the ringleader, the one who kept thinking up even wilder antics for us."

"You were young," she whispered. "Boys are often wild and uncontrollable."

"But it didn't stop when we grew up. It became worse." At the somber darkness that flashed across her face, he turned his head to kiss her palm. He appreciated her concern, if not the pain she was forcing him to dredge to the surface. "I was a grown man and old enough to know better, yet I kept partaking in the same wild debauchery as I did at university, racking up huge gambling losses, and damaging the family's reputation. Finally, Father had enough."

A knowing empathy lit her green eyes. "He spoke with you about it?"

"More of a lecture, in public and with every intention of trying to bring me to my senses." Even now he could hear his father's deep voice speaking the words as clearly as if he'd said them only minutes before rather than two years ago...*I raised you to be a man. But when I find you like this, behaving as you are, I am disappointed in you.*

She asked softly, "Why did he lecture you?"

"Because I'd launched into a spree of drinking, gambling,

and whoring of such infamous proportions that it threatened the reputation of the Carlisle family and the new title." He wasn't exaggerating, and he could tell by the emotion in her eyes that she realized that, too. "I'd been missing for three days when Father came after me. When he found me, I had just lost five hundred pounds in a game in which I'd been too foxed to see the cards clearly and was attempting to assuage the grief of my losses by letting the barmaid...*comfort* me in the back room."

She swallowed hard at that bit of news, the only outward sign that his actions shocked her. "He was worried about you."

His chest tightened with guilt. "And what kind of son makes his father worry about him?"

"*Every* son," she whispered.

He shook his head. "Not like that."

She knew not to press the issue and turned her attention instead to caressing her thumb across his chin. "What happened then?"

"He'd pulled me out of the hell, stumbling drunk and furious," he explained, his voice raspy with emotion. "He ordered me back to Park Place with him, but I had every intention of finishing my spree." The bitter taste of grief rose in his mouth. "After all, I wasn't a child to be ordered about by his father. I was a man, and I was going to prove it by gambling away even more money and tupping as many women as possible." Then he added quietly, "An hour later, he was dead."

She gasped, the breath tearing from her in her pained surprise.

He squeezed shut his eyes, unable to bring himself to look at her for fear of the shock he'd see on her face, or the pity. Or worse—the same condemning disappointment he'd seen on his father's face.

He forced himself to continue. "As he was mounting his horse to leave, someone fired off a pistol. The horse startled and threw him, and he struck his head." Sharing what happened that night was brutal, but he *had* to tell her everything now. Telling Mariah was the only way to purge the shaking that gripped him and the metallic taste of helplessness forming on his tongue. "I heard the shot and saw him fall backwards, saw his head hit the cobblestones and the blood pool around him..." He shuddered violently. The same helplessness that had consumed him that night returned as the image flashed through his mind, branded there forever. So much helplessness that it choked the air from him even now, and he had to force out around the knot in his throat, "For Christ's sake! I was less than twenty feet away, and I couldn't do anything to save him."

Her arms tightened around him as she silently tried to console him, but even her loving embrace wasn't enough to ease the guilt he'd carried since that night. And always would.

"I never had the chance to apologize, to promise to correct my ways," he murmured, burying his face against her shoulder. "He died thinking I was a drunkard and a scoundrel. That I was nothing more than a worthless scapegrace who didn't give a damn about the family's reputation. Or mine."

"He didn't think that," she whispered soothingly. "He knew you would change your ways."

"Did he?" he bit out. "Because I sure as hell didn't. Not until it was too late."

She cupped his face between her hands and gently lifted

his mouth up to kiss him, her lips touching his in a kiss so tender, so filled with comfort that he trembled.

When she lowered herself away, he opened his eyes, expecting to see pity on her face. What he saw instead ripped his breath away. Her eyes glistened brightly with unshed tears for him, and her compassion tore deep into his heart.

"That's why you've been pushing yourself so hard, why you're so driven," she whispered. "Because you're trying to prove that you're worthy of the Carlisle name. And your father's love."

A ragged sigh tore from him, and his shoulders sagged, his head hanging. "Yes."

She hesitated before gently whispering, "But you're never going to."

His heart stuttered painfully. Then he narrowed his eyes. Did she think so little of him after all? "I am well on my way to being successful—"

"You're never going to," she repeated, more forcefully despite the tremor in her voice, but this time she blinked hard to keep back tears.

Surprise turned to anger that even now she would be concerned about that blasted partnership. How could she hold that over his head, now of all times? He'd placed his trust in her, damn it! Only to have it thrown back into his face.

He forced back a curse and ground out, "Because of Winslow Shipping?"

"No." A tear escaped down her cheek. "Because he's dead, Robert. No matter how hard you work, no matter how successful you become, he'll never know, and you'll have spent your life chasing after an approval which will never come. It cannot, not now—" A soft sob choked in her throat. "It never will."

Guilt that he was causing her pain clawed at his gut, but she didn't understand. Could *never* understand. "So I should just give up," he drawled bitterly, "surrender the partnership?"

"No!" She cupped his face and brought him down for another kiss, this one meant to both silence and reassure in equal measure. "I'm not saying that."

He turned his head away before her lips could touch his, and she stiffened at his rejection. "Yes, you are."

He untangled her arms from around his shoulders and shoved himself out of the bed. She scrambled to sit up, clutching at the blanket to cover herself as he stomped away.

"Perhaps I am," she explained calmly, yet the frustration in her voice was palpable. "But not for the reason you think."

"Oh, I think it's *exactly* the reason," he muttered. He snatched up his breeches and yanked them on. "Even now you can't stand the thought that I'll be able to prove myself to my father's memory when you'll never be able to prove yourself to yours."

She flinched at the harshness behind his attack, yet he only felt a momentary pang of guilt that he'd wounded her. She was overstepping now, by a goodly ways, and the prick of chastisement he'd leveled was *nothing* compared to the anguish she set burning inside him.

He pulled his shirt on over his head and didn't bother with the cravat as he slipped into his waistcoat. The faster he could dress, the faster he could leave. And to think that less than an hour ago he didn't want to let her out of his arms.

"What happened to your father was an accident," she tried again. "And you need to stop blaming your—"

"Don't," he ground out, his eyes narrowing on her. "*Don't* tell me what I need to do, Mariah. What happened between us tonight does not give you that right."

She fell silent. He expected her chin to rise, for the pride in her to surge to the surface the way it always did whenever they fought, for her to retort with some scathing reply—but she didn't. She only sat there unmoving on the bed, her eyes glistening in the dim light from the stove.

He turned away to stomp into his boots, doing his best to ignore the tightening of his chest at the sight of her tears. And the unbearable knowledge that he'd put them there. He muttered, "You don't understand. You never will."

"I lost a parent, too," she whispered softly, so softly that the sound sliced into his heart, "and I used to blame myself. But I know that—"

"You don't know a damned thing!" He wheeled on her, fury pulsing through him. He clenched his teeth so hard that the muscle jumped in his neck. "You didn't kill your mother!"

She inhaled sharply, her eyes widening. For a heartbeat she said nothing, stunned into silence as she stared at him.

Then she breathed out, so softly that her voice wasn't even a whisper, "And you didn't kill your father." She leaned toward him, as if she could physically convince him. "His death was an accident."

"It wasn't an accident that he had to hunt down his son from a gambling hell, smelling of gin and prostitutes." He angrily began to pace the small room, too furious at himself to stand still. "He shouldn't have been there. He should have been safe at home with Mother." His hand shook violently as he raked it through his hair. "If I hadn't been there, if I had been the son he deserved—"

"You *are*, Robert," she insisted softly.

"Not that night I wasn't. Not only was I the son who disappointed him—" The words choked around the knot in his throat. He sucked in a ragged breath, then admitted in a hoarse voice, "I was too drunk to help him."

"He hit his head," she whispered with a soft shake of hers. "There was nothing you could have—"

"You weren't there! You didn't see the look on his face or hear his words, and you'll *never* be able to understand the hell I've gone through since."

She reached for him. "Robert, please—"

"Stop," he hissed, pulling back to keep her from touching him. He couldn't have borne it.

He started toward the door. The urge inside him to flee was overwhelming...from the ghosts of what happened that night, from her kindness and sympathy that only brought more pain, from having to face the truth of what she was saying.

From the moment he'd learned she'd lost her mother, he'd hoped she'd be able to understand his pain, but that was *all* he'd wanted—understanding. He sure as hell wasn't seeking absolution in her arms.

He paused at the door, his hand on the handle, as he tried to think of something to say to her, some parting comment to make her understand. But nothing came. His mind spun too fast to sort through all that had occurred between them tonight. So he stood there, breathing deeply and trying to find his way through the riot of emotions that engulfed him. That pulled at him to finally take him under and drown him.

"It wasn't your fault," Mariah said softly.

He felt the heat of her as she came up behind him and squeezed his eyes shut against the pain. "He was there because of me."

"It was an accident, my darling." Her arms slid around his

waist, and she gently pressed herself against him. She laid her cheek against his back, and he sucked in a mouthful of air through clenched teeth at the scalding torture of her consoling touch. "A terrible, horrible accident."

"Mariah—"

"It wasn't your fault," she repeated, tightening her arms around him, unwilling to let him go. "Just as it wasn't my fault that Mama took us to the park and came down with fever. People die, and there's nothing we can do to stop it. No matter how much we love them. No matter how much—"

A sob fell from her lips as her words choked off, and the sound broke his heart.

He turned and took her into his arms, pressing her tightly against him as she began to cry softly. For him. For both of their losses. He buried his face in her hair to take comfort in her, to breathe in her strength and certainty. To grieve together. As he held her, tears stung in his eyes, and for the first time since his father's death, he released the blame he'd carried inside him.

He exhaled a jerking, anguish-filled breath as he finished for her in a rasping whisper, "No matter how much they love us."

She nodded, unable to speak as she cupped his face in her hands and rose up on tiptoe to kiss away the tears on his cheeks. Then she kissed his lips with such tenderness that he felt the first stirrings of healing deep within his heart. Slowly, the pain eased away until there was only Mariah.

As he lifted her into his arms and carried her back to the bed, he knew he'd been wrong. He *had* found absolution in her arms, and he prayed that she could help him find redemption in the days to come. But more than that. As he lowered her onto the bed and followed down to make love to her, he knew the truth.

Mariah had undone him.

He'd never experienced such a connection with any other woman as he did with her. Physically, emotionally...*never*. Never had he shared such soul-wrenching release. And never had he bared his heart so vulnerably as he just had with her.

He'd fallen in over his head. Because it was more than the partnership that tempted him now. It was the Hellion herself.

And he had no idea what to do about it.

CHAPTER THIRTEEN

❧

*M*ariah's heart skipped. Robert was staring at her. Again.

Sitting at a desk the next morning in the shipping office, Mariah tried to pay him no mind, but he wouldn't stop staring. As if he could see right through her dress to every naked inch of her beneath. Blast the hot blush threatening at the back of her neck at everything that stare implied! And oh, how *very* much it implied.

Even now, surrounded by office workers, she couldn't help but remember the pleasure of being in his arms last night, how he made her feel special and beautiful. Just as she couldn't stop the urge rising inside her to somehow get him alone right now, scandalously in the middle of the afternoon when she was supposed to be going over the warehouse lists for anything Papa might be willing to donate to the school. A flimsy excuse for why she'd come to the office, when the truth was that she'd simply wanted to be near Robert.

But every time she looked at him—and every time she caught him looking back with that knowing twist to his sensuous lips—her mind blanked and her body tingled, in all kinds of wicked ways.

She hadn't known what to expect this morning when they saw each other again, after sharing themselves both physically and emotionally last night. Oh, they would always argue. A tiger would still be a cat even if it managed to change its stripes. But they were no longer enemies.

As for how he felt about her as a woman... well, *that* one she had no answer for. Although they'd spent the night in each other's arms and he'd made her happier than she'd been in her entire life, he'd not once admitted to having feelings for her. And she'd not asked for fear of hearing an answer that might destroy her. Because no matter what he felt for her, she had fallen in love.

He glanced up and caught her watching him. Their gazes locked, and a pulse of heat curled down her spine.

Oh my.

As her cheeks flushed, she looked away. Yet she couldn't stop the flutter of happiness low in her belly.

Without drawing attention to himself, Robert rose from his desk and casually approached her. He leaned over her shoulder as if reaching for the papers in front of her. The nearness of him sent an electric shiver spiraling through her.

"You look beautiful," he murmured low enough that none of the office workers could overhear.

Drat him for making her heart stutter! Yet she somehow managed to roll her eyes at the compliment. "I'm wearing last year's dress."

"Can I help it if you'd look beautiful wrapped in gray drab?" His hand brushed hers as he pretended to examine the inventory, sending a warmth up her arm. "I want to see you tonight."

A soft ache began to throb dully between her legs in quick arousal. How was it possible that he could affect her so viscerally with only a husky murmur? Yet he did just that.

"You *are* going to see me," she reminded him a bit cheekily. "We're having dinner with Lord and Lady Hammond."

"We'll have to beg off, then." His eyes sparkled wickedly. "Because that kind of feast is not what I had in mind."

At his rakish innuendo, she lowered her face and cleared her throat to keep the hot blush at bay as she enticed with a breathy purr, "What, exactly, did you have in mind?"

"Dinner by ourselves at Park Place."

She wheeled around on her chair to face him, unable to stop the happy dancing of her heart. "Park Place?"

Oh, that meant so much more than only a physical intimacy! He was letting her into the most private aspects of his life, and surely, that meant he held affection for her...didn't it?

"Hmm." He reached for the papers to continue the pretense that they were only speaking of business, although from the amused curl threatening at his lips, he knew exactly what she'd been thinking. "I've given the entire staff the night off, down to the last scullery maid. They've all been warned not to step foot inside the house until midnight." He pretended to sort through the lists. "Just you and me, laughing and talking and...*other* things."

That was exactly what she'd longed for. Another night in his arms, another night spent making love to him. "Heavenly," she breathed out. The happiness that sent her heart leaping into her throat made it impossible to speak.

With a slight hesitation, he set the papers onto the desk. "Is it truly?"

"Yes." Instant nervousness knotted her belly. "Why would you doubt that?"

He looked away guiltily. "I wouldn't dare presume that after last night, after the things I revealed to you—"

"Presume it," she whispered breathlessly.

His eyes sparkled with relief as they returned to hers, and with an affection in their sapphire depths that stirred warmth inside her. "So you like me after all."

"Stunned the daylights out of me to realize it, I daresay." She smiled when he chuckled at her. But then it was her turn to hesitate, before she asked nervously, "Does that bother you?"

There was a world of deeper meaning in that simple question. An exploration of emotion neither of them had yet dared to raise.

"There are a great many ways in which you bother me, Mariah Winslow," he admitted, his voice husky and low. "Many tantalizing ways…and many more I hope to teach you tonight."

She lost the battle with her blush, and it sped hotly across her face and down beneath her neckline.

"But you liking me," he assured her quietly, "doesn't bother me at all."

Hope sparkled inside her. "I'm glad." *Very* glad.

His eyes flared possessively, and from the way his body tensed, she knew he felt the same frustration of not being able to reach for her that she did. They hadn't been alone all day, not since they left the offices last night, and not being able to hold him or kiss him was driving her mad. For one desperate moment, she considered the wanton thought of finding some excuse to accompany him upstairs where they could be alone, if only for a few minutes—

The bell over the door jangled as a rush of wintry air blew in from the street, seemingly carrying Whitby along with it. He'd pulled his beaver hat low over his ears in defense against the blustery day, which only served to make his already outsize ears appear even larger. The usual goofy grin lit his face.

"Whitby, you're here!" Mariah came forward to greet him, although more to recover herself and slow her pounding heart than to welcome him. Robert had just admitted to holding affection for her, and while liking was a great long ways from loving, her heart still flipped joyous somersaults. The wait until tonight would be interminable. "I didn't expect you to stop by."

"I wanted to make certain you were feeling better." He frowned at her with concern. "You left the ball so quickly that I didn't get to say good-bye."

She cast a quick glance at Robert. "I—I had a terrible headache and needed to go home." Swift guilt pierced her at the pretense they'd been forced into. But if she had her way, they wouldn't have to lie much longer. "I'm feeling much better today."

Papa's office door opened, and Mr. Ledford stepped out, as always with stacks of ledgers and ships' manifests filling his arms. Distractedly, he nodded to them as he hurried past toward his own desk in the corner of the outer room.

"Carlisle," her father called out from his office doorway, his serious gaze sliding awkwardly past her to Robert. "A word with you."

Mariah stiffened. Her father wanted to talk to Robert? Surely, it was about business. *Couldn't* be about last night. It was impossible that her father could have discovered what they'd done. Not when Robert had returned her home by the time the ball would have ended. Not when they'd given excuses to his mother and Evie that she'd fallen ill and had to leave early. Nothing had appeared amiss.

But if they were found out, *oh God*, it really would be the convent for her!

"Of course." Robert solemnly met Mariah's gaze, not a stray emotion revealed on his stoic face when she was certain that a wealth of guilt and panic gripped hers.

Without a lingering look to betray them, he followed her father into his office.

* * *

Robert closed the door. If this conversation with Henry Winslow was about what happened last night, then he wanted no witnesses to his murder.

He sucked in a deep breath. "You wanted to speak with me?"

Gesturing for him to sit, Winslow crossed to the cabinet in the corner and pulled out a bottle of bourbon. "This requires a drink."

He stiffened. "Oh?"

"And it involves Mariah," Winslow muttered.

Robert's heart skipped. He wasn't ready for this conversation.

After last night, he had every intention of winning both the partnership and Mariah. After he'd taken her home, he'd spent the hours until dawn walking the snow-covered streets of Mayfair and letting the icy air quell the heat of physical desire, until he could think clearly about what happened, what he wanted for his future, and what Mariah deserved for hers. By the time he'd watched the sun rise over Hyde Park, he knew exactly what he wanted. And would settle for nothing less.

But he also knew that he had to tread carefully on both fronts. Because as far as Henry Winslow was concerned, the two were mutually exclusive. The man who claimed his daughter could never assume a position in his business. Yet Robert hoped that Winslow was smart enough to recognize both his business acumen and his affections for Mariah and welcome him into both the family and the company with open arms.

Which was why he wanted to spend the evening with Mariah. More than time together to laugh and talk freely, more than a chance to make love to her again, tonight would be an opportunity to discuss their future.

But being confronted by her father was certainly *not* part of the plan.

"I only want the best for her," Robert admitted quietly. If Winslow realized that, perhaps being force-marched to the altar—and out of Winslow Shipping—could be avoided.

"And she's going to have it! More than her wildest dreams could ever have imagined."

That was unexpected. He blinked. "Pardon?"

Winslow laughed as he splashed golden liquid into two glasses, the sound one of arrogant victory. "Ledford just gave me good news about the docks project."

"The docks." Relief sank through him. He would have to have a conversation about Mariah with her father eventually, but thankfully, not today. "What news?"

With a triumphant smile, he handed a glass to Robert. "The first round of offers to buy up property has gone out to the owners. We've heard back from ten of them who are eager to sell and another five who want to negotiate."

He clinked his glass against Robert's to toast their success. "There's nothing to stop us now!"

"You sent out offers?" Confusion gripped him. So did a sinking feeling of icy dread. "But nothing has been finalized with Parliament. Those docks might never go in, let alone in St Katharine's."

"But they will." Winslow took a long swallow of bourbon, his eyes shining with certainty. "It's more than simply a rumor now. Thomas Telford's been contacted by the crown. They're creating plans as we speak to dredge up the land. And it will be Winslow properties they'll have to purchase to do so. Winslow properties that the traders and captains will have no choice but to use for their warehouses. We've done it!" Another lift of his glass. "*You've* done it, Carlisle."

Dear God, he didn't want responsibility for *this*! "Nothing is certain," he cautioned, praying Winslow would listen to reason. "We should have waited—"

"And give someone else the opportunity to sweep in and take our profits from us?" He shook his head and sank into the large leather chair behind his desk. He gestured for Robert to sit, but Robert remained on his feet, too troubled by Winslow's news to take a seat. "Those docks *will* happen."

"And if they don't?" His chest tightened. It was one thing to speculate about the whims of the king and investigate real estate purchases, but it was something altogether different to commit capital to the scheme. Massive amounts of capital. "We'll be stuck with slum properties, perhaps for years."

Winslow dismissively waved a hand. "Then we profit from our renters until Parliament agrees to put in docks."

"And if they don't?" he repeated grimly.

Winslow's exuberant expression faded, his smile hardening as his eyes cooled. "Then you make them." His voice turned brittle. "That's why you're here. Your connections in Parliament." A pause, so fleeting as to almost be missed, but Robert heard it and understood the silent threat behind it. "Unless you're not up to the task, after all."

He returned the man's stare, his jaw clenching tightly. Winslow wanted him to deny it, to pledge himself even more adamantly to the project to prove his worth. But Robert wouldn't be played. Not this time.

"My reputation"—and now his entire future—"is resting on this company's success. I won't take the blame when your plans fall through, or become a pariah to my friends and family for pushing for these docks just to make a profit."

Winslow's eyes flared with icy anger at being challenged. But he'd damned well better get used to it. When Robert became both the man's partner and his son-in-law, he planned to challenge him at every opportunity.

"Our plans will *not* fail," Winslow returned in clipped tones. "You might have the determination of a man on the rise, but I've got instincts honed over twice as many years in business as you've been alive. My gut is telling me with certainty that we'll be successful, *if* we've got the courage to see it through. So you are either in this with me, or you can walk away now." His eyes narrowed. "So which will it be, Carlisle?"

Walk away and destroy his future? *Like hell he would.* And yet, something ominous ate at him and sent up a cold warning he couldn't ignore. "You said this involved Mariah," he pressed. "What does this have to do with her?"

"Ledford's other good news for us." Winslow leaned back in his chair. "Baron Whitby has agreed to sell us his property."

The school. His body flashed numb. He asked slowly, praying he'd somehow misunderstood, "You're going to close Gatewell?"

"Not close it—move it to another property that Ledford just found. One that Winslow Shipping can purchase and give outright to the school." A pleased smile stretched across his face, thrilled to be doing such a grand gesture for his daughter. "And twice as big as the current building. New construction, too, without drafts and holes and broken windows to worry about fixing. And in a far more respectable part of town."

"Where?" he demanded, fearing that a new building wouldn't be enough to compensate for Mariah's attachment to the old one. She loved that old house, every drafty, broken inch of it.

"Lambeth, right near the old bishop's palace."

And a world away. Leaning over the desk on his palms, Robert shook his head. "There aren't any wharves in Lambeth."

Winslow laughed. "That's the whole point, my boy!"

He tapped a finger against the desktop to make Winslow listen. "Which means there aren't any children of sailors or longshoremen to help."

"But still plenty of poor urchins." He frowned as he finished off the last of his bourbon. "Although I'm hoping that after this season Mariah won't feel the need to spend so much time among them. That she'll understand how much better it is to be a fine lady than a reformer."

"She's already a fine woman," Robert bit out. If Winslow couldn't see that, then he would never understand his daughter.

"One who will appreciate what new docks in St Katharine's

will do for the company's accounting books," Winslow added. "What are a slum and an old school building compared to that?"

Robert stared at him, feeling the world tilt beneath him. Not until that moment did the full ramifications of Winslow's real estate plan sink into him, along with the realization of what it would mean to Mariah. To see the buildings of St Katharine's torn down, its streets dredged up—

Good God. It would destroy her.

"We're wrong," he said quietly, remembering the vulnerability he glimpsed in her regarding the school and her mother. "We can't do this to Mariah."

"You knew when you agreed to help with this project that it would mean the destruction of St Katharine's," Winslow reminded him, sitting up in his chair. "You knew the role you would play in bringing it about."

"I did." But *Christ*! He'd thought the project didn't have a prayer of coming to fruition, knowing how fickle the king could be. He'd thought of the destruction of the school and the neighborhood as something distant and abstract, no more tangible than any other grand plans tossed about by gentlemen over drinks and cigars.

And it wasn't until recently that he understood the truth about Mariah. It wasn't the school or the company that mattered to her. It was what they represented—being close to her parents, returning to those happy days before her mother died, having her father's nearness and protection.

Destroy all that, and they might as well extinguish the fire in her soul.

"I did everything you asked," Robert admitted, praying that Winslow would listen and understand. "I tracked down the owners, found out the property values, traced bills of sale and liens—for God's sake, I set up *everything* so that we could make a profit when St Katharine's is torn down and the docks go in."

And every step of the way, he'd been certain that he was doing the right thing. That he'd secure the partnership and his reputation as one of England's most successful men. But that was before Mariah got under his skin, before he realized how important the area and school were to her. Before he realized that he cared about her.

"But this—what this will do to Mariah…" He sucked in a deep breath and shook his head. "I *never*—"

"Robert?" Mariah whispered.

He wheeled around. Mariah had opened the door while they'd been arguing, and neither man had heard her.

She stood in the doorway, close enough to have overheard, and a horrified look darkened her face. One that told him that she fully understood now exactly why Winslow Shipping had been interested in acquiring so much property in St Katharine's. Why her father chose him of all the businessmen in England to bring into the company.

She stared at him, as if she couldn't believe… Then she breathed out, so softly he almost couldn't hear her but felt the painful slash of it through his heart, "You bastard."

She spun on her heel and walked away.

"No!" he said firmly, rushing after her and grabbing her shoulders to stop her, to make her listen. "It's not what you think."

She fought to twist out of his hold, but he refused to let her go. "All those properties, the church—" She choked out, "*The school.* All of it destroyed and flooded, the children abandoned… and you knew."

God help him, he'd known all along. "Mariah—"

"You *knew*!" Her angry cry reverberated through the office, and the assistants stopped what they were doing to stare. In the office behind them, Winslow rose to his feet. "No—oh so much worse than simply knowing..." Her voice lowered to a pained whisper. "Dear God, you *made* it happen!"

He couldn't deny it. He'd done exactly as she accused, and he respected her too much to lie to her. But he could make her understand why. And why he was now completely done with it.

He took her arm and pulled her into the corner, where they would have privacy to talk. But she flinched and shrank away. The anguish in her green eyes nearly undid him.

"Listen to me, please," he urged. If they had any chance at a future, she had to trust him. "I can explain."

"All that time we spent together, what we did—" She pressed the back of her hand to her lips as humiliation flushed her cheeks. She breathed out past her fingers, "You used me."

His head snapped back at that, stunned. He forced out in a low voice through clenched teeth, "I did *not* use you."

But she said nothing, her silence a damning accusation.

His heart slammed against his ribs. Everything he'd worked so hard to obtain during the past two years was suddenly spinning out of his control, and he felt as if he were now grasping at straws blowing in the wind. The more desperately he tried to hold on, the more they slipped through his fingers.

"I care about you, Mariah." He tried to keep from hurting her the only way he knew how, by stating the truth. "Very much."

"But you care about the partnership more," she accused in a heart-wrenching whisper. "Even now, even after all we shared..." She gave an anguished shake of her head. "You're still trying to prove yourself to your father."

He bit out a curse of frustration. "It isn't as simple as you—"

"Then end the project right now," she challenged. Twisting free of his hold, she ran through the office to his desk and snatched up the papers lying there. "Destroy all your notes, tear up all the sales offers—do it!" She shoved the papers at him. When he wouldn't take them, she thrust them into his arms. "If St Katharine's means anything to you—if *I* mean anything to you—" Her voice choked with desperate hope. "Then walk away."

And with that, to completely end all possibility of proving himself to his family.

As he stared at her, unable to do as she wanted, the silence reverberated between them like cannon fire. The wounded look of betrayal on her face cut through him. A look so raw and anguished that it stole his breath away.

In that moment's silence, he knew he'd lost her.

She stepped back and raised a hand to keep him away. "You told me how much this partnership meant to you, how you'd do anything to prove yourself." Her rasping voice broke with emotion as she struggled to fight back the sobs. A tear spilled down her face as she whispered, "But I underestimated how far you were willing to go."

"You're wrong." Dear God, why wouldn't she believe him? He tossed the papers aside and reached for her shoulders. "Mariah, listen—"

She slapped him, so hard that the crack of her hand against his cheek echoed through the office.

"Congratulations, Carlisle," she choked out as she wrenched herself away from him. "You've proven yourself a true beast after all."

CHAPTER FOURTEEN

*O*h, she'd been such a fool!

Swiping at her eyes with the back of her hand, Mariah stopped in the basement hallway of the Gatewell School and leaned against the wall.

Breathe…just breathe… If she focused on the simple act of breathing, then perhaps she wouldn't crumple to the floor in tears.

But each beat of her heart brought a jarring stab of self-recrimination inside her hollow chest of how stupid she'd been to fall for Carlisle's charms. And oh God, what she'd done with the man! How she'd behaved no better than a wanton, foolishly believing that he found her desirable and beautiful. That he'd cared for her…

She squeezed her eyes shut, thanking heaven that the school was quiet for once, that the children were at their studies upstairs and the basement was silent except for the faint noises coming from the kitchen. But even that moment's calm wasn't enough to fight down the emotions churning inside her, so much so that she pressed her hand against her stomach to keep from being sick.

Oh, what a goose she'd been to trust him! To so blindly give herself to him—worse, to have fallen in love with him...only to have her body used and her heart shattered. Dear God, how would she ever recover?

From Papa, profiting from the new docks made sense. He'd never understood how much Gatewell and St Katharine's meant to her, and working to increase the company's profits was simply how he strove to protect his family. To him, the company's future *was* the family's future.

But Robert wasn't some mindless soldier blindly following her father's orders. He had more resolve than any other man she'd ever known, certainly enough to stand up to Papa about this project. She'd been convinced that he'd understood what this place meant to her. He'd lost a parent himself, knew what grief could do. She thought she'd come to know him...but apparently, she hadn't known him at all.

No. She knew exactly what he was.

He was the devil, and she'd let him take her soul.

"Mariah, oh thank goodness you're here!"

She opened her eyes and stared through the watery blurriness as Mrs. Smith hurried down the basement hallway. Mariah couldn't answer for fear of breaking into fresh sobs.

The housekeeper stopped suddenly and stared at her. Her lips pressed together at the sight of her red-rimmed eyes and puffy nose, and her face softened sympathetically. "So you've heard already, then?"

Confusion added to the swirling emotions inside her. "Pardon?"

"Evelyn." Worry darkened the older woman's face. "I just received her note."

With a stab of dread, she shoved herself away from the wall. What had her sister done now? "About what?"

Mrs. Smith blinked, now confused herself. "You don't know?" Deep worry wrinkled her brow. "But your tears—"

"Aren't important." The last thing she wanted to do was explain why she was crying. "What's happened?"

Mrs. Smith fished the note from her apron pocket and gave it to Mariah, then lowered her voice for fear of being overheard, "She's run off."

Oh God. Mariah quickly unfolded the note and scanned the message. With every word her heart fell further toward the floor. "To Scotland to elope," she whispered, in her shock unable to speak any louder.

"To run off like that..." Mrs. Smith twisted her hands in her apron as she fretted with worry. "It's not like her."

Unfortunately, it was *exactly* like Evie. To follow her heart and leap without looking. But this leap might just ruin her life.

"Mariah!" Whitby's voice boomed through the school as he charged down the steps into the basement. He hurried toward her, concern for her plastered all over his ruddy face, now made even more red from chasing after her all the way from Wapping. "Are you all right? You ran out before I could—"

"It's Evelyn," she interrupted. She couldn't bear to face Whitby's pity now. She pressed the note into his hand. "She's run off with Burton Williams."

"Williams?" He stiffened with surprise. "That fortune hunter? But surely he knows that Evelyn doesn't have a dowry."

"No, I don't think he does." Or that Papa expected his sons-in-law to work for their money. Burton Williams was not the kind of man who seemed willing to work for anything. Including a wife, apparently, when he could simply steal her. "She's making a terrible mistake." She looked frantically between Mrs. Smith and Whitby as the helplessness raged inside her. "We have to stop them!"

Mrs. Smith interjected. "We'll tell your father, and he can send a man after them."

Her shoulders slumped in defeat. "They've already been gone half a day." Which was exactly why Evie had sent the note to the school instead of to the house, so that Mariah wouldn't learn of what she'd done until it was too late to stop her. She rubbed her forehead and groaned in frustration. "By the time Papa sends someone after her, they'll be halfway across England and impossible to catch."

"I'll go after her, then," Whitby piped up, the bravado of his words undercut by the uncertainty on his face. "I'll take my phaeton and catch up with her—"

"And throw another unmarried gentleman into the mix?" Mariah shook her head. "Her reputation would never recover, then."

"It won't recover at all if we don't stop her one way or another," Mrs. Smith muttered worriedly.

Whitby pleaded, "Which is why you have to let me go after her."

Her head swam with worry, her own troubles with Robert pushed aside. For now. All that mattered at this moment was saving her sister from making the biggest mistake of her life. And there was no way to stop her, unless—"I'm coming with you!"

Mrs. Smith gasped, appalled at the idea. "Absolutely not! The last thing we need is for your reputation to be ruined on top of Evelyn's."

"I don't signify in this." A stab of guilt pierced her chest. She was already ruined, her heart past saving. "But if anyone finds out that Evelyn ran away, I'll never forgive myself if I could have stopped her but didn't."

"Then I'll come, too." Mrs. Smith's lips pressed into a determined line. "I'll be your chaperone, and then no one can say that you two girls did anything improper."

"We'll take my father's carriage," Whitby offered, already running down the hall toward the door. "He's got the sleekest coach and six in London. I'll fetch it and be back in less than an hour. We'll catch them before they reach Leicester!"

An hour later, all three of them had settled into the coach and set out toward the Great North Road. There hadn't been time to pack anything more than one bag of essentials between the two women, and in his rush to be the chivalric hero, Whitby hadn't thought to bring anything with him at all. But even in their hurry to leave and her anger at her father, Mariah made certain to have Whitby send word home that they were chasing after Evelyn. He hadn't had time to scrawl out more than a few sentences, but it would be enough to put Papa's fears at ease until she could send a more detailed message herself from one of the posting inns. And put enough distance between them to keep Evie safe from the brunt of Papa's anger until it was all over and she was tucked safely back into her room in Mayfair. This time, Mariah was certain, it would be back to Miss Pettigrew's for both of them.

Mariah leaned against the squabs and tried to concentrate on the city passing outside the window. But her thoughts were racing too wildly for her to calm her pounding heart or put at ease the dread weighing upon her chest.

"Are you all right, Mariah?" Whitby asked, his long face drawn with concern.

She nodded. "We'll catch up with them before they reach Gretna Green. They'll have to stop every hour or so." A wry smile tugged grimly at her lips. "Evelyn can't travel far without having to use the necessary."

"No," he corrected gently. "I meant about Carlisle."

Her body flashed numb at the mention of Robert, then a thousand pins pricked at her as the numbness eased away and the pain returned in force. Yet she somehow kept her composure, despite the deep concern for her that she saw on Whitby's face. And the pity.

She forced a sniff and turned toward the window. "I don't know what you mean."

Sitting next to her, Mrs. Smith slowly put down the knitting she'd brought with her. Mariah felt her concerned gaze land on her. "So *that* was why you were crying."

"Mariah was crying?" Whitby asked, incredulous.

She rolled her eyes, wishing for nothing more at that moment than to be alone to wallow in her misery. "It was nothing."

"It was Carlisle," he told Mrs. Smith, leaning forward and somehow managing to sit on the edge of the seat despite the long length of his legs in the small space between the benches. "They had a row."

Oh, she truly wanted to be alone! She shrugged it away. "We always have rows."

"That's true," Mrs. Smith agreed, yet frowned at Mariah, her knitting forgotten in her lap. "But the man's never made you cry before."

"She cried when they met," Whitby reminded her.

"Oh that's right, I remember now. Well, he's not made you cry since."

"Usually he just makes her furious—"

"The way you two are doing to me now?" Mariah interrupted, letting the frustration and irritation replace the sorrow inside her.

Immediately, she regretted her outburst. Her friends were only trying to help, not realizing they were making her feel worse. Oh, she knew how to deal with anger, but she didn't know how to deal with love. Especially when that love had been nothing more on Robert's part than calculated manipulation.

She admitted, "Yes, we had an argument. But it was nothing." Only the shattering of her heart.

"She slapped him," Whitby added solemnly for Mrs. Smith's benefit.

The housekeeper glanced curiously at her. "That sounds like more than a simple row to me."

"Yes, it was, all right?" Her eyes stung, and she blinked hard as her vision began to blur again. "We had a terrible fight, and I slapped him."

Mrs. Smith reached to gently pat her hand. "Whatever for, my dear?"

"Because she loves him," Whitby explained.

Mariah stared at her two best friends with mortification swelling inside her as they looked at her with expressions of confusion and pity. Her lips parted as she readied to dissemble, to hide the truth from them—

"Yes," she whispered instead, so softly the sound was almost lost beneath the rumble of the carriage wheels. She lowered her gaze to her hands, which were folded uselessly in her lap, and she sat stiff and unmoving despite the bouncing of the carriage. There was no point in denying what was so obviously visible on her face. "I do love him—*did* love him…but it doesn't matter now how I feel."

"Oh, sweeting." Mrs. Smith slipped her arm around her shoulders in a motherly embrace. "I'm certain the man cares about you. You two can work past whatever little problems are between you."

Little problems? The destruction of an entire neighborhood lay between them. She laughed at that bitter irony, but the sound emerged as a soft sob. "No. We have no future." She swiped her hand at her eyes as she admitted, "I was nothing to him but an obstacle between him and the partnership. I got caught up in his charms and forgot that."

Across from her, Whitby said nothing, but his face fell, right before all his features blurred beneath the hot tears welling in her eyes. And thank goodness, because she didn't think she could stand another look of pity from either of them.

"I was a fool," she breathed out, finally giving voice to her most tortured emotions. "He called me beautiful, said I was special, and I thought…I thought…Oh, it doesn't matter!"

"Did he make promises to you?" Mrs. Smith pressed gently.

Mariah's heart would have broken at the older woman's innocent questions if it hadn't already shattered. Even now Mrs. Smith thought the best of her, and it never occurred to the woman that Mariah might have lost more to Robert than her pride and dreams of the future.

Wordlessly, she shook her head as new humiliation heated through her.

"When we return, I'll call him out," Whitby assured her, making her tear-blurred eyes grow wide. "Pistols at dawn."

Even as he made the promise, though, his face paled with the realization of what he was saying. "I think."

"Oh, Whitby!" She smiled through her tears and reached across the compartment to hug him. "Thank you!"

He tensed. "You mean—you mean you really want me to duel for you?" Panic cracked his voice as he added, "With Carlisle?"

"No, you silly goose! You are *not* dueling with him." She didn't know which was more amusing—the image in her mind of Whitby attempting to duel or the panicked expression on his face. "I meant for being such a good friend."

"Oh. *That.*" He leaned back against the squabs with visible relief, the color returning to his face. "Well. It's a good thing that you won't let me duel with him. Because I'd have put a ball in him. I'm quite a good shot, you know."

"La!" Mrs. Smith arched a dubious brow as she picked up her knitting again. "Not better than Robert Carlisle."

"I most certainly am."

"Mr. Whitby, do you even know how to fire a pistol?"

"Of course I do! I won the spring marksmanship in Buxton last year, I'll have you know."

"Out of how many shooters?"

"That's not important..."

As her two dearest friends argued about Whitby's prowess with firearms—or lack of it—Mariah leaned against the side of the carriage and stared out once more at the passing city, but she didn't see any of it. She was too worried about Evelyn and too hurt by Robert to pay it any attention.

Only sheer resolve kept back a new round of tears. The three of them *would* find Evelyn and stop her from marrying Williams, which was all that mattered now. She couldn't go back in time and stop herself from falling in love with

Robert, but she could stop her sister. And she would never let Evelyn make the same mistake she had.

Never.

* * *

Robert hunched his shoulders against the cold as he made his way through Mayfair, but the bitter self-recrimination that swept through him burned hot.

Frustrating woman! To slap him and then run away before he could stop her—

No. It wasn't the slap that bothered him, but that she'd left. Yet even if he'd been able to keep her from fleeing, most likely having to resort to binding her hand and foot, she wouldn't have listened to reason. She was too angry and hurt to understand and accept his apologies. Or to believe his promise to never have a hand in the docks project again.

Damn Henry Winslow for catching him up in this mess!

And damn Mariah for not having more faith in him.

Although, had he really given her much cause to trust him? After all, he'd gone willingly into that damnable agreement with her father to find her a husband, despite what she wanted. An agreement he should never have entered into in the first place. So of course, when she'd overheard about St Katharine's, she'd believed the worst of him.

But then, she wasn't wrong. He *had* done exactly what she'd accused him of—attempting to profit by destroying what she loved. Abandoning that plan had simply come too late, the damage already done.

Which was why he'd chased after her as soon as he could free himself from Henry Winslow, after dodging the man's prying questions about his fight with Mariah. She might never understand or accept his apology. In all likelihood she would probably still hate him, still blame him for the destruction of St Katharine's and the school. But damnation, she *would* hear him out. Even if he had to tie her to a chair to do it.

But she wasn't at home, and by the time he'd reached the school, she was gone, with no one there able to tell him where she'd gone or when she would return. After two hours spent crisscrossing London in the cold, he'd decided to return to Park Place, to give her time to calm down. And to give himself time to figure out what exactly he would say when he saw her.

He raced up the steps of Park Place and through the front door, desperately needing a glass of something strong to calm the frustration in his chest. To put him into a stupor that would take two weeks from his life and six months to recover.

He flung open the door to the billiards room and the largest collection of spirits in the house—

"Robert!"

Christ.

His brother Quinton lounged in one of the red leather chairs lining the wall, his leg crooked akimbo over the rolled arm and a cigar clenched between his teeth. He poked his cue at their eldest brother Sebastian as he leaned over the billiards table to line up his shot.

Quinn grinned. "Told you he'd be happy to see us."

Sebastian quirked a brow at the expression on Robert's face. "That's not happy to see us." He sank the ball in the corner pocket, then gave him an assessing look. "*That's* what the cat dragged in."

"Half-eaten," Quinton added, taking a second glance at him.

"Then promptly cast back up," Sebastian finished.

Robert rolled his eyes. "Good to see you, too," he muttered dryly and continued across the room to the liquor cabinet. He pulled out the bottle of whiskey and a glass. "What are you two doing here?"

"Do we need an excuse to drop in on our brother?" Quinn shoved himself out of the chair and held out his own glass for a pour.

"Yes." Especially today, the second worst day of his life. With a grimace, he refilled Quinn's glass. "Does Mother know you're here?"

He jerked a thumb toward the front stairs. "She's up with Annabelle right now, helping her get settled."

"You brought your wives to London?" Robert glanced across the room at Sebastian, surprised that he'd allow his wife to travel. "In Miranda's condition?"

"He didn't," Quinn answered for him. When Robert pulled the bottle away, Quinn gestured for him to keep filling his glass.

"She's still in Islingham," Sebastian explained.

Quinn grinned. "Which is why Seb's in London."

Sebastian interjected with a hand going to his heart, "I love my wife." He defended himself smoothly enough for Robert to suspect that he'd been practicing his answer all the way from Lincolnshire. "She is the light of my life, and not a day goes by that I don't thank God for her." Then he blew out a long-suffering sigh and reached for his own glass of cognac as he admitted, "But this pregnancy is going to kill me. She's laughing one moment, bursting into tears the next—and the food she's been craving..." He shook his head, a bewildered expression gripping his features. "Who eats salt-cured ham with sweet cream at three in the morning, for God's sake?"

Robert cast him a knowing look. "So you fled Lincolnshire."

"Like a scared rabbit," Quinn laughed.

Sebastian slid a murderous glance at Quinton that only made him grin more broadly, then explained, "I'm here to collect Josephine and bring her home for Miranda's confinement. And it's a good thing I arrived when I did, too." He lined up the cue for his second shot. "There was some misunderstanding among the servants. They thought they'd all been given the night off."

Robert tensed.

"I said it couldn't possibly be true," he continued wryly with forced bafflement. "After all, why would my younger brother clear out the staff from *my* town house—"

"And *his* current bachelor's residence," Quinn interjected.

"Getting rid of all possible witnesses—"

"If he didn't have plans to do anything scandalous—"

"Like spend the night with a woman," Sebastian finished, no amusement on his face as he sank the second ball.

Robert replaced the bottle into the cabinet and dropped into the nearest chair. At times like these, he dearly wished he were an only child.

"I'm not spending the night with a woman," he corrected. Not a lie, now that Mariah most likely never wanted to be alone with him again.

"I don't believe him." Quinn looped his arm over Sebastian's shoulders and gestured at Robert with his glass. "Do you?"

Sebastian swept his gaze over him from head to boots. "No."

"He's lying."

"Like a rug."

"Like a *lying* rug."

Robert rolled his eyes as a headache began to pound at the base of his skull. Not this. Not them. Not today of all days.

Sebastian laid his cue stick across the table, then leaned back against the railing and stared at Robert with that imperious expression he'd perfected since becoming duke. "You're a bachelor and entitled to partake, but this isn't the place to entertain mistresses or widows."

"I'm not," he snapped. His brother was unknowingly poking at a raw wound.

Not believing him, Sebastian arched a warning brow at Robert. "As long as it's not some actress or singer determined to separate you from your blunt."

"No one's separating me from anything," he half growled at their prying.

"Or trap you into marriage."

The very *last* thing— *Christ!* "It's Mariah Winslow," he bit out, reaching the end of his patience and scrubbing his hand over his face in frustration. "She's the woman I planned on seeing tonight, all right?"

His two brothers stared at him, stunned and wide-eyed. And for once, speechless.

Then Quinton blinked. "The Hellion?"

"Oh good Lord," he muttered and tossed back the rest of his whiskey in a single gulp.

Sebastian and Quinn exchanged bewildered looks. Then Seb asked deliberately, as if he hadn't heard correctly, "The woman Mother has been sponsoring this season? The same woman whose father wants to give you a partnership in his business?"

"Yes." He pushed himself out of the chair to refill his glass but snatched up the bottle instead. A bottle's worth of whiskey wasn't such a bad idea, given how this day was going.

"Nodcock." Sebastian crossed his arms over his chest. "Are you and she—"

"Yes, damn it!" And damn the whole situation for having to admit this to his brothers. Although one look at his face would reveal everything about his feelings toward Mariah, as well as the torment of knowing how much she most likely hated him.

"Nodcock."

He glared at Sebastian. "You are *not* helping."

"But I thought..." Puzzled, Quinn frowned at Robert. "Does Mother know you're planning on proposing to her?"

"No." He refilled his glass and took a large swallow of whiskey. But even it didn't dull the pain in his chest as he admitted, facing the horrible truth, "Because I'm not."

"Nodcock," both brothers said at the same time.

The glare Robert gave them was murderous. "Damnation, I *can't* propose!"

Unable to remain still a moment longer, he began to pace, dragging his fingers through his hair. But the room wasn't big enough to exorcise the frustrations, anger, and anguish from inside him. St James's Palace wouldn't have been big enough for that.

"Why not?" Sebastian challenged.

"Marriage isn't an option." *Not anymore.* He'd lost Mariah and was now on the verge of losing the partnership. The most he could hope for was that Mariah wouldn't spend the rest of her life hating him.

"Seems like a fine one to me," Quinn muttered, taking back his glass.

Robert glared at his younger brother. "Says the man with the doting wife."

Quinn lifted the empty glass in a toast and grinned. "And a baby due in the fall."

Robert stopped in mid-stride at the news. *A baby?* "You're going to be a father?" His chest panged with something close to covetous longing as he offered quietly, "Congratulations."

He was happy for Quinton, of course, but he also couldn't help the fierce sting of envy. Or the unbidden image of Mariah, full with child and glowing happily. With *his* child.

But that future would never be his now.

Pacing once more, he snatched up his glass and took a gasping drink. With each turn of the room, and many swallows of whiskey, he told them what had happened between him and Mariah. And why.

Marriage must have mellowed his brothers, because they listened without interrupting, and when he finished, instead of laughing at him as they would have done in the past, both looked at him with solemn empathy. His shoulders slumped. For once, it was a relief to confide in them.

Sebastian studied the glowing tip of his cigar and asked quietly, "Does she know you're in love with her?"

"No," he admitted, rubbing his hand at the hard knot at his nape. "She doesn't know."

"You should start by telling her that, I think," Quinn pressed sagely. "I've found that it smooths over quite a bit of female anger."

Knowing Mariah, though, it might just cause her to kill him. Robert asked wryly, "When did you become so wise?"

"The moment I told Belle that I loved her." Quinn's grin

faded into a solemn expression. "So what's stopping you from doing the same?"

He bitterly quirked a brow. "The small problem that she hates me."

He set down his glass of whiskey, no longer having a taste for the stuff. There wasn't enough drink in the world to dull the desolation aching hollowly in his chest where his heart had been.

Crossing his arms, he leaned back against the wall and grimly shook his head. The only way he could receive the partnership was if he helped Winslow to profit from the destruction of St Katharine's, and in the process, lose all chances at a future with Mariah. But if he chose Mariah, Winslow would think him too cautious and weak-willed to deserve the partnership... and with that, lose the best opportunity to prove himself worthy of the Carlisle name. Mariah and the partnership—he knew now that he could never have both.

"Love her or not," he muttered, "either way I'm damned."

He turned his face away before his brothers saw the emotions burning inside him. The last time he'd felt this frustrated, this powerless, was the night Father died. With Mariah's help, he thought he'd healed that wound, only for it to return with an intensity so strong that it was nearly blinding.

"When have you ever let anyone stop you from getting what you want?" Seb asked.

Robert sucked in a harsh breath. His brothers were right. He'd never backed down from a fight in his life.

But they didn't understand the choice he was being forced to make. "It's a helluva lot more complicated than you realize," he ground out. Then he succinctly summed up the torment that had been engulfing him since last night when she'd shattered in his arms, "If I marry her, I lose the partnership."

Quinn shrugged as if that meant nothing. "You've a brilliant business mind, Robert. You've only been making business ventures for the past two years, since after Father died." Robert felt Sebastian's gaze dart to him and pin there, even as Quinn continued, "But it's only a matter of time until you're successful. You *will* become a partner, if not in Winslow Shipping then in some other business."

"No," he argued, jabbing a finger at the floor. "It has to be *this* company. It's the best opportunity at the best company. The *best*, damn it! And I will not fail at this. I will *not* be another disappointment, not in this."

Struck by the force of his words, Quinn was taken aback. "You've never failed at anything in—"

"That's not it," Sebastian interrupted. His eyes narrowed as they studied Robert, then flickered knowingly as understanding dawned on his face. "His problem has nothing to do with this partnership, not really."

Quinn blinked. "Then what is it?"

"It's about Father."

Fresh grief spread through Robert as he returned Sebastian's stare in the sudden silence that fell over all three brothers, unable to deny it. The tension suddenly grew so thick between them that each heartbeat only added to it, each ticking second growing the silence deeper. Robert wasn't used to such silence when the three of them were together, and it rattled him. So did the implication behind his brother's quiet accusation.

"You still blame yourself, don't you?" Sebastian asked somberly.

Robert refused to look away. This conversation had been two years in coming, along with the punishment he deserved. "Don't you?"

"No," Sebastian answered honestly. "But there was a time when I did. When the grief was still fresh and I needed someone to blame."

"I sure as hell did," Quinn put in, the raw honesty in his brother's voice tearing through his chest like a knife. "But I stopped eventually."

"We both did, while Mother and Josie never blamed you in the first place," Sebastian divulged with a faint shake of his head. "The only person who hasn't stopped blaming you, Robert, is *you*."

His eyes stung as he glanced between his brothers. Because of Mariah, he'd found a way to realize that his father's death had truly been only an accident. He'd been able to find his way out of that torture.

But he hadn't been able to let go of everything regarding that night.

"The last moments of his life were spent dragging me out of a gambling hell," he bit out hoarsely, the self-recrimination inside him so brutal that he flinched. "That's how low I'd fallen. How much of a mockery I'd made of him and the family."

"You think you're the only son he ever had to bring home?" Sebastian slowly shook his head. "He dragged me out of a tavern."

His heart pounding, Robert looked at Quinton. "You, too?"

"Twice," Quinn admitted ruefully.

He vehemently shook his head. It hadn't been the same for them, it *hadn't* been! "He lectured me right there in the street, told me that I—"

"Had been raised to be a better man than that?" Quinn interrupted gently.

Sebastian's eyes softened sympathetically. "That he was disappointed in you?"

His heart leapt into his throat. He admitted in a rasping whisper, "Yes."

Quinn and Sebastian exchanged a solemn look, then Quinn nodded slowly. "The same things he said to us."

"And if you would have had the same chance," Seb assured him, "you would have done exactly what we both did, which was to apologize and work to change your ways."

Quinn added somberly, "And be told by Father a week later that you were forgiven."

"But you weren't given that chance, so you've spent the last two years trying to force it to happen." Sebastian shook his head. "But you'll never be able to now, no matter what kind of success you reach, no matter how respected a name you make for yourself. And you will, because you're capable and hardworking."

Mariah had told him the same thing, and he'd attacked her for it. A new guilt rose inside him, one that began to replace the guilt he carried for his father. And a new grief, as well. This time for losing her.

A paternal expression fell over Sebastian's face as he said quietly, "You *are* the good man Father raised all of us to be."

Silence fell over them again, and Quinn turned his face away, but not before Robert saw the glistening in his eyes. Sebastian pushed himself away from the billiards table and reached for the bottle of cognac on the side buffet to refill his glass.

"So you don't need to prove your worth to any of us, and least of all to Father. We've all come to terms with what happened that night, and now you should, too," Sebastian assured him, taking a slow sip of brandy. "But if you are determined on that path anyway, then you don't need to worry. Another company *will* come along, one just as good in its own way as Winslow Shipping."

"But there will never be another Hellion," Quinn added quietly.

Robert blew out a breath, his heart racing beneath the twisting coils of emotions. Gone was the guilt over his father and the need to prove himself, but in its place came a terrifying fear of losing Mariah. The woman was the toughest challenge he'd ever encountered in his life. And the one challenge he most wanted to win.

"Think of it this way," Sebastian told him. "Propose to her, and the happiness you've had this season has a chance of continuing, and for the rest of your life. But if you don't, all the happiness she gives you will be lost. You'll never be able to laugh with her again, or kiss her, or—"

"Make her toes curl," Quinn put in with a grin. Then his smile faded as he murmured sardonically, "But at least you'll have your business to give you satisfaction."

"It's that simple. The partnership or the woman you love." Sebastian's voice was quiet as he laid a hand on Robert's shoulder, his eyes grave. "Now, which do you choose?"

Ten minutes later, Robert charged up the steps of the Winslow town house and pounded his fist against the door.

He had no intention of leaving until Mariah had heard him out. He would explain everything to her, make her understand how he'd gotten caught up in her father's plans, and ask forgiveness for being so blind to what mattered most to her. Then he would convince her to marry him.

He grimaced. No matter how many months it took.

The door opened, and the butler peered out. "Yes?"

His heart pounded, nervousness gripping him at what he was about to do. "Robert Carlisle for Miss Winslow."

"I'm sorry, sir, but Miss Winslow isn't at home." The butler blocked the door, refusing to admit him. "Would you care to leave a card?"

Absolutely not. What he needed to say to Mariah was delicate and required the kind of finesse that a card or note could never convey—it more than likely would also require ropes and a chair to tie her to. "I need to speak with her."

"Might I suggest, then, that you call again in the morning? Good day, sir."

As the butler began to shut the door, Robert slapped his hand against it and held it open. With anger and frustration speeding through him in equal measure, he pinned a hard gaze on the man that told him he'd tolerate no dissembling and repeated through clenched teeth, "I need to speak with her."

The butler lifted an indignant brow, a gesture that told him exactly where Mariah had learned that haughty look of hers. "As I said, sir, Miss Winslow is not at home, and I do not know when she will return."

Damnation. "Then I'll wait."

Robert shoved past the butler and into the foyer. He glanced up the grand stairs toward the upper floors. He didn't expect to see Mariah, yet he couldn't help but hope. And hoping she wasn't standing up there with another bucket of water to dump over his head. Or a pistol.

The butler took his hat and coat and handed them to a waiting footman, then gestured down the hall. "The drawing room is this way, sir."

"I'll wait here," he insisted.

The butler stared at him, his mouth falling open, stunned. For a gentleman to wait in the foyer—it simply wasn't done.

But Robert didn't give a damn about propriety. There was no way he would risk letting the minx come home and sneak past him to her room. There was too much of his future riding on the conversation they needed to have to chance missing her tonight.

When it became obvious that Robert was going nowhere, the butler snapped his mouth closed, bowed stiffly, and turned on his heel to leave. The footman lingered for a few more awkward minutes, still holding his coat and hat in hand, as if waiting for Robert to change his mind, take them back, and leave.

Robert held out his hands. The relieved footman gladly handed them over, only for Robert to toss his hat onto the foyer table and fling his coat over the nearby stairway banister. He folded his arms across his chest and arched a brow at the gaping footman, who slowly backed out of the foyer, then turned and hurried away.

"Smart man," he muttered, then set to pacing the length of the black-and-white draughtboard marble floor.

He'd wait here all night, if necessary. It would be a damnably sticky spot he'd find himself in if Winslow arrived home before Mariah, but one that couldn't be helped. He knew the truth now, that he'd never met a more perfect woman for him than the one who drove him absolutely mad, and that he wanted to spend the rest of his life fighting with her and making up.

A knock rapped at the front door.

Without waiting for the butler to return, Robert hurried to the door and flung it open wide, his heart pounding. "Mariah?"

Instead, a young man in household livery stood at the doorstep and held up a folded note. "A message, sir. To Mr. Winslow from Mr. Hugh Whitby."

Whitby. His eyes narrowed. What did that dandy want with Mariah's father? He held out his hand. "Thank you."

The footman handed over the note, then pulled at the brim of his hat and hurried away, not caring who took the note as long as he'd done his duty in delivering it. As if nothing were out of the ordinary about a well-dressed gentleman answering the door.

"Good to know I can always have a career in service," he muttered to himself, "when I'm denied Winslow's partnership."

With only a fleeing stab of remorse at reading someone else's message, he snapped the wax seal and opened the note, scanning over it.

Robert's heart stopped. And when it began pounding again, each beat cut a blindingly painful pulse through him.

Sir,

Your daughter is eloping to Scotland. Mariah and I will be back—with Evie and Mrs. Smith—in a few days. Will send more information as soon as we can. Do not worry.

Hugh Whitby

A searing pain stabbed through him like a knife, so intense that the scrawled handwriting blurred beneath his eyes.

Crumpling the paper in his fist, he spun on his heel and

charged from the house, muttering a string of curses beneath his breath. He had to leave. *Now.*

She had two hours' travel on him, and judging from the way she'd raced down St James's Street, the woman wasn't afraid of speed. But he'd catch her before she reached Gretna Green, even if he had to ride through the night. And God help her—and Whitby—when he did.

CHAPTER FIFTEEN

Along the Great North Road
Two Hard-Traveled Days Later

Mariah rushed inside the Dragon Inn and stopped to let her eyes adjust to the dim light.

Her heart pounded as she scanned the common room. Her sister was here somewhere. The men in the last carriage they'd passed confirmed that they'd seen a couple fitting Evelyn and Burton Williams's description staying at the inn. Oh, she just *had* to be here!

"Pardon me." She hurried up to the counter where a man stacked pewter tankards on the shelf behind it. "Have you seen a young woman traveling alone with a man, about my height and age, reddish brown hair, amber eyes?"

"Aye. There's a young lady here like that." He flipped a towel over his shoulder and pointed toward a private dining room in the rear of the inn. "But she's not traveling with a man."

Her hope sank through the floor. "She's not?"

If she wasn't with Williams, then the woman wasn't Evelyn. Her eyes stung with fatigue and frustration. After traveling almost nonstop to catch up to Evie, with barely any food or sleep, the thought of having to travel on nearly undid her.

"Not no more," he answered. "He took off on a hired horse this mornin'. Left her standin' there in the coach yard—"

Mariah ran. She reached the dining room and froze in the doorway.

Evelyn stood at the dirt-covered window overlooking the innyard, keeping watch for Williams to return to her. Her face pale, she clutched a handkerchief to her breast with a trembling hand. Streaks from shed tears glistened on her cheeks.

"Evie," Mariah whispered, her heart breaking.

Evelyn glanced up, and as their gazes met, a tangle of emotions darkened her face. But most of all, there was pain. A soft sob escaped her.

Mariah rushed across the room and pulled her into her arms, and the sobs turned into shuddering wails as they clutched each other close. They sank down onto a settle along the wall, with Mariah stroking Evelyn's trembling back to soothe her in an attempt to ease her pain. But it was impossible, she knew, because she now knew herself the agonizing pain of a shattered heart, and as she held her sister, her own tears began to fall.

"I'm here, Evie," Mariah whispered, rocking her in her arms as her sister gasped between cries to catch her breath. "I'm here, and you're safe...everything will be all right." A bald-faced lie—nothing would ever be all right for the Winslow sisters again. They had both crossed lines that could never be uncrossed. The fact that they had done so for love meant nothing. "We'll go home, and everything will be fine."

"He left me," Evelyn choked out between sobs. "He rode off without even looking back..."

"I know." She placed a kiss on her forehead. "But I'm here now, with Mrs. Smith and Whitby. We're here to take you home."

"I didn't know what I was going to do. I was so frightened," she admitted, and Mariah realized that part of her sister's tears were also cries of relief. "I don't have any money, barely any clothes...I didn't have any way to buy a seat on the coach, or even to purchase food."

Anger burned inside her. If Mariah ever saw Burton Williams again, she'd flay the man alive! Evelyn could have been hurt. Or worse. "I'm here now, so you don't have to worry about any of that. Everything will be all right." Perhaps if she said it enough, she'd believe it, too. "It will all be fine."

"How?" She lifted her head and looked at Mariah through tear-blurred eyes. "I ran off with a man," she whispered, as if afraid she might be overhead. "I'll be ruined!"

"No, you won't. I'll make certain of it." *Somehow.*

Mariah refused—absolutely *refused*—to let Evie's life be ruined over a mistake of love. She would find a way to keep her sister's reputation intact, whatever it took. Williams was an arse, yet she suspected that even he would keep quiet. After all, if he dared to utter a word about this, he'd be forced to marry her anyway, plunging himself into the meager life he was so desperately attempting to avoid. And since she, Mrs. Smith, and Whitby were all here now, anyone who saw them returning to London would assume they were all traveling together and that Evelyn had been accompanied the entire time.

Together, on the ride home, they would come up with

some reason for why they'd traveled north in case they ever needed an explanation, then never speak of it again. Mrs. Smith would keep her silence because she loved Evie like a daughter, and Whitby wouldn't speak a word if Mariah asked him. He might be a bit of a dandy, but he was also loyal to a fault.

Evelyn shook her head, swiping the handkerchief at her eyes. "I'm such a fool!"

"It isn't your fault," she countered firmly, not wanting Evie to blame herself. "He's the blackguard in this, not you."

"He didn't force me to go." Her shoulders sagged, as if those few words thoroughly explained the ruin that her life would now become. "I went willingly."

Mariah's face softened as she brushed a stray curl from Evelyn's cheek. "Because you loved him. There's no sin in that."

"Is there sin in being a reckless goose?" Evelyn gave a self-deprecating grimace. "I should have known better. You tried to warn me, but I didn't listen."

For once, Mariah took no pride in being right.

"He stopped by the house and surprised me," she explained, the sobs finally dying away. "He had a ring, said he wanted to talk to Papa to offer marriage...but Papa was out, so of course he couldn't."

"Of course." And highly convenient, since he most likely knew that Henry Winslow would refuse.

"So we sat in the garden, talking and planning about how our life together would be...I was so happy." But the look on her face now was one of pure misery. "I don't remember who brought it up first, but we agreed that we hated to wait to be married."

"So he suggested that you elope instead," Mariah added gently.

"No," she whispered, guilty recrimination darkening her face. "I did."

Anguish tightened her chest. "Oh, Evie."

"He agreed, and the next thing I knew, I was packing a bag and writing that note to explain where I'd gone so you wouldn't worry."

And cleverly sent it to the school instead of to the office so that she and Williams would have time to get a head start before anyone realized they'd run off. But Mariah knew not to bring up that bit of recklessness. Evie already felt humiliated enough.

"I thought he was being romantic, that he loved me too much to wait to make me his wife." Shamefully shaking her head at her gullibility, Evelyn closed her eyes. "How could I have been such a fool?"

"Because we always want to believe the best of the men we love," Mariah whispered.

The truth behind her words was brutal. Her eyes blurred, and she inhaled a pain-filled breath to fight back new tears. Evie had been wrong about Burton Williams, but how had Mariah been so blind about Robert? She thought she'd come to know him well during the past several weeks, that those hours spent bare and vulnerable in each other's arms only confirmed the goodness she saw in him. When in fact he'd only been scheming to make certain that the partnership was his by working to destroy all she held dear.

She'd been so *very* wrong.

"When the mail coach stopped here yesterday evening, we decided to spend the night," Evelyn continued, dabbing at her eyes and the last remnants of tears even as her voice grew steadier. "But nothing happened between us, I swear to you. *Nothing.* I'd never be so foolish as to give myself to a man who hadn't yet married me."

Mariah winced. *She* had been exactly that foolish. And where had it gotten her? More misery than she'd had in her entire life.

Most likely, Robert did care about her, enough to make love to her so tenderly that it had brought tears to her eyes. But in the end, he'd cared about the partnership more. When she'd stood there in the shipping offices and heard him admit to what he'd done, the shock and pain at losing her last connection to her mother at his hands had been unbearable. The sudden grief had been overwhelming, and she'd felt as if she lost her mother all over again.

"We were never alone together," Evie explained, misunderstanding Mariah's silence. "I slept in a shared room upstairs, and he slept down here on one of the benches. We *never*— I promise you!"

"I know," Mariah reassured her grimly. But she also knew that all her sister's protests wouldn't make one whit of difference if anyone in London ever found out that she'd run away with a man. She'd be ostracized from society. Simply riding with him in a mail coach without a chaperone, even surrounded by a half dozen other people, was enough to ruin her. No one would ever believe they'd slept apart or that Evie had remained innocent. Especially not with a scoundrel's excuse for a rake like Burton Williams.

"I think he changed his mind about marrying me last night during dinner," Evelyn admitted, her body sagging against the settle, "when I commented that reserving a private dining room was too expensive. He said that I needn't worry because we'd have plenty of money once we married and received my dowry." She plucked idly at the lace edging the handkerchief, in her shame not raising her eyes to look at Mariah. "I thought he knew. I thought for certain that he *knew…*"

That the Winslow daughters had no dowries, that there was no guarantee that the daughters would inherit any part of the business… Williams must have realized the truth then— he would never see a penny of Winslow Shipping money.

A rush of relief cascaded through her that Evie had escaped that horrible man.

"When I woke this morning and went downstairs to join him for breakfast, he wasn't inside. He was in the yard saddling a horse to ride back to London." She raised her eyes, and the haunted look on her face took Mariah's breath away. "He said he'd changed his mind," she whispered, so softly that it was barely more than a breath on her pale lips, "and he didn't want to marry me anymore."

Mariah hugged her tightly, but this time, thankfully, no new tears fell.

"I'm such a fool!" Evelyn choked out against Mariah's shoulder, "I thought—I thought he loved me."

Her own voice cracked with emotion as she whispered hoarsely, "Then he's the bigger fool because he doesn't."

A loud commotion went up outside in the innyard, followed by shouts and the noise of running feet and galloping horses. Then came arguing voices raised in anger. A smash of furniture, the splintering of wood and crash of broken bottles—a barmaid screamed.

"What on earth…?" Mariah hurried across the room and opened the door.

Staring wide-eyed, she was stunned into speechlessness at the sight of the bar brawl that had broken out. A handful of men flung fists at one another, smashing up tables and tumbling over chairs, while the few women travelers rushed outside to avoid the melee. Stable hands and grooms running inside to join the fight were caught up by the women in the bottleneck of the narrow doorway.

A bottle shattered against the wall. When the innkeeper poked his head up from behind the bar to curse at whoever had thrown it, an ale tankard flew past his head. He ducked back down, this time staying put and leaving the fight to play out without interference.

At the center of the fray stood three large, golden-haired men with broad shoulders, clenched fists, wide grins—

Robert.

She gasped. Impossible! Yet there he was, standing back-to-back with two other men who looked so much like him that they could only be the Carlisle brothers. The scourge of Mayfair and the bane of Lincolnshire. And right now, three men well on their way to destroying the inn.

One of the grooms who had pushed his way past the women grabbed the youngest brother by the back of his coat and tossed him across a table. When he landed, he jumped to his feet, then went running back into the brawl, fists flying. Seconds later he was thrown over the table again, and this time when he scrambled to his feet, a broad grin of unabashed joy lit his face. Without pause he rushed back into the fray.

The other man to Robert's right—good heavens, was that the Duke of Trent? And were dukes supposed to be so skilled in bare-knuckle brawling? But this man was. He lowered his shoulder and plowed into a hostler who swung a wide punch and missed his target, bodily tossing the man through the door and out into the yard.

But her eyes kept returning to Robert, who simultaneously ducked and landed punches with the ease of a well-trained pugilist. Her heart lurched at the sight of him, and in that moment's confusion, she didn't know whether to rush forward to throw herself into his arms or join the other men in swinging at him.

In the middle of the skirmish, Whitby stepped inside the inn. "What the devil—"

Robert lunged.

* * *

Burning with jealousy, Robert grabbed Whitby by the lapels and shoved him against the wall.

"She belongs with me," he growled through clenched teeth. "You don't get her. Not now, not ever."

"I don't—I don't know—" Whitby's eyes grew large. But Robert wasn't going to be fooled by that bewildered look on the man's face. "Why are *you* here?"

Or fooled by feigned innocence. "To stop you from—"

A pint of ale poured over his head.

"What the hell!" He released Whitby's coat, and the man fell to the floor in a heap. He wheeled around.

He should have known—"Mariah."

Tossing the empty tankard aside, she knelt beside Whitby, who now sat on the floor, dazed, although not a single punch had been thrown at him. Around them, the fight continued, with more broken pieces of furniture, more smashed bottles, and a solid string of curses coming from the innkeeper still hiding behind the bar.

"What did you do?" she accused, shooting Robert a dark glare.

"I didn't lay a hand on him," he refuted, wiping the ale from his hair. "For god's sake, he fainted!"

She pulled Whitby into her arms. "Leave him be!"

Her defense of Whitby flamed the anger inside him. He ground out, "The hell I will!" He took her arm and lifted her to her feet. She tried to yank herself away, but he held tight. He'd come too far to let her go now. "You are *not* marrying him."

Stunned by his words, she froze. Only her eyes moved as she stared at him, growing wide in surprise as if he'd just admitted to attempting to kill the king.

Taking full advantage of the moment, he grabbed her into his arms and carried her swiftly through the fight and up the stairs.

"Put me down!" Mariah demanded, kicking her legs and hitting at his shoulders to make him release her.

"No," he answered flatly, trying the door handle of each guest room. One of the handles gave way, and the unlocked door swung open wide to reveal an unused guest room.

He carried her inside, shut the door with a kick of his boot, and rolled her onto his shoulder, to free his hand and flip the lock.

When she kicked a knee into his stomach, he sucked in a mouthful of air and slapped her bottom. "Stop that!"

He carried her across the room and dropped her onto the bed. With a gasp, she bounced on the mattress.

Placing his hands on either side of her, he leaned over to bring his face level with hers. "You are not marrying that man," he repeated, wanting no mistake between them on this point. "I won't let you elope with Hugh Whitby."

Her mouth fell open. "You think that Whitby and I—that we're—"

He gritted his teeth. He didn't need feigned innocence from *her* right now, either. "Running away to Scotland, yes," he drawled acidly.

Her eyes grew impossibly wider. Then she laughed, so hard that she had to place her hands over her stomach.

He glowered at her. *Damnable woman.* "This isn't funny."

"Oh yes, it is!" she choked out between laughs.

"I've been riding nearly nonstop for two days to catch up to you," he bit out, fighting to keep his patience. "When that message from Whitby arrived at your house—"

"You were at the house?" The laughter died on her lips, replaced instantly by suspicion. Her distrust of him cut nearly as painfully as her laughter. "Why?"

"Because I wanted to explain to you about St Katharine's." He clenched his jaw in anger as the memory of reading Whitby's note flooded back, carrying with it the sharp stab of her rejection. "Only to learn that you'd fled north. With Whitby." He paused and stared down into her green eyes, seeing the pain and anger in their depths that he'd put there. For the first time since leaving London, uncertainty that he'd be able to change her mind gnawed at his gut. His shoulders slumped as he asked quietly, "Do you hate me so much that you'd marry another man just to spite me?"

For a moment, she didn't answer. Then her chin somehow rose defiantly into the air even as she lay on her back. "Why do you care whom I marry, as long as I wed?"

Her anger wasn't strong enough to hide the pain he heard in her voice, which only added to his guilt and frustration. She wasn't wrong to doubt him. A few weeks ago, he wanted exactly that. But now he wanted so much more.

"Because you're not going to marry Whitby," he said

with complete resolve. He leaned in closer, so close that he could feel her breath fanning across his lips. "You're going to marry me."

Stunned by his words, she stared at him, wide-eyed and incredulous. He could almost see the thoughts whirling inside that sharp mind of hers.

Then her eyes narrowed to slits. "Is that why you bedded me, Carlisle?" Her voice was a scornful hiss. "So you could secure the partnership through marriage, if not by merit? To hedge your bet in case my season failed you?"

Hell no. "I made love to you," he said, deliberately correcting her description of what happened between them, "because I wanted to be with you. No other reason."

"I don't believe you," she whispered. Despite her fury, anguish dulled the light in her eyes and traitorously revealed how much pain pulsed inside her. "Besides, Papa won't let—"

"I don't give a damn about that partnership," he growled. For God's sake, how did he make her believe him?

Her eyes glistened with suffering and rage. "And you don't give a damn about St Katharine's, either!"

With a fierce cry, she shoved hard at his shoulders to push past him and scramble off the bed. But Robert grabbed her around the waist and pulled her back down, pinning her beneath him. The minx was going nowhere, not until she'd heard him out.

"I care about St Katharine's," he explained calmly, despite an elbow she threw into his ribs, "because *you* care about it."

She punched at his shoulder. "I don't believe you! I heard what you said to Papa—"

Grabbing her wrists, he pinned her arms to the mattress

to hold her still so she would have no choice but to look at him as he admitted grimly, "Yes, and every word was true."

She stopped struggling and stared at him, blinking in bewilderment. From her reaction, she certainly hadn't expected to hear him confess to that. But it was true. And it was time he took responsibility for it.

He sucked in a deep breath, then explained, "At the start of the season, I wanted nothing more to marry you off, secure the partnership, and wipe my hands of you. You were nothing more to me than a means to an end, and I had no intention of getting to know you better." His shoulders slumped with remorse. "So when Winslow proposed buying up properties in St Katharine's to profit off the new docks, I was certain you'd put the company before the school, that you'd be happy to move it once you saw the company's earnings."

She sniffed haughtily, still unwilling to let go of the anger pulsing inside her. "You were wrong."

His chest squeezed hard around his heart. He deserved every bit of her rancor. "And I am truly sorry for it," he murmured, his voice growing raspy with regret when he saw the hurt on her face.

She said nothing, the accusatory glint in her glistening eyes cutting into him like glass. She was going to make this difficult on him, and he didn't blame her. He'd hurt her too badly for the wounds to heal with only a few words of explanation and an apology. No, he had to lay bare his heart before he could be absolved.

"By the time I realized how much St Katharine's and the school meant to you, your father had already made offers to the property owners. *That* I did not know about." He punctuated that with a lift of a brow. "I would have tried to stop him if I had." He risked a caress to her cheek then, and relief filled him when instead of turning away she trembled beneath his touch. "You should have been told from the beginning."

"Yes," she whispered, "I should have."

He bit his cheek to keep back a smile at her obstinacy, yet noted with chagrin that she'd ignored his apology. "I can't change what I did in the past, but I can promise you that I'll have no hand in the project going forward except to use my influence in Parliament to *stop* those docks from being built. To save the borough and the school."

She turned her face away, but not before he saw the glistening of tears. "You're just saying that to get what you want." She shook her head. "You want Winslow Shipping."

"I want *you*, you stubborn hellcat!" His patience snapped, and exasperation poured from him. "For God's sake, Mariah, if all I cared about was the company, I never would have made love to you, and I certainly wouldn't have ridden after you. I would have let you elope with Whitby and gotten my reward for it."

"Then why didn't you?" she demanded, then shook her head. "I'm just supposed to believe that everything has changed? That your motives are selfless—"

"*Not* selfless," he corrected firmly, knowing how much choosing Mariah was costing him when it came to the memory of his father. Choosing her meant never having a place within Winslow Shipping. "Marrying you is the most selfish thing I've ever wanted in my life."

She stared up at him with uncertainty as she searched his face for answers. Yet she gave him an opportunity to change her mind when she grudgingly asked, "Why should I believe you?"

Hope surged through him. "Because I know now what's truly important. Because now I'm willing to lose everything I have if it means being with you." He paused, his eyes staring deeply into hers. Then he threw all caution to the wind—"And because I love you."

Her breath caught with a loud gasp of stunned surprise, and for a heartbeat, she froze as she looked up at him, incredulous. Then, she asked so softly that he could barely hear her, "You...love me?"

"Of course I do," he confessed. Then, blowing out an aggravated breath, he added, "Although you make it damned hard at times, Mariah, you truly do."

The distrust melted from her flushed face, replaced by a look of contrition as she blurted out, "Evelyn."

His turn, then, to stare in confusion. He blinked. What did her sister have to do with this? "Pardon?"

"She's the reason Mrs. Smith and I traveled north, to stop her from eloping with Burton Williams. Whitby agreed to be our escort." Contrition flashed across her face. "I never wanted to marry him."

Relief swelled inside his chest as understanding sank through him. The note was simply Whitby being Whitby. *Thank God.*

But his plea for forgiveness wasn't yet finished. Resting his forehead against hers and helpless to stop the nervous pounding of his heart, he sucked in a deep breath, held it a moment, then—"Marry me, Mariah."

Her lips parted as she stared up at him, stunned. But the love he saw in her watery green depths ripped his breath away. "You can't!"

He grinned, happily looking forward to a lifetime of arguing with her. "I think I can."

"No, Papa won't let you. He'll think you a fortune hunter."

"I don't care if I never have a position with Winslow Shipping," he assured her quietly, meaning every word, "as along as I get to spend the rest of my life with you."

"I don't understand," she whispered, frustrating him to no end because she hadn't answered him. "You wanted that partnership so much..."

"You were right about my father," he admitted softly. "I'm never going to be able to prove myself to him. All I can do is live the life he wanted for me, which wasn't one of wealth and power. He wanted me to be happy, to marry the woman I love and create a safe and loving home for her and our children, just as he'd done for us." His voice choked. "Marry me, Mariah, and give me that life."

Her eyes glistened, and he feared she might cry. "You hurt me, Robert," she whispered, barely a breath on her lips.

"I know." He soberly tucked a stray ebony curl behind her ear. "I can't ever make up for that. All I can do is promise that I will never knowingly hurt you again." He dropped his hand away, his eyes staring pleadingly into hers. "Can you forgive me?"

"Yes," she whispered.

That single word warmed through him. Then she sent his heart somersaulting—

"I will marry you."

He captured her mouth beneath his as joy filled him, hungrily kissing her with all the love and desire inside him. Her arms wrapped tightly around him, as if she were afraid he might slip away from her even now. But she had nothing to fear. He would *never* let her go.

"Minx," he purred, lowering his head to tongue her throat and the pulse beating wildly there.

She whispered as she blinked back tears of happiness, "Make love to me, Robert."

With a groan of desire, he seized her lips in a blistering kiss, and to his delight, she met his mouth eagerly and with equal passion. He rose up on his knees to strip out of his coat and waistcoat, neckcloth and shirt...Damnation! He would have to leave the bed to remove his boots and breeches, and letting her out of his arms was the last thing he wanted to do.

Before he could move away, Mariah rolled onto her stomach beneath him and gestured toward the row of tiny buttons down her back. "Undress me?"

"Anything you want," he promised as his fingers worked loose the buttons, only to open the dress to find a stay and chemise beneath. He groaned in frustration. Women wore too many damned layers.

"What I want...is you, Robert," she panted out. "The only man...I will ever give myself to."

His cock flexed, already straining hard against the tightly fitted material of his riding breeches. Giving up on attempting to unlace the stays, he grabbed her skirt in his hands and pulled it up her legs, revealing her stockings and smooth stretches of thigh beyond their lace edges, the round curves of her bare buttocks and hips above.

She tensed. "What are you doing?"

"Making love to you," he answered huskily.

Unable to resist her siren song a moment longer, he slipped his hand between her legs to stroke her from behind. She moaned with a shudder at the unexpected caress.

"That's nice?" he murmured into her ear as he leaned forward to cover her with his body.

"Oh that's *wonderful*," she sighed as he dared to take another caress, this time deeper than before.

He smiled against her ear, marveling that she was already wet and slippery, her body quivering with arousal. As he fluttered his fingers against her, she shivered and fisted the coverlet in her hands with a whimper. She shifted her hips to spread her legs wider, and he groaned at her wanton invitation. His minx was no passive flower. She was brazen and bold, and he loved her for it.

"Robert," she whispered and tried to raise her hips from the mattress, in an attempt to roll over to give herself to him.

But he wanted her too badly to wage the war with skirts and breeches that rolling her onto her back would entail. He needed her. *Now.* He grabbed a pillow and shoved it beneath her hips, raising her bottom into the air.

She glanced warily over her shoulder at him as he unbuttoned his fall and freed himself from the unbearably tight breeches. Her eyes widened as she realized what he intended. "But we— Can we?"

"Deliciously so," he assured her in a rakish murmur. "Like this." He gently nudged her thighs apart and settled himself between them, sliding his cock down against her feminine core from behind. He drew a deep breath and lowered his hips, sheathing himself completely in her tight warmth, his hips resting fully against her round buttocks. He groaned against her neck. "Sweet Lucifer...just like this."

Wrapping his arms around her, he gathered her close beneath him and made a teasing plunge and retreat with his hips. The movement drew a soft *oh* of surprised pleasure from her and had him longing to stroke inside her like that again. A pulsing sensation cascaded through him, all the way down to his toes curling inside his boots. To be able to hold her this close while being so deep inside her—*exquisite*.

He whispered her name around the knot of emotion in

his throat and placed a delicate kiss between her bare shoulder blades, not ceasing in the gentle rocking of his body into hers.

"Please, Robert," she pleaded, attempting to wiggle her bottom against him to beg with her body to give her what she needed but not finding enough room. She shook with frustration. "Oh, please..."

With his arms sliding low around her waist to keep her tight against him, he shifted back onto his knees and brought her up onto all fours. She gasped in surprise, then sighed with pleasure as he grasped her hips and stroked powerfully into her.

With her hands planted on the mattress, she pushed back, meeting each hard movement thrust for thrust.

Joy flooded through him. That she enjoyed letting go of her inhibitions and giving herself over to her desire made him shake with sweet satisfaction. She was shamelessly demanding her own pleasure from him, and he would gladly give it. He thrust into her fast and hard, driving them both on, and each thrust of his hips made a slapping sound against her buttocks as their bodies met.

He felt the tension curl inside her like a coiling spring, in the way her folds began to quiver and flex around his cock, and in her frustrated whimpers as her body strained to reach for its release. He bent over her back and wrapped his arms around her. One hand fondled her breasts through her loosened bodice as the other reached down between her thighs to seek out her most sensitive spot—

Her hips bucked as a gasping spasm of pleasure shot through her. "Robert!"

"Minx," he returned with a possessive bite at the back of her neck.

As his teeth sank into her flesh, she shattered in his arms, and a throaty cry of pleasure tore from her as she collapsed limply onto her forearms beneath him. A heartbeat later, his own release tore from him, and he poured himself deep inside her. As the waves of release swept through her, her sex clenched and quivered around his cock, greedily milking every last drop of his essence from him.

With his spent body folded over hers, he rested his cheek against her bared shoulder where her dress had slipped away, and closed his eyes. Each racing beat of her heart beneath his cheek brought him intense satisfaction, the force of which he'd never known before.

At that moment, with bliss flooding through him, he wanted nothing more than to spend the rest of his days loving her.

* * *

Mariah lay nestled in Robert's arms, happier than she'd ever been in her life. What he had done—what *they* had done together! Oh, she was certain she'd been completely corrupted now into a life of wanton behavior and wicked pleasure.

And she didn't regret one heartbeat of it.

"Where will we live?" she asked softly, drawing patterns across his chest with her fingertips. "I mean, once we're married."

"Wherever you want, darling." He grinned and tipped her face up to kiss her. "But not with your father."

He smothered her laughter with his lips.

He'd been kissing her nearly nonstop since they made love, as if he couldn't get enough of her, even as she lay half-naked in his arms. They hadn't taken precautions, and a part of her was glad. She could think of nothing more wonderful than his child growing in her womb.

But best not to terrify him with thoughts of a baby so soon. After all, it must surely be bad luck to give the groom a heart attack before the wedding.

So she said instead, "The fighting has stopped."

He cocked his head to listen, then languidly kissed her again. "Sounds like it."

She frowned. "Aren't you worried about your brothers?"

"No." He placed delicate kisses to her brow to soften it. "My attention's needed right here." More kisses to her eyelids, her cheeks, and the tip of her nose. "On you."

"Robert," she chastised, but her scolding was undermined by a silly smile on her lips and the happiness swelling inside her chest.

"Well, they've either won, in which case Trent is now settling up the bill with the innkeeper for destroying the furniture." The ease with which he said that made her wonder exactly how many times he and his brothers had gotten into bar fights and ended up doing just that. "Or they've lost, in which case they're dead and beyond help."

"Robert!"

With a teasing grin, he ignored her rebuke and tugged down the neckline of her rumpled bodice to place a kiss on the swell of her breast. "Most likely, though, they're in gaol, where they'll keep safely until I pay their fines."

Her eyes widened. "Gaol?"

He shrugged, unperturbed. "It's happened before," he murmured as he slipped his fingers beneath her stays and freed her breast from its confinement. "So there's no hurry to leave." He placed his lips around her nipple and gave it a soft kiss though the thin chemise. "No hurry at all."

With a sigh of happiness, she eased down onto her back and ran her fingers through his hair as he continued to gently suckle at her breast. Already, a warm tingle stirred between her thighs. How long would they have to wait before he could be hard and inside her again, once more making love to her?

No, she decided as she ran her hands over his bare back, no reason to hurry.

"Where will we be married?" She smiled at him as he released her right breast and began the same sweet torture on the left. They had a future to plan, and discussing it brought her more joy than she thought possible.

"I've been thinking about that, actually." He rested his chin between her breasts as he looked up at her with a grin. He appeared so boyishly earnest and happy that she couldn't resist smiling at him. "How about over the anvil?"

Her mouth fell open. He couldn't mean... "Elope?"

"Why not? We're halfway to Scotland now. In two days we could be at Gretna Green, then married and back to London by the end of the sennight. Then we wouldn't have to wait to be married." He arched a brow. "Or give your father the chance to refuse my offer."

"You truly mean it?" she whispered, not daring to believe he could be hers so soon, finally, and in every way.

"Whatever you want, love." His grin faded into seriousness. "I don't care how or where, Mariah, as long as I get to be your husband."

Tears of happiness stung her eyes as she whispered, "I love you, Robert."

"Dear God, I hope so! I'd hate to think how you'd torment me if you didn't." When she slapped gently at his shoulder at his teasing, he caught her hand. He rose up to touch his lips to hers, a slow and lingering kiss that tasted of both promise and possession. "On to Scotland, then?"

She nodded, unable to speak around the knot in her throat.

"Just one more thing," he added in afterthought.

Her heart skipped with a spark of dread that something might stop them after all—

"Instead of bringing my brothers with us, can we pick them up on the way back?"

She laughed, then her hand flew to her mouth in horror at how she'd just reacted at his brothers' expense. The two men were now going to be brothers to her, as well.

He pulled her hand away, his eyes gleaming. "I love you, Mariah," he murmured, his voice hoarse with emotion. "And my family loves you, too. They'll think you the best decision I've ever made."

Her smile faded. "Even if I cost you a place with Winslow Shipping?" Her chest grew heavy with remorse as she admitted, "You deserved it, Robert. You truly did."

"There will be other partnerships, other business opportunities." He leaned in to kiss her, so softly and with so much love and tenderness that a tear slipped down her cheek. "But I'll always have you, Mariah."

"Yes, you will," she breathed, unable in her joy to find her voice. *Always.*

He murmured against her lips, "I won't need anything else."

EPILOGUE

A Warm Spring Day in London
One Month Later

here you are." Robert leaned against the doorway to the small office in the basement of the Gatewell School and smiled at Mariah as she sat behind the desk, still wearing her wedding dress even as she combed through the school's account books. Typical Mariah. And he loved her for it. "It isn't proper for a bride to flee her own wedding breakfast."

She looked up at him and gave the guilty smile of a caught-in-the-act criminal. "It's such a crush upstairs that I wanted a few moments to myself."

He corrected with a lift of his brow, "You wanted to go over the books one more time, you mean." That, too, was typical Mariah.

She grimaced, not even bothering to pretend that he was wrong. "Can you blame me? I've handled the school's accounts for the past five years. Now I'm supposed to simply hand them over to a stranger."

"To a well-trained and greatly qualified accountant," he corrected. And a man whom she interrogated for over an

hour when she interviewed him for the position of oversee-
ing the school's funds. "Our lives have changed, darling.
You have to learn to adjust."

She stood and circled around the desk to him, slipping
her hands around his waist as she stepped into his arms. "I
think I've done a good job of adjusting to all the changes
recently."

He only smiled at her, knowing better than to engage in
that battle.

At least she was right about one thing. There had certainly been an immense amount of change in their lives since
they returned from Scotland.

The first change was Henry Winslow himself, a transfor-
mation that Robert never would have imagined would have
come to pass. When they first returned to London and told
him they'd eloped, her father had reacted exactly as Mariah
had predicted—denying her a dowry and refusing to give
Robert a position within the company. He didn't understand
why an attack on St Katharine's felt like an attack on her
mother or that relocating the school made her grieve all over
again. She and her father had never talked about Beatrice
Winslow or how her death affected all of them, but Robert
insisted that they did so now, having learned himself the importance of sharing grief.

Her father grudgingly came around. Not only did he welcome Robert into the family, he also gave both of them
joint partnerships. To Mariah because Winslow now realized
why she needed to be part of the company the same way
she needed air to breathe, and to Robert because Winslow
couldn't afford to lose his political connections. But a lingering distrust borne from the debacle with her uncle made
him carefully split their interests. Robert would work with

him on the shipping interests, while Mariah would oversee the expansion into stores, selling exotic merchandise from all over the world and bringing the faraway places and foreign ports she loved to London society.

Scuttling the king's plans for new docks in St Katharine's, however, had been more of a fight. Robert did what he swore he would never do—he used his influence with friends and family in Parliament. But he did it to halt the new docks rather than to profit from them. St Katharine's and the Gatewell School for Orphans of the Sea were both given reprieve.

And for the first time, the company truly belonged to the Winslow family. *All* of the family.

"Did you see Evelyn before you left the party?" she asked, a frown creasing her brow. "Is she all right?"

"Whitby's guarding her like a bulldog," he assured her. "She's fine." And she *was* fine…for now.

They'd managed to keep the scandal of her elopement secret, and so far, Burton Williams was smart enough to keep his silence. Perhaps because he realized he'd just barely escaped marriage to a woman who had no money. Or more likely because the Carlisle brothers had vowed to tie him up and toss him onto a ship bound for Australia if he uttered one word about Evelyn. And anyone who asked about her absence during those days were all told the same story—that Mariah couldn't have possibly gotten married without her sister at her side, even over the anvil in Gretna Green.

In fact, at this morning's formal wedding for their friends and family at the medieval church of St Katharine's by the Tower, Evelyn had stood up with Quinton for the ceremony, while his mother and his sister-in-law Annabelle sat in the front pew and wept. *Good Lord.* It was as if a spring had opened up in the church for all the waterworks that had gone on. The only flaw in the day was that Sebastian wasn't there to share their happiness. But news arrived from Blackwood Hall just as the wedding breakfast was beginning and the first toasts were going round that Sebastian was now the proud father of a beautiful baby girl, whom they'd named Rose.

Distracted, Mariah looked down at the desk and the account books, and worry crossed her face. "What if there's a problem and the accountant doesn't know—"

He silenced her with a kiss. "Everything will be fine, darling," he murmured, sliding his lips away from hers to kiss his way along her jaw to her throat.

Her pulse raced tantalizingly beneath his lips. Not for the first time since he saw her standing there in the church aisle on her father's arm, he wondered how long they had to stay at the breakfast before he could take her home, carry her to their bedroom, and make love to her.

While he would have to wait for that, he couldn't resist stealing a caress of her cheek. "Your mother would have been so proud of you today. I know that my mother is. Already she loves you like a daughter."

Her eyes glistened, and she could say nothing, bringing her lips to his with a love and happiness so powerful that she trembled from it.

His arms tightened around her, and he brushed his mouth against her temple. "Think you can handle it—continuing to support the school while running the stores?"

"I can, with you at my side," she whispered. "I can do anything as long as you love me."

Closing his eyes, he held her pressed against him. He'd never been happier in his life.

A soft sound came from the doorway.

He looked up at his mother, a smile on her face at catching them in such a loving embrace. He stepped back from Mariah, but he didn't lower his arm from around her waist.

"I thought I might find you two here." She came forward and took their hands in hers, squeezing them affectionately. "I am so very happy for both of you."

"Thank you, Mother." He placed a kiss on her cheek.

She arched a brow. "Although it certainly took you long enough to figure out what the rest of us already knew."

He rolled his eyes and repeated dryly, "Thank you, Mother."

She smiled lovingly at him. "I know you want to get back to your guests, but I have something that I thought you might want to see."

She pulled a small book from her reticule, and her smile saddened with wistful melancholy.

Robert tensed. "What's that?"

"Your father's journal. Annabelle found it while she was looking through the books in the library at Park Place." She handed it to him. "I marked an entry that I think you should read."

With a kiss to his cheek and another to Mariah's, she retreated toward the door.

She called back to them, "Of all the accomplishments your father achieved, the one that he was most proud of was his family. He always believed that it was his children who gave him his greatest purpose in life." She paused, a look of love shining in her eyes for her son. "He would have been so proud of you, Robert."

She slipped away to go back upstairs to the party.

As Robert stared after her, the journal heavy in his hand, he felt Mariah's reassuring touch on his shoulder. He ignored the stinging in his eyes and looked at her.

She said gently, "Read it, my love."

Nodding wordlessly, with a dark dread settling on his chest, he opened the book and flipped through the pages filled with his father's distinctive handwriting to the last entry. The one written just hours before his death, while he had once again been waiting up for Robert to return home. Holding his breath, he read over the entry.

Still sowing wild oats, yet with the potential to be the most successful of all my sons... Then his heart lurched into his throat— *He tries my patience, but I take such great pride in him. He has become the good man I have always known he would be.*

"I knew it," Mariah whispered as she read over his shoulder. "Your father loved you, Robert, and he believed in you, always."

He blinked hard as he tore his gaze away from the page, but her face blurred. He forced out hoarsely around the knot chocking in his throat, "How did you know when I didn't?"

"Because I love you myself, and I recognized the same signs in all those stories your mother told about you and your father." She wrapped her arms around him. "And just like him, I am so very proud to have you in my life."

She pressed into his embrace, and he welcomed the softness of her body against his, the warmth and love she carried for him.

"We found a true partnership after all, minx," he murmured.

Then he lowered his head and kissed her.

AUTHOR'S HISTORICAL NOTE

In 1825, Parliament authorized the building of new docks at St Katharine's. As Henry Winslow knew, the only way to increase the quayside was to create more riverbank, exactly what engineer Thomas Telford designed—two joined inland basins connected to the Thames by an entrance lock. Ultimately, construction consumed approximately twenty-three acres. Over 1,250 houses were demolished, along with the twelfth-century medieval church and the hospital of St Katharine's by the Tower, for which the area was named. Nearly 12,000 inhabitants, who were mostly poor dockworkers living in slum-like conditions, lost their homes. Only the property owners were compensated.

Unable to accommodate large ships, the docks were never a commercial success, and in 1968, the St Katharine's Docks were closed. Development of the site as a residential and leisure complex commenced in the 1970s. Now known as the Docklands, the area comprises luxury apartments, upscale shops and restaurants, and a yachting marina. It is a model of successful urban redevelopment.

I would like to believe that the Gatewell School for Orphans of the Sea shared a similar fate to St Katharine's by the Tower. The hospital lost its buildings in 1825 but relocated its services to nearby Whitechapel. After several more moves around London, it relocated in 1948 to its present location in Limehouse, one mile from its original site. Its mission continues today.

Miranda Hodgkins has only ever wanted one thing: to marry Robert Carlisle. And she can't wait a moment longer. She boldly sneaks into his bedchamber with seduction on her mind and is swept into the most breathtaking kiss of her life. But she never dreamed that kiss would be with Sebastian, the Duke of Trent—Robert's formidable older brother...

An excerpt from

If the Duke Demands

follows.

CHAPTER ONE

Islingham, Lincolnshire
January 1822

*M*iranda Hodgkins peeked out cautiously from behind the morning room door. The hallway was empty. *Thank goodness.* Drawing a deep breath of resolve, she hurried toward the rear stairs and reached a hand up to her face to make certain that her mask was still firmly in place.

The grand masquerade ball that had been held in celebration of Elizabeth Carlisle's birthday had ended, and now the guests were dispersing...those who had come only for the evening's ball into a long line of carriages, those few remaining for the last night of the house party into their rooms in the east wing. And the family would eventually make their way to their rooms in the west wing. *Exactly* where Miranda was headed.

She scurried up the dark stairs, knowing the way by heart from years of playing at Chestnut Hill with the Carlisles when they were all children. She knew which steps squeaked and how to move over them without making a sound, just as she'd attended enough parties here to know that the servants would be busy in the lower rooms of the house and that the family would take several minutes to say good night to all their guests.

If this had been any other night, she wouldn't have been sneaking around like this. She would have gone home with her auntie and uncle and stayed there, instead of changing into her second costume of the evening and sneaking back to Chestnut Hill. And she would have entered right through the front door instead of through the cellar, with no one thinking twice about seeing her in the house that bordered her auntie and uncle's farm and that felt like a second home to her.

But this wasn't just any other night. Tonight, she planned on declaring her love for Robert Carlisle. The man she wanted to marry and spend the rest of her days making happy.

And the man she planned to surrender her innocence to tonight.

She reached the landing and felt carefully in the darkness for the latch to release the door. She'd known Robert since she was five, when her parents died and she came to live with Aunt Rebecca and Uncle Hamish, when she'd met the entire Carlisle family and been welcomed warmly into their embrace as if she were a long-lost relative instead of the orphan niece of one of their tenants. Seldom a day went by that she hadn't been at Chestnut Hill, playing in their nursery or gardens. But a stolen kiss from Robert when she was fourteen changed everything. For the first time, she had evidence that Robert thought of her as more than a friend, even if he'd never attempted to repeat it. She hadn't stopped dreaming of him in the intervening years, and during the past two years, since his father passed away and he returned to live at Chestnut Hill, she'd dared to dream of more.

Oh, he was simply wonderful! He'd always been dashing, with that golden hair and sapphire blue eyes that all the brothers shared, along with the tall height and broad shoulders, that same Carlisle wildness and charm. The three men were so much alike physically that they even sounded the same when they spoke. But their personalities were completely different, and so was the way they'd treated her. Sebastian had already been sent to Eton by the time she arrived in Islingham and so was too busy to pay her much mind, and Quinton had been...well, *Quinton*. But Robert had paid the most attention to her, had always been kind and supportive, even when he'd teased her mercilessly, just as he had his sister, Josephine. Since he'd returned to Islingham to help Sebastian with the dukedom, though, he'd also matured. Bets placed in the book at White's had *never* thought that possible. But Miranda had always known how special he was, how dedicated to his family and especially to his mother. And tonight, she planned on showing him how she felt about him.

Her hands shook as she silently closed the door behind her and paused to let her eyes adjust to the dim light in the hallway. Heavens, how nervous she was! Her heart pounded so hard with anxious excitement over what she'd planned for tonight that each beat reverberated in her chest like cannon fire. She'd never attempted to seduce a man before, had never even considered such a thing, and her entire knowledge of how to please a man came from the barmaid she'd paid to tell her everything the woman knew about men. Which had proven to be a great deal, indeed.

Yet Miranda had no choice but to carry out her plan tonight. Time was running out. She could no longer afford to wait for Robert to tire of temporary encounters with the string of women he was rumored to have been involved with since university and crave something deeper and more lasting. Or wait for him to realize that *she* could be the woman to give him that. He would be in London soon for the season, and once there, he'd court Diana Morgan, the general's lovely daughter he'd talked about since last fall. And the woman he'd spent the house party chatting with in quiet conversation, taking for turns about the gardens, waltzing with tonight…If Miranda didn't take this chance now, she would lose him forever. And how could she ever live with herself then, knowing she'd never dared to reveal her true feelings?

She knew tonight could go horribly wrong, that he might not return the feelings she had for him…But she also knew it could go perfectly right. That he might finally see her as the woman she'd become and the seductress she could be rather than as nothing more than the friend who had always been there, like a comfortable piece of furniture. How would she have lived with her cowardly self if she didn't at least *try*?

Drawing a deep breath, she pushed herself away from the door and hurried down the hall, counting the rooms as she went…two, three—*four*! This was it, the one the footman had told her was Robert's.

She slipped inside the dark room, then closed the door and leaned back against it, to catch her breath and somehow calm her racing heart. There was no turning back now. In a few minutes, Robert would walk into his room and find a masked woman draped across his bed. By the time her mask came off and he realized that the woman was her, he would be too enthralled to see her as simply plain Miranda Hodgkins any longer. She would show him that the same woman who was his friend could also be his lover and wife.

And finally, he would be hers.

Her eyes adjusted to the dark room, lit only by the dim light of the small fire his valet had already banked for the night. A new nervousness swelled inside her that had nothing to do with her planned seduction. Heavens, she was in Robert's room. In his *room*! His most private space. But instead of feeling like an intruder, she felt at home here amid the large pieces of heavy furniture and masculine furnishings. As she moved away from the door and circled the room, her curiosity getting the better of her, she passed his dresser and lightly ran her hand over his things...his brushes, a pipe that she was certain had belonged to his father— Her fingers touched something cold and metal.

She picked it up and turned it over in her palm, then smiled. A toy soldier from the set Richard Carlisle had given to the boys over two decades ago for Christmas and long before she'd come to Chestnut Hill. Her throat tightened with emotion. The set had always been the boys' most prized possession, and several of the soldiers had been secreted away in Sebastian's trunks when he left for school, much to Robert and Quinn's consternation. That Robert would be so sentimental as to keep such a memento of his father...just another reason why she loved him.

Lifting the soldier to the faint smile at her lips, she circled the room to take in as much of this private side of him as possible. A typical bachelor gentleman's room, she supposed. Then she laughed with happy surprise when she saw the stack of books on the bedside table. Of course, he was well-educated; Elizabeth and Richard Carlisle had made certain of that for all their children. But Shakespeare,

Milton…*poetry*? A warmth blossomed in her chest. She loved poetry, too, and discovering this romantic side to Robert only made her certain that they belonged together.

A noise sounded in the hall. With her heartbeat thundering in her ears, she raced to the bed, kicked off her slippers, and draped herself seductively across the coverlet. That is, as seductively as possible, because her hands shook as they pulled at her costume to spread it delicately over her legs and to check once again to make certain that her mask was still in place.

The door opened, and her heart stopped.

Miranda stared at the masked man silhouetted in the doorway and swallowed. Hard. The only conclusion to this night would be her utter and complete ruination.

Exactly what she hoped for.

Praying he couldn't see how her fingers trembled, she reached a hand toward the draping neckline of her costume to draw his attention to her breasts…er, rather to what there was of them.

Robert's sapphire blue eyes flickered behind the panther mask. The shocked surprise in their depths faded into rakish amusement, and his sensuous mouth curled into a slow, predatory smile.

Her belly pinched. *Oh my.*

Without shifting his eyes away from her, he closed the door behind him.

Oh. My. Goodness.

He stalked slowly toward the bed, reminding her of the graceful panther his papier-mâché mask proclaimed him to be. He stopped at the foot of the giant four-poster bed, and his gaze heated as he stared down at her through the soft shadows.

"Well, then," he drawled in a voice so low that it was almost a whisper and one as deep as the darkness surrounding them. "What have we here?"

She drew a breath for courage. "I saw you at the masquerade tonight." Her nervousness made her own voice far huskier than she intended. *Thank God.* She had to carry off this seduction tonight. She simply *had* to! "And I wanted time with you." She paused for emphasis. "Alone."

He smiled at that. "You weren't at my mother's party." With a slow shrug of his broad shoulders, he slipped off his black evening jacket and tossed it over the chair in front of the fireplace. "I would have remembered you."

Miranda nearly scoffed at that. He would have remembered her? From among the two hundred other females of all ages crammed into Chestnut Hill's ballroom for the Duchess of Trent's birthday? Hardly!

From behind his mask, his eyes drifted over the dress, and heat prickled across her skin.

Well…*maybe* he would have remembered *if* she'd been wearing the same flimsy crêpe dress currently draped over her rather than the costume in which she'd arrived. A clinging, sleeveless rose-colored gauze creation with matching mask, this dress had cost her a small fortune from months of saved-up pin money and her salary from the orphanage. It had also required several secret trips to Helmsworth to visit the dressmaker there, whom she'd hired so that no one in Islingham would suspect what she was up to. But all the subterfuge was worth it, because the whole effect turned her body into a long-stemmed rose. Instead of this, though, she'd been announced to the party at the beginning of the evening wearing the pumpkin costume that her auntie had made for her, complete with a stem sticking out of her hat, and Robert hadn't given her a second glance all evening.

But he certainly noticed her now as she reclined across his bed, her back propped up by a pile of pillows and the hem of her skirt scandalously revealing her legs from the knees down. *Bare* legs, too, because she couldn't afford to purchase the lace stockings that matched the dress.

"Perhaps you didn't notice me because I was dancing with other men," she offered coyly. Tonight, her mask made her bold and free to say flirtatious things she never would have had the courage to utter otherwise. "But I'd much rather have been dancing with you."

She saw his hand freeze for just a heartbeat as he reached for his cravat. "Then the loss was definitely mine." His eyes trailed from her low neckline down her body, across the curves of her hips, and over her legs. "And your name, my lady?"

Her heart jumped into her throat. Oh no, she couldn't tell him *that*—not yet! She'd worn the mask and costume purposefully so that he would see this other side of her before he dismissed her outright. So that he would have an opportunity to see her through new eyes, to look upon her as a woman instead of the girl he'd always known. If she revealed her identity so soon, he'd never see her as anything more than a friend.

So she whispered, "Rose."

He untied his black cravat and tossed it away. "Lady Rose," he murmured. Knowing amusement touched his sensuous mouth at her completely fabricated answer. "Is that why you're in my room, then?" His sapphire eyes stirred heat beneath her skin everywhere he looked. And dear heavens, he was looking everywhere! "Because you want to dance with me?"

Dance. The word shivered down her spine as she watched him slip free each button of his black waistcoat. They both knew he didn't mean waltzing.

Electric tingles of excitement raced through her. This was it. The moment that would bring her the man she'd loved. The moment when her life would change forever...

She drew a shaky breath. "Yes." The word came out as a husky rasp. "Very much."

His full lips tugged into a seductive smile, and he slipped off his waistcoat, then dropped it to the floor. The muscles of his arms and shoulders rippled beneath his black shirt as he reached up to unfasten the half dozen buttons at his neck, the firelight playing across his golden blond hair and his handsome face still hidden behind the mask. Her heart thudded painfully against her ribs when he tugged his shirttail free from his black breeches to let it hang loose around his waist.

He was undressing. And not for sleep. For a moment, she forgot to breathe.

When she remembered again, her breath came in a soft sigh. Which caused his blue eyes to darken with quick arousal as he took the sound as an invitation to...to—

She swallowed again. *Very* hard.

Well, that *was* why she was lying on his bed, for goodness' sake. To be ravished. But heavens, she was nervous! Trying to hide the trembling in her hands and be the seductress he would want, she ran her palms up and down her thighs, each stroke upward pulling the crêpe material with it until her legs were bare to her thighs. His eyes keenly followed every caress she gave herself. Because of the mask, she couldn't see whatever other emotions might be flickering across his face, but she could see his eyes and mouth, and those both struck her as intense. Predatory. Aroused.

Goodness.

He reached up to remove his mask—

"No!" she gasped.

He froze at her outburst. Then curiously tilted his head as if he'd misconstrued her meaning.

But he'd understood perfectly. She couldn't let him remove his mask. If he did, then he'd expect her to remove hers—oh, she wasn't ready for that! Not until she was certain that she'd made him want her as much as she wanted him, and somehow not just for tonight but always.

"The masquerade was so much fun," she explained quickly, silently praying that he'd believe her, "that I should hate for it to end so soon."

"It won't." He stole a wandering glance down her body. A heated promise lingered in that sultry look.

"Please don't remove your mask, not yet." Then she added as enticingly as possible, "My Lord Panther."

He inclined his head toward her in a gentlemanly nod.

A thrill raced through her. Robert had never shown her such deference before. Of course, though, he didn't know that it was her in this costume, she thought with a twinge of chagrin. But he would soon, and then everything between them would change.

"As you wish, Lady Rose." Another heated smile, this time as he stepped forward to lean his shoulder against the bedpost and stare unapologetically at her body. "Your costume is quite beautiful."

"Do you like it?" She raised her hand to her neckline again, drawing his attention back to her breasts as she arched her back in an attempt to make them appear as full as possible.

"Very much," he murmured appreciatively.

"Good." Her trembling fingers trailed up to her shoulder and to the satin bow holding the bodice in place. "Because I wore it just for you."

He parted his lips as if to say something, but she pulled loose the ribbon in a seductive move she'd practiced all afternoon. The shoulder of her dress fell down, nearly baring her right breast. He fixed a hungry stare on her, whatever he was about to say lost forever.

With a sound that was half groan, half growl, he grabbed his shirt and yanked it off over his head, then started forward, crawling up the bed toward her on hands and knees. Very much a panther stalking forward to claim its prey.

Her eyes widened, and she slowly sank down onto her back as he crawled up the length of her, trapping her between his hands and knees. She certainly hadn't expected *this*! Or the way he lowered his head to lick his tongue across her bare shoulder, as if he were tasting her before deciding whether to toy with her a while longer or devour her whole.

"Mmm," he purred against her flesh as his mouth moved to her neck, where she was certain he could feel her pulse pounding beneath his lips. "Perhaps it's good that I didn't notice you at the party after all."

"Why is that?" She shivered as his teeth nipped at her throat, unprepared for the pulse of heat that shot straight down to her toes. This was nothing like the kiss he'd given her all those years ago.

"I would have embarrassed myself in the middle of the ballroom trying to get to you." He traced his fingertip over her bare shoulder, drawing invisible patterns across her skin and down toward the swell of her breast. "We would have danced, I'd have made certain of it."

His finger dipped under the edge of her dress and, finding no stays nor shift to impede him, grazed seductively over her nipple still hidden beneath. She gasped, and he smiled delightedly at her response. Apparently he had decided to toy with her after all.

Then he slipped his hand completely beneath the gauzy bodice to cup her bare breast. "So we'll dance now," he murmured.

Heat radiated into her from his large hand as he gently massaged her, and she wiggled beneath his touch, suddenly unable to lie still as she bit back a moan of happiness. She'd dreamt for years about having his hands on her like this, touching her, caressing her... but she'd never once imagined it would feel so warm and wonderful. So soft yet urgent.

"Lovely dress." Shifting his weight back onto his knees, he reached his free hand toward her other shoulder and deftly untied the bow. With a tug, her bodice fell away and revealed both breasts to the firelight. And to his eyes, now dark with desire as he gazed hungrily down at her. "So very lovely."

Despite the goose bumps that sprang up across her skin everywhere he looked, she resisted the nervous urge to cover herself. This was Robert, and he, of all people, had the right to see her. Because she'd known him since she was five. Because she loved him. Because she wanted no one else but him to ever see her like this, tonight and for the rest of her life.

She shyly bit her bottom lip. "You don't find me... plain?"

He gave a laugh, and the deep sound rumbled through her, swirling down to land between her legs. He lowered his head toward her. "Hardly."

Her breath strangled. For a moment, she thought he was lowering his mouth to kiss her...*there*, on her bare breasts. Instead, his fingers gently lifted her chin, and his lips met hers in a kiss so tender that it left her shaking. His mouth was warm, surprisingly soft, and oh-so-wonderfully skilled as he languidly explored and tasted hers, with none of the boyish eagerness she remembered from before, none of that sloppy, inexperienced kissing. This was a man who was confident in himself and knew what he wanted.

And what he wanted—she shivered—was *her*.

"You're trembling." He touched the tip of his tongue to the corner of her lips.

She shook so hard that she had to grasp the coverlet beneath her to hold herself still. "I-I'm n-not."

"Now you're lying," he scolded, smiling against her mouth.

He caught her bottom lip between his teeth, and as he bit down gently, he lowered himself over her.

No, she thought as his hard body sank onto hers, definitely nothing boyish about him any longer.

"What else can I do to make you tremble, hmm?" His hand reached down for her skirt and pulled it slowly up her thighs. The promised shivers trailed in its wake.

Miranda rolled back her head and gave herself over to him. She'd wanted this moment for so long, and now that it was finally happening—oh, dear Lord, *it was happening*! She could hardly believe it wasn't still only a dream. Robert in her arms, his lips on hers, his hands caressing her seductively. Her heart pounded so hard she could hear the rush of blood in her ears, so rapidly she was certain he could feel it, because when she placed her palm on his bare chest, his heart raced beneath her fingertips.

He nipped his way down her throat, then farther down to lick his tongue into the valley between her breasts. When she shuddered and wrapped her arms around his neck to bring him closer, his lips closed around her peaked nipple and sucked.

She moaned, her back arching off the mattress. "Robert..."

He froze, his mouth stilling on her. Then slowly, he released her breast and lifted his head. His blue eyes pinned hers. "*What* did you say?"

"I didn't say anything. I just—"

"Christ!" He pushed off the panther mask and revealed his face.

Oh God.

The air ripped from her lungs. "Sebastian."

Oh God oh God oh God oh God!

"Who are you?" Sebastian Carlisle grabbed her mask and yanked it down. His eyes widened in stunned surprise. "Miranda?"

He stared at her as if he couldn't believe— Oh, he was *looking* at her! Red heat flushed her face, and she slapped hard at his bare chest. "Get off me! Get *off*—"

His hand clamped down over her mouth. "Shush!" Anger furrowed his brow. "Someone will hear you."

"I don't care!" she mumbled against his palm.

"You will if they find us together"—another sweep of his gaze down her body—"like this."

With a mortified groan, she rolled her eyes. She wanted to die!

He crooked a brow in warning to keep her voice down, then withdrew his hand and rolled off the bed, muttering angrily beneath his breath as he snatched up his shirt from the floor and yanked it on.

Miranda scrambled to cover herself, but her fingers shook so hard that she could barely retie the bows at her shoulders. One knotted pathetically.

He wheeled on her. "What are you doing here, Miranda?"

"Me?" she squeaked, her hand jerking and creating another knot. "What are *you* doing in Robert's room? You'd better dress and leave before he—"

"This is my room." He pointed possessively at the floor.

"Your— *No*," she protested firmly even as she took a frantic glance around, although she wouldn't have known the difference between any of the brothers' bedrooms at Chestnut Hill. But this was Robert's, she was certain of it, along with the toy soldiers and poetry books. "I asked the footman. He told me *this* room."

His eyes narrowed. "You asked a footman which bedroom belonged to Robert?"

"I was discreet." She sniffed at his insinuation that she'd been reckless enough to confide her plan for seduction to a footman. If a woman planned to drape herself across a would-be-lover's bed, she certainly wouldn't announce it to the household staff. Even she knew that much. "And I wore a mask."

He placed his palms on the mattress and leaned toward her, bringing his face level with hers. "Exactly how does a masked lady go about asking a footman which bedroom belongs to a bachelor gentleman?"

Ugh, he was so frustrating! She pushed at his shoulders to shove him away, but of course he didn't budge. The man was a veritable mountain of muscle and aggravation.

With a huff, she folded her arms across her chest and raised her chin. "Wearing *her* mask, she goes to a footman at the party, slips him a coin, and points to the gentleman in *his* mask, then asks in complete anonymity which room is—"

He held up a hand, stopping her. "If the gentleman was wearing a mask, how did you know which man you pointed to?"

"Because I bribed Robert's valet yesterday to find out what mask he'd . . ." The blood drained from her face as she realized her mistake. "Oh no."

"Oh yes." With a grimace, he tossed the panther mask onto the bed at her feet. "We switched masks before the party. The man you pointed to tonight, Miranda, was me."

Her stomach plummeted. "Sebastian, I had no idea."

"Obviously." He drew up to his full six-foot height and looked down at her with that authoritative look that all the Carlisle brothers—and *especially* Sebastian—thought they could level on her simply because they'd all grown up together. "Now, we've determined *how* you ended up here." He folded his arms across his chest, the intimidating pose one she knew well. "Tell me why."

But she had absolutely no intention of telling him *that*. Wasn't she already humiliated enough? "It doesn't matter. I—I need to leave."

She scooted to the edge of the bed, her hands tugging at her skirt with each wiggle of her hips to keep her legs covered, although she didn't know why she bothered, considering he'd just had his mouth on her breast.

Her face burned. Oh God—Sebastian's mouth had been on her *breast*!

"Now—" Her voice choked with panic and mortification. "I need to go *now*."

"Stay," he commanded with that regal air all three brothers had inherited in varying degrees from their father and which Sebastian as the current Duke of Trent owned in spades.

She stilled at the edge of the bed, silent in her humiliation.

"You expected Robert to come to his room and find you lying in his bed, dressed like that." His blue eyes flashed with incredulity. "Are you and he..." At least he had the decency to look away as he stumbled over the accusation. "Intimate?"

"No!" She blinked back the stinging tears. Her humiliation had reached new heights now, never mind the fact that intimacy with Robert was exactly what she'd hoped for tonight.

"Then why were you waiting in bed for him?" he pressed.

With a groan, she hung her head in her hands. All she'd wanted was a simple seduction, but her dream had become a nightmare. "Oh, what does it matter?"

He arched a brow. "Because he's my brother, and I care about him." His voice softened. "And about you."

Ha! She didn't believe that for a second. The oldest of the three Carlisle brothers, Sebastian was the one she knew the least well yet the one who had annoyed her the most, probably because he was a decade older than she was and impatient with the games she and his siblings had played. He'd been fifteen when she arrived at Islingham, already enrolled at Eton and so away most of the time. Even on those rare visits home on holiday, he'd been too interested in spending time with his father and learning about the estate to be anything more than distantly friendly to her. By the time he'd reached university, he was more concerned with chasing women and having a good time with his brothers carrying out whatever wild scheme they could concoct than whatever was happening in Islingham. And the wilder, the better.

Until Richard Carlisle became a duke. Then the rowdy, unmanageable brothers became more serious, especially Sebastian, who as the heir had always felt the weight of the responsibilities he would someday bear. He'd paid her scant attention before; now that he was the duke, he barely noticed that she existed at all.

"Miranda," he sighed patiently, "I can't think of any good reason why you'd be in Robert's bed."

She grimaced. "No, of course not—I mean— Oh, blast it!"

She didn't care that she'd cursed in front of him, especially since the Carlisle brothers were the ones who taught her to swear when she was a child. Especially since Sebastian would never have seen her as a demure, polite society lady in the first place. And especially since she knew he wouldn't care that she'd made such a muddle of things tonight.

But she also knew that he fiercely protected his family and that he wouldn't let her leave until she explained what she'd planned for his brother.

So she grimaced in defeat and admitted softly, "Robert's going to offer for her, I know it."

"Who?" he puzzled.

"Diana Morgan." Her eyes blurred with a hot mix of anger and humiliation, and her shoulders sagged beneath the weight of it. "General Morgan's daughter. He invited her to the house party, and he's going to court her this season in London."

"What does that have to do with— Oh."

"Yes." She rolled her eyes. "*Oh*. Tonight was my last chance to be noticed by him as someone other than a friend.

So I wore this costume." She gave a hopeless wave of her hand to indicate the dress that now crumpled with wrinkles from him lying on top of her. Good heavens, how could something cost so much when there was so little to it? "And the only person who saw me in it was you. No one important."

His mouth twisted dourly. "Thank you."

"Oh, you know what I mean!" Her hand darted up to swipe at her eyes. "But I thought that if Robert could see me like this then maybe... just *maybe* he'd..." She shrugged a shoulder, feeling utterly pathetic. "Notice me."

"But... *Robert*?"

With a cringe of humiliation, she shoved him away to scramble off the bed. She barely remembered to snatch up her mask before rushing past him toward the door.

A sob strangled in her throat. What a horrible, horrible night! All she wanted to do now was flee and never again show her face at Chestnut Hill, or in Islingham Village, or anywhere in England for that matter, so she wouldn't accidentally run into Sebastian. Or Robert, because Sebastian was certain to tell his brother about this. Oh, what a hearty laugh the two of them would—

"Wait." He grabbed her arm and tugged her back toward him.

Set off-balance, she stepped backward, and her legs tangled in the gauzy skirt. She fell against him, and his arms went around her to steady her.

Fresh mortification heated her cheeks. She'd tripped in front of him like some graceless dolt, then fell right into his arms. So pathetically. Her eyes blurred. Tonight was proving to be nothing but one humiliation after another.

"Let me go," she pleaded.

His arms stayed firmly around her. "Miranda, I am sorry." His apologetic voice was surprisingly kind. "I had no idea that you…"

Raising her gaze to his, she steeled herself against the pity she knew she'd see on his face.

What she saw instead was incredulous curiosity. "I'm just surprised," he explained gently.

Her throat tightened. Surely he hadn't meant that as an insult, but when heaped on top of the other humiliations she'd experienced tonight, his words hurt. "Surprised to find me in your room?" She stuck her nose into the air with a peeved sniff. "Or surprised that I might possibly have feelings for your brother?"

"Yes," he answered honestly, "to both."

With an angry groan, she pushed against his chest to shove herself away.

He took her shoulders and held firm, his solid body not budging an inch. "And, frankly, that you would want Robert in the first place instead of some nice man from the village."

She bit her lip to keep from screaming. Was that how all the Carlisle men saw her? As a silly country gel destined to marry a boring vicar or farmer and spend her life polishing church pews or chasing pigs on a farm? Was that the best they thought she could do with her life? Oh, she wanted so much more than that! She wanted adventure and excitement, a large family of her own to love, and a home right here in Islingham, surrounded by the people she loved and would do anything for. She wasn't daft enough to think that she could marry someone of rank, like a landowning gentleman or a peer.

But the *brother* of a peer…

Yet if Robert thought no more of her than Sebastian did,

then he would never notice her as a woman with whom he could spend the rest of his life, and everything she'd gone through tonight was a thoroughly humiliating, horrible waste of time. And money. She might as well have been placed on the shelf tonight and marked *Do Not Touch*, because her life as she wanted it to be was irrevocably over.

She turned her face away, blinking hard. She wanted to laugh! And cry bitterly.

"For what I did earlier," Sebastian apologized as he sucked in a deep breath, "I am truly sorry."

Yes, she supposed he was, now that he knew it was her and not some temptress he thought had wantonly sneaked into his room for a night of bed sport with the duke. After all, he hadn't appeared particularly apologetic when he'd been pulling up her skirt.

He squeezed her shoulders in a gesture of friendly affection. The same hands that moments before had been caressing her naked breasts and had her liking it, that even now sent tingles through her—

"Oh God, no!" She pressed her fingers to her lips with horror at her sudden outburst—and even more horror at herself for liking the way he'd touched her. *Sebastian* of all men!

"Pardon?" He frowned, bewildered at her behavior.

"I mean, no apology is necessary. It was nothing." She stepped back, and this time he let her go. "A mistake, that was all. And I would greatly appreciate"—another step away, because if she kept putting steps between them she could reach the door and flee into the hallway before the tears overtook her—"if you would kindly keep what happened here tonight a secret."

"Of course," he agreed solemnly.

Embarrassment burned her cheeks. "I mean it, Sebastian. If you tell anyone, especially Robert or Quinton, I'll… I'll…"

"You'll do what?" he challenged at her weak attempt at a threat and lowered his head to bring his eyes level with hers. Drat the man for being so tall! And so…duke-like.

She boldly stuck up her chin as inspiration struck and blurted out, "I'll tell your mother what really happened to that Chinese vase your father gave her for Christmas!"

For a moment he stared at her blankly, simply unable to fathom her. Then his eyes narrowed, as if he were sizing up an opponent in Parliament instead of the annoying gel from next door, and he drew himself up to his full height…So *very* tall. Odd, how she'd never noticed that about him before. Or how much more solid that very tall body was than Robert's, or how his golden hair fell rakishly across his forehead and made her want to brush it away.

It was amazing, the details a woman noticed about a half-dressed man after he'd had his mouth on her.

"Do we have an agreement, then?" she pressed.

A lopsided threat at best—her reputation for a vase that had met its shameful demise years ago during a secret spread that the brothers had thrown while their parents had been away in London. But his mother had loved that vase, and Miranda wasn't afraid to use it to her advantage.

"Agreed," he said.

Thank God! She turned toward the door, taking a deep breath to run—

He reached over her head and pressed his hand against the door to keep her from flinging it open. "Wait."

Wait? Her heart skipped, then thudded so hard in her

chest that she winced. The infuriating man was also terribly cruel... *Wait?*

When she looked over her shoulder at him, she thought she saw his gaze dart up from her breasts. But that was impossible. Sebastian wouldn't be looking down her dress like that, not now. Now when he knew who she was... would he?

But when he reached back for the jacket he'd tossed over the chair and held it out to her, she rolled her eyes, feeling like an absolute cake. Oh, he'd been looking at her breasts all right... and pondering a good way to hide them.

"Best not to be seen sneaking out of my room, Lady Rose," he cautioned. "In that dress."

She slipped on the jacket, and knots tightened low in her belly when she breathed in the scent of him wafting up from the superfine material. She bit back a defeated groan. *Of course* he would have to smell good.

Then he gestured for her mask, and she handed it over. He lifted it into place and tied it behind her head. When he rested one hand on her shoulder while the other slowly cracked open the door, the heat of his fingers seeped into her skin, all the way down her front to her breasts. Beneath the gauzy costume, her nipples tightened traitorously at the memory of his hands on them.

At that, her stomach plummeted, her humiliation complete. Even her own body was conspiring against her tonight by fraternizing with the enemy.

He peeked past her into the hallway, then lowered his mouth to her ear. "Go down the back stairs to the ground floor. The downstairs hall will be empty and dark by now. Go out through the terrace door in my study, and stay close to the garden wall where the shadows are darkest until you get past the stables. And *don't* let anyone see you." His deep voice tickled across her cheek, and she shivered. "Especially my mother."

"How do you know so much about sneaking out?" she asked in a whisper, surprised by the detail of his instructions.

He answered with a sultry chuckle that rumbled through her. "Because I'm a Carlisle brother."

When she turned her head to look at him over her shoulder, his hand slapped against her bottom. She jumped.

"Go!"

She stepped into the hall and fled from Chestnut Hill as fast as her feet could take her. Her *bare* feet. Groaning at her own foolishness, she rolled her eyes because she'd left her slippers behind in his room. And there was no going back for them.

Ever.

ABOUT THE AUTHOR

Anna Harrington fell in love with historical romances—and all those dashing Regency heroes—while living in London, where she studied literature and theater. She loves to travel, fly airplanes, and hike, and when she isn't busy writing her next novel, she loves fussing over her roses in her garden.

You can learn more at:
   http://www.annaharringtonbooks.com
   Twitter at @AHarrington2875
   http://facebook.com/annaharrington.regencywriter

   Sign up for Anna's newsletter to get more information
on new releases, deleted scenes, and insider information!
   http://eepurl.com/cX3AmP

If you love Anna Harrington, don't miss *New York Times* bestseller Grace Burrowes's *A Rogue of Her Own*, available now!

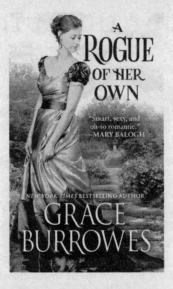

"Grace Burrowes is a romance treasure." —Tessa Dare

With one well-placed rumor, Charlotte Windham can ruin her reputation and be free to retire to the countryside in peace. Except when the rumor of a steamy kiss turns into the real thing, her only option is the one thing she never wanted: a husband. Lucas Sherbourne has no title but more than enough ambition and wealth to make up for it. But to advance his business schemes he now needs the prestige of nobility. He's proven that he and Charlotte have plenty of sizzle, but with each hiding what they really desire, will this marriage of convenience ever become true love?

Fall in Love with Forever Romance

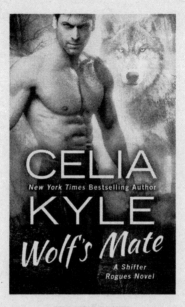

WOLF'S MATE
By Celia Kyle

From *New York Times* bestselling author Celia Kyle comes the first book in the Shifter Rogues series! Cougar shifter Abby Carter *always* plays it safe. That's why she's an accountant—no excitement, no danger, and no cocky alpha males. But when Abby uncovers the shady dealings of an anti-shifter organization, she'll have to trust the too-sexy-for-her-peace-of-mind werewolf Declan Reed...or end up six feet under.

Fall in Love with Forever Romance

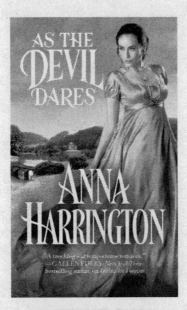

AS THE DEVIL DARES
By Anna Harrington

Lord Robert Carlisle never backs down from a challenge, but finding a husband for the captivating Mariah Winslow seems impossible. Mariah knows Lord Robert is trying to secure a partnership in her father's shipping company, a partnership that is rightfully hers. She'll play his game, but she won't be tempted by this devil—even if she finds him wickedly irresistible. Fans of Elizabeth Hoyt, Grace Burrowes, and Madeline Hunter will love the newest book in the Capturing the Carlisles series.

Fall in Love with Forever Romance

CHANGING THE RULES
By Erin Kern

The next stand-alone novel in Erin Kern's Champion Valley series! Cameron Shaw knows how to coach high school boys on the football field, but caring for his six-year-old niece, Piper, is a whole different ballgame. Audrey Bennett wasn't planning to stick around once she delivered Piper to her new guardian, but the gruff former football star clearly needs help. And the longer she stays—watching Cameron teach Piper to make pancakes and tie her sparkly pink shoelaces—the harder it is to leave.

THE SWEETEST THING
By Jill Shalvis

Now featuring ten bonus recipes never before seen in print! Don't miss this new edition of *The Sweetest Thing*, the second book in *New York Times* bestselling author Jill Shalvis's beloved Lucky Harbor series!

Fall in Love with Forever Romance

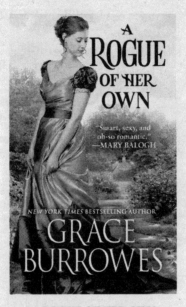

A ROGUE OF HER OWN
By Grace Burrowes

From Grace Burrowes comes the next book in the *New York Times* bestselling Windham Brides series! All Charlotte Windham needs to maintain her independence is a teeny, tiny brush with scandal. What she doesn't count on is that one kiss will lead her straight to the altar with a brash, wealthy upstart she barely knows.